PUSHKIN PRESS CLASSICS

HIDDEN
FACES

SALVADOR DALÍ (1904–1989) was a Spanish surrealist painter renowned for his striking, bizarre painting style that drew deeply on his explorations of the subconscious. He was strongly influenced by the writings of Sigmund Freud, as well as the Paris Surrealists who sought to establish the "greater reality" of the human subconscious over reason. Some of his most famous works include *The Persistence of Memory*, and the two Surrealist films *Un Chien andalou* (*The Andalusian Dog*) and *L'Âge d'or* (*The Golden Age*), made with the Spanish director Luis Buñuel. *Hidden Faces* is his only novel, and was first published in 1944.

HAAKON CHEVALIER (1901–1985) was an American writer, translator, and professor of French literature at the University of California, Berkeley. Chevalier translated the work of a number of writers, including André Malraux, Louis Aragon and Salvador Dalí.

HIDDEN FACES

SALVADOR DALÍ

TRANSLATED FROM THE FRENCH
BY HAAKON CHEVALIER

PUSHKIN PRESS CLASSICS

Pushkin Press
Somerset House, Strand
London WC2R ILA

© Salvador Dalí 1944
English translation © Haakon Chevalier 1944

Hidden Faces was first published in 1944 by Nicholson & Watson
First published by Peter Owen Publishers in 1973
First published by Pushkin Press in 2024

1 3 5 7 9 8 6 4 2

ISBN 13: 978-1-80533-055-4

All rights reserved. No part of this publication may be reproduced,
stored in a retrieval system or transmitted in any form or by any
means, electronic, mechanical, photocopying, recording or otherwise,
without prior permission in writing from Pushkin Press

Designed and typeset by Tetragon, London

Printed and bound in the United Kingdom by Clays Ltd, Elcograf S.p.A.

www.pushkinpress.com

Cover art for the original edition of *Hidden Faces*.
© Salvador Dalí, Fundació Gala-Salvador Dalí 2023

Le rêve by Salvador Dalí. Reproduced in black
and white from colour original.
© Salvador Dalí, Fundació Gala-Salvador Dalí, DACS 2023

Contents

Larvatus prodeo
(I advance masked)

DESCARTES

Translator's Foreword

When this book first appeared in the United States nearly thirty years ago, Dali's admirers and the many who knew him only from having seen his paintings and having heard, perhaps at second hand, of his eccentricities and his antics in the Paris of the twenties and thirties greeted the announcement of its publication with incredulity. He had a prodigious gift, they recognized, when it came to projecting his vision of the world in form and colour. But what impelled him, what qualified him, to venture into the realm of fiction, to build an imaginary world through the medium of words?

The novel was written in 1943 when the world was still plunged in the most destructive and lethal war in history, with battles raging on many fronts, from Russia, across Europe and North Africa to the Far East. It is, in the perspective of Dali's own development, an epitaph of pre-war Europe and reads like a period piece, its stylized characters reliving scenes that are bathed in an aura of decadent romanticism reminiscent of Barbey d'Aurevilly, of Villiers de l'Isle-Adam and of Huysmans, taking the English reader back to Disraeli, Bulwer-Lytton and Ouida with its ringing aristocratic names, its men and women of resplendent beauty, its luxury and extravagance. The action of the novel, with the scene shifting from France to North Africa, Malta, United States and back to France, roughly covers the period of the war, anticipating its end with the inclusion of a hallucinatory scene in which we see Hitler, against a background of Wagnerian music, awaiting his imminent doom with mingled fascination and horror.

Dali has always envisaged the world, his art and himself in cosmic terms, with God ever-present, whether as myth or as reality. It is a tormented world, with apocalyptic overtones, in which passions, elemental and perverse, strain the human psyche to the limit. This world, with which his paintings have made us familiar, has its own laws, its own monsters, chimeras and myths. It is a world of desolate mineral landscapes, centuries-old ruins and blanched Spanish villages beneath skies of infinite aspiration, peopled with figures caught in expressions and postures of anguish or ecstasy; a world obsessively strewn with fetichistic objects – bedside tables, sometimes cut out of the plump flesh of nurses sitting on the seashore, fried eggs slithering down banisters, dripping telephones, kidneys, beans, limp watches, crutches; a world of metamorphoses in which phenomena are constantly subject to strange deformations, shapes and contours repeating one another in a dynamic imitative interplay. There is in Dali a fascination with magic, necromancy, spells, incantations, superstition, ritual and pageantry. He is haunted by what lies beyond the limit of the conceivable. It is hardly surprising that his fertile genius should have sought to encompass a new dimension in the form of a novel.

The basic theme of *Hidden Faces* is love-in-death. We here have a treatment in modern dress of the ancient and perennial Tristan and Isolde myth. Nothing gives greater intensity to love than the imminence of death, and nothing gives greater poignancy to death than its irremediable severing of the bonds of love. The motif of death, however, is balanced by its counterpart: resurrection. This secondary but pervasive theme of new life emerging out of decay and destruction runs through the whole novel, and it is symbolized from the first page to the last by the forest of cork-oaks which pushes forth tender yellow-green shoots every spring in the plain of Creux de Libreux.

But perhaps the chief interest of this novel lies in the transposition that the author makes from the values that are paramount in the plastic arts to those that belong to literary creation. For if it is true that Dali's painting is figurative to the point of being photo-graphic, and is in that sense 'old-fashioned', his writing is above all *visual*, although as in his painting the images shown and evoked are enhanced by a stimulation of all the other senses – sound, smell, taste, touch – as well as by adumbrations of the ultra-sensory, the irrational, the spiritual and the other-worldly that are interwoven in the warp and weft of human life as reflected in a hypersensitive consciousness. The story of the tangled lives of the protagonists – Count Hervé de Grandsailles, Solange de Cléda, John Randolph, Veronica Stevens, Betka and the rest – from the February riots in Paris in 1934 to the closing days of the war constitutes a dramatic and highly readable vehicle for the fireworks of Dali's philosophical and psychological ideas and his verbal images.

Have I succeeded in carrying over the flavour and texture of Dali's style into our alien English tongue? I cannot claim to have done more than approximate it. I spent several weeks with him and his wife Gala in Franconia, New Hampshire, on the estate of the Marquis de Cuevas, when he was writing *Hidden Faces* in the late fall of 1943. The leaves of the maple trees on the mountain slopes all around us were turning from yellow to glowing orange to fiery red and then russet, and it was there that I drafted the first hundred or so pages of my translation. Dali speaks a rich, colourful French that is neither too idiomatic nor too correct, full of Spanish spice and thunder. As is usually the case with people who are not primarily writers, the peculiarities of his spoken language tend to become exaggerated in writing, as if to compensate for the absence of vocal modulations, facial expression and gesture. My problem was to temper the native exuberance of his expression and reduce it to written language with-out losing its essential qualities. Sometimes, exhausted from hours of ploughing through the lush jungle of his prose, I would turn to him in exasperation and say, 'You never use one word where two

will do. You are a master of the mixed metaphor, of the superfluous epithet; you weave elaborate festoons of redundancy round your subject and illuminate it with glittering fireworks of hyperbole....'
To this he would smile with apologetic self-assurance, a diabolical glint would come into his eyes and balance on the waxed tips of his mustache, and with great gentleness he would improvise a little piece on the violence of his Spanish temperament and the volcanic excesses of his imagination.

Whether or not Dali paints as effectively with words as he does with brush and paint, those who have been fascinated by his pictorial creations cannot fail to find his venture into this new medium absorbing.

HAAKON CHEVALIER

I dedicate this novel to Gala, who was constantly by my side while I was writing it, who was the good fairy of my equilibrium, who banished the salamanders of my doubts and strengthened the lions of my certainties…. To Gala, who by her nobility of soul has inspired me and served as a mirror reflecting the purest geometries of the aesthetic of the emotions that has guided my work.

Author's Foreword

Sooner or later everyone is bound to come to me! Some, untouched by my painting, concede that I draw like Leonardo. Others, who quarrel with my aesthetics, agree in considering my autobiography one of the 'human documents' of the period. Still others, questioning the 'authenticity' of my *Secret Life*, have discovered in me literary gifts superior to the skill which I reveal in my pictures, and to what they call the mystification of my confessions. But as far back as in 1922 the great poet Garcia Lorca had predicted that I was destined for a literary career and had suggested that my future lay precisely in the 'pure novel'. Also, those who detest my painting, my drawings, my literature, my jewels, my surrealist objects, etc., etc., proclaim that I *do* have a unique gift for the theatre and that my last setting was one of the most exciting that had ever been seen on the Metropolitan stage…. Thus it is difficult to avoid coming under my sway in one way or another.

Yet all this has much less merit than it seems to have, for one of the chief reasons for my success is even simpler than that of my multiform magic: namely, that I am probably the most hard-working artist of our day. After having spent four months in retirement in the mountains of New Hampshire near the Canadian border, writing fourteen implacable hours a day and thus completing *Hidden Faces* 'according to plan' – but without ever retreating! – I came back to New York and again met some friends at El Morocco. Their lives had remained exactly at the same point, as though I had left them but the day before. The following morning I visited studios where artists had for four months been patiently waiting for the moment of their inspiration…. A new painting had just been begun. How many things had happened in my brain during that time! How many characters, images, architectural projects and realizations of desires had been born, lived, died and been resuscitated, architectonized! The pages of my novel form only a part of my latest dream. Inspiration or force is something one possesses by violence and by the hard and bitter labour of every day.

Why did I write this novel?

First, because I have time to do everything I want to do, and I wanted to write it.

Second, because contemporary history offers a unique framework for a novel dealing with the development and the conflicts of great human passions, and because the story of the war, and more particularly of the poignant post-war period, had inevitably to be written.

Third, because if I had not written it another would have done it in my place, and would have done it badly.

Fourth, because it is more interesting, instead of 'copying history', to anticipate it and let it try to imitate as best it can what you have invented…. Because I have lived intimately, day by day, with the protagonists of the pre-war drama in Europe; I have followed them in that of the emigration to America, and it has thus been easy for me to imagine that of their return…. Because since the eighteenth century the passional trilogy inaugurated by the divine Marquis de Sade had remained Incomplete: Sadism, Masochism…. It was necessary to invent the third term of the problem, that of synthesis and sublimation: Clédalism, derived from the name of the protagonist of my novel, Solange de Cléda. Sadism may be defined as pleasure experienced through pain inflicted on the object; Masochism, as pleasure experienced through pain submitted to by the object. Clédalism is pleasure and pain sublimated in an all-transcending identification with the object. Solange de Cléda re-establishes true normal passion: a profane Saint Teresa; Epicurus and Plato burning in a single flame of eternal feminine mysticism.

In our day people are afflicted with the madness of speed, which is but the ephemeral and quickly dissipated mirage of the 'humorous foreshortening'. I have wished to react against this by writing a long and boring 'true novel'. But nothing ever bores me. So much the worse for those who are moulded of boredom. Already I wish to approach the new times of intellectual responsibility which we will enter upon with the end of this war.... A true novel of climate, of introspection and of revolution and architectonization of passions must be (as it always has been) exactly the contrary of a five-minute Mickey Mouse film or the dizzy sensation of a parachute-jump. One must, as in a slow travel by cart in the epoch of Stendhal, be able to discover gradually the beauty of the landscapes of the soul through which one passes, each new cupola of passion must gradually become visible in due time, so that each reader's spirit may have the leisure to 'savour' it.... Before I had finished my book it was claimed that I was writing a Balzacian or a Huysmansian novel. It is on the contrary a strictly Dalinian book and those who have read my *Secret Life* attentively will readily discover beneath the novel's structure the continual and vigorous familiar presence of the essential myths of my own life and of my mythology.

In 1927, sitting one day in the spring sunshine on the terrace of the café-bar Regina in Madrid, the greatly lamented poet Federico Garcia Lorca and I planned a highly original opera together. Opera was indeed one of our common passions, for only in this medium can all existing lyrical genera be amalgamated in a perfect and triumphant unity, in their maximum of grandeur and of required stridency, which was to permit us to express all the ideological, colossal, sticky, viscous and sublime confusion of our epoch. The day when I received news in London of the death of Lorca, who had been a victim of blind history. I said to myself that I would have to do our opera alone. I have continued since in my firm decision to bring this project to realization some day, at the moment of my life's maturity, and my public knows and is always confident that I do approximately everything that I say and promise.

I shall therefore make 'our' opera…. But not immediately, for as soon as I have finished this novel, I shall retire again for a whole consecutive year to California, where I want to devote myself again exclusively to painting and put my latest aesthetic ideas into execution with a technical fervour unprecedented in my profession. After which I shall immediately begin patiently to take music lessons. To master harmony thoroughly, two years is all I shall need – have I not indeed felt it flowing through my veins for two thousand years? In this opera I plan to do everything – libretto, music, settings, costumes – and moreover I shall direct it.

I cannot guarantee that this fragment of a dream will be well received. But one thing is certain: with the sum total of my phenomenal and polymorphous activity I shall have left in the hard skin of the bent and lazy 'artistic back' of my epoch the unmistakable mark, the anagram sealed in the fire of my personality and in the blood of Gala, of all the fertilizing generosity of my 'poetic inventions'. How many there are already who are spiritually nourished by my work! Therefore let him who has done 'as much' cast the first stone.

SALVADOR DALI

PART ONE

The Illuminated Plain

1

The Friends of Count Hervé de Grandsailles

For a long time the Count of Grandsailles had been sitting with his head resting on his hand, under the spell of an obsessing reverie. He looked up and let his gaze roam over the plain of Creux de Libreux. This plain meant more to him than anything in the world. There was beauty in its landscape, prosperity in its tilled fields. And of these fields the best was the earth, of this earth the most precious was the humidity, and of this humidity the rarest product was a certain mud.... His notary and most devoted friend, Maître Pierre Girardin, who had a weakness for literary language, liked to say of Grandsailles, 'The Count is the living incarnation of one of those rare phenomena of the soil that elude the skill and the resources of agronomy – a soil moulded of earth and blood of an untraceable source, a magic clay of which the spirit of our native land is formed.'

When the Count went down toward the sluice-gates with a new visitor on a tour of the property he would invariably stoop to the ground to pick up a muddy clod and as he showed it, modelling it with his aristocratic fingers, he would repeat for the hundredth time in a tone of sudden improvisation, 'My dear fellow, it is undoubtedly the somewhat rough ductility of our soil that accounts for the miracle of this region, for not only is our wine unique, but also and above all we possess the truffle, the mystery and treasure of this earth, on

3

whose surface glide the largest snails in the whole of France, vying with that other oddity, the crayfish! And all this framed by the most noble and generous vegetation, the cork-oak, which treats us to its own skin!'

And in passing he would tear off a handful of cork-oak leaves from a low branch, squeeze them tightly and roll them in the hollow of his hand, enjoying the sensation against his fine skin of the prickly resistance of their spiny contact whose touch alone sufficed to isolate the Count from the rest of the world. For of all the continents of the globe Grandsailles esteemed only Europe, of all Europe he loved only France, of France he worshipped only Vaucluse, and of Vaucluse the chosen spot of the gods was precisely the one where was located the Château de Lamotte where he was born.

In the Château de Lamotte the best situation was that of his room, and in this room there was a spot from which the view was unique. This spot was exactly limited by four great rectangular lozenges in the black-and-white tiled floor, on whose four outer angles were exactly placed the four slightly contracted paws of a svelte Louis XVI work-desk signed by Jacob, the cabinet-maker. It was at this desk that the Count of Grandsailles was seated, looking through the great Regency balcony at the plain of Creux de Libreux illuminated by the already setting sun.

There was nothing that could so lyrically arouse the fervour of Grandsailles' patriotic feelings as the unwearying sight constantly offered him by the changing aspect of this fertile plain of Creux de Libreux. Nevertheless one thing egregiously marred for him the perennial harmony of its landscape. This was a section about three hundred metres square where the trees had been cut away, leaving a peeled and earthen baldness which disagreeably broke the melodic and flowing line of a great wood of dark cork-oaks. Up to the time of the death of Grandsailles' father this wood had remained intact, affording to the vast panorama a homogeneous foreground composed of the dark, undulating and horizontal line of oaks, setting off the luminous distances of the valley, likewise horizontal and gently modulated.

But since the death of the elder Grandsailles the property, burdened with heavy debts and mortgages, had had to be subdivided into three sections. Two of these had fallen into the hands of a great landed proprietor of Breton origin, Rochefort, who immediately became one of the Count's bitterest political enemies. One of the first things Rochefort did on entering into possession of his new property was to cut down the three hundred square metres of cork-oaks which fell to his title and which had lost their productive value by being separated from the rest of the great wood. They had been replaced by a planting of vines which grew poorly in the exhausted and excessively stony soil. These three hundred square metres of uprooted cork-oaks in the very heart of the family wood of Grandsailles not only bore witness to the dismemberment of the Count's domains but also this gap had brought completely into view the Moulin des Sources, now inhabited by Rochefort – a place keenly missed, for it was the key to the irrigation and the fertility of the greater part of Grandsailles' cultivated lands. The Moulin des Sources had formerly been completely hidden by the wood, and only the weather-vanes of the mill tower, emerging between two low oaks, had been visible from the Count's room.

Next to his devotion to the land, his sense of beauty was certainly one of the most exclusive passions that dominated Grandsailles. He knew himself to have little imagination, but he had a deeply rooted consciousness of his own good taste, and it was thus a fact that the mutilation of his wood was extremely offensive to his aesthetic sense. Indeed since his last electoral defeat five years previously the Count of Grandsailles, with the intransigence that characterized all his decisions, had abandoned politics, to await the moment when events would take a critical turn. This did not imply a disgust with politics. The Count, like every true Frenchman, was a born politician. He was fond of repeating Clausewitz's maxim, 'War is only the continuation of politics by other means.' He was sure that the approaching war with Germany was inevitable and that its coming was mathematically demonstrable. Grandsailles was waiting for this moment to enter into politics again, sincerely wishing that it might come as quickly as possible, for he felt his country day by day growing weaker and more corrupt. What, then, could the anecdotic incidents of the local politics of the plain matter to him?

And while he was impatiently waiting for war to break out, the Count of Grandsailles was thinking of giving a grand ball....

No, it was not only the proximity of his political enemy that oppressed him at the sight of the Moulin des Sources. In the course of these five years, during which the heroic and unswerving devotion of Maître Girardin had succeeded in stabilizing his fortune and in organizing the productivity of his lands, the last wounds that the division of his property had inflicted upon his pride and his interests seemed slowly and definitely to have healed. It should be added that if Grandsailles had been relatively indifferent to the dwindling of his former domains, he had never despaired of buying back the properties that had been taken from him and this idea, dimly nursed in the depths of his plans, helped provisionally to make him feel even more detached from his ancestral estates.

On the other hand he could never become accustomed to the mutilation of his forest, and each new day he suffered more acutely at the sight of that desolate square on which the wind-broken grape-vines of a moribund vineyard pitifully wrung their twisted arms at geometrically distributed intervals, an irreparable profanation on the horizon of his first memories – the horizon and stability of his childhood – with its three superimposed fringes, so lovingly blended by the light: the dark forest of the foreground, the illuminated plain and the sky!

Only a detailed study of the very special topography of this region, however, could satisfactorily make clear why these three elements of the landscape, so linked and constant, achieved such a poignant emotional and elegiac effect of luminous contrast in this plain of Libreux. From early afternoon the descending shadows of the mountains behind the Château would begin progressively to invade the wood of cork-oaks, plunging it suddenly into a kind of premature and pre-twilight darkness, and while the very foreground of the landscape lay obscured by a velvet and uniform shadow, the sun, beginning to set in the centre of a deep depression in the terrain, would pour its fire across the plain, its slanting rays giving an increasing objectivity to the tiniest geological details and accidents – an objectivity which was heightened even more paroxysmally by the proverbial limpidity of the atmosphere. It was as though one could have taken the entire plain of Libreux in the hollow of one's hand, as though one might have distinguished a slumbering lizard in the old wall of a house situated several miles away. It was only at the very end of twilight and almost on the threshold of night that the last residues of the reflections of the setting sun regretfully relaxed their grip on the ultimate empurpled heights, thus seeming to attempt, in defiance of the laws of nature, to perpetuate a chimerical survival of day. When it was almost nightfall the plain of Creux de Libreux still appeared illuminated. And it was perhaps because of this exceptional receptivity to light that, each time the Count of Grandsailles experienced one of his painful lapses of depression, when his soul darkened with the moral shadows of melancholy, he would see the ancestral hope of perennial and fertile life rising from the deep black forest of the spiny cork-oaks of his grief – the plain of Creux

7

de Libreux bathed in warm sunlight, the illuminated plain! How many times, after long periods spent in Paris, when Grandsailles' spirit would sink into the idle scepticism of his emotional life, the mere memory of a fugitive glimpse of his plain would revive in him a new and sparkling love of life!

This time Grandsailles had found Paris so absorbed by political problems that his stay in town had been extremely brief. He had returned to his Château de Lamotte without even having had time to be affected by the progressive disenchantment eventually produced by a too continual indulgence in relationships based exclusively on the tense drama of social prestige; this time on the contrary, the Count had come back to his domains with an unquenched craving for sociability, which induced him to invite his closest friends, as he once used to do, to come and spend weekends with him.

It was two weeks now since Grandsailles had been back and dined as usual on snails or crayfish in the company of his notary, Pierre Girardin. These were meals over which they held interminable low-voiced conversations, served on tiptoe by Prince, the old family servant.

Maître Girardin, as has been noted, concealed turbulent literary leanings beneath the strict and modest severity of his profession, just as his everyday laconic and objective phraseology concealed a succulent, metaphoric and grandiloquent verve, a modest expansiveness to which he gave free rein only in the presence of intimate and trusted friends, among whom the Count of Grandsailles was the first to be privileged.

Grandsailles took a voluptuous delight in his notary's long tirades, full of images and often touched with grandeur. And not only did he savour them, but he also put them to good use. For if it is true that the Count possessed a remarkably eloquent style and spoke the French language with a wholly personal elegance, it was no less true that he was incapable of inventing those unexpected images that came so naturally to Girardin, images of a slightly acid and cynical fancifulness that had the peculiar faculty of effectively penetrating the vulnerable zone of seduction and of dream in the suggestible and chimerical minds of women of refinement. Grandsailles would note Girardin's lyrical inventions and bizarre ideas in his memory and often, not trusting his memory, would jot them down in a tiny social engagement book in handwriting fine as a gold thread. On such occasions Grandsailles would often beg Maître Girardin to repeat the end of a sentence, and the latter then experienced the moments of his greatest pride and was forced, in spite of himself, to display the double row of very white teeth in an almost painful smile wrenched from the severe contraction of modesty. Maître Girardin would lower his head, respectfully waiting for the Count to finish his fine scrawl, and on his bowed forehead blue-tinged veins, normally quite visible and prominent, would swell even more and reach that swollen and shiny hardness characteristic of arteriosclerosis.

In Pierre Girardin's set and embarrassed expression there was not only pride compressed by the humble willingness to keep his distance, but also there was a shade of uneasiness, barely perceptible yet impossible to dissimulate. Yes, Maître Girardin was embarrassed, he was ashamed of Grandsailles, for he knew exactly the use the latter made of his notations, which was simply to enable him to shine in society, and it was in truth thanks to the occult inspiration of his notary that the Count had acquired his unique reputation as an original conversationalist. He availed himself of these jotted notes also and more especially to seduce women, and above all to keep alive that latent and consuming passion, composed of idle talk and artificiality, which by the growing addiction to its slow and fatal power linked him to Madame Solange de Cléda.

9

In fact Grandsailles, who had a poor memory, would go so far as to study the course of his meetings with Madame de Cléda in advance, and his conversations were always woven around three or four lyrical and flashing themes that had usually developed in the course of the long evenings spent in the company of his notary. It is true, to do justice to the Count, that with his natural gift of speech and his mastery of the art of social intercourse, he would often achieve real gems of style, while with the restraint of his rare good taste he developed and polished the excessive, succulent and picturesque elements which had sprung from his notary's somewhat plebeian lips but which, if he had presented them without modification in an ultra-Parisian salon, might have seemed pretentious, ridiculous or out of place, if not all three at once. Grandsailles, who had had Pierre Girardin as a playmate at the Château during his whole boyhood, had also gained from his notary an immediate, trenchant and elementary understanding of human relationships, which only a person sprung from the most authentic stock of the common people, like Girardin, could have given him. Thus each time it was said of the Count that he was a great realist in spirit, it was in large part to the logical virtues of his notary that people unwittingly alluded.

The Count of Grandsailles not only usurped his poetic images, his profound remarks and his almost brutal sense of reality from Maître Girardin, but he had even imitated the latter's way of limping. Five years previously in an automobile collision during the tragi-comic events of the electoral campaign, the Count and his notary had both suffered a similar injury in one leg. Maître Girardin was completely cured in three weeks, but the Count, whose leg was badly set, retained a limp. He had nevertheless time to observe the way his notary walked during his convalescence, and immediately took to imitating his limp, which struck him as having an impressive dignity. Indeed, by giving a slower and more serene inflection to the rhythm of his defective walk Grandsailles only added to his perfectly proportioned and manly physique a note of melancholy and refined distinction. The Count also kept from this accident a long and very thin scar, which extended in a straight vertical line from the left temple to the middle of the cheek. Now this cut, which was very deep, was barely visible, but like a barometer it would appear sharp and purplish on days of storm, and at such times it would itch violently, forcing the Count who did not want to scratch himself to bring his hand sharply to his cheeks, to which he would hold it pressed with all his might. This was the only incomprehensible tic among all his gestures and movements, which were so deliberate as to touch the fringe of affectation.

The Count of Grandsailles was giving, that evening, a dinner by candle-light to twenty-five of his closest friends who, having all arrived in the course of the afternoon, were now in the midst of 'primping' before going down into the reception room at half-past eight. Grandsailles was all dressed an hour ahead of time, and as in the case of his love-trysts, his evenings in society or even a meeting with an intimate friend, he liked to sip without haste a long, slightly and delightfully anguishing wait, during which he had time to prepare himself for the kind of effect and the situations he would like to bring about. He had a horror of anything that betrayed the barbarous love of improvisation, and on this particular evening, ready even earlier than usual for the reception, the Count sat down to wait at the desk in his room. Pulling his little engagement book out of the drawer, he began to consult the notes taken in the course of these last two weeks by means of which he expected to give brilliancy to his talk. He neglected the first three pages, written confusedly and with little conviction, and containing phrases and themes intended for general conversation, then smiled as he came upon a page full of surprises exemplifying clever ways of breaking into a discussion, and finally stopped at a page on which was written only the phrase, 'Notes for tête-à-tête with Solange'.

He remained for a long time absorbed in the contemplation of this page, and a kind of invincible indolence prevented him from proceeding, at the same time urging him irresistibly to follow the confused and agreeable course of a seductive reverie.

It was a bizarre passion that united Hervé de Grandsailles and Solange de Cléda. For five years they had played at a merciless war of mutual seduction, more and more anxious and irritating, having as yet crystallized only to the point of exacerbating a growing impulse of rivalry and self-assertion which the slightest sentimental avowal or weakness would seriously have threatened with disillusionment. Each time the Count had felt Solange's passion yield to calms of tenderness he had come forward eagerly with new pretexts to wound her vanity and re-establish the wild and rearing aggressive attitude which is that of unsatisfied desire when, whip in hand, one obliges it to overcome more and more insurmountable obstacles of pride.

It is for these reasons that after their long sessions carried on in the semi-languorous tone of a light idyll sprinkled with feigned indifference and delicate play of wit, while both of them were in reality stubbornly hiding from themselves the frenzied gallop of their passions. Grandsailles was always tempted to tap Solange on the buttocks and give her a piece of sugar, as one does to a thoroughbred horse prancing up with the supple elegance of his movements to place his boundless energy at your disposal. For the Count regarded all this with the same good-nature as a horseman covered with dust and bruises who has been thrown several times during a spirited ride. Nothing is more fatiguing than a passion of this kind, based on an integral coquetry on both sides. Grandsailles was telling himself this when he heard the clock in the drawing-room strike half-past eight. He raised his head which he had held for a long time bowed, leaning on his hand, and looked for a few moments at the plain of Creux de Libreux, which because of its special topographical configuration still held the reflections of the last gleams of day in spite of the reigning semi-darkness.

Casting a last glance at the plain the Count of Grandsailles promptly got up from his desk and, limping in his characteristic fashion, crossed the corridor that led to the reception room.

He walked with that free, calm elegance so well set off by a last nervous touching of the hand to one's hair, a final clumsy straightening of one's tie or a suspicious and casual passing glance at a mirror, characteristic of the most highly bred Anglo-Saxon timidity. The Count advanced to the middle of the room where he encountered the Duke and Duchess of Saintonges, who had entered through the opposite door at the same moment, and gave them each in turn a kiss on both cheeks. The Duke looked extremely moved, but before he had time to open his mouth there was heard the approaching sound of a violent discussion which suddenly ceased at the threshold. The young Marquis of Royancourt, with his head swathed in bandages, appeared, flanked by Edouard Cordier and Monsieur Fauceret, and all three came rushing over to Grandsailles, trying to outdistance one another. Seizing and softly pressing the Count's hand, Camille Fauceret exclaimed, 'Fine messes your protégé, the Marquis of Royancourt, gets himself into! On the very evening of the day when he becomes a King's Henchman he fights side by side with the communists to overthrow the only government that knew what it wanted and that had the guts to impose it, a government of order!'

'Damn it!' the Marquis de Royancourt broke out jovially, touching with his finger a fresh patch of blood that had just appeared through his bandages. 'It's bleeding again. I'll run up and change the dressing. It will only take me ten minutes, and I leave it to these gentlemen, my dear Count, to tell you everything that happened.

By the time I get back all the spade work will have been done, and I will only have to add the truth.'

In a few seconds the room was almost completely full and Grandsailles, while he was busy receiving his guests, began through fragments of conversation coming to him in a jumble from all directions at once to learn the tragic events of the day before. It was the Sixth of February, as it was already being called, which had just brought about the resignation of the Daladier cabinet.

The Count of Grandsailles had an invincible antipathy for the radio – indeed did not own one – and having spent the day without reading the newspapers, he now listened with a kind of voluptuous intoxication to the avalanche of sensational news to which the names of almost all his acquaintances were closely linked. He would interrupt from time to time to have some detail clarified, but before the person had had time to explain, his attention would already be drawn by the surprise of fresh revelations. The Count of Grandsailles limped back and forth from group to group, his head thrown back, his face slightly turned to the left, lending an equally attentive ear to everyone and with his glance fixed on some indeterminate point in the ceiling. By this detached and superior manner he wished to show that while interested in these events in a general way, not only was he not astonished at them but refused to be drawn into the feverish atmosphere of the conversations which only the decorum of the place prevented from becoming acrimonious.

The women especially appeared really overwhelmed by what had happened, for to the forty killed and several hundred wounded was added the blatant and romantic truculence of the organizations involved. The Croix de Feu, the communists, the Cagoulards, the Acacia conspirators, the Camelots du Roi were such melodramatic names that by themselves alone they were enough to bring goose-flesh to the most delicate skins exposed above the low-necked dresses.

The Count of Grandsailles observed all his friends, among whom
there were in fact Croix de Feu, Cagoulards, Acacia conspirators,
King's Henchmen, members of the resigned cabinet, even communists, and with the indulgence which his vivid love of literature
rendered just a little perverse he imperceptibly winked his eyes and,
taking in the motley collection of his guests, decided that his salon
was 'quite impressive'.

A little overwhelmed by so much sudden actuality, he ceased to pay
attention to his friends' narrative avalanche, and with his back lightly
resting against the marble of the fireplace, the Count began to see
rising before him, as in a cinema montage, the disorderly succession
of the most striking images of everything that he had just learned.
He saw the setting sun disappear behind the Arc de Triomphe while
the Croix de Feu demonstrators came down the Champs Elysées in
serried ranks of twelve, with unfurled banners in the lead; saw the
motionless, black, expectant barrages of the police ordered to hold
them back yield one after another at the last moment, without even
appreciably slowing the intrepid march of the demonstrators; now
the latter were heading straight towards the Pont de la Concorde,
cluttered with army trucks and troops protecting the access to the
Chamber of Deputies.

Suddenly the chief of the municipal police advances a dozen yards
to meet the demonstrators. He parleys with the banner-carriers and
then the procession, first hesitating, then changing its direction, heads
toward the Madeleine and there is a redoubling of the cries. 'Daladier
to the gallows! Daladier to the gallows!' In a flash the iron castings
that form protective gratings round the trees are torn up, violently
hurled on the cobble-stones and broken in pieces, which become
fearful weapons; with iron bars the gas conduits of the streetlamps are
smashed and, as they begin to burn, project furious whistling flames
that rise obliquely like long-contained geysers to a height of ten feet

toward the sky in which the twilight deepens. Another! Then another! And as if by a destructive contagion bonfires of popular anger form gala festoons, with their fiery plumes, over the seething tide of the crowd. From the sidewalk opposite Maxim's, rocks are thrown on the Navy Ministry, a leather-gloved hand introduces kerosene-soaked rags through a broken window, a *porte cochère* opens and the livid face of a vessel-commander appears. 'I don't know what you want,' he says, 'but I see the tricolor among you and I am sure you will not want to shed the blood of French sailors; Long live the Navy! Long live France!' And the crowd surges on toward the Madeleine. It now fills the Rue Royale. A chambermaid leaning on a balcony is killed by a stray bullet, and an ample amaranth-coloured dressing-gown that she was holding in her hand drops into the street. Grandsailles sees this sinister piece of fabric flutter over the heads of the crowd, momentarily distracted by such incidents, but immediately caught up again by the unsated frenzy which, like that of rutting dogs, drives it on at a pulsating and uncontrolled pace to pursue the magnetizing and bitter odour of revolt.

All these visions were beginning to follow one another in Grandsaille's imagination with an accelerated rhythm, without apparent continuity but with such visual acuteness that the animated spectacle of his drawing-room became an indeterminate background of confused murmurs and movements.

He sees a great pool of blood from a horse with its belly ripped open, in which the journalist Lytry, enveloped in his invariable yellow raincoat, has just slipped. The flowershop window of the Madeleine (where the Count used to buy his little yellow lilies with amaranth leopard spots which he sometimes had the audacity to pin in his buttonhole) now reflects in the stalactites of its broken glass the burning hulk of an overturned bus on the corner of the Rue Royale. They are unbuttoning the trousers of Monsieur Cordier's fat chauffeur, whom two friends have just stretched out on a bench; his flesh is very pale, the colour of a fly's belly, and right beside his navel, ten centimetres away, there is another little hole, without a drop of blood, smaller but darker, just as Monsieur Cordier himself had described it. 'It looked like two squinting little pig's eyes.'

The Prince of Orminy, pale as a corpse, goes in through the service-entrance to the Fouquet bar; he has a fine iron rod, fifteen centimetres long, nailed like a small harpoon just below his nose and so solidly anchored in the bone of his upper jaw that even with the full strength of his two hands he is unable to dislodge it, and he falls unconscious into the arms of the manager, the faithful Dominique, crying. 'Forgive me....' Then at nightfall, the cafés on the Place Royale crowded with wounded and the last belated recalcitrants driven back toward the far end of the Champs Elysées, closely pursued by the stray bullets of the Garde Mobile sub-machine guns; the deserted Place de la Concorde, with the dripping indifference of the elegant bronzes of its fountains and the residues of passion – guttered lamp-posts with their jets of flame unfurled in the starry night in a sheaf of aigrettes.

Just at this moment Madame de Cléda entered the drawing-room wearing a sheaf of aigrettes in her hair. Grandsailles gave a start on seeing her appear and, as if abruptly awakening from his waking dream, instantly realized that she was in fact the only person he was waiting for. He stepped forward with unhabitual eagerness to receive her and kissed her on the forehead.

Madame de Cléda, with her sun-tanned complexion, so sculptural and adorned with diamond necklaces and cascades of satin, so completely personified Parisian actuality that it was as if one of the fountains of the Place de la Concorde had just broken into the room.

Madame de Cléda's entrance was not quite what the Count would have wished. He was uncompromisingly zealous of the 'tone'

of his salon, and although this unwonted disorder, with everyone
trying to out-talk his fellow, had intrigued him for a moment, now
before Madame de Cléda's somewhat startled and ironic gaze the din
became intolerable to him. He immediately assumed an indulgent
and slightly acid smile as if to say, 'Well, children, we have enjoyed
ourselves long enough, now we have to put an end to play.' Burning
with a controlled impatience which cast a shadow of concern over his
face, Grandsailles discreetly ordered dinner to be served ten minutes
ahead of time, thus hoping to re-establish the fluid course of well-
ordered conversations, foreseeing that the ceremonious descent down
the broad stairway to the dining-room would canalize the impetuous
torrent of budding polemics into a calm river of politeness.

The Count's dinner, however, only restored the dialectical equilibrium for a very short time, for almost immediately the burning
issue of the bloody events of the Sixth of February again rose to the
surface of all the conversations. This time they began to slide down
the dangerous slope along which one passed imperceptibly from the
descriptive phase of the beginning, to the ideological phase, which
would inevitably crown the end of this meal – a meal which, if not
historic, was at least dramatically symptomatic of this decisive and
crucial period of the history of France.

Madame de Montluçon was seated at Senator Daudier's right, and
at the left of the political commentator, Villers. She was a member
of the Croix de Feu because the husband of her lover's mistress
was a communist. She wore a Chanel dress, with a very low neck,
edged with roses cut out of three thicknesses of black and beige lace,
between which were hidden rather large pearl caterpillars.

Senator Daudier always stood in opposition to every political
opinion with which he was confronted and invariably defended the
person criticized by whomever he happened to be talking with, and in
the last part of a speech he systematically and intentionally tore down

what he had built up in the first, so that while giving the impression that he had very precise opinions on every subject the unvarying result of what he said was a draw. He delivered a dithyrambic encomium on Madame de Montluçon's dress concluding, as he turned to her, 'The neck of your dress, Madame, is quite edible, including the roses, but for my own taste I should have preferred to have the caterpillars served in a separate dish, so that one could just help himself.'

Villers thereupon told about the latest Parisian extravagance – the edible hats exhibited in the surrealist show. Politically, Villers belonged to the Acacia conspirators, for the simple reason that, being a writer, he composed the political speeches of one of the prominent leaders of this faction.

He spoke fawningly to Madame de Montluçon, trying to interest her in his pseudo-philosophic work on contemporary history. Madame de Montluçon, giving up trying to follow him in his frenzied cavalcade of paradoxes, finally exclaimed, 'But I really can't make out which side you are on!'

'Neither can I,' Villers retorted with a note of melancholy. 'You see, I am in my way a kind of artist, and my attitude is exactly like that of Leonardo da Vinci, who left his famous equestrian statue unfinished while he waited to see who was going to win. I keep working away on my book and I'm making it a veritable monument; it is grandiose, imposing, finished in its slightest details, but there is no head; I am leaving that till the last moment so that I can give it the head of the conqueror.'

And as a calf's head trimmed with laurel leaves was just being served at that moment he added, pointing to a leaf with the tip of his fork. 'As a matter of fact what really counts, you know, is not so much the head as the laurel.'

Monsieur Fauceret and Monsieur Ouvrard, since the beginning of the meal, had been carrying on an acrimonious debate on the

Paris riots. They were the most antagonistic political adversaries of the moment because, having the same position, the same platform and the same approach to all political questions, they were obliged to perform masterpieces of interpretation in order to give their followers the impression that they were in constant and flagrant disagreement, so as to outdistance each other in the frenzied race of their immediate and daily ambition, which confused their vision and prevented them from seeing their still uncertain goal of power.

Simone Durny who for some moments had furiously and obstinately been devouring her asparagus to the ends, chewing and rechewing their fibrous residues without knowing what she was eating, finally broke hysterically into the conversations that were going on around her. 'No, I say, No! I would a thousand times rather see a communist France than a France dominated by the Boches!'

Monsieur Fauceret looked at her pityingly for a moment, then peering straight into her eyes said with an air of solemnity, and as if trying to remember, 'Madame... what is your son's name, now?'

'Jean-Louis,' Simone answered, her lips trembling with anticipation.

'Well, Madame,' answered Camille Fauceret gently, 'with remarks like that you do nothing less than blindly sign your son Jean-Louis' death warrant!'

Madame Durny sat as if congealed, her face suddenly motionless, and her eyes slowly filled with large tears: she had just swallowed an asparagus the wrong way.

Béatrice de Brantès felt some tenderness for radical-socialism because she had an intuition that it was in the untidiness of the trousers, in the stiff collars and the unkempt moustaches of its leaders that the authentic jesting, ribald spirit of France had found refuge.

She was seated at the right of Monsieur Edouard Cordier, a radical-socialist because he was a Mason, and at the left of the Marquis of Royancourt, a royalist as his very name indicated.

Béatrice de Brantès, fresh and exuberant, was lightly leaning on Monsieur Cordier's well-padded shoulder, paying homage to his political affinities by telling him risqué stories; she had so much grace in her diction that she could say anything without losing an iota of her elegance, but contrary to all usage, she would whisper the innocuous passages of her anecdotes and raise her voice just for the most ribald parts, coquettishly trying by this device to attract the attention of the Marquis of Royancourt, whom she felt to be too much absorbed in the general conversation.

'Imagine,' said Béatrice to Monsieur Cordier, 'Madame Deschelette, with her Schiaparelli dress and hat – that monumental hat – mounted on top of a taxi to get a better view of everything that was going on, tapping with her feet and alone against the crowd pouring a torrent of violent insults on the demonstrators.'

And as Monsieur Cordier was listening with great absorption, she went on, 'Naturally this could last only so long. (She lowered her voice.) A group of the King's Henchmen seized her by the legs, laid her on the pavement, pulling up her skirts… (raising her voice) and burned her with the tip of a cigarette in one of the most sensitive and delicate parts of her anatomy.'

'The baptism of fire!' exclaimed Cordier, apoplectic and with eyes sparkling.

'Well, no,' Béatrice answered with a drawling inflection, feigning innocence. 'It appears on the contrary that it was the cigarette that was baptized – with water.'

'What water?' asked Monsieur Cordier in momentary perplexity.

With a lazily astonished and infinitely voluptuous expression, Béatrice answered between her teeth, almost hissing the words, 'It wasn't really water….' And as some very frothy champagne was just being poured into her glass she added, giving even more emphasis to each syllable, 'Nor was it exactly champagne.'

She looked at Monsieur Cordier with such an air of malice that he remained flabbergasted for a moment.

'Yes, I assure you, this incredible story is quite true,' the Marquis of Royancourt broke in, highly amused, and trying to help out Monsieur Cordier in this moment of embarrassment. 'It was Madame Deschelette herself who told it to me. You can imagine that having been hemmed in by the crowd for two hours she really needed to go – it couldn't have happened more opportunely.'

'My dear Marquis,' said Béatrice, delicately placing her plump hand on his arm, 'having waited in vain for the homage of your Gallic wit, since you're submerged in politics, I'm pouring my charms over poor Monsieur Cordier.'

'You won't be wasting them, my dear,' the Marquis responded with liveliness. 'He could tell you some that would make you blush to the tips of your hair, but you have to get him in his own element. As for me, my dear Béatrice, I apologize for not making love to you, but I'm sure you understand, with such events going on....'

Saying which, he playfully pressed his thigh, hardened by horseback-riding, against Béatrice de Brantès' soft one, and she accepted the attention with a charming laugh.

Senator Daudier was creating a sensation at his end of the table by expounding a highly original theory.

'Hitler wants war,' he said, 'not in order to win, as most people think, but to lose. He is romantic and an integral masochist, and exactly as in Wagner's operas it has to end for him, the hero, as tragically as possible. In the depth of his subconscious, the end to which Hitler at heart aspires is to feel his enemy's boot crushing his face, which for that matter is unmistakably marked by disaster....' And Daudier concluded, with a note of concern, 'The trouble is that Hitler is very honest.... He won't cheat. He is willing to lose, but not to lose on purpose. He insists on playing the game to the end according to the rules, and will give up only when he is beaten. That's why we shall have so much trouble.'

The Count of Grandsailles had at his right the Duchess of Saintonges and at his left Madame Cécile Goudreau. Politically the Duchess of Saintonges was rather leftish, while Madame Cécile Goudreau was definitely rightist. With the leftist ideas of his right-hand partner the Count would mildly bring out the rightist ideas of his left-hand partner, and with the rightist ideas of his left-hand partner, he would moderately develop the leftist ideas of his right-hand partner. This was all executed with the exaggerated opportunistic politeness of the subtle game of balance which distinguished not only the Count's personal attitude, but also that of the great powers in the European situation at this moment.

Toward the end of the meal the ideological effervescence gathered around the Count de Grandsailles who, resigning himself to listening, had lapsed into silence. With the proselytizing zeal of bellicose charlatans devoid of all conviction, each one brought forward his own political solutions, with which everyone else unanimously disagreed. The Acacia conspirators saw France's only hope of political health in a Latin bloc, composed of France, Spain and Italy, set off against England and Germany; those who belonged to the Comité France-Allemagne demanded that for once an attempt be made to create a frank and unqualified friendship with the Germans; others wanted an immediate military alliance with Russia, to isolate England and nip the communist organizations of the country in the bud. All these theses were simultaneously investigated in the light of the subtlest legalistic interpretations, to the great delight of Monsieur Ouvrard who kept breaking into the discussions and who observed:

'France's situation is indeed grave, but one thing is certain: in spite of the political chaos which we are undergoing, our notions of law and order are becoming more refined and specialized day by day. Yes, gentlemen, on this score we continue to lead all other nations and it is impossible not to recognize that the growth of our jurisdictional institutions constitutes the very health of our nation.'

'In short,' the Duke of Saintonges sighed, remembering Forain's famous last words, 'we are dying – but we shall at least die cured!'

Grandsailles smiled bitterly, puckering up his eyes which became edged with a multitude of tiny and almost invisible wrinkles. He remembered the Hitlerian hordes, the Congress of Nuremberg, on the occasion of his last sojourn in Germany, and from the light of each of the syllables and of the candles that illuminated his table with a fanatically witty and Socratic atmosphere he saw emerging the spectre of the defeat of 1940.

Like Socrates, France was preparing for death by uttering witticisms and discussing law.

Grandsailles brought a last glass of champagne to his lips and swallowed it stoically, as though it had been hemlock, while the oratorical fervour of his guests crystallized in the great bilious eloquence of recrudescent sarcasm as coffee was about to be served. Grandsailles lent a more and more absent ear to what was being said and, drowsy from eating, let himself relax in the absorbed contemplation of the thousand movements that the light of the candles, the gesticulations of the dinner-guests and the ceremonious comings and goings of the servants communicated to the impassive impartiality of the crystals and the silverware. As if hypnotized, the Count looked at the Lilliputian images of his guests reflected in the concavities and convexities of the silver pieces. He observed with fascination the figures and faces of his friends, the most familiar ones becoming unrecognizable, while reassuming by virtue of the fortuitous metamorphoses of their rapid deformations the most unsuspected relationships and the most striking resemblances with the vanished personalities of their ancestors, mercilessly caricatured in the polychrome images that adorned the bottoms of the plates in which the dessert had just been served.

Thus in one of these reflections, fleeting daughters of the magic of chance, it was possible to see emerging from the outline of Béatrice de Brantès, vertically draped in a Lelong dress, the corseted and strangled figure of Marie Antoinette, or the infinitely more extended one of a hunted weasel, which the Queen hid in the depth of the destiny of her decapitated royal head. And in the same way the Viscount of Angerville's rectilinear nose which aspired to Anglo-Saxon dandyism could suddenly swell into the pear-shape of the succulently Gallic nose of his grandfather, which in turn could recede until it became like that of a marmot, covered with hair and earth, lost in the infernal subsoil of its atavistic origins.

Exactly as in the famous series of monstrous faces drawn by Leonardo, one could here observe each of the faces of the guests caught in the ferocious meshes of anamorphosis, twisting, curling, extending, lengthening and transforming their lips into snouts, stretching their jaws, compressing their skulls and flattening their noses to the farthest heraldic and totemic vestiges of their own animality. No one could escape this subtle and cruelly revealing inquisition of optical physics, which by the imperceptible torture of its constraint was able to snatch the avowal of degrading sneers and unavowable grimaces from appearances that were the most dignified and set in nobility. As if in an instantaneous demoniac flash one saw the dazzling teeth of a jackal in the divine face of an angel, and the stupid eye of a chimpanzee would gleam savagely in the serene face of the philosopher.

Each reflection was a divination; for even better than in a gazer's crystal, one can discover a natural son's uncertain origin in the suavely deformed reflection of a face on the delicately curved back of a fork-handle.

The congested epiderms of the concluding meal empurpled the candelabra. Each candelabrum was a sanguinary genealogical tree, each knife was a mirror of infidelity and each spoon an escutcheon of infamy.

A stark naked young Silenus, masterfully chiselled in oxidized silver, was holding down a rough branch of the candelabrum, bringing the light very close as if in calling attention to the budding curves of Solange de Cléda's breasts exposed above her décolleté. Here her skin was so fine and white that Grandsailles, looking at her, cautiously dipped his dessert spoon into the smooth surface of his cream cheese, taking only a small piece to taste it, snapping it adroitly with the agile tip of his tongue. The slightly salt and tart taste, evoking the animal femininity of the she-goat, went straight to his heart. With a faint but delightful anguish he continued to cut into the immaculate turgescence of his Homeric dish and as he finished his cheese he decided that the familial undulations of his silverware harmonized so well with Solange's matt and oxidized pallor that the thought of marrying her sprang into his mind for the first time. Solange happened to catch the Count off guard in this moment of his equivocal concupiscence and, also for the first time, she made him a humble, almost slavish bow, while the moist slit of her lips half opened in a feverish smile imperceptibly tinged with pain, expressing the almost sensorial emotion of a violently physical pleasure.

Grandsailles seized the knotty trunk of a candelabrum, which he lifted without effort in spite of its heavy weight, and brought it close to light his cigar without waiting for the match which the servant was about to offer him, indicating by this impatient and energetic movement that he had just made an important decision.

With the coffee the conversations assumed the grave note of synthesis, for the fervour of the guests had by now somewhat cooled, and they looked back a little shamefacedly at the orgiastic ideological chaos of their opinions and were anxious to reach some common ground that might seem more or less like a conclusion. The Duke of Saintonges, especially, had assumed an insistent and superior tone which while remaining quite general was unmistakably aimed at the political indifference displayed by Grandsailles, who seemed to withdraw more and more into his shell as the meal was coming to an end.

'Whether we wish it or not,' Saintonges exclaimed, addressing himself now directly to the Count with almost a note of impertinence, 'contemporary history is so dense and dramatic that each of us in his own sphere, even the most aloof, even without knowing it, is involved in what is happening, each of us already has a decisive card to play.'

'Banco!' Grandsailles exclaimed, abruptly letting the candlestick fall back on the table. An expectant silence suddenly held all conversation in suspense, and there was only the bustle of the servants' imperturbable movements, which heightened the tension by its subdued and respectful little sounds. Without ceasing to gaze at Solange de Cléda, Grandsailles calmly took several puffs on his cigar. Having assured himself that it was well lit he remained silent for a moment; then, in a perfectly natural tone, but measuring his words, he said, 'Saintonges is right, and it is precisely to announce my decision to you that I am giving this dinner.'

The moment was so dramatically charged that it was with a kind of anguish and a sharper beating of all hearts that attention gathered more closely round Grandsailles.

'I have been thinking it over for three days,' the Count finally announced, 'and I have decided to give a grand ball.' A murmur of enthusiastic exclamations crowned the announcement with a flurry of unanimity and sympathetic warmth and in a moment, breaking all rules of etiquette, the women gathered in a cluster round the Count, besieging him with the grace of their blandishments.

The Duke of Saintonges, who had barely had time to regret the incident, seized Grandsailles' hand with his two effusive ones, sincerely grateful to him for having so skilfully turned aside a polemic which because of his ineptitude had nearly become dangerously personal.

Solange de Cléda was deeply upset by the scene. For since the moment when she had made her curtsey to the Count, the latter had not averted his eyes from her for an instant. During this whole time, with her head slightly bent back and her eyes lowered, she had pretended to be listening attentively to Dick d'Angerville's confidences, but in reality she had only been furtively watching, through the luminous rainbows that formed in the long lashes of her half-closed lids, the parsimonious ascension and the seductive movements of the candles, with which Grandsailles chose to light his cigar.

Unaware of the conversations that had been going on around the Count, Solange did not understand what he meant when he exclaimed, 'Banco!' This word indeed reached her only through the hubbub of the general conversation, as a passionate appeal addressed to her, after which an unexpected abruptness in the Count's gestures made her tremble. Without moving her head she merely opened her eyes a little further and then clearly saw that as the candlestick was heavily put back on the tablecloth, a profusion of large drops of wax were spattered at its feet.

After a mortal silence the sound of Grandsailles' voice seemed to her to possess an infinitely and inexplicably sweet languor, especially when he said, '... it is precisely to announce my decision to you that I am giving this dinner. I have been thinking....'

Solange, who since the enigmatic word, 'Banco', felt as though she were living a waking dream, was quite aware of the ridiculousness of the mortal fear that beset her: she was afraid Grandsailles was publicly going to announce their engagement, which had never been discussed between them. Nevertheless, in spite of the absurdity of this conviction, her heart beat so tumultuously that she thought she would be unable to breathe, yes, she was sure of it! Graindsailles was going to speak about the two of them.

But now how stupid, childish and delirious this all seemed! Disconcerted, mortified, and overcome by a kind of sudden complete disenchantment, she thought for a moment that she would be unable to go on for the rest of the evening. A warm drop of perspiration formed in each of her armpits and slowly flowed down the whole length of her bare sides, and these two drops were black because each of them reflected the black velvet arms of the chair she was sitting in. But she was so supernaturally beautiful that one might rather have thought that the wings of melancholy hovering near were now folding over her, darkening and transmuting this magnetizing and desirable physical secretion of her anguished flesh into two black pearls of precious grief.

As everyone had got up from the table the Viscount of Angerville, who was standing behind Solange waiting to pull back her chair, placed his hand on her shoulder and whispered close to her ear, '*Bonjour, tristesse!*'

Salonge quivered, tried to get up. But feeling dizzy, she was obliged to sit down for a moment on the black velvet arm of the chair, the end of which was ornamented by a sphinx's head of carved bronze. She bowed her head against Dick d'Angerville's chest and shut her eyes. The sphinx's head felt so cold through the thin fabric of her dress that she thought she had sat down on something wet.

The 'Grandsailles ball' was going to be her ball? She opened her eyes again, pressed her thighs together and, leaping up unexpectedly, whirled round several times in an impassioned waltz step. And as d'Angerville remained glued to the spot, registering only a faint astonishment through his incurably blasé air, Solange said, with a final whirl, '*Bonjour, tristesse – Bonsoir, tristesse,*' tossed back a smile and ran up the stairs to the drawing-room.

Monsieur Edouard Cordier, who was lingering over his armagnac and had been a witness to this scene, came over to the Viscount of Angerville.

'My dear Vicomte, our epoch is slipping out of our hands, it's getting beyond our comprehension – but I am resigned to it. At one moment we think our ladies are about to die of God knows what, right in our arms, and suddenly they revive and dance away, and it's exactly the same in politics. Just now we were on the very verge of a fight, and we thought we were hearing the first clarions of civil war.... Well, it was merely the announcement of a ball. As a matter of fact one of the most deeply rooted notions of the human spirit, the sense of the right and the left, has been completely lost and scrambled by our contemporaries.'

He glanced down with perplexed anxiety at each of his robust hands with their fingers outspread, and continued. 'Do we know, today, which is our right hand and which is our left? No, my dear Vicomte, we have no idea! When I was a young man it was still possible to form an opinion about great events according to the ideology of the political party to which you belonged. But that is no longer possible today. You read a piece of sensational, vital, decisive news in the paper – well, you have no way of knowing whether it is good or bad before the specialists of your political party have pondered over it and decided it for you. Otherwise we would run the risk of making fools of ourselves and reaching exactly the same opinions as the newspapers of our worst political enemies the next day.'

The Viscount of Angerville, who, while this peroration had lasted, had gradually drawn Monsieur Cordier toward the door to the foot of the stairs, said by way of conclusion, 'In any case, if Grandsailles goes ahead with his ball we might as well dance at it. Is there anything better for us to do while we await developments?'

The Grandsailles balls, since the beginning of the other post-war period, had all been brilliant moments in the history of Parisian life, and this refined society which now again filled the Count's drawing-room instinctively felt that their rôle as a ruling class gained more reality and social meaning by their continuing to maintain the prestige of French elegance and wit than by wallowing in suicides and sterile political fumblings. So it was that this rallying of forces, this revival of the consciousness of its historic rôle, which the most cleverly calculated slogans of the ideological jargon of the moment had not been able to bring about, had been achieved by Grandsailles with *his* slogan, 'a ball'.

And through this single word, which kindled the deep essence of frivolity of their common tradition into a hot flame, the Count saw re-established around him that indestructible unity of the national 'character' which was to be that of the whole French people on the day when the tocsin of war should sound-so true was it, according to one of Grandsailles' theories, that wars are rather a question of character than of ideology, and that the historic constants of great invasions often only mask the geo-political frivolities of nations.

After this Socratic dinner, in the course of which no one had attempted to shut his eyes to the fate of his country, the plan for the great ball now began in the Count's drawing-room to be illuminated by all the fires, the fiery crosses, the hooked crosses, the fleurs-de-lis and the hammers and sickles which had caused the Place de la Concorde to swim in blood the evening before.

Grandsailles who, contrary to his usual habits, had announced his long-caressed plan for the ball on the spur of the moment, was surprised at his success, and immediately gave up the idea of the tête-à-tête with Solange de Cléda so carefully worked out with the aid of his notebook – that tête-à-tête which, also against his habits, he had had the indolence not to prepare, and which would have committed him to psychological ineptitudes which he would never have forgiven himself.

He accordingly decided to exploit the opposite of that affectionate and attentive tête-à-tête which he had looked forward to for weeks, and to pretend to ignore and to neglect Solange's presence for the rest of the evening. This distant attitude, following upon the admiring glances he had bestowed on her at the conclusion of the dinner, could not fail to create a desirable disturbance in this woman whom he had just now had the ephemeral idea of marrying.

The almost turbulent manner in which Solange had been behaving since they had left the dinner-table gave Grandsailles additional reasons for treating her acidly as a too noisy and inexperienced child whom only her undeniable charm and the radiance of her beauty rendered indispensable for filling the gaps in the decorative atmosphere of his salon, in which if it was true that there were never lacking sensational specimens of the rarest and smartest femininity, it was also true that the prestige of birth, joined to the even more rigorous distinction of intelligence, constituted the dominant note.

Spurred to audacity by the vague presentiment of her impending triumph in the 'Grandsailles ball', Solange de Cléda heroically accepted the rôle which the Count had just assigned her – accepted it with such disconcerting malice and charm that Grandsailles immediately felt his evil intentions had been unmasked. In a kind of continual dance, she progressed from one flower display to another while the guests looked on with amusement, forming adornments for her hair, each more captivating than the last, with the blossoms which she plucked, then pitilessly tore off and tossed away. According to the inspiration of the moment Solange would accompany each of her improvised effects with the pantomime and the interpretive language of the flowers she was dramatizing. Each new parody received an acclamation and Grandsailles himself, hypocritically overcoming his reticence, began to pretend to be touched by the pastoral poetry of her play.

Now Solange gathered some long trailers of star-shaped ivy-leaves which she fastened together and draped over her head, letting them droop behind her ears down to the floor. Then she made little holes in two ivy leaves which she held over her eyes like a mask. Everyone applauded this new transformation, that would have graced the purest fairy-tale, and a fresh silence awaited the scene that Solange would enact on the theme of the ivy.

She tripped forward quickly on tiptoe, and stood for a moment motionless, all quivering, before the Count of Grandsailles. Falling suddenly at his knees she delicately but firmly wound her arms around them, and in a suppliant and pathetic voice, with a barely perceptible barb of irony that stung the Count, she feebly declaimed, 'I must cling, or I die!'

There was no more talk of the ball. Bérard, the painter, his beard trimmed à la Courbet, was sitting on the floor with both his elbows resting on the Duchess of Saintonge's knees and was making everyone turn to admire Solange, who had run to the far end of the drawing-room where Dick d'Angerville helped her remove her leaf-ornaments, by a large malachite table where the flowers she had been using for her acts lay scattered.

Solange was immediately surrounded and the drawing-room became divided into two groups, the one gathered round Grandsailles, and the other in which Madame de Cléda reigned. Presently exclamations of astonishment and delight rose among the latter's admirers. She had just invented a new game. With the three diamonds of her earring that were mounted on the ends of three trembling stems, she had composed a flower of surprising effect by taking a mauve-tinged lily and substituting the three diamonds for the real pistils. Immediately all the women stripped off their jewelry, strewing the table with a new disorder of precious stones which with their intact fires seemed to arouse the dulled and faded fires of the flowers.

'*Messieurs, Mesdames, faites vos jeux*,' said Dick d'Angerville in a polite, insistent voice. 'Green wins!' exclaimed Béatrice de Brantès, who had placed a small turtle of emeralds on a darker gardenia leaf; the effect was so homogeneous that it looked as if the two had been made for each other. Thereupon they began to vie with one another in making the most unexpected and ingenious juxtapositions spring from the chaos. There was a lively flutter of hands avidly trying out combinations, their frenzy and emulation growing so violent that presently it looked like a mock-battle, with each one attempting to seize the same flower, the same jewel, the same leaf, the same idea. But all at once the game ended, as abruptly as it had begun, everyone having grown bored with it. By way of conclusion Solange placed between her breasts a yellow rose in which she had pinned a big Fabergé beetle of rubies and diamonds a little off centre. The unexpected effect of this combination was that the rose immediately looked artificial, while the beetle appeared so living and real in spite of the stones that Solange was again acclaimed.

But the centre of gravity of the salon had shifted elsewhere. Somewhat shamefacedly they abandoned this childish play (which nevertheless on the morrow was to become incorporated in the most mannered chichis of Parisian fashion) and the interest now reverted to the incidents of the Place de la Concorde and the ball.

'The list,' exclaimed Bérard, the painter, 'let's have the list!' and he waved a sheet of white paper which he had gone to fetch from Grandsailles' desk. Solange, seating herself humbly at the Count's feet, said candidly, 'What an exciting moment it is – to begin the first list of the Grandsailles ball!' By this ingratiating remark she hoped to gain his forgiveness for her triumph of a while ago.

'But my dear,' he said, stroking her hair paternally, 'you know perfectly well that it isn't the guests who count on such occasions.' And he added, with the air of someone who repeats a thing that has been said again and again a thousand times, 'One gives balls for those one doesn't invite.'

'What fun it's going to be to plan a ball in that spirit!' Solange exclaimed with annoyance.

'Of course it won't be fun,' Grandsailles replied acidly, and then with indulgence, 'You know, darling, at our age we don't go to balls for fun any more!'

Oh yes, she knew – Grandsailles never did anything for fun!

Solange spent a sleepless night, did not go down to eat, and Prince brought her breakfast in bed, announcing at the same time that tea would be served the guests in the Count's room before they left. Dick d'Angerville was to bring her back to Paris in his car in the late afternoon.

Madame de Cléda, who was a prey to a kind of childish fear which made her believe that her rather frequent insomnias were undermining her health to the point of endangering her life, forced herself by an almost superhuman exertion of will to swallow a little food, after which she let herself sink into an anguished semi-slumber, the slightest sound inducing in her spasmodic shiverings which, according to the changing course of her reveries, she was often able to transform into voluptuous sensations.

Toward four o'clock Solange began to get herself ready for tea. She felt weak, with a heaviness about her chest. A vague desire to vomit obliged her to dress slowly and now and again remain motionless to

35

listen to the beating of her heart. The lack of sleep tugged all around the orbits of her irritated eyes: she felt discouraged, afraid of the moment when she would have to appear in this new disadvantageous light before Grandsailles, knowing moreover that it would be difficult henceforth to equal the image of herself she had succeeded in creating on the previous evening, which was the result of three weeks of studied preparation, of special, daily, minute, uninterrupted, exclusive and desperately heroic care. At last, facing the dreaded moment, she approached the mirror, looked at herself and was delighted with her appearance. Never, she thought, had she looked so seductive. The look of weariness in her eyes had only accentuated the consuming and burning expression of her gaze. Her mouth was so white and its outer edge was set off so faintly from the olive pallor of her face that her smile appeared only as the single warmly shadowed and sinuous line that marked the joining of her almost translucent lips, looking now like those of a spectral and immaterial alabaster sculpture, now like the carnal and equivocal ones drawn with a single mysterious line by Leonardo's ambiguous charcoal pencil.

Madame de Cléda bowed her melancholy head till her brow touched the mirror. Smiling at herself at such close range that her breath obliterated her own image it was then as if, during the interval when she remained thus motionless, the immateriality of her reflection was transferred to her body to bring her back to life, awaking all her movements with a new burst of anxious and determined energy.

If it was impossible for her to resemble the woman she had been the previous evening, she could perhaps do just the opposite and speculate on the infinite treasures of tenderness of her lividity, draw the maximum effect from her pallor.

Solange did her hair with maniacal care and perfection, but she put on no make-up, and immediately decided on a costume that would be at once tantalizing and severe, that would sharply set off the spiritual tension of her face. Over her bare torso she slipped a black silk blouse, very heavy and shiny, opening down the front to the middle of her stomach.

Solange's breasts were small, almost like an adolescent's, and so hard that the vertical folds of the silk slid over them with the lively movement of eels caught between two polished stones in a salt marsh from which the water devoured by the sun has evaporated. Each of her movements, characteristically abrupt and unpredictable, had a tendency to expose the compact and dazzling roundnesses of her bosom, producing an effect of innocent impudicity befitting the Spartan pride of an ancient Amazon.

To this somewhat informal and scanty upper attire Solange added the sparkle of several strings of uncut emeralds and rubies whose smooth, cold and mobile hardnesses gave a slightly more dressed appearance to the turgescent and feverish hardness of her flesh. Then she squeezed her waist violently, till it hurt, into a wide, brand-new gum-coloured belt of dull leather, and this barbarous compression gave a cynical emphasis to the two very prominent bones of her pelvis which, pointing toward heaven, fine as two knife-blades, seemed as though they might cut right through the wool of her skirt that fitted smoothly over her thighs.

There was a knock at the door. 'Are you ready?' Dick d'Angerville asked.

'Yes,' said Solange, and asked him to come in. She stood in the middle of the room, her arms folded across her chest as though she felt cold. D'Angerville took hold of her arms, opened them and held them outspread.

'It looks ravishing, and above all, it's so intelligent.'

'What is?' said Solange, pretending not to understand.

'Everything,' he said, 'your dress, the deliberate absence of make-up, the whole effect makes one think insistently of....'

37

'Of what?' Solange asked eagerly.

'Of love,' said d'Angerville.

'Idiot!' said Solange indulgently. 'You were going to say something much better.'

'Yes, you're right,' d'Angerville responded with passion. 'I was going to say that you make one think of a bed – of a terribly luxurious and half-unmade bed.' Then he added, changing his tone, 'Your eyes are red.'

'Run along now,' said Solange with hurried insistence. 'I'll meet you right away in the Count's room, it'll just take me a moment,' and she offered him the palms of both hands to kiss.

She shut the door and ran into the bathroom, made the water run very hot, soaked a folded wash-rag with it and pressed it for several minutes against her eyelids. Her eyes were red – well, they were going to be even redder!

Red eyes, too, could be seductive, for 'he who beguiles his sorrows enchants them'.

Solange de Cléda made her entrance into the Count's room brusquely, as he was sitting talking with Dick d'Angerville and Maître Girardin around the table that had been set out for tea in the centre of the room. They immediately ceased their conversation and Grandsailles, who always required a little time to get to his feet, had not yet risen from his seat when Solange was already beside him, quickly offering him her cheek to kiss and seating herself at the same time on the edge of his armchair. Grandsailles then sat back to leave her room, and while adjusting himself to his new position familiarly passed his hand behind the back of Solange, who felt the Count's hand descend the whole length of her spine and attach itself to the leather belt, linger to appraise the slenderness of her waist, then pause motionless for a moment on the very prominent pelvic bone, which he seized with the hollow of his hand, with a movement as natural as if it had been an object. Now the Count's fingers were softly caressing it and, encountering a seam of the skirt passing just over the middle of this ridge, he seized it with the tips of his nails, and using it as a rail to guide the movements of his hand suspended over the hip, followed it down its length, barely grazing it.

In spite of the feigned assurance verging on indifference of all his movements, Solange immediately guessed by imponderable shades of trembling awkwardness that Grandsailles' hand was excited. She had thus successfully achieved her first effect: intimidation. And she was determined to keep this advantage, knowing that it was one of the surest ways in which she could wield her influence over the proud Count, for Grandsailles was undoubtedly immediately overwhelmed by Solange's disconcerting appearance, though he had no time to analyse exactly wherein the change in her looks consisted.

Solange was too close to him to allow him to examine her at leisure, which only added to Grandsailles' somewhat confused feelings. He had the impression of finding himself suddenly holding in his arms the body of a new being who, to the seductions of a very relative, unsatisfied intimacy constantly tantalized by the play of studied reticences, now had unexpectedly added those of another, totally unknown and desirable being, glimpsed for just a second as in a flash of lightning.

Solange, guided by the feminine instinct of her passion, had indeed an almost miraculous gift of metamorphosis. For who could have believed, not only that she was the same woman as the one she had been the evening before, but that this same Madame de Cléda who had burst into the Count's room with such haughty, wilful and intrepid ease of manner was the same Solange who a little while before had crouched in the depth of the solitude of her room, full of anguish, assailed by childish fears and annihilated by the dizzying agonies of doubt.

39

'You seem to enjoy testing the solidity of my skeleton, my dear Hervé,' said Madame de Cléda, stopping his hand. 'But of all my bones I prefer those of my knees.' And as she spoke she lifted Grandsailles' hand over and let him touch her knees, that were fresh, smooth and blue-tinged like riverstones shadowed by the pallor of twilight.

Then, addressing Dick d'Angerville with a somewhat theatrical impatience, she said, 'I have to be in Paris not later than six o'clock tomorrow. You promised me, so we mustn't leave too late. I have a terribly important dinner.'

'A boring one?' Grandsailles asked.

'No, a charming one!' Solange replied, cutting him short with a laconic inflection that conveyed her firm intention to give no further details on this subject.

A silence fell, then Madame de Cléda, changing her tone and helping herself to tea, continued, 'And what is the bad news that Maître Girardin brings today? Is Rochefort still asking one and a half million for the repurchase of the Moulin des Sources?'

'Far worse than that, my dear Madame!' answered the notary, after having assured himself by a glance that Grandsailles would approve bringing up this subject of discussion.

'Just think,' Girardin went on, 'this feeble creature, Rochefort, yielding to the pressure of an indescribable intrigue on the part of our political enemies, has just signed a will whose terms are intended solely to prevent the lands attached to the Moulin des Sources from ever again becoming incorporated in the former Grandsailles domains.'

'It is really incredible,' Dick d'Angerville added, barely controlling his indignation. 'And do you know what the political reason for all this is? Simply that the Count of Grandsailles, because of his eminently anti-national spirit, is unworthy of ever buying back his former domains!'

'Is there anyone in the world who is more authentically French than the Count!' asked Solange, nervously shrugging her shoulders, pretending not to understand what was at issue.

'Why yes, of course,' Girardin replied.

'Who?' asked Solange.

'The Russians,' said the notary, looking crestfallen. D'Angerville greeted this with a faint smile.

'You must understand, my dear Madame de Cléda,' Girardin began again, 'that the Count has dedicated his life to the realization of a single plan: to preserve the plain of Creux de Libreux, to prevent at all costs the demoniacal nightmare that would follow in the wake of the industrialization of this eminently agricultural countryside, favoured since antiquity by the fertility of the gods. But our parties of the left, inspired by Moscow, have different ideas. They prefer the well-paid ignominy of the bourgeoisification of a miner to the noble and well-to-do austerity of our peasants. As a matter of fact these progressives, who clamour for mines, don't even have the pretext of war in their favour, for they are the very ones who systematically vote against all armament plans!'

A new silence fell, and this time no one thought of interrupting him, plunged as they all were in the problems raised by the notary's words.

Grandsailles was in fact haunted by the fear that some day his Virgilian plains of Libreux might be invaded by the fatal advance-guards of industrial progress. This could never have happened at the time when he owned almost all the lands, but at present he was powerless to prevent anyone's coming to exploit the mineral wealth of the territory that no longer belonged to him.

'We shall no doubt have to resign ourselves in the end,' sighed Grandsailles, 'and admit our historic rôle as enemies of progress, for it is certainly going against the progress of our epoch to try at all costs to prevent this countryside which inspired Poussin's finest landscapes from being transformed before our very eyes into the ignominious and degrading soot-covered ugliness of a panorama made vile by the mechanical junk of industrial buildings. The day this happens I shall consider my country dishonoured,' Grandsailles raged, struggling to his feet, no longer able to stay put.

Dick d'Angerville took him by the arm and led him toward the desk, reassuring him in a semi-confidential tone.

'My dear Count,' he said, 'take my word for it, I shall be able to use my influence with the British – nothing will be done without British capital, and besides, the proverbial apathy and lack of initiative of the government will be extremely valuable to us in this matter.'

Maître Girardin, who in his pessimism considered the industrialization of the plain as an inevitable misfortune, which at best could be delayed, brought his chair close to Madame de Cléda who had remained alone, leaning back in her armchair, sipping her tea in little gulps.

'My dear Madame,' said the notary, 'we're powerless, and I keenly regret that this unpleasant subject should have been brought up solely through my fault and that it should so unhappily have disturbed the charming intimacy of this gathering. We notaries should really keep away during these pleasurable moments and appear only at the historic hour, at ten o'clock in the morning, to announce either ruin or fortune.'

And as Madame de Cléda did not respond, he felt it his duty to justify the Count's neglect. The latter was deeply involved in a conversation with d'Angerville, both speaking in low and excited voices.

'I have known,' the notary tried to explain, 'the Count's attachment for the plain of Libreux since his childhood. But believe me, Madame, I would never have suspected that the news I was obliged to bring him today – Rochefort's categorical refusal – could have affected him so deeply. Few people can flatter themselves that they know the Count's heart so well as your humble servant. There are people who imagine him to be so ambitious as to wish ardently for the outbreak of war, which might return him to political power, but really the Count's only ambition is to preserve the heritage of Libreux and be able some day to replant the three hundred square metres of cork-oaks that Rochefort cut down at the time of the division.'

'Then according to you,' said Solange, in a tone of slightly sarcastic reproach, 'a few hundred cork-oaks would suffice to gratify the ambition of the most handsome and brilliant of the Grandsailles?'

Maître Girardin bowed his head with respectful dignity and said laconically, 'Yes, Madame, a single one would suffice!' Taking the sugar-bowl from the table he showed her the escutcheon prominently engraved on its convexity. 'You see, three roots suffice!' and he pointed to the three roots of the solitary cork-oak, like those of a molar – the sole symbol, against a field of fleurs-de-lis.

'I can't help it, I still think it's a little arid,' Solange observed. 'I like escutcheons sprinkled with claws, rivers, flames, stars and even dragons, and observe, dear Maître Girardin, what self-restraint and good taste I am showing in not asking for angels and hearts to boot!'

Maître Girardin, touched by Madame de Cléda's affectionate tone, eagerly pulled out his glasses which he lent her, so that by holding them against the sugar-bowl they would serve as magnifying glasses. Now Solange was able to read distinctly the heraldic device inscribed on a band disposed across the upper branches of the cork-oak:

JE SUIS LA DAME

Solange at once looked more attentively at the image as a whole, instantly grasping its anthropomorphic significance. She had discovered a small woman's face emerging from the centre of the foliage, and a bare torso belonging to the face, forming the whole part of the trunk which had been stripped of its bark, while the dress of cork modestly covered the rest of the body from the navel down, with its three roots planted in the ground.

Likewise, in the upper part of the tree-woman the bare shoulders disappeared in their turn into the rough surfaces of the bark, becoming transformed into tufted branches which, in spite of the confusion of their interlacings, preserved an unequivocally human character in their open and suppliant arms.

The old servant, Prince, came silently into the room, announcing to Grandsailles that the mayor of Libreux would like to speak to the Viscount of Angerville. The latter, deciding to stop at the mayor's office for a moment, promised Solange to come and fetch her in time for them to leave at half-past six, and Maître Girardin took advantage of this occasion to retire. While Grandsailles was seeing d'Angerville as well as Maître Girardin to the door, Solange after putting the sugar-bowl back on the table went and sat down on a small tabouret standing in one corner of the large balcony. The moment Prince had come to make his announcement she had glanced furtively at the clock on the mantelpiece. Unexpectedly she was going to have a tête-à-tête of exactly three-quarters of an hour with the Count, and for nothing in the world did she want their conversation to take place in the frigid, too ceremonious centre of the room.

With her eyes fixed on the plain, Solange made herself very small, curled up, resting her chin on her knees violently pressed together till they hurt. She felt Grandsailles' uneven steps slowly approach, and then his lips fervently kissing the top of her head, while with his hands he took her under each arm, trying to lift her.

'You're not comfortable here,' said Grandsailles, 'come and stretch out on my bed.'

Solange then bent her head back, for the first time offering her full face to his gaze, and asked, 'Do I look so much as if I were dying?'

'No, you are divinely beautiful, but you look tired, very tired.' And with these words Grandsailles, slipping one arm under Solange's legs, lifted her easily to the height of his chest and carried her thus to the bed, where he put her down gently, careful to make her head rest exactly in the centre of a small, very thin pillow covered with steel-grey silk.

Grandsailles immediately went to fetch the table and bring it close to the bed. Solange lazily stretched her legs and the bones in her knees cracked one after the other with the same sound and at the same moment that the vine-stumps, which Prince had added to the fire a while ago to revive it, were beginning to kindle and crackle in the fireplace.

'You're completely worn out!' said the Count as he brought the table over, 'you went to such great pains last night to dazzle me.'

'What makes you think that?' asked Solange, not giving much weight to her question.

'How could it be otherwise?' answered the Count with an air of amusement, 'when just now you tried to make me believe in front of d'Angerville that you had a dinner engagement, which you don't have at all and which you invented purely to excite the weakness of my curiosity. But unfortunately for me and in spite of myself, I have seen so much of that kind of thing that it's impossible for me to be mistaken as to the substantiality of a real or an imaginary dinner. In my own world I have become like those peasants, in theirs, who can tell, just by holding an egg in their hand, whether or not a chick will hatch from it.'

Solange did not answer. She was so happy to feel her body, that constantly ached from the superhuman rôle she was playing, now rest softly on the bed of the being she adored, that the Count's provocative teasing slid over her heart without leaving the slightest trace of rancour. Grandsailles could have insulted her, and she would not have been in the least disturbed by it.

In the languorous bliss of her abandon she shut her eyes, feeling the presence of the Count standing at the foot of the bed before her, looking at her with his scrutinizing eyes, yet seeming not to see her.

'What are we thinking of?' asked Solange in a low, dreamy voice. 'I am thinking about the two of us for it was lovely, after all, to have tried to believe in our desire. *You* are thinking about your wood!'

'It's true,' Grandsailles answered. 'I've been thinking about my wood. And why shouldn't both of us try, in all humility, to find what is natural to us? After all, it's really too stupid to try at all costs to convince ourselves, by an irritating exertion of our imaginations, that we have been devoured by a mutual passion through all the five years that our flirtation has lasted. If we had wanted to ever so little, we could have found a hundred occasions to make love and to unmake it. We would even have had time to follow d'Annunzio's advice, when he said…', and Grandsailles recited in a ringing and slightly mocking tone, '"Each of us must kill his love five times with his own hands for this love to be born again five times, five times as violent."'

Solange, touched to the quick by his mockery, felt as though she could die, and Grandsailles continued in a friendly note of hypocritical gentleness,

'By the way, I should like to give Madame de Cléda a bit of advice: she has reached such a refined level of beauty, of elegance and distinction that it is extremely regrettable that she should continue, with an utterly childish and romantic shamelessness, to try to create around herself a literary and poetic atmosphere that betrays her bourgeois origins all too clearly.'

'Just as in the case of the Count of Grandsailles,' Solange retorted, aping his tone of voice, 'the senile shamelessness with which he exhibits his prosaic mediocrity too clearly betrays the country squire!' And she underlined the last two words with a passionate burst of sarcasm.

Grandsailles turned his back and, limping a little ridiculously, walked toward the balcony door, which he opened with a violent movement, as though the air of the room were choking him.

'Country squire! It's true!' shouted Grandsailles. 'You see,' he said, pointing with his finger to the gap in the wood of cork-oaks, 'those few trees that are missing matter more to me than your life! It is because of such things that wars are waged. The smile of our dead fathers fades in our memory with the years, but one does not forget a piece of land that has been snatched from one, or an uprooted tree. One also forgets five years of stupid and snobbish flirtation – but a single claw-mark in the heart of one's property, no! That one never forgets.'

All this Grandsailles had spoken with his back turned, facing the landscape, while he tried to tear loose a big section of moss that had grown in a joint between the stones on the balustrade of the balcony. Finally the moss yielded, pulling with it a piece of the cement that filled the fissures in the stone. Seizing it in his hand Grandsailles hurled it forcefully in the direction of the wood.

Solange suddenly gave vent to a great theatrical burst of laughter, and just as suddenly stopped, for Grandsailles had turned round and was approaching the bed, his face ravaged by emotion and so full of menace that she was frightened. Never would she have thought him capable of such passionate hatred. But it was too late to change attitudes, and Solange's expression remained fixed in a contemptuous smile, which Grandsailles could no longer bear to see, which he decided to eradicate by main force. He bore his hands down on her face, burying it in the pillow, pressing with all his might.

Solange remained motionless, with the dilated eyes of an animal at bay.

'I don't want to see that smile on your face,' Grandsailles growled. 'Idiot! What do you know about my world!' And as he spoke, pressing down more and more convulsively, his little finger slipped into the wet slit of Solange's mouth in such a way that his large gold ring struck savagely against her gums, which immediately began to bleed. Abruptly recovering possession of himself, the Count fell conscience-stricken to his knees at the foot of the bed and begged forgiveness.

Solange got up, leaning for a moment on Grandsailles' shoulder, and in turn walked over to the balcony, but instead of going outside, she remained standing in a corner, protected by the dark shadow of the heavy curtain. Presently her shoulders, lifting and falling with her hurried breathing, were shaken by convulsive sobs.

Then Grandsailles went over to her, and taking her face this time with infinite gentleness, kissed her on the mouth. It was the first time he had ever kissed her thus, and it was done only to obtain forgiveness. Solange reflected, as she stopped weeping.

'Forget all that, dear,' she said, 'I was too happy just now on your bed. I don't want to play any more – I love you madly, whether you like it or not!'

At this moment they heard the footsteps of Maître Girardin, accompanied by Dick d'Angerville, who was coming to fetch Solange. The latter withdrew to the mirror over the fireplace, pretending to fix her hair and wiping the blood from her chin, while Grandsailles was busy talking with d'Angerville and the notary about the visit they had just paid to the mayor of Libreux.

When Solange was ready, the Count said goodbye to them all at the door to his room. In the courtyard Prince helped d'Angerville, who had an obsession about the arrangement of luggage, insisting on loading everything in the car himself, and on using the least possible space. Madame de Cléda paced back and forth, then went over to a semi-circular stone bench which stood behind a very old cypress-tree and on which had been placed a wicker basket with fresh eggs. She leaned one knee against the bench, took an egg, broke it and swallowed it. Then she swallowed another, and still another, and so on up to five.

She must eat more. As soon as she got back to Paris she was going to begin taking care of herself as she never had before. Feeling that they were about to leave, Solange took a last egg, broke it and swallowed it in the twinkling of an eye. Thus far she had performed all these little operations with extreme care and without spilling a drop, but this time a little of the white slid down her chin and dropped to the ground. As she had no handkerchief she wiped herself with the back of her bare hand, remained for a moment motionless with her head bent forward in the attitude she had assumed to prevent the white of egg from spilling on her dress, and held her two hands out with the fingers widespread for the tips to dry.

At this moment she heard the deck of the trunk-compartment slam inconclusively, then bang down a second time with more force and with finality. Eager to drive, Solange took the driver's seat, and presently they were entering the anticipatory night of an immense forest of giant chestnut trees that formed a tunnel across the road as in the famous Fragonard painting in the Chester Dale collection. Twenty minutes passed in silence, and as Solange's hands were engaged at the wheel she felt the dried white of egg tugging at her chin, causing her periodically to twist her face into a little grimace that imparted an infinitely touching and unhappy expression to it.

Dick d'Angerville, discreetly observing her, already had on the tip of his tongue his habitual expression. '*Bonjour, tristesse*,' but this time, since her tears in the Count's room as well as the little scratch on her lip had not escaped him, d'Angerville remained silent and turned the radio on softly. Solange let herself sink into an intricate reverie, tenacious and all-absorbing, broken and begun again a hundred times with growing insistence. Through a thousand heroic adventures she imagined herself buying back Grandsailles' ancestral domains, thus preventing the industrialization of the plain of Creux de Libreux by her tireless perseverance, and in the end replanting the three hundred square metres with cork-oaks. Thanks to her sacrifice, Solange de Cléda saw the heraldic oak of the Counts of Grandsailles grow again and become perpetuated.

Besides, was she not the Lady, the cork-oak?

In the Château de Lamotte, left to his habitual solitude, the Count and his notary were preparing to dine. That morning Grandsailles had told Prince. 'For tonight I feel like having a *salade au coup de poing!*' And Prince had set out on the table everything that was needed to make this 'fist-blow salad', as it was called in that region.

When the Count and his notary were seated, Prince placed before the Count a large bowl, from which emerged the rough back of half a loaf of peasant bread which had soaked for some time in a dark-red juice composed of a mixture of oil, vinegar, blood sausage finely diced, and a soupçon of grated chocolate. Maître Girardin then took a large peeled onion that Prince handed him on a folded napkin and placed it in the very centre of the bread, continuing to hold it with his fingertips to keep it in place. Now Grandsailles shut his fist, held it suspended for a moment menacingly over the onion, taking his aim. Thereupon he struck it vertically with a vigorous fist-blow, crushing it into numerous pieces that scattered over the crust of the loaf, which in turn was shattered to bits. At this point the whole was strewn with fresh escarole, and salt and pepper were ground over it with a mill. The successful blow was the signal at which Prince, who had been following his master's ritual with extreme and anxious attention, returned to the kitchen reassured, while the notary, as though struck by a sudden vision and without detaching his hallucinated gaze from the salad bowl, exclaimed:

'A miracle! From the Count's blow I see rising the entire plain of Creux de Libreux. Tell me, is it madness or am I right?' And, bringing the candles closer to give better light to what he wanted to show, Maître Girardin began his description of the salad bowl standing there before them, with an eloquent enthusiasm stimulated by the fact that he felt himself honoured by the admiring perplexity of Grandsailles, to whom these whimsical and ingenious sallies of the notary's had the gift of communicating a sudden joviality.

'Look, my dear Count,' said Girardin, pointing with his pale writer's fingers to the undulated and broken protuberances of the loaf, 'if that isn't the very configuration of our crusty and golden hills of Libreux, of the gentle slopes, the abrupt and unexpected ridges, the deep ravines in which cascades of fresh onions flow, for it is those thin, snake-like and shiny slices that represent the hard opalescent tension of our swift streams, with their silvery foam, as they break away from the snows piled up at the far end of the bowl. The luxurious escarole represents the leafy foreground of the fertile and well-irrigated vegetation of the plain. While beyond, emerging from the forests of dark lettuce, appear the first solemn and pastoral undulations, where the grains of rye lying prone and baked into the crust represent to the life the ruminating attitude of motionless and meditative cattle, while the brilliant salt crystals sprinkled over the illuminated heights in turn represent the windows of the distant villages sparkling in the late afternoon sun. There, by chance, is a large grain of salt clinging solitary and lustreless to a steep bank: that's the whitewashed Saint Julien hermitage; And there is more. Look, my dear Count, at the little pieces of pepper, ground somewhat irregularly, slightly elongated – some even look as if they had heads – they walk, they are our peasants, dressed in black; they fill the hollows of the highways and the twisting roads in teeming processions as they return from the day's tilling....'

Grandsailles sat there fascinated and melancholy. 'All this that you are telling is beautiful as an Arcadia by Poussin,' he sighed, then avidly launched into the salad with all the energy of his knife and fork which had remained suspended in his hands during Maître Girardin's whole exposition.

After the salad, Prince served truffles covered with ashes, in their little immaculately white paper wrappings, and poured a red wine of 1923 vintage which, as Girardin put it, had a bouquet of sunshine. They ate the truffles in silence, and when the goat cheese was served the Count said to his notary.

'Well, my dear Girardin, now talk to me about Madame de Cléda.' He uttered this request in the same tone in which he might have asked him to play a favourite piece of music.

'I was just thinking of her,' answered Maître Girardin, 'as we were eating the truffles. Everyone sees things according to his own lights. The Viscount of Angerville no doubt imagines that Madame de Cléda's body of a goddess harbours the soul of a queen, and many of her numerous admirers, misinterpreting the permanent fire of her gaze, attribute to her the unsociable temperament of a courtesan. And I, being a notary, ought to see her above all from the point of view of my profession, as a fine match, or else from the point of view of my rustic and poetic naïveté, as a fairy. Well, neither satisfies me. I see Solange de Cléda rather as a kind of saint.'

And as Girardin detected a shade of irony in the Count's eyes he went on to explain, 'By the grace of God saints often possess bodies as beautiful as Aphrodite's. Now this afternoon, during the whole time we were having tea, I was observing Madame de Cléda. She was dressed so scantily that there was no mistaking the sovereignty of her body, yet she would often keep her arms crossed over her bosom, as though she felt chilly, suggesting at one and the same time the pose of a sculptured nude coming out of her bath and that of a saint listening to a message from heaven. I was struck, as I watched her, by the purity reflected in the oval of her face. And her lips were so pale that I could only think of the nun in the song they still sing in Libreux: "The Feast-Day of the Hermit of Saint Julien".'

'I don't know it,' said Grandsailles.

'According to the local legend,' Girardin explained, 'Saint Julien in passing through this region accompanied by his faithful followers discovered the tomb of a nun who had been famous for her beauty. When the coffin was opened the entire body had turned to ashes, and thistles and clover had grown in its place. Only the nun's head, covered by the white and dazzling hood, remained intact, but her mouth had become white as chalk and jasmines grew from the corners of her lips.'

'I see!' said Grandsailles in a whisper, as if to himself, 'the truffles under the ashes… the paper wrappings: the headgear….'

Girardin concluded, 'And the refrain of the song, sung with a melancholy inflection, to the accompaniment of the flute, the bagpipe and the tambourin, goes as follows:

> Her breasts were two live stones,
> Her legs were the green grass,
> And jasmines were her lips.'

'Sing it to me, I think I know the melody,' Grandsailles begged him.

Girardin needed no urging, and after taking a sip of wine he clicked his tongue and in a falsetto voice, with the perfect and quavering intonation characteristic of the peasants of Libreux, he sang snatches of the ballad of the nun of Saint Julien, then sang the entire song and sang it again and this time the Count accompanied him with his deeper voice, marking the rhythm by striking his gold ring against a crystal dish which he held with his other hand to produce a sharp sound without resonance.

53

When they reached the refrain Maître Girardin pinched the tip of his nose with his fingers to sharpen and refine the plaintive inflection of the song by the somewhat strident tone of his nasal voice.

'Her breasts were two live stones,' Girardin sighed, in a voice as delicate as a mosquito's whine.

'P-m, p-m, p-m,' Grandsailles responded, marking the last 'p-m' with a sharp tap of his ring.

> 'Her legs were the green grass!
> P-m, p-m, p-m,
> And jasmines were her lips!
> P-m, p-m, p-m,
> P-m, p-m, p-m,
> P-m, p-m, p-m.'

Girardin always left at ten-thirty. He now got up and said goodnight. The Count remained for ten long minutes in the dining-room, writing down the song in his notebook as slowly as possible, and then did not know what else to do. For a moment he thought of saying something to Prince, who seemed to be lingering intentionally, as if in the hope of starting a conversation. But the silence remained unbroken, and Prince then smiled a sad little smile, as if wishing to apologize because Grandsailles had found nothing to say to him.

Removing the last pieces of the service he withdrew, wishing the Count a goodnight. Then Grandsailles finally got up from the table and, slowly ascending the wide staircase, went to his room.

The electric light of the Château, always a little feeble, quivered almost imperceptibly, and the single globe, hanging rather low from the ceiling above the exact centre of the Count's bed, was so worn that its ambered and dying pallor barely cast a glow over it.

On the pulled-back sheet a mite-coloured silk nightshirt was meticulously folded. As was his nightly habit, Grandsailles provisionally laid on it the little notebook with his jottings and got undressed. When he was completely naked he remained thus for a few moments, absentmindedly stroking a slight bruise he had given under the left pap with a button when he had crushed the onion in the salad a little while ago.

The Count's body was perfect, tall and handsome, and to visualize him one may recall the famous drawing of Apollo in the Milan museum, executed by Raphael. When the Count had slipped on his nightshirt, which was just a little longer than his day-shirt, he picked up his notebook and went to the end of the room where a large, dark mahogany chest stood, very narrow but so tall that it reached the ceiling.

This rigid chest rested on four little human feet with long, slender toes in the Egyptian style, sculptured in very shiny golden bronze. Grandsailles opened the two doors of the chest, the interior of which was empty except that on one of its central shelves and within reach of the hand there lay a series of objects: at the left, a tiny child's skull crowned with a delicate gold aureole, attributed to Saint Blondine, which Grandsailles had kept here since the restoration of the church of the Château had been begun: beside this relic of the child martyr, a violin and bow, and next to these a black key adorned and inlaid with a silver crucifix which went with the coffin that contained the remains of the Count's mother. As he did every night, Grandsailles deposited his notebook there and picked up the violin, but just at the moment when he inclined his head to seize the instrument between his chin and his shoulder he heard a noise which made him turn around. The smiling face of an old woman appeared in the partly opened door.

It was Grandsailles' faithful governess, whom the Count always called 'the Canoness of Launay' in reminiscence of Stendhal's *The*

Charterhouse of Parma. 'Good evening, canoness, 'said the Count, putting his violin down on the bed. The canoness entered, bearing in one hand a dish with two boiled artichokes, for which the Count had a mania when he was taken with insomnia in the middle of the night. In the other hand the canoness carried a great shaggy glove made of cat hair with which she regularly rubbed the Count's limping leg, which was subject to seizures of acute rheumatismal pains. The canoness was almost diabolically ugly, but she exerted a certain attraction by her intelligent vivacity and her wide-awake look. She was clean to the point of exaggeration; her skin was fine, but monstrously wrinkled, and her right eye was continually running, which obliged her to wipe it periodically with her white lace-edged apron.

The Count had no secrets from his canoness. She was the only one allowed to enter and leave his room without even knocking. She decided everything in the Château, and as the Count was unable to do without her ministrations, he always took her along when he went off to Paris. The canoness, who had not yet opened her mouth, got down on her knees and began patiently and conscientiously to rub the Count's leg. In the course of one of her rhythmic movements, a little more vigorous than the rest, the Count's intimate parts were half exposed.

Respectfully she pulled his shirt down again with her gloved hand, but her other bare and wrinkled one she slipped underneath and, pressing the flesh with the chaste joy of a mother, looked at him tenderly and exclaimed, 'Oh my, oh my, what a blessing from heaven!' Then with the same hand she tapped him on the knee as she leaned on it to get up with the full weight of her body resting on it. 'You ought to take Saint Blondine's little head out of the chest,' the canoness advised, as she started to leave. 'I could never go to sleep with that in my room.'

From the doorway, as with great deliberation she wiped her eye which had had time to wet the whole length of her neck while she had got to her feet, she twice repeated this sentence by way of a conclusion, 'For nothing keeps you awake so much as always thinking about death.' And as she walked down the length of the corridor he heard her mutter, 'Blessed be God! Blessed be God!'

The clock struck eleven. Grandsailles then again picked up his violin and, pressing it serenely but firmly against his cheek, launched with his virtuoso's bow into Bach's D Major Aria. He stood leaning a little forward, the knee of his injured leg against the edge of the bed, the slit in the side of his nightshirt partly baring the thigh which had turned bright pink from the stimulation of the rubbing. In the centre of this irritated skin the old scar spread its branches like a dark eggplant-coloured vegetation.

Grandsailles' eyes rested on Saint Blondine's little skull, with its tiny intact teeth, as smooth and white as a riverstone. Its purity made him think of Solange de Cléda's knees, and the memory of her haggard face, ennobled by the brightness of her tears, seemed to lend precision and divine beauty to the melody as it developed, majestic and all-powerful.

Grandsailles breathed deeply, moving his head to the melodic inflections of the burning river of the sonata, but his impassive features reflected his determination not to allow the emotions of his heart, with their weaknesses, to cloud the limpid purity of his interpretation of the music. As the aria neared its final bars, in which all the anguish of the night seemed to reach a geometric point at which it would remain suspended for eternity, he could feel the tip of the little finger of the hand with which he held the bow, as though it were still wet with Solange de Cléda's warm and desirable saliva.

2

The Friends of Solange de Cléda

A T ABOUT HALF-PAST ELEVEN in the morning Barbara Stevens, the wealthy American widow and heiress of John Cornelius Stevens, hurried out of the Hotel Ritz in Paris with her daughter Veronica. They walked down the sidewalk some fifty paces and entered Madame Schiaparelli's dressmaking establishment. At ten minutes past one, mother and daughter came out of Schiaparelli's and returned to the Hotel Ritz where they lunched on a salad served to them with due obsequiousness and ceremony.

They swallowed two different kinds of vitamins with the aid of two martinis, which made them long for a third, and a chocolate and pistachio panaché ice cream; after which, without waiting for coffee, they set off again for Schiaparelli's, whence they emerged to return once more to the Ritz in time for five o'clock tea.

Barbara Stevens had succeeded in composing for herself a special facial expression by virtue of which she made it apparent when she entered Schiaparelli's that she had just come from the Ritz, and another whereby she showed on returning to the Ritz that she had just left Schiaparelli's. The first of these expressions consisted in keeping her mouth constantly half-open in a kind of disillusioned languor, which was exactly the contrary of the gaping mouth of surprise; she never answered the questions which the saleswomen asked her; she would let her gloved hands linger on the various articles and, tactlessly pretending to look at nothing, she was secretly astonished at everything. The second of these faces, the one for her return to the Ritz, she achieved by means of a closed, or rather a contracted mouth, for she would pucker her lips with an air of annoyance, which expressed a shade of disgust so frivolous that it could arise only from the little tyrannical worries peculiar to the exigencies of fashion, that must always remain unsatisfied in an ultra-sophisticated lady like herself. Barbara Stevens had had herself awakened this morning at half-past nine on the pretext that she had a six-thirty appointment with her hairdresser, which she had wrung from him by main force and which she was coldly resolved to break. Like many weak creatures chained to their absolute caprice, she felt free and at ease only when she could arbitrarily abolish the cares and obstacles with which she had purposely strewn her way the day before.

For that matter, each of her little worries could become for Mrs Stevens a precious source of distraction in case she should find herself in the alternative of being bored. Thus when her day looked too empty to her she always had something with which to encumber, if not to fill it; on the contrary, when a morning started out auspiciously with more exciting occurrences, Mrs Stevens would begin voluptuously to rid herself of all her obligations, though to do her justice it is true that she did so with a correctness, a rigour, a meticulous care in the choice of excuses, which represented a real effort on the part of her secretary, who adroitly utilized all pretexts of politeness with an exclusive and unequivocal eye to publicity.

'Mrs Barbara Stevens regrets her inability to come for her last fitting as she needs her shoes with the little diamond watches inlaid in the heels in order to attend the charity affair at the British Embassy.'

'Mrs Barbara Stevens wishes to cancel her luncheon at Larue because of the arrival of the King of Greece.'

'Mrs Barbara Stevens begs Monsieur or Madame Fernandez kindly to telephone her tomorrow morning, she is sorry she cannot be present at their cocktail party for she is being detained by her lawyers on an urgent matter.'

'Mrs Barbara Stevens begs to be forgiven for having to put off her visit until her return from Versailles next Friday, and asks to have put aside for her the two rose tourmaline clips and the necklace of emerald cabuchons that Bérard the painter liked so much.'

'Yes, indeed, yes, indeed,' the jeweller would answer at the other end of the wire. 'I believe she is referring to the Renaissance necklace with the little centauresses. Why yes, certainly, we shall put it aside.'

Hanging up the receiver, he would say to himself, 'Hm-Versailles... it must be the dinner at the Windsors'... let's see, what day is that dinner?... the sixteenth, yes, Friday. But in that case the secretary must be mistaken. Mrs Stevens will never get back before Saturday morning. We will have to wait till Monday or telephone again... no, we must wait – Monday morning....'

This kind of little calculation, infallibly set in motion by the telephone conversation in the jeweller's platinum-mounted brain, was the speciality of Barbara Stevens' secretary.

Miss Andrews, for her part, possessed a small brain moulded of newspaper pulp, irregularly sprinkled with lugubrious black squares combined with the dirty grey ones of half-effaced and dreary pencil-scribblings of a crossword puzzle left lying around. She derived an almost savage joy from being able to shine for a moment in her mistress's eyes, when she came in the evening to get her orders, by fawningly displaying the Machiavellian resources that enabled her, with unparalleled mediocrity, to weave filigrane ornaments of stupidity to dress the too-naked and impulsive desires which Mrs Barbara Stevens often just left where she dropped them.

'Taking upon myself the responsibility of cancelling your Friday appointment.' Miss Andrews would say, jubilant over her find, 'I achieved four different results. First, that of adding a margin of two days for Madame's decision; second, of informing them of Madame's dinner at the Windsors' in Versailles without mentioning it; third, of informing the Fernandezes of your choice, for they are to go tomorrow morning to see the same jewel, which Cécile Goudreau has called to their attention. They are bound to become interested in it. Then they will be told that Mrs Barbara Stevens has had it put aside.'

'I'm sure Madame Goudreau must have heard about it from Bérard, for they say she has absolutely no taste,' Barbara broke in, a little pricked by jealousy.

'And fourth,' Miss Andrews continued triumphantly.

'What do you mean, fourth?' Mrs Stevens asked in surprise, having only vaguely followed her secretary's social expatiations while slipping on a lace dressing-gown splashed with large and loud-coloured violets. She wore this garment (which clashed outrageously with the chasteness of her white-and-gold drawing-room, decorated by Jean Michel Frank) with the pleasure of satisfied self-love. In the intimacy of her room, at least, and before the sole secret witness of her secretary, she could give herself over without restraint to the natural penchants of her execrable taste.

'Fourth – the fourth advantage is having chosen Friday,' Miss Andrews resumed, rattling off her words in fear of not being able to get to the end of her explanation. 'Friday the Fernandezes are dining at Solange de Cléda's where Madame is so sorry she cannot be present because of the Windsors! The Fernandezes cannot fail to speak jealously of your latest extravagances, so it will be exactly as if you had been there.'

'Who answered the telephone at Cartier's? The little dark fellow with the Spanish accent?'

'I think so. He was very pleasant. He said twice, "Tell Madame I am entirely at her disposal".'

61

'Entirely at her disposal. Yes, it's surely the little dark fellow. Did you telephone Monsieur Paul Valéry for my luncheon of the twentieth?'

Miss Andrews again plunged into the exhausting description of the diplomatic advantages of her manner of telephoning, while Barbara Stevens, with her head between her hands, remained bowed attentively over her engagement book with her eyes shut, imagining with a scenic precision worthy of the best stage designer each of the reactions and the facial contractions which her new appearance in Paris would produce in her circle of acquaintances, advised in advance of her recent activities by her secretary's mystifying zeal. Then she studied her rôle according to each of the circumstances and, exacting, dissatisfied, she obliged herself to begin again a hundred times the same movements, the same grimace, the same inflection of voice, coming in, going out and coming in again imaginatively and tirelessly in order to achieve perfection. It was exhausting! And it was only then that she ventured to be pleased with herself, having in turn become her own spectator.

She saw herself enter Cartier's as the vermilion climax of all the gossip of the Versailles dinner, going to the Fernandezes as the gavel of high finance, and to her booter's as though she were merely the Duchess of Kent. It was a curious thing: although Barbara did not take such effects very seriously, it was nevertheless certain that she thus obtained the most eager cajoleries from her shopkeepers, the promptest whistles to call her car, the deepest bows from doormen and society people; and all this contributed to make her unsure of herself and she would wonder. 'Am I perhaps not altogether a bluff?'

'Enough, darling,' Barbara implored, cutting short her secretary's inexhaustible chattering, 'tell me, what does destiny hold in store for us today?'

She knew, alas! And by her tone of fatality she was only preparing the naturalness of her reaction.

'There is nothing,' Miss Andrews replied a little embarrassed, 'except the fittings and the hairdresser at six-thirty.'

'At last,' Barbara sighed, 'a day of happiness!'

Miss Andrews was already standing with her feet together like a military rigidity waiting to be dismissed; her slightly shiny and Lilliputian face had the same pink colour and the exact form of a little toe with a large greenish tooth – that is, a tiny nail – placed in the middle of it.

'You may go – thank you. I'll see you tomorrow.'

At this moment Veronica entered the room and came up and kissed her mother on the corner of her mouth. Eluding the kiss Barbara again sighed. 'At last, we're going to be able to spend a pleasant day, just the two of us, but in any case I'll have to go to that confounded hairdresser instead of staying and catching up with my correspondence.' She did in fact detest her new hairdresser's too glacial manner of treating everyone alike, and she would gladly have avoided the appointment with this rebel... 'a communist, undoubtedly,' she thought. But the frightful emptiness of the end of her day chained her hopelessly to her appointment: after the hairdresser, nothing! She looked furtively and resentfully at the telephone as it quivered and gave a timid tinkle without sequel, which made all the mortal silence of this morning beat painfully upon Barbara's already empty heart. She felt herself grow faint and averted her face with disgust from the spot where it slumped like a motionless sleeping white lobster, stupidly caught on its fork, incapable of coming to her rescue.

'How restful,' said Barbara, 'a morning without telephone calls.'

'Who do you expect to telephone? Everyone has gone to the country,' said Veronica.

'Why, is this a holiday?' her mother asked weakly.

'It's a half holiday. Some of the shops are open, but the people have left. There's a new Fred Astaire film, by the way.' Veronica threw out this suggestion for the fun of teasing her mother.

'I should say not! For nothing in the world!' Barbara burst out with annoyance, while she hastily ran over and took back her nail-file which she had just discovered in her daughter's hands.

'I should say not!' the girl said in turn imitating her mother's tone, 'you know that the manicure forbade you to touch your hands.'

Barbara acceded poutingly and went back to lie down on her couch.

'I can stand the manicure getting on my nerves; I can stand Miss Andrews getting on my nerves; I can stand my daughter Veronica getting on my nerves, but not Fred Astaire – enough tapping; I can stand anybody getting on my nerves, but not with their feet!'

In a moment Barbara's face became covered with barely perceptible nervous quivers. It was as though one could see the little grey spiders of dissatisfaction running in all directions on the mother-of-pearl of her carefully tended epiderm. Veronica came and sat down beside her: motionless and steady-eyed, she could feel her mother's eyes already turning moist and expected her to cry. Barbara Stevens had that faculty for fleeting emotivity that gives sparkle to certain faces, in which the dew of large and facile tears enhances and polishes the shades of sentiments at the same time that it removes the slightest trace of their dust. Barbara was forty-three, but her little chisel-shaped nose was sixteen, and the blue-tinged dimples at her mouth were barely twelve.

Was Barbara really beautiful? She gave exactly the contrary impression. She seemed to have been beautiful, just recently. And this was perfectly true. Ugly as a child, passable at the time of her marriage, beautiful yesterday, ravishing today, Barbara Stevens was one of those rare beings capable by their nature's very essence of all the transformations and rejuvenations so glibly promised by beauty parlours. Through an innate sense of imitation her face could with deceptive accuracy reproduce the most antagonistic expression of any being – man, woman and even animal. Plunged in the mythology of fashion shops, she expended all her mimetic faculties in contaminating herself at will with the virtues and attitudes of the divinities of the day who succeeded most imperiously in fascinating her: thus Barbara Stevens, in the frenzied race of her depersonalization, spent the treasures of her energy in resembling all the pretty women of her period, while keeping of herself only what was strictly necessary to remain alive. All that was natural about her was limited – her legs were rather short, her forehead small, she was plump without generosity and just passably blond. What contrast could be more startling than that offered by the river-like and golden exuberance of her daughter!

Veronica was blond, by virtue not only of her golden hair that cascaded over her shoulders, but of the kind of light than emanated from her whole body: when she was beside her mother it was as though she lent her some of her blondness, and when she was alone she made the very furniture that surrounded her turn blond. Unlike Barbara, Veronica had a large serene brow, rounded, slightly meningitic, and long, sculpturally modelled legs that one never saw, for in her presence one could not help looking constantly at her eyes, and one could not help looking at her eyes because in her gaze one saw absolutely nothing; foreign to tears and to frowns her eyes were fixed and dry like two immense deserts, and their pupils were of a blue so pale that they blended into the whites, and it was only in their depths and on the horizon of their translucent vista that a bit of moonlight and gold-dust shone. Barbara's defect of having rather short legs was undoubtedly nature's ungracious way of bringing her closer to the earth, and at the same time making her more human. Veronica, on the other hand, did not need her long legs of a goddess to lift her heart to a different level. She was one of those who trample on human feelings with the light feet of an antelope. Barbara, like most weak creatures, was kindly, disposed to forgiveness, to pity, and was cruel only unconsciously. Without being cruel, Veronica was neither good nor bad, like the gods of ancient Olympus, and like all combative creatures belonging to an élite she was pitiless, vindictive and subject to irretrievable passions. She was the praying mantis that devours its love through a biological need for the absolute.

Barbara Stevens felt her daughter's inquisitorial gaze resting on her. But she was attached to this gaze, for its ponderable transparency was like a crystal-ball paper-weight resting on the lightness of her feelings written on the fluttering tissue-paper of her frivolity. She was attached to it, above all, because she might need it at any moment if a crisis should presently occur. Barbara expected from Veronica's inflexible gaze no consolation, but she nevertheless liked to feel herself looked at while she wept, for it was the only way in which she could bring herself to feel sorry for herself. While waiting for such a scene Barbara had recovered her engagement book which she placed on her lap, she leaned her elbows on the arm of the couch, her forehead resting on her hands, her eyes wide open, concentrating without seeing anything on a page opened at random. Presently out of the darkness of her mind, she saw a little hat emerge, a hat of such a violent metallic blue that it appeared red: as a matter of fact, it appeared red only because it *was* red, and it was not blue because the sole thing that was blue about this hat was the blue veil that covered it. This hat flashed in her brain for an instant, like an electric spark which changes from blue to red with such rapidity that once it is gone one can no longer tell which of these colours was perceived first. Nevertheless the instantaneous and blinding apparition of this hat had sufficed to illuminate the face of the person who wore it for a moment and as Barbara recognized this person she uttered a cry of fright and called out her name, 'Mrs Reynolds!'

'I had completely forgotten that I have a dinner this evening at the Reynolds',' she said, letting her two arms drop on the couch in a theatrical abandon by which she seemed to beg for pity from Veronica, who smiled at her in a fashion which could have been a little more tender and a little less malicious.

'I can't just not go to the dinner at the Reynolds',' Barbara continued. 'I'm already being accused of neglecting my compatriots. Besides I like them, but they're so naive! I don't like to be able to lie without having to watch myself. Remember this, my daughter: in order to be carried away by a lie, one must be able to lie to others as well as to oneself.'

The prospect of her mended evening had given her back wit, kindness, beauty, and had restored to her soul a serene calm that made her yawn long and gratifyingly between her teeth. This compressed yawn made her lips quiver imperceptibly and was a sign that she was going, after a last relapse into indolence, to make a decision.

'Ai, Dio!' she exclaimed, getting up.

Barbara dragged herself aimlessly about the room, enjoyed its silence which a while ago made her nerves feel raw, and was even prepared to feel indulgent about the large cubist painting of Harlequin by Picasso, which she had had to buy so much against her will.

'You know,' she said, 'what reminded me of my dinner? You'll never guess – the Picasso! Exactly the same colour as Mrs Reynolds' hat, the one she was wearing the day she invited me as we crossed downstairs in the lobby: that same blue, and that same flame-red....'

Thereupon Barbara half pulled out, then immediately put back into their envelope, some photographs of herself that she had not yet had time to look at carefully, and going into the bathroom she put them provisionally on the washstand. Then she returned to the room, looking for something else, hesitating between a German book on Renaissance jewels and the *New York Times* of the previous Sunday. She finally chose the latter, took it under her arm and once more, lazily and with finality, headed for the bathroom, dragging her feet as she went. There she locked the door and remained a good long three-quarters of an hour.

In the course of the afternoon Barbara Stevens found time, besides, to choose between three cocktails, of which she accepted four, for she invited two Venetian friends whom she met by chance to join her at the Ritz bar for a quarter of an hour, substituting this for her appointment with the hairdresser, which she had cancelled. From this moment on it might be said that her time was organized with the precision of a military manoeuvre: twenty-four minutes to get to Neuilly, ten minutes to enjoy a cocktail; then back to the Ritz, eight minutes to change dresses, then two more appearances, each of five minutes' duration, for final cocktails; and lastly, to the Reynolds', where she arrived twenty-three minutes late.

At six o'clock Veronica came back to the hotel alone, and by the special immobility of the disorder in the living-room she realized that her mother had left a long time before. She immediately stretched out on the same couch where her mother had reclined during the greater part of the morning; she planned to have dinner here later, and to go to bed immediately after. She would have liked to get undressed right away and slip on a glazed piqué dressing-gown, her latest acquisition, so fresh, smooth and starched that Veronica had said, in answer to her mother's reproaches the first day she had worn it. 'It's the first time in my life that I realize what it's like to feel completely naked.' Barbara, in fact, always protested when she caught Veronica in her room without any clothes on, but since the discovery of this dressing-gown her nudism had become transformed into the pleasure of the direct contact of her firm flesh with the somewhat rigid, slippery and immaculately white fabric. She was also having her sheets glazed with a very substantial quantity of starch, and when one struck them with one's finger they gave off a little sound like cardboard. All day long Veronica would stoically wait for this delightful moment when, exhausted with fatigue after her shopping, she could at last slip her naked body into her starched robe and eat an apple.

But today something prevented her from changing immediately – one of those premonitions that were so habitual with her. She had just had a strange, fixed and very clear impression that someone would come and fetch her at the last moment to take her out. Veronica puckered her brows with a characteristic stubborn, ill-humoured expression, that was neither the grimace of migraine nor that of melancholy, but rather the contraction of her concentrated and permanent interrogation as to what was about to happen to her. Nevertheless, and in spite of the deep absorption of her mind, she took off her shoes and with one hand pressed a pale apple which had the same lustre as her brow. And while with the other hand she held a knife, one foot perseveringly struggled to enlarge a hole in her stocking till it was big enough for a whole toe to slip through. It was as though she were merely waiting for this result as a signal to start to peel her apple, that is to say her life. And by her calm and resolute manner any humble peasant of the plain of Creux de Libreux might have divined that the first man Veronica met in her life would be hers, and that she would marry him.* For Veronica was one of those who, when they peel an apple, carry the operation to its conclusion with a sure regularity and an awe-inspiring skill that enable them, by their steadiness, not to make a single 'break' through the irregular incisions of doubt in this skin of their own destiny, no matter how finely they cut it. No symbol in the world is more powerful and real than this one, for having relearned, thanks to Freud, that automatic

---

* *According to a very ancient peasant superstition, 'if a girl peels an apple and continues to the end without once breaking the strip of skin, she will marry the first man she meets'.*

actions (the language of the subconscious) always prophetically reveal the secrets of our souls, we now know for certain that the girl who peels an apple and continues to the end without once breaking the peel gives proof of a constancy of character and a level-headedness such that when instead of the apple she confronts the man whose emotional relations to herself she has to peel, she will never break her idyll and will bring it to a happy final result. The girl who on the contrary breaks the peel of her apple into a thousand uneven pieces will behave in the same way with her loves; being inconstant, she will break and cut all her relations, and at the end of her life, instead of the continuous and melodic line of her conduct, she will see the skin of her destiny lying in a thousand shreds at her feet.

Without in the least suspecting what a magic operation she was performing, as with impeccable assurance she peeled the fruit among all fruits most heavily weighted with symbols.* Veronica, who would probably have been the first to laugh at this kind of exegesis, nevertheless felt it in all the fibres of her intact organism. She knew that the first love that would be born in her life would be definitive, and so the least accident threatened to be irreparable and fatal. She would not begin again, she would not mend: one single life, one single line of absolute perfection. But the man's apparition was not yet imminent, and she even knew approximately the moment when it would occur. She would meet him this summer, toward the end of summer, perhaps in the beginning of September.

While waiting for love, Veronica ardently imagined friendship, of a woman, which she also wanted to last as long as she lived, a beautiful creature who would feel as she did, riveted to her body,

---

*   *The apple of sin in the terrestrial paradise: Adam and Eve.*
    The apple of beauty in the judgment of Paris.
    The apple of sacrifice: William Tell and his son.
    The apple of physics: that of Newton's law of gravitation.

protecting her by the double cuirass of spirit and of flesh, in anticipation of the great ordeal. She wanted a woman-friend with whom she might share the anguishing springtime of her passion, the ferocity of her midsummer embraces and the elegy of autumnal caresses. The friend she was expecting must be as feeble as her own mother and at the same time, unlike the latter, she must have a big mouth, a great devotion, no frivolity and arms habituated to and expert in pleasure, capable of guiding hers, which would be resolute but perhaps trembling at the supreme moment of the annihilating sexual embrace. For she was preparing herself to be the immolated victim – like the legendary beings of the ancient sanguinary religions of the Aztecs. Veronica sitting in the shadow of the fertile coolness of the great tree of her blood was waiting, and her paralysing immobility became like that which precedes aggression. She was getting ready for the great ordeal of giving her life, she was arming herself with a dangerous force, for at the least flinching of her partner in the accomplishing of the rite – that of tearing out her heart, she knew herself capable of sealing the climax of their absolute embrace with the force of her own jaws, and thus by the death of one of them concluding her pact of conformity with the grandiose rules and laws of the nature of her love.

Veronica thus needed more than a woman-friend of epic stature, she had to have a complex being who would be at once the mother offering her ecstasy in witness of Veronica's passion, the virgin-flower of the ritual of her sacrifice, the lascivious slave who unveils the secrets of the initiation, and the messenger from heaven, the priestess of her faith.

Up to this moment in Veronica's life, each time she had wanted something with intensity her destiny in the guise of an objective hazard would regularly come to her rescue, bringing her at the exact hour the precise object of her wish. And again today, this evening, presently, this same hazard was preparing to materialize by fulfilling her desire.

The doorbell rang. Veronica did not quiver, and without waiting for Miss Andrews to announce who it was, ordered her, 'Have her come in!'

It was indeed she – Betka!

Betka had a big mouth and she was wearing a raincoat. A choking heat rose from the street, and the heavy atmosphere of a storm which for three days had not made up its mind to break loose over Paris charged her heavy red hair with electric sparks.

'What do you wish?' said Veronica, unhurriedly putting on her shoes again.

'I wanted to speak to Mrs Barbara Stevens. May I introduce myself? I am the young woman who last week wrote all the invitations for Veronica Stevens' coming-out party. You are Veronica, aren't you?'

Veronica nodded her head.

'Your mother expressed her satisfaction with my work, as well as her intention to avail herself of my services again shortly.... It's true that I did pretty well to write all those addresses at the last moment in one night, and by hand, for we had to check them with Miss Andrews one by one.... So I hope that I may be able to make myself useful again....'

Veronica waited for a long time before answering her, in order to be quite sure that Betka's embarrassment tacitly implied a request. Then, her already assured friendship prodding her intuition, she anticipated herself by guessing.

'Yes, my mother did tell me she was going to employ you again, and probably in a more regular way; meanwhile I'll be delighted to give you an advance on your future salary.... Oh, no! it's quite natural. I'm always running out of pocket money myself!' And, as Betka still seemed to protest, Veronica concluded. 'I really must insist, it means so much to me – I want awfully to make you happy!'

Betka was flabbergasted by the violent and elementary sincerity of Veronica's tone.

'No,' said Betka, 'I don't want an advance on my salary. I can return this money to you in exactly two days; I only need enough to send a telegram to my parents in Poland.'

Veronica promptly handed her a pad of telegraph blanks which Betka seized avidly while at the same time she pulled off her raincoat so hurriedly that she tore it. She tossed back her hair that kept falling over her eyes, and with her trembling hands she tucked in her blouse which again emerged from her belt, exposing a little lozenge of bare stomach which she vainly tried to hide. Veronica looked with stupefaction at this whirl of disorganized, communicative and irresistible life that seemed to be in the throes of perpetual torment – a frenzy of flesh – and as she gazed at her she compressed her lips on her gold cigarette-holder, biting it harder and harder with her teeth till she left their marks in it.

Feeling that Veronica was watching her intently. Betka moderated the disorder of her excitement and it then became apparent that it was a strain for her to keep relatively calm. She sat down in a business-like way before the desk and began, with a worried look, to fill out blanks which she would immediately crumple, dissatisfied, looking up each time with pleading eyes full of apology and encountering the other's impassive gaze. Veronica's dark and unbending face rarely smiled, but when it happened (not more than three times a week) her smile of a melancholy angel became illuminated by celestial gleams that transfigured her for a few seconds to such a point that all who observed her at such moments would wait for this smile to be repeated in order to convince themselves that they had not been the victims of an illusion. This evening, since Betka had entered

73

the room, Veronica had smiled at her four times already in this way, and one might have said that Betka had lived during the intervals only to wait each time for the reappearance of this new light from her lips which seemed to warm her eyelids from afar, as must be the case when one approaches the gates of Paradise.

'Read it,' said Betka, handing the telegram to Veronica, who merely took it, folded it, and put it back on the desk; then Betka picked it up again and read it aloud: 'RECEIVED NO MONEY FOR THREE MONTHS LIFE VERY HARD PLEASE TELL ME TRUTH ABOUT AJALE MARRIAGE WITH MY SISTER HAVE RIGHT TO KNOW YOUR DAUGHTER BETKA' – followed by her address: '17 Quai des Orfèvres.'

'Ajale was my fiancé,' Betka added, putting the telegram down again, and abruptly picking up her raincoat.

'Thank you, thank you so much!' said Betka, her smooth face contracted by suffering. She was beautiful as a Dolorosa by Bernini would have been, if his subject had been like Betka, an adolescent with very young breasts. She was eighteen.

Veronica went up to her and gave her a kiss.

'Wait for me a second, we'll have dinner together!'

The storm broke loose, accompanied by a few large gumdrops of hail, just at the moment when their taxi stopped in front of the Tour d' Argent restaurant. Merely in crossing the sidewalk they were soaked to the bones and felt that sudden and delightful cold of the gluttonous downpour of summer which made them shiver as they climbed to the summit of the tower. There they sat down at a table which Veronica purposely chose as being a little too large for intimacy, but which on the other hand stood directly in front of the inaugural crackling of a wooden fire which had hurriedly been lighted the moment the first claps of thunder had burst. At the beginning of their dinner they spoke little, like the new mate and the captain who eat their first meal together on the eve of the day when their ship hoists anchor for a long voyage. Betka and Veronica each silently watched in the depths of the other's eyes the receding wake of the laughing foam of illusion, which the little they had lived together already stirred behind the rudder encrusted with blackish barnacles and dark algae.

Betka, who was still unconscious of the fact that they had launched on a common voyage, and to whom the encounter appeared like the mirage of a moment, lived each second as though it were a miracle, and in each of her glances she gave everything: feeling, pleasure, and even remorse.

Veronica, on the contrary, 'quiet and concentrated like a blind statue',[*] kept that restraint of apparent icy indifference which, far from being avarice or aridity of heart, was but the necessity of dividing the latter into little even slices, corresponding to each of the seconds which the continuous and uninterrupted passion of her life was to last: she would never love more than she loved at this moment, she would merely live her long cycle. Betka, on the other hand... poor moth! At each of Veronica's steely glances Betka would laugh, while her pure teeth savagely crunched stalks of celery that broke in her mouth like icicles of spring.

'I like your big mouth,' said Veronica, leaving Betka's childish, almost frenzied voracity in suspense.

'Too big!' the latter pleaded.

'Yes, a little too big,' Veronica continued reticently, watching for the effect of her agreement.

'I know. A horror!' Betka exclaimed, sighing, discouraged, and on the point of tears.

'My angel!' Veronica reassured her, 'don't you know that you are divinely beautiful?'

---

[*]   *Federico Garcia Lorca, speaking of his friend.*

'Yes, I think I am!' Betka answered, with a soft inflection of regret, 'I don't consider myself ugly, and I might even enjoy looking at someone like me... I don't care for my mouth, and I detest the colour of my hair... I like the rest – especially my body. But for myself, I should prefer to be like you.'

'With me it's just the opposite,' Veronica replied, her gaze suddenly absent. 'I don't like myself at all, but I should like to find someone absolutely like me, whom I could adore.'

Betka preferred to be lulled by the intoxication which Veronica's personality communicated to her rather than try to understand and discover the strange and somewhat fateful meaning of the latter's severe tone. Betka seemed to be listening with her lips, which were slightly parted in a semi-ecstasy of virginal innocence by which she betrayed the eminently physical character of all her feelings. This expression which was a familiar and almost constant one with her became a grimace under the impact of the slightest emotion, and then it was difficult to distinguish whether it expressed pleasure or pain, so common and interpenetrated an existence did these two tyrants of her soul lead in the flesh of the single person of her body. Nevertheless intense pleasure manifested itself in her through a more violent contraction of her facial muscles extending her mouth to the maximum in a laugh which exposed the generous and total sparkle of her teeth. Their desperate effort to remain closed rendered Betka's expression of joy fetchingly mad and infinitely touching.

Champagne was poured. Veronica wriggled in her chair as though she were about to pounce on her friend, but feeling the latter so confident and defenceless that she kept delaying the moment of aggression with voluptuous delight. Finally she confronted her point-blank with the long-premeditated question, thee- and thou-ing her for the first time: 'Tell me, *chérie*, are you a virgin?'

Betka did not answer and merely looked at her, her face beet-red, humble and yet proud, making her all the more attractive.

'Eat!' Veronica cried to her with a sigh, as she cut the string that held a little strip of bacon surmounted by a large muscat grape between the open legs of a rum-glazed quail. Veronica lightly seized the grape with her fork and offered it to Betka as if to console her.

'Here, angel, catch this!' And Betka reached her head forward and crushed the smooth, sweet grape between her teeth, as two bitter tears flowed down her cheeks. Veronica knew perfectly well she was not a virgin! But she felt pacified now at having succeeded so quickly, so easily in making her weep.

To reward her, Veronica was immediately going to confide in her, and still later, over the dessert, she was going to blot out every trace of bitterness making the enchanted cavalcade of her inexhaustible seductive imagination sweep past her dazzled eyes, as she could do when she set out to please and to enslave.

Having decided to resort to these charms, Veronica moved back her chair a little from Betka's, wishing her to get the full impact of all her impetuous gestures, often incomprehensible and always fascinating like those used in spells; abandoning her habitual immobility, she gave herself over to an amazing exhibition of equivocal mimicry. 'I am a virgin,' she said softly, in a troubling tone of innuendo, and still more softly, 'I swear I am! And yet I don't weep, as you see!' With a solemn gesture she pretended to wipe her eyes to show that they were dry.

Betka laughed.

'And now,' continued Veronica, 'look at the proof of what I'm telling you,' and she slowly, very slowly raised her closed hand till it was higher than her head. Then she opened it maliciously, and meaningfully shook her ring-finger which had a little gauze bandage held in place by a strip of pink adhesive tape. 'You see? A wound!' she said blinking her eyes.

Betka was utterly bewildered, but she blushed nevertheless, accentuating her weakness by shaking her head with a charming look of annoyance that was meant to disavow her blushes. Then Veronica brought her chair close to Betka's in sign of tenderness and as she was preparing to begin her confidences she gave Betka her injured finger to hold.

'Take it,' she said, 'but don't press unless I make you blush.'

Betka took the finger with her two hands and lifted it to her lips, barely grazing it with a kiss. Veronica then began her tale with diabolical animation.

'I, Veronica Stevens, am a virgin – married and chaste. I am a virgin, because instead of being married to a man I am married to a woman. You know her – Barbara, my mother. We sleep together whenever she feels like weeping. This happens about twice a week; I have to console her, from time to time, for the heavy burden of her frivolity; she comes running into my bed and makes me put something on; otherwise she would feel shame; then I have to snuggle up to her from behind, hold her tight, rest my cheek against the back of her neck to warm it. That makes her sleep. Then immediately I slip out of my pyjamas and get rid of them; and if she wakes up in the middle of the night she screams with fright as if my body were a demon's. Will you believe that my mother never kisses me? She cares for me only as a warm hot-water bottle that sometimes calms her insomnias. Just as she can't stand the direct contact of hot-water bottles either. She always has to have everything covered.

'The day after our curious love-nights, I always receive a present; I let Mama give me all these presents in the same way that Mama lets me love her – that is to say, without noticing it. Here is the most recent of these presents,' and she showed Betka the belt she was wearing, whose clasp was a gold padlock.

'As usual, I didn't notice it,' Veronica continued. 'I had made a date with a man, a Frenchman, in his apartment. He immediately noticed it, and while he was pouring a cocktail he said to me. "I feel that destiny has chosen me to free you of your chastity belt." I didn't answer. I like the reputation of being a cold and inaccessible woman. For me love must be severe, like a kind of military pact between two conquerors, and no confusion of the senses must precede the signing of the treaty. Perhaps it was in the spirit of this kind of treaty that I went to his apartment. I was wearing a sober tailored suit, cut like armour, and he received me in slippers. I recognized immediately by these slippers that he was not "the one". Instead of a treaty he simply tried to wrench his pleasure from me and he went about it so awkwardly that he couldn't undo my belt, whose new clasp was a little hard to open. I told him to wait a moment, that I would take it off myself, and I stepped back two paces and tried. In the clumsiness of his haste he had only succeeded in jamming the buckle, and I had to press so hard that the clasp cut my finger. But nothing in the world could have stopped my growing exertion just then, and I finally could feel the metal enter to the bone like a Gillette blade. None the less. I carried out this whole operation with so much calm and stoicism that he had no suspicion of my pain. I saw him standing there in front of me, very pleased with himself, his two hands stuck in the pockets of his cashmere dressing-gown, and yet trembling with desire like a leaf. Then I pressed on the lock even harder, and it was my bone that finally released the spring. The sound of it made him shudder, as well as my look, and without having had time to realize what I was about to do he was already drawing back. At that I grabbed the end of my belt and struck his yellowish feet so hard that with a single blow I made him fall on his knees, at my knees.... You see? I guess I can't have any temperament....'

Betka, who had been looking at her worshipfully during the whole telling of her story, again lifted the injured finger to her lips to kiss it.

'I never want to think of love,' Veronica went on, putting some sugar in Betka's coffee, 'I feel that in my case it's too important. The day he comes it will be terrible, and if I began I should never let go, to the end. But I won't change the look in my eyes. You understand, Betka? For me the sensation of love is that of a single glance which has become emotionless through so much, so much confidence, just as a red-hot iron turns white! You see? A kind of burning calm. What about you, Angel?' Veronica then asked her, obliging her to lose herself in the depths of her eyes to tear from her all her sincerity.

'With me,' Betka said, yielding with a fragile smile by which she implored her pity, 'with me it's only a kind of continual toothache in the heart!... without let-up.'

How it was raining outside now!

The dessert arrived, borne in triumph on a beribboned silver chariot adorned with huts with illuminated marzipan windows, wax roses and sugar squirrels.

Veronica laughingly exclaimed, 'Now you've got something for your teeth and for your heart ache!' And immediately she became tyrannical. Betka had to try everything, from the melancholy chocolate tart's sentimental flavour of a Viennese Sunday interior lighted by the rays of a pagan sun, to the Smyrna figs stuffed with walnuts, and the pastries drunk with rum, passing through the surprises of the melting and Mohammedan skies of liquor-filled candies and reaching at last the voluptuous and slightly nauseating suffocation of the ultimate *petit-four*. During all this time, as she had likewise premeditated, Veronica bewitched her friend by the unbridled galloping of the thousand-and-one nights of her fantasy with which she would eventually enchain her friend's wonder-starved spirit. It was a kind of delirious fairy-tale, with just two fairies: the two of them.

Veronica had the idea of projecting coloured moving pictures on Betka's teeth, with a different film on each tooth! She was going to make her a present of a dress that would be lighted from within by mercury rays that would make the whole surface of the body erogenous. She was going to lend her a salve by virtue of which one could appear at a dinner with one's head invisible. She would show her obsidian earrings into which living cholera microbes had been inserted; she knew how to carve a love poem in the immaculate white of a tender almond, just as it was shaping: later, when she broke it and removed the skin her handwriting would appear on it! Also how to provoke dreams of flight at will, how without sleeping to see a man advance, masked in white. Betka, dumbfounded, with teeth clenched, tried to follow this dizzy flight of images, and as when one approaches certain too rapid turns, she would often shut her eyes and, smiling at her fear, would reopen them immediately after each of these dangerous curves.

Her face suddenly darkening, Veronica said, 'I shouldn't have drunk champagne. I have my migraine; and here I've been talking like a madwoman!'

Veronica dropped Betka at the Quai des Orfèvres, gave her a rapid kiss and flung out the words, 'I'll telephone you tomorrow!'

Betka went to sleep delightfully exhausted, in a happy confusion from which emerged a single gaze and a single head of hair – Veronica! But she awoke late and frightfully anguished, and an absurd fear immediately assailed her: she would not see her friend again. Betka said to herself, 'How is she going to be able to telephone me? I didn't give her my address.' This animated her for a moment, justifying her, she thought, in telephoning her herself, but she immediately became gloomy, convinced that Miss Andrews did in fact have her address and telephone number. What a day to look forward to! All her hours taken, and so it was always – never anything, then all of a sudden everything happened to her at once! She had waited for months, she had written, forced herself into offices, telephoned and re-telephoned without results, all in vain. But since yesterday everything got into motion at once: she had to be at Mademoiselle Chanel's to try out as a model, be at half-past four at the Propaganda Bureau for a radio test, then she had had to drop in at the editorial office of *La Flèche* to do some typing, and so on and so forth! Yet she had already resolved not to go out on any pretext before Veronica's telephone call, for it would come as always just at a moment when she was out.

Toward four o'clock Betka said to herself, 'I'll wait another fifteen minutes. If she hasn't called, I'll phone her.'

But at seven neither of them had called the other and Betka, stretched out on her bed, reflected that the meeting with Veronica had occurred at the most critical and unhappy moment of her life. Not that her childhood had been happy, quite the contrary. But now it was as though the persistent rains of the bitterness of her childhood were oozing through the walls of the present prison of her guilt-feelings; how dearly, with what hell of anguish and remorse she had to pay for every little bit of pleasure that her body managed to snatch from her daily life so harassed with cares! As an adolescent in love with love, she had feared pleasure; now pleasure goaded her with new fears, the lugubrious fears of disappointment and disenchantment. Never yet had she had the courage to 'begin again' with the same person, so hideous did these experiences become in her memory. The only pleasure without shame that she had found in her whole life, she knew it now, was that of her meeting with Veronica; aside from this, ever since she had acquired the use of reason, she had known only the anxiety of her body and a fearful wish to end everything. She remembered having felt an irresistible urge to suicide. It was when she was eight years old, in a little village near the Russian frontier, that she had lived her martyrdom. All the visions of this period had the gall-taste of punishment and she had had more than sufficient motives to convince herself that the life she endured with her brothers was not a happy one! Their mother mistreated them pitilessly with words and acts; one day she strapped Betka's big brother to the bars of his bed and threatened to put out his eyes with her red-hot curling iron. Yet her mother was an intelligent and very beautiful woman, with fiery red hair. She was refined in manner, and for all who did not know her domestic furies she must have appeared to be a creature full of distinction. Seeing her appear among her friends, the soft curves of her bosom swelling from her low-cut dress and her eyelids, always half shut, bespeaking gentleness, no one in the world would have suspected her inhuman cruelty, her systematic, persevering and meticulous way of making her children suffer. She was astute, possessed a will of iron and was a fanatic on cleanliness, which did not prevent her from having a peculiar smell, as of burnt coffee. With her strange instinct that enabled her to discover all the most vulnerable points in the little souls of her children, she would contrive to sink the needles of her arbitrariness into them, pinning them to the four walls of her bedroom, papered in a pattern of corn and poppies, where she would lock them up and exercise her despotic domination. Never were they allowed to go out and play! Oh, thistles by the roadside, evening star!

Sometimes Betka would feel violent hatreds for her mother, and this curiously made her weep and feel infinite tenderness toward her; for nothing plunged her into a more inconsolable state than to imagine her mother as a victim of her chimerical vengeance. In spite of the fact that her mother made her suffer so greatly she admired her as a being endowed with an all-powerful sovereignty. Yes, her mother was superior to all other mothers, and in the depth of her unhappiness she venerated her like a divinity. She saw the other children around her, wasteful, gluttonous and heedless, lost in the sweet and peaceful unconsciousness of their lives; yet she did not envy them, she would not have changed places with them! Her youth did not allow her to understand her mother's injustice. The latter was always right, and they were monsters. She recognized this of her own accord, for no injunction could prevent her from sinning. Thistles by the roadside, evening star! And each of her tiniest impulses of pleasure was born already shrunk, sickly and bent by the stronger impulse of begging forgiveness. If her mother chastised her, it was of course to curb her evil instincts, her innate perversion; she was still sure of this today! And was she not even now, in the depth of her anguish, fondling herself, taking advantage of the agony of her emotions to clutch once more at pleasure?

Betka closed her gown again and held herself rigid. She belonged to the race of animals. She would have liked to die. Veronica! Angel! Never despise me!

At ten o'clock Betka received a telegram from Poland, signed by her mother, which contained one single word in Russian, '*Suka!*' (bitch).

The following morning at a quarter-past ten Betka telephoned to Veronica who was sitting naked before the desk in the living-room, trying to rub out the remorse of not yet having telephoned to her friend, and at the same time trying to think of the most tactful way of being of service to her. Four times she had carefully folded and unfolded a five-hundred franc bill which she had slipped into a little envelope and immediately pulled out again. She also had the receipt of Betka's telegram which had gone to Poland the day before yesterday. Should she put it into the same envelope, or simply keep it? For that matter, she would have to give her this envelope in person. Otherwise she might be offended. 'I must telephone her immediately!' And at the very moment when she was reaching for the receiver, the telephone rang.

Veronica got up and unhooked the receiver. She leaned her icy knee against the warm satin of the chair where she had just been sitting; but realizing suddenly that she was cold, she sat down again. Gathering her feet under her thighs she curled up, transforming her slim tall figure of a moment ago, as if by a miracle of the elasticity of her body, into a regular ball composed of all the intermingled confusion of her knees, her shoulders, her golden hair, her silver medals and her pearls. From this ball emerged a free arm, with which Veronica definitely put away the telegram receipt in a box of envelopes, keeping the five hundred francs in the hollow of her hand.

'Hello! My angel, it's you?'

'... Why yes. I'm fine. When can I see you?'

'... No, I can't today, shall we make it tomorrow?'

Barbara, who had just finished her own telephoning in her room, came in to the living-room at this moment and began from a distance to grimace incomprehensible words at Veronica, who looked at her without seeing, not trying to understand what she was saying. Then Barbara cried to her. 'Tell Solange we'll be at her cocktail party tomorrow!' Veronica merely responded with a furiously impatient shake of her head, but suddenly decided to make use of the information.

'Hello, *chérie*, hello! Is tomorrow all right? At Solange de Cléda's?... No, no, that doesn't matter, *mon chou*, I've already told her about you, she wants to meet you. You'll adore her.... Why of course it's true! Yes, wait, I'll give it to you... listen to me! Rue de Babylone, number....'

'Number 107,' said Barbara grumpily, tossing her daughter's dressing-gown at the feet of her chair.

'107,' Veronica repeated. 'Will you remember?... 107... Madame Solange de Cléda... Rue de Babylone... 107... Yes, *chérie*... as you wish... seven or half-past six... and afterwards I'll take you to dinner. Did you get a telegram in answer to yours?... Not yet.... Listen, my angel, you'll need some cash!... Don't be an idiot, will you?... Don't bring that up.... Of course, *chérie*, I'm listening to you, go ahead.... Yes, *chérie*.... Yes, *chérie*....'

During this time Veronica with her free hand folded the banknote three times, slipped it inside a small envelope, folded the latter in turn twice, and by pressing it with her wrist and holding it thus, managed to pass a brand new celery-coloured rubber band around it. Veronica's fingers, long, pale and blue-tinged at the joints, had executed all these complex operations with the inexorable, somewhat frightening and almost inhuman calm precision of those metallic phalanges that catch, turn over and mechanically change the records in automatic phonographs.

'Listen to me, don't worry about that. I've just put it into a visiting card envelope; I'll give it to you tomorrow. Don't lose it-it's so tiny!... Don't say that... don't be an idiot, now... I've already explained to you.... Why yes, *chérie*.... Just what you had on the other evening, but wear black shoes – and no raincoat, even if it rains! No, *chérie*, no hat.... Yes, at half-past seven, *chérie*, and we'll go out. I kiss you, *chérie*!'

'My angel, *mon chou*! Yes, *chérie*! No, *chérie*! The tiny, tiny ones, in the tiny little envelope. I can just see it!' exclaimed Barbara, imitating her daughter's tone of voice, both tender and vivacious. 'A windfall for another poor, pretty, idle girl!' Then she asked more energetically, 'Who is she?'

'It's your new secretary whom I've just invented, but whom I'll never let you see. It's none of your business,' answered Veronica, curtly. Then she went on in a honeyed voice, as if seeking forgiveness from her mother's disapproving glance, which was riveted on her nakedness: 'Thank you, Mama, for having rescued me with the dressing-gown; but you know perfectly well I only like to put on the other one which we sent out to be starched; this one is too thin, it's like a silk handkerchief,' and as she spoke she caught it between her toes that were almost as agile as her fingers. Then she began to swing the dressing-gown capriciously from the end of her extended leg, and suddenly – whish! – she tossed it with an impulsive kick up to the ceiling, catching it with her two uplifted arms. Then she began coquettishly to roll it like a turban around her head, while at the same time she purposely and negligently spread her legs open with an air of candour and as if forgetting herself.

'Tell me, Mama, did you go and look at the streamlined car you promised me?'

'Yes, but I don't like it at all,' answered Barbara in an uncompromising tone.

'Why not, Mama?'

'Because it's like you – it's too naked, it's really embarrassing to look at it – too many curves, too many roundnesses, too many lights, too many buttocks, too much of everything! I said without batting an eyelash to the salesman who showed it to me, "I'll only take it if you dress it for me!" As he seemed overcome with surprise I explained to him, "What I mean is this, my dear man: it's too naked. You'd have to dress it up in a cover cut in the shape of a scotch tailored suit!"'

Barbara had drawn close to her daughter, seeming unaware of her nakedness at the moment, and continued with exaltation. 'Don't you think that's amusing? A dressmaking establishment for automobiles! Very formal evening dresses, with low necks, the radiator of their bosoms emerging from the organdie, and long, dragging satin trains, to go to opening nights! This would automatically double our fashion collections – spring, summer, fall and winter collections. Convertible tops lined with ermine, door handles lined with seal-fur, and bison muffs to wrap on the radiators. Can't you just see the effect of our Cadillac travelling through an icy landscape in the vicinity of Leningrad?'

Veronica sneezed, and with the jolt her turban became undone, and fell in a mass over her, concealing her head and her shoulders. Veronica remained thus without moving, as if comically expecting to be rescued.

'It serves you right!' cried Barbara, and she added with a false note of concern, 'Don't move, I'll go and get you some nose-drops.'

*

In her private mansion on Rue de Babylone, Solange de Cléda was preparing to receive her guests for cocktails. Since the incident in the Count of Grandsailles' room some five weeks before she had not seen him again. The latter, still obstinately keeping to his solitary retreat in the Château de Lamotte, had given her no other sign of life than to send her flowers. Those flowers of his were something to die and to laugh over! One Thursday morning her chambermaid, Eugénie, had opened before her wonderstruck eyes a large square lustre-lilac box from one of the best Parisian florists. Inside an immaculate starched nun's head-dress serving as a vase was a homogeneous mass of tightly packed jasmines filling it to the brim, and in the centre of this fragrant blinding whiteness, the Count of Grandsailles' card, with nothing on it but his own engraved name.

Since the moment when she had abandoned in an outburst of tenderness all the artifice of pride which had nourished her exasperating flirtation with the Count of Grandsailles for five years, Solange had felt distraught and lost. Yet Hervé's flowers had a smell that was not the insipidity of pity – they were so fragrant! And the nun's head-dress – she attached no other symbolic significance to it than that of purity, if indeed there were any other reason than the Count's original taste. During these last four weeks it was as if in spite of the fact that Solange's bewilderment had grown, her anxiety on the other hand had relaxed by virtue of the very fact of having given up the struggle, and her anguish thus tended to become stabilized in a vague continual torment, in an uninterrupted suffering of her spirit, which she had decided by all human and superhuman means to prevent from marring the glorious integrity of her beauty, the pole star of her hope. She had often observed, in Grandsailles, the kind of earthy taste that bound him so much to the flesh. That need in him, always a little crude, to tap her to test the solidity of her body before taking her affectionately in his arms. No! No spectre, even the most fascinating, could ever have arrested his attention.

The afternoon of the very day when Solange had received the jasmines, she could not resist dropping in, as if by chance, at the florist's from whom the flowers came. While waiting to have a bouquet of lilies of the valley made up she caught sight of a suspicious case, on whose cover the place from which it had been sent could be distinctly read: the station of Libreux. As she was waiting Solange went over to where the box stood, with her gloved hand arranged two lilies that emerged from a large basket beside it, loosened a bouquet of bachelorbuttons, and at last casually lifted the cover of the mysterious object. Her legs nearly gave way: that's what it was – rows of nuns' headpieces, carefully folded one on top of the other, at least fifty of them! So Grandsailles had generously supplied his florist with his original wrappings. The sudden idea that this kind of bouquet had been invented and destined for other persons than herself made the marble-dust of her resentment grind between the acerbated teeth of her jealousy. These nuns' headpieces that had a moment ago been pure and celestial now appeared to her a veritable abomination. Of all that whiteness, the receptacle of an offering, of the most delicate feelings, there remained only the degrading reality of a basely utilitarian fabric, similar to and as vile as that of the clean napkins that the chambermaid hurriedly and noiselessly brings in at the last moment to the bathroom – the vile linen of the unavowable intimacies of her own rivals. Nuns' headpieces, well folded, arranged in rows, waiting in turn for the consummation of the libidinous ignominies with which, she knew, Grandsailles would finally tear out her heart.

But the next day Solange received a bouquet just like the first, and the same the following day: soon she had proof of her certainty that at least this kind of bouquet was destined exclusively for her.

From this moment the flowers became one of her dearest reasons for hope, but at the same time subjected her to the cruellest of all ordeals. For what would become of this insinuation of a nuptial way if at the end of these assiduous offerings there was to be nothing but the sweetness of the light fragrance of a homage and if the fragility of its cloying aroma was not to be mingled at last with the bitter and permanent odour of love? In any case Solange knew that the way of her passion would be long, and while preparing to become the slave of the torments of her spirit she had decided to care for her body as a thing apart. Convinced of the error it would have been to wish to try the impossible, to daze herself or even distract her moral anxiety by events of a different nature from those of her own feelings, she neither sought nor expected from the physical world any 'consolation', for the heart can be healed only by the heart.

Beginning an imaginative life apart, Solange was preparing to pursue the realization of the unique miracle of caring for the physical person of her anatomy as an independent being. Thus, while she delivered only her spirit to her passion, she provisionally lent the inexhaustible biological resources of her body to the studied mouldings of masseurs, beauticians, surgeons, dressmakers and ballet teachers. But before all and at all costs, one thing was certain: she must be able to sleep, and for this Solange de Cléda had recourse to an astute and unscrupulous woman doctor, Dr Anselme, who gave her regularly every night before she went to bed a rather large injection of luminal – a drug by means of which she obtained a refreshing sleep, and whose effects on her organism might be harmful only a few years later. Solange ordinarily awoke without anguish, but after some ten minutes it began to invade her as in the phenomenon of capillarity which makes coffee rise in a lump of sugar, and it came over her, progressively darkening the whiteness of her waking soul with its sombre ideas through the fine capillarity of her sensibility.

Having given herself over to the cares of specialists – all but her sentiments – Solange knew less and less about herself, and each morning she anxiously questioned Doctor Anselme. 'Did I sleep well?' She had dreamed so much about being able to sleep that now when she slept she no longer dreamed.

That evening, when Solange heard her first guests ring the bell at the door to her garden-court she wondered, '*Mon Dieu!* Why am I seeing all those people?' Yet she knew quite well why. People came running to her to admire her, to serve her, to help her to climb, she still needed their fawning adulation to progress toward the all-powerful goal of her growing social prestige which would enable her to approach Grandsailles' level. She had already yielded in her pride by admitting to the Count the nature of her feelings. Now she wanted to maintain her inferiority with nobility: on an equal footing.

At Solange de Cléda's there was much talk of the Count of Grandsailles' forthcoming ball, and already several 'small souls', with their sharp and wholly Parisian intuition of social Machiavellianism and believing themselves already predestined to be numbered among those who would not be invited, were beginning to prepare the platform of their social battle. They were trying to impose themselves by the terror of their malicious gossip or by the histrionic platitude of their servility, or else by the two methods combined, all without any of them forgetting at the same time to prepare for themselves a favourable terrain of retreat, so that in case of defeat the latter might be interpreted in all possible ways, human and divine, except the true one, namely the Count of Grandsailles' intentional, pure and simple omission.

Madame Claudine Druett, with a cup of tea in one hand, was helping herself to cakes which she chewed languorously one after another with a heartbroken expression. In her pearl-grey tailored suit, with a corsage of lilies of the valley pinned at a melancholy angle, she was preparing to launch upon a polemic.

'A Grandsailles ball is always a success,' she said, while she lifted her white veil with her little finger, the only one that remained free and dry. 'It's as clear as day! The Count succeeds because he never runs the risk of failing. These affairs of his are always masterpieces, but in the long run the lack of spontaneity becomes deadly for those who have lived too long in his drawing-rooms.' She sighed with the ethereal but four-edged breath of her tiny nacreous nostrils, while resting the tips of her pointed buttocks on the knees of Farges, the plump poet, who obliged her to let herself go in his arms. 'I like balls that grow in twenty-four hours like mushrooms,' Claudine continued, in a naive and capricious intonation, 'balls with new faces, dresses that are hardly sewn, and smacks!'

'Why yes, why yes! my Claudinette, my Claudinette, my beautiful reine-claude,' Farges buzzed, 'your old Farges is the only one who understands what is on this child's mind! You remember Venice,' he continued, addressing Solange de Cléda who had just stretched out at his feet, looking like an oxidized-silver greyhound in her tight-fitting dress of dull silver that accentuated her ribs as they stirred to her breathing. 'Well, in Venice,' Farges continued, 'every time we decided to go off on an excursion to visit a Paladian villa, it would rain – it never failed. In the evening the sky would clear, and someone would point to a cloud of May-bugs dancing in a Saint Andrew's cross before a cypress, and on returning to Venice we would learn that a ball had just grown.'

Farges had the reputation of being very witty because he was fat, because he spoke in a very nasal voice, choked and interrupted by a great variety of respiratory troubles and accidents, and finally because he was really very witty. He now dandled Claudine in his arms, and the black, hairy holes of his nose grazed his protégée's bouquet of lilies of the valley like two buzzing bumblebees. Each of his syllables, barely distinguishable and murmured into Claudine's ear through the screen of the diverse pollens of the forests of hair of his nose and his ill-kempt beard reached the other auditors confusedly like the unintelligible hum of poetry.

'What is he saying?' young Ortiz asked, radiant with anticipation. He was shiny and new, as if just out of a box, and he brought his chair up to Farges. Claudine uttered a hysterical cry. 'It's wonderful! He says that the Grandsailles ball has to simmer on a low fire in the back of the kitchens of all the Parisian salons. It will only be good once it's warmed over!'

'I adore warmed-over dishes!' Ortiz exclaimed.

'What snobbery! You couldn't tell by looking at her dress,' muttered Farges, frowning in his annoyance. 'Warmed-over or not,' Cécile Goudreau broke in, shouting from a distance, 'the worst of all will be to stay home on the night of the ball, trying to convince yourself that your own warmed-over dish is the best of all!'

'And the Banco?' exclaimed young Ortiz, laughing till the tears rolled, and trying in this way to wipe out the bitterness of Cécile Goudreau's last words. 'Each one of us should begin right now to prepare his Banco for the night of the ball. Mine will be the costume!'

Others had just arrived to swell the group, in which the debate over Grandsailles was but in its preliminary phase. Then Solange, gliding like an oxidized-silver eel, went over to talk with Dick d'Angerville, who was observing everything with his sceptical air, seeming to see nothing. Solitary, standing, continually manipulating something near the bar-table, Solange de Cléda was a little frightened as she observed the animation of her drawing-room, which today seemed to her just a little too boldly picturesque. There were indeed some quite extraordinary people there: Soler, the Catalonian, was in a state of constant agitation, spilling his martini, burning himself on his cigarette, dragging the armchairs about and being of service to everyone; what a 'specimen' he was – he did ultra-sophisticated fashion photographs, claimed to have invented a new religion and made leather helmets for automobile drivers by hand!

Now he was shaking little Mademoiselle de Henry, who as usual was covered – one might say devoured – by clips, brooches, pins, necklaces, bracelets, amulets, bells; it looked as if he wanted to dust her, deliver her of all that. Soler hesitated, but he was certainly going to end up by doing something with her. There he goes! It was inevitable, he had just sat her on top of the piano! Her ruby brooch had become unpinned and fallen on the floor. The better to see, Solange kneeled on the third step of the little library ladder and looked up. She thus resembled a silver hawk. Judging the total effect of her guests from the 'Grandsailles point of view', her drawing-room struck her as incoherent; all her friends who saw one another constantly, accustomed to being together almost every day, gave, on the contrary, the agitated impression of people who have just met by chance, and their familiarity seemed out of place.

At Grandsailles' it was the reverse; everything held together so well that since there was nothing that could change places, nothing was 'out of place'. And even the people who met at his house for the first time seemed to have just left one another two or three hundred years before.

'What are you thinking of, *tristesse*?' d'Angerville asked her, taking Solange by the arm and helping her down from her stool. Solange remained for a moment with her arms crossed over her bosom in her characteristic gesture of fearful melancholy; she now resembled a Solange de Cléda of oxidized anguish.

'I find all this frightfully *patchy*,' she exclaimed, shaken by a smothered laugh as she pressed a cigarette between her lips. 'It lacks distinction.'

'The thing that gives distinction – class in the true sense –' said d'Angerville, offering her the flame of his lighter, 'is oneness with destiny. The same is true of the famous equestrian statues of the Renaissance – that had class only if they were cast, horse and horseman, in a single mould. "The man mounted on the horse of his destiny" – all of a piece! Just look around: no one seems to be completely finished! And most of the time it's even worse. They all seem to be made up of parts, rented, subrented, from other persons and put together with a thousand pieces not one of which goes with the rest.' Then with a sigh, 'It's even more pitiful when they try to create an ensemble.' And as Solange repressed a sudden laugh, pretending to cough into her hand, 'Yes, *tristesse*, don't laugh, I beg you; I was looking at the same person.' Then, taking inventory, as though he were telling something very serious, he enumerated, 'The hat with the bag, the clip with the buttons, the buttons with the tics, and the shoes with....'

'The nose!' Solange exploded.

Indeed the lady in question had pointed shoes exactly the shape of her excessively powdered nose.

One could say whatever one liked about Grandsailles, thought Solange, but he at least was moulded all of a piece.

'Mon *Dieu*!' Solange exclaimed, becoming despondent again, 'What's to be done? Only you, dear d'Angerville, could help me do my salon over properly.'

'That's easy,' answered d'Angerville. 'Some beautiful old furniture – and limit the pederasts to a strict minimum.' As he spoke he turned his eyes to a large divan near the entrance in the centre of which Cécile Goudreau reigned in a well-fed group of cynical women among whom several notorious pederasts were indulging in all sorts of pantomimes for their own amusement.

'But Cécile Goudreau is received at Grandsailles'.'

95

'Yes, but she's too highly flavoured for you,' d'Angerville advised.

Cécile Goudreau was in fact a kind of Balzacian character, intelligent, *déclassée*, having become a real Parisian institution by dint of intrigues, whose strong personality Grandsailles had admitted and recognized just at the opportune moment, as an established government does with a revolutionary power when the latter threatens to become too important.

'And Barbara?'

Barbara had just entered the drawing-room, and her decorative effect was undeniable.

'She,' said d'Angerville, 'can do you no harm; on the contrary, she belongs to the species of Grandsailles' forbidden fruit, and to the "dissidents that have their place in the centre".'

Solange went to meet Barbara, who kissed her on the cheeks, on the ears and excused herself for arriving so late. But anyway she brought the photograph she had promised for Solange's scrapbook of society notes – 'a picture of Princess Agmatoff as a contortionist!'

'But where did I put my bag?'

Solange ordered a servant to fetch the bag. Almost at the same time as Barbara, Betka appeared. For two hours she had waited in vain for Veronica, so that they might go in together, for she was intimidated by the constant arrival of all those luxurious cars. Then, finally, she had recognized Veronica's mother and had followed her closely. Dazed, she immediately found herself with a Bacardi cocktail in her hands which an attentive servant came and offered her. There was a stir of curiosity in the group that surrounded Cécile Goudreau, and all the admiring eyes wondered. 'Who is that big, beautiful redhead?'

Immediately Cécile Goudreau came to her rescue. 'Put that nasty stuff down for a moment, you can pick it up later,' she said, taking her glass from her and putting it cautiously down on the table next to the divan. 'Come with me, I'll introduce you to your hostess, and when you've got rid of your things you can come back here to our group. Don't pay any attention to anybody else, we're the only intelligent ones you'll meet in this gathering.'

Betka gratefully took Cécile by the arm and let herself be led. Several people were already beginning to leave, and Solange standing near the hall, escorted by d'Angerville, exchanged with them the usual amenities, while in each interval, pretending to carry on a conversation with d'Angerville, they simply passed the guests through the sorter, saying. 'This one, yes – that one, no....' When Betka had withdrawn, Solange said to d'Angerville, 'Beautiful teeth!'

'Yes, but they won't do her much good.'

'Weak?' asked Solange.

'A premature death, a violent death surely,' concluded d'Angerville in the swift and convinced manner he had of expressing his premonitions of the destinies of most of the beings he encountered.

Betka came back to Cécile Goudreau and drank her Bacardi in two swallows. Never had she felt so intimidated; never in a social group had she heard such cruel, acid and cynical talk. They were in the midst of debating the following question. 'What do women prefer, men "to go out with" or men "to go home with"?' One woman said, 'Why to go out with, of course!' Another broke in, amid acclamations from the pederasts, 'I like a man to go out with and a woman to go home with.' Still another one said, 'With me it's just the opposite, I like a woman to go out with and two men to go home with.'

'Why not all six, like the Greek courtesans?'

'Ah, that's the temperamental kind,' sighed Cécile Goudreau, 'Isadora's kind. But you know, *chérie*, we in Auvergne in the country achieve the same result with two hardboiled eggs and a guitar string!'

Betka, fearing she would be asked the same question, which would have paralysed her with shame, broke away from the group

97

and made for a solitary corner near a great balcony that overlooked the garden. But feeling even more lost here, she immediately decided to go and introduce herself to Barbara to ask her news of Veronica.

'My daughter has gone off to Fontainebleau for the weekend, but she left me something for you. Oh, there is my bag!' she exclaimed, taking it from the hands of the servant who was just bringing it to her. 'Here is the picture of the princess!' Barbara announced, signalling to Solange, who came over, accompanied by d'Angerville, and Barbara went and sat down in the midst of Cécile Goudreau's group, where they made room for her, avid with curiosity.

Barbara began to rummage in the bottom of her bag with both hands, making all her bracelets tinkle, displaying the inattentive eagerness of a little lap-dog that has just buried its toy, through no other need than that of the play of its instinct.

'I hide everything in my bag, and then I can never find anything! Too many secrets... too many scandals rolled up in newspaper clippings... too many vitamins. There! This is from Veronica for you,' said Barbara to Betka, handing her with a postman's bureaucratic gesture the little folded envelope held by a celery-green rubber band. Betka blushingly took the envelope. 'At last!' Barbara exclaimed triumphantly, 'this is for Solange!' From among the jumble of objects in her bag she had managed to extract a slender postcard, turned very yellow, which from having remained folded in two for a long time had an irresistible tendency to close again on its worn hinges. With her outstretched arm Barbara made this fragile souvenir flutter coyly before all eyes, and at each jerk of her department-store saleswoman's superficial exaltation it seemed as if it must inevitably break in two.

'Isn't it amusing? Isn't it darling? Isn't it a unique, sensational document?'

It was simply the printed photograph of a beautiful 'talking head' – that of Princess Agmatoff, at the time when she had to find refuge, on the morrow of the Russian revolution, among the vermin-infested stalls of the Prater amusement park in Vienna. At the sight of this picture the pederasts burst into loud exclamations and sobbing laughs that modulated all the shades of hypocrisy included between sarcasm and pathos. The cynical women uttered contradictory yelps. Cécile Goudreau was silent, and the Viscount of Angerville darkened disapprovingly. Then Solange de Cléda kissed Barbara in the neck, pressing the postcard to her bosom, and holding it thus as if to protect it from further curiosity, pleaded.

'May I really keep it?'

Betka was so overcome by the emotion of finding herself in possession of a message coming from Veronica that she choked for a moment and had to lean on Cécile Goudreau's arm. The latter made her sit down beside her on the large couch and kept an eye on her.

'I'll be back in a moment,' said Betka to Cécile, getting up, her legs weak from emotion and her heart pounding. She went back to the window which was still deserted, bathed now in a soft bluish light, which was nevertheless sufficient to reveal in all its crudity the frightful disappointment that the contents of this envelope contained for Betka. Before opening it Betka's fingers had several times snapped the celery-green elastic. Overcome with hesitancy she seemed thus to wish to put off the moment of knowing everything. Already fear had begun to mingle with her hope, and poisoned it. But no suspicion could have equalled the cruelty, the bitter and wounding reality that awaited her, for within the envelope there was neither a message nor the money promised with such insistence over her own protests. Instead of the gift she had not asked for, or the friendly word she had tried to deserve, there was only the blue receipt of the telegram to Poland which Veronica had sent for her, carefully folded in four, and in the centre of which was conspicuously and carelessly scribbled in red pencil, probably in Veronica's own mocking and

99

pitiless handwriting, the defaming mark of the trivial figure of her debt – forty-eight francs and fifty centimes! At this moment, in the new light of her disenchantment, Betka saw the unfolding of all the reverses and mishaps of her last days, which she had managed to banish, forgetting everything, and wanting to live in the sole illusion and the single hope of seeing her friend again. Now she felt assailed by the remorse of all those meetings neglected, missed and abandoned without excuses, her lost opportunities either of being hired as a mannequin or on the radio or on the newspaper; then that refusal of her parents to help her, the almost absolute certainty that her sister had married her fiancé....

But none of these reverses, even the dreadful stigma of her own mother's insult, could wound her more poignantly than Veronica's contempt, and she seemed to glimpse, in the inhuman hardness of her act, something strange and monstrous that she could not understand by any rational process. Why had Veronica feasted her so sumptuously at the Tour d'Argent? Why had she expended so much charm, lavishing upon her for several hours all the resources of her seductive fancy? Was it only to fill the emptiness of an evening of boredom? Or to satisfy the caprice of her exhibitionistic desire, if not merely for the amusement of a few hours of feeling herself looked at and of dazzling, with the flash of her diamond personality, a being like herself, so feeble, without any other resources than her hunger for affection, her readiness and eagerness to give her heart?

Betka felt Veronica's gaze harden in the depths of her own until it hurt, wrenching tears from her. It was as though her friend's impassive eyes, so gentle a while ago, were even more materially present and enigmatic as they grew inflexible. And now, was she going to love Veronica less because of all this? Assuredly not! On the contrary she loved her all the more as Veronica's reality became chimerical and her own reasons for despair augmented; her passion grew apace with her misfortune. She had never been able to hate her cruel mother; how she could worship Veronica, if the latter would deign to accept her martyrdom! But would Betka ever see her again? Just now, looking out into this same garden in the anguished uncertainty of expectation – fool that she was – she had felt the spring rites of their imminent reunion beating in each of the flowers of the chestnut trees; now at the approach of night these same flowers had become snowflakes in the winter of her disillusion, and a cold hand, clutched like a bird's claw, had alighted on her still burning flesh.

Cécile Goudreau, whom Betka had felt breathing beside her for a moment, seized her by the arm. 'You're upset, eh? Come on, let's leave! It's deadly here, everybody is busy. We'll just slip away.... Tonight Cécile Goudreau is taking you out, and not a word – we'll go home together!... And how!'

'Where are we going?' Betka asked Cécile after they had walked in silence halfway down the Rue de Babylone.

'Not to a restaurant, in any case, after all that swill we've been putting away!' Then, after a long pause, 'Aren't you afraid I'll seduce you?'

'Pleasant things never happen,' answered Betka, laughing.

'They do happen, just the same, but by halves!' sighed Cécile.

'Do we walk? It'll do us good to go up the Champs Elysées. It's soothing sometimes. What about your anguish?'

'What anguish?'

'Come, *chérie*, don't put on any chichi with me. I'm anguished, too, and anyway, why are we walking together? Because we're anguished!... It's the malady of our time. Why are we preparing for war? Because we're bored and we're anguished. Boredom and anguish combined have become a terrible power. It is they that rule our world! Taxi!' shouted Cécile Goudreau. The car stopped short, and drew up to them with the faithful obedience still commanded by those who by the 'irrevocable' tone of their voice knew how to convey the inflexible authority of the master.

As soon as they were in the taxi Cécile, slumping in the seat, exclaimed. 'It's good for the legs to say to yourself from time to time, "we'll walk up the Champs Elysées," provided you immediately find a taxi. I'm tired, *chérie*. I'm very, very fond of Solange; besides which she's eating her heart out over that Grandsailles of hers. But I can't stand Barbara's kind. I'm supposed to be a cynic – well, Barbara is beyond me!'

'She's so kind to everyone,' Betka feebly protested.

'I'll grant you that, *chérie*. Unconsciousness is what it really is, but it amounts to the same thing. Imagine daring to show the picture of the "talking head" of poor Agmatoff? Barely two years after she was guillotined, so to speak, by the windshield of her car. And you think the way she handed you Veronica's little envelope was tactful? You know Veronica well?'

'Very slightly,' Betka answered, blushing.

'There's a girl who's tempered in steel! Her mother, at least, is kind. She paid Princess Agmatoff's rent for five years. An immense apartment on the Rue de Rivoli... the dressmakers' bills... and everything. It's true that she can afford it.'

'She's been perfect to me,' said Betka, bluffing about her almost non-existent relations with Barbara.

Then, after a long silence, and as if continuing her reflections, Cécile concluded, 'Why, yes. I'll grant you Barbara is a real angel. Which doesn't prevent her always putting her wings in it.'

The taxi had just stopped so smoothly that it was as though in the course of the whole trip the passengers' prestige had grown and become consolidated.

*

Cécile Goudreau's *garçonnière* was situated in a recess with damp and moss-green old pumice-stone walls, behind the Palais Galiéra. When they arrived it was not yet quite dark, and the brief immobility of their taxi, though it was exactly like that of any other taxi, became immediately suspect, solely because of the moss that covered the oozing walls. It would have been even more so if it had been observed by an imaginary spectator, preferably placed on the fourth storey of a neighbouring house, if such a person had existed in this rich but sparsely inhabited quarter of Paris. The stairway was so dark that when they entered the house Cécile Goudreau took Betka by the hand to guide her.

'Don't stumble... there! We'll thee-and-thou each other, shall we?'

They were now climbing a long spiral staircase.

'There's one more floor before we get to my door, wait a moment!'

Goudreau had just got down on all fours, looking under the carpet for the key to let herself in. 'There, my lovely redhead. I've got it! The worst is over!' said Goudreau, slipping her key into the lock and opening the door noiselessly. They passed through a large room in the dark, and their heels resounded as in an Ambassador's antechamber, clicking as on marble. Then they passed between heavy curtains into a second, feebly-lighted room, much smaller but with a very high ceiling, which gave it a character both of intimacy and of solemnity. It was entirely covered with broad bands of daisy yellow and black satin folded vertically all along the walls, carried to the ceiling in the form of a cupola, and joining in the centre in an immense rosace trimmed with silver braid, from which hung a heavy black cord sprinkled with silver grains and at the end of which was attached, rather low and in the exact centre of the room, a very large but fragile Japanese lantern of an indeterminate mite-coloured rose – assuming there were mites of this colour. Along the four walls of the room, facing one another, four wide, very low divans, uniformly covered in chinchilla and strewn with large antique oriental cushions, were separated only by the entrance door and a window in the opposite wall. These two openings were hidden by great curtains of the same material and imitating the same folds as those of the walls, so that when everything was closed one had the impression of being shut in by an absolute uniformity of materials. Beneath the lamp, but a little toward the angle between the door and the window and level with the divans stood a rectangular black lacquer table on which were disposed in perfect symmetry two pipes for smoking opium, the little alcohol lamp, the needles, the metal boxes. Two further details completed the atmosphere of this spot: a little niche situated in the same angle as that in which the table stood, halfway up the wall, set in the satin, containing a Russian icon lighted by an oil night-lamp. On the floor a thick hairy all-over carpet the colour of wine-lees, on which one walked as on flexible needles, was still further softened by four immense polar-bear rugs, their four open jaws, their eight crystal eyes facing one another.

'Peel off your clothes!' said Cécile Goudreau, tossing to her a shiny tobacco-coloured dressing-gown, while she undressed and slipped on a kind of pale blue quilted robe, brown-stained in spots around the black holes of several burns.

Betka took everything off in a few seconds, and while she adjusted the sleeves of the dressing-gown she had been offered she observed Cécile Goudreau out of the corner of her eye with an anxious heart. The latter was making herself comfortable, as much at ease as if no one had been in the room. Cécile Goudreau's nude body showed ravages, and her breasts were shrivelled, but she had divinely beautiful and slender legs. She had the face of a bird that looked like a cat, and the body of a cat that looked like a bird without in the least resembling an owl, as one might first be tempted to think. In fact what was birdlike about Cécile Goudreau was the extreme fragility of the joints of her ankles, of her wrists, of her hollow and greenish neck, the exiguous volume of her tiny skull with its small brainpan, and her hair curling in light separate ringlets, smooth and regular as feathers; what was catlike about her was the fixed green gaze and the masculine cynicism of her pointed teeth. Everything else about her was catlike; her elastic and arching movements, the feline and concentrated languor of her indolence, and even her mews, for it could be said that her famous witticisms, brief and shaded with voluptuous inflections, were mewed rather than spoken.

'Do you like this?' Cécile Goudreau mewed, making a circular nod, with which she seemed to caress, from a distance, all the satin that hung from the walls. 'I don't give a damn about the decoration, it's much too Paul Poiret, but I like its *gaga* and anachronistic side. I bought the whole thing at an auction, just as it is, from the Prince of Orminy, who was sick of it, you understand? But you'll see, my puss, as soon as you get used to the whole business all this excessive luxury will begin in spite of everything to strike you as very appropriate for smoking. For all this isn't rabbit, you know! Real chinchilla, my lass. And is there a lot of it!' said Goudreau, crushing the fur with her bare bird-foot. 'Orminy doesn't wipe his nose on his sleeve, I can assure you! You see that thing, that kind of soup-bowl for puking into? Well, it's solid gold!'

As she spoke, Cécile Goudreau stretched herself out and drew up the lacquered table with the smoking accessories set out on a level with her chest. Betka came and lay down beside her, pressing her own body lightly against hers. Then Cécile, with a quick and casual movement, passed her arm around her neck, thus holding Betka's face glued to hers. Intently their two pairs of eyes watched the preliminary ritual of Cécile's two hands busily preparing the first pipe. At the tip of her needle, with the consummate skill of an old mandarin, she rolled a tiny pellet of opium, heated it, brought it close to the flame, till it crackled, but just at the moment when it was about to catch fire she withdrew it in order to mould, press, play with it voluptuously, as though this were a matter as precious to her as that which great narcissists pull out of and put back into their noses and ears with such great delight. Cécile Goudreau must have been thinking the same thing, for she said laughingly to Betka:

'Anyway, it's less dirty than picking your nose, eh? What an occupation! Take that poor Orminy, who smokes like one of the blessed and who got fed up with his atmosphere! You understand, my child, there are two kinds of smokers, those who smoke to create an atmosphere for themselves and, once they succeed, get fed up with it; and the others who smoke simply because they are fed up with the atmosphere. The first are almost always the aesthetic kind, the slightly imbecilic kind, the Orminys; and the second is me, the real thing – dogmatic, without chichi. But you see how curious it is: in the end we buy their atmosphere readymade, with all their chichi, and their trouble thrown in. Suck my ear, *chéri*, it pricks me... a little lower – thank you, my girl. Will you press a button-just under the table, to put out the light-simply with your foot. There! That's better, isn't it, with just the little flame? It's really nice-the night – lamp near the icon now. Orminy must have been proud of that effect, the poor bastard! How old are you?'

'How good it is to be here!' Betka sighed.

'Come, now, are you listening to me? You must be twenty?'

'Worse than that,' Betka laughed. 'Eighteen!'

'That's too bad! Just what I thought-the stupid age! Here, my treasure, inhale this fragrance,' continued Cécile Goudreau, putting the pipe to her lips: 'some day you'll thank your old Goudreau for having taught you to smoke this vile stuff. You're made for it – one can tell by taking just one look at you! Your anguished face and your big sensual mouth. Don't you see, they don't go together! Only a good dose of opium can put them into harmony. I've had experience. I can tell a future smoker in a bullfight crowd. Will you remind me to tell you the story of young Ortiz whom I picked up in Madrid? Today I'm not talking, you understand? I just say anything that comes into my head. But now we're going to have several years ahead of us, you'll hear some good ones from your Cécile. I can give you any literary flavour you like, Marcel Proust, for instance, the real, living thing, not like his; I can also do you some Lautréamont, but I need a piano for that. This place lacks a piano, don't you think?'

Betka had just finished the pipe with the avidity of a nursing babe. She was beginning to derive pleasure from her disappointment over Veronica, and to launch on reveries in which the latter was 'amazed' at her new life of debauchery which already appeared to her as endowed with a unique distinction, and beyond the scope of anything she had known. 'Only among a few vice-addicts is there a certain honesty and frankness,' she reflected, wholly won over by Cécile Goudreau's irresistible personality....

'I feel nothing, no effect,' said Betka, gently benumbed as she took a third pipe that Cécile offered her.

'This one is stronger, it's a very full-bodied opium, but you won't feel anything either: opium doesn't produce any effect, but it does what is more important – it makes the nastiness of this world cease to have any effect on you. At your age people believe either that they can banish unhappiness, or invent an artificial life. There is no artificial Paradise, there is only the way to convert that fine and gelatinous pain which is anguish into something agreeable. Are you all right? I'll fix one for myself now.'

'How good it is here!' sighed Betka, picking up her fifth pipe.

'You can live here as much as you like. There is always a little pocket money, you'll never guess where-well, it's under the gold soup-bowl, you see.'

Cécile had just picked up this receptacle which rested on a large box, likewise of gold – a polo trophy of the Prince of Orminy's – whose lid was scrawled all over with engraved autographs. Goudreau opened it and stirred with her hand several rolls of bank bills, among which there was also an ivory elephant, broken, tied to a very dirty red ribbon. 'You can take whatever you want from here, without asking, my girl. What's the matter with you, *chérie*?'

'I don't know. I suddenly feel a dreadful anguish again,' said Betka, uttering a deep sigh and pressing her brow with her hand moist with cold sweat. It's Veronica, she thought to herself: it was too good to last – oh, if only the thought of her doesn't come and harass me with grief!

'I thought so,' Cécile Goudreau grumbled, bringing the gold recipient close to her, 'go to it, my girl! It's because of all the swill you had at Solange de Cléda's. Opium purifies.'

Betka began to vomit.

'Go to it, my girl! I'm holding you, *chérie*. I'm here, *chérie*,' and as she spoke Cécile tenderly pressed her brow with her two little hands which were always slightly contracted like bird-claws. 'Wait a second, I'll give you a clean towel sprinkled with ether.' And Cécile immediately returned, bringing the gold basin….

At the end of three hours Betka murmured, 'I think I've been sleeping.'

'I'll say you have! It's half-past four in the morning: it's raining outside now. I never sleep! Do you still feel like vomiting?'

'A little,' said Betka. 'I'll go – don't you bother!' And she went, all dazed, and shut herself up for some time in the bathroom, which was finished entirely in black marble. 'What a dog's life! It's wonderful!' thought Betka, making the last contractions to assure a longer period of rest for her stomach.

Cécile Goudreau, seeing her return, brought a fresh pipe close to her. 'Here's another one all ready, that I just fixed for myself; it's good!

I'll have to teach you to make them; I shan't always be there.... Did you notice that fine green moss that covers the front of the house? Oh, no, you can't have observed it – it was almost dark when we came in. I'll show you, the wall of the façade is almost entirely covered with a very fine moss, of a sinister green,' said Cécile Goudreau, smiling strangely, and continuing in a disturbing tone of voice. 'Before I used to like that moss! and on days like today I would imagine it dripping in the rain; then the vision of it appearing between pipes only augmented the obscure pleasure of huddling even more madly in the depth of my cushions. But for the last week that confounded moss has had a very funny effect on me, and it's idiotic how a stupid thing like that can become so anguishing... yet that horrible moss is so pretty when you look at it close! It's like very fine hairs with what look like flowerlets at the ends, like little yellowish crosses...!'

Betka listened to all this with half an ear. Rigid, she felt herself floating above the starless and oily marsh of her first opium night, on whose black horizon Veronica's cruel gaze, blended into a single flame of regret, remained suspended, oscillating like the half-drowned flicker of the night-lamp of her bad conscience.

'Faithless friend! You'll see! You'll see!' Betka kept reproaching her in a bare whisper, without yet knowing whereof her vague threat consisted. For a long time she had been watching the dying light of the night-lamp and saying to herself, trying to play at frightening herself, 'That would be frightful – Veronica's face vacillating in place of the icon's!' But fear did not take up its abode in her spirit that evening; on the contrary, instead of the barking pack of the stirred-up hounds of her rancour against Veronica, and instead of the terrors which she would have liked to awaken in her spirit, she felt only a limitless sensation of undefined happiness that she had never experienced before, which made her ready to weep with joy. Cécile Goudreau, with an obsessed air, her hands joined on her burnt-out pipe, murmured in a low voice and as if telling the beads of her anguish:

'That horrible green! That awful moss!... Yet it's funny.... It was just nothing at all, the way this new phobia started... I was walking, feeling very low, and then, bang, I found myself before the wall of the Montmartre cemetery drenched with a moisture that struck me as abominable and covered by exactly the same moss as my façade... and that's all there was to it... yes, there was also the dream with the business of the coffin in light walnut and then... and then the cards that don't work, and everything, and everything. I should have been suspicious of Orminy. I remember now the day when the Prince called my attention to that accursed moss, pointing to it with the tip of his ebony cane, and laughing between his yellow teeth he said, "It's very damp, there's no denying it, but it doesn't penetrate. The interior is dry and in perfect condition to preserve people like us... embalmed creatures!" Lord, what a lugubrious creature that Orminy is! My God! that moss, how sticky it can become, an idea, a fixed colour in the night. Green! how I detest you-green! colour of the demon.'

Betka, who no longer listened to this interminable wail, rubbed one foot against the other. 'If only this would never end! Now the night-lamp is going to go out,' she thought, 'and I'm not at all sleepy.'

'Stop!' she said, passing her arm around Cécile's neck, and shaking her head as if to rid herself of a fixed idea. Cécile readily lent herself to this, and once her little head was warm and snug in the hollow of the nest of Betka's armpit she said to her with a sadness that seemed to have neither beginning nor end, 'You're going to be very disappointed with your Cécile Goudreau? So cynical! And here she is, capable of getting all upset over nothing but a little tuft of fresh moss. Bizarre, eh?'

Betka, who during all this time heard silent and slow steps coming and going across the hall and now already nearer, in the bathroom, turned her face toward the entrance door. A tall skeleton dressed in black silk pyjamas, with a high, tight Russian-style collar, looked at her from a distance as if not daring to approach. It was Countess Mihakowska who lived with Cécile in a separate sickroom. Betka in her drugged state was in no way astonished at her presence, and with a friendly gesture begged her to come and stretch out beside her on the other side of Cécile. Mihakowska shook her head in a sign of refusal that was infinitely gentle and came up to within a few feet of Betka as if to make an explanation. Then, leaning one knee on the divan and with the aid of her hands that seemed to want to draw attention to her left breast, she said, with an exaggerated grimace at each syllable and in a voice so effaced that it was barely audible. 'I can't – operation, o-o-operation.' Betka tried to catch the words by the movement of the Countess's lips, but she did not succeed in understanding them.

'She has just had her left breast operated on for cancer.' Cécile Goudreau explained, 'they've removed everything, and she has tuberculosis of the throat – a real angel!'

Betka then gave the Countess a long smile, and the latter stood up again, with a kind of childish pride at feeling herself at last understood and admired.

'Don't pay any attention to her,' said Cécile, 'she never disturbs anybody; a regular dove – she doesn't talk, she coos like a dove, and like a dove, too, she has just one breast… a little lopsided, to be sure!' Cécile Goudreau exclaimed, as if suddenly recovering her desire to chatter. 'You understand, my child, between myself and the Countess, never been anything,' and lifting her forefinger and her thumb in the form of a cross to her mouth, she kissed it, swearing, 'I keep her here solely out of kindness. She's the Prince of Orminy's former mistress, he had set up this apartment to be able to come and smoke with her; it was more or less her house, you understand?

So when I bought the whole thing from Orminy, I also kept his mistress – thrown into the bargain, you understand; a Countess sort of goes with this kind of a house. I've just had her disintoxicated and operated on (with Orminy's money, of course, that would be the last straw!) She's perfectly well now; she doesn't talk much, but she never did say much, poor woman; she's happy; she busies herself with little nothings – especially her icon. Look! Look!'

Countess Mihakowska had got up on the divan and was adding oil to the little night-lamp; after which she got down, took the gold basin and disappeared. 'You know, she's so clean, she wants everything to shine; have you ever seen anything more aristocratic than that skeleton?'

Time had dropped the mauve veil of heedlessness on the polar night lighted by the aurora borealis of opium, and Betka felt herself barely living, crouching in the royal eskimo hut of her new vice, in the heart of the twilight of her winter, without light and without cold. She smoked, vomited, swallowed orange juice, vomited again, and this curious activity, far from appearing exotic to her, seemed to her on the contrary the most natural thing in the world. How was it that she had never thought of it before? Thus she lived three days and three nights consecutively in an almost complete absence of the notion of time. She had vaguely the idea that Cécile Goudreau during all this time went in and out of the house several times, but she did not know when or how.

Now Betka had just awakened; she stretched herself for a long time and her outspread hands rubbed back and forth across the chinchilla fur on which she was lying, as if discovering for the first time the sumptuous luxury in which she was living, yet barely perceiving it. After a few moments during which she was astonished not to feel even the slightest trace of the feeling of guilt which gripped her at each of her anguished awakenings, Betka lazily lifted herself

up and leaned her back, a little stiff from having remained too long
in the same position, against a heavy cushion swathed in tiny silver
beads that pleasantly pricked her spine. Then she had the sensation
of feeling the emptiness of her stomach close to her back, overrun
with little ants circling in all directions.

'I'm hungry as a bear,' she said to herself, yawning, and imitating,
as was her habit, the feline jaw-stretching of the Metro-Goldwyn-
Mayer 'emblem lion'.

It must have been towards the end of the day, judging by an orange
ray from the setting sun which pierced through a crack between the
high closed curtains and drew a diagonal purple line on the garnet
of the carpet, climbed the adjoining divan and somewhat timidly
followed the yellow-satin-draped wall. Lying on her side on this divan,
Countess Mihakowska was peacefully sleeping, her mouth half open,
and the fine line of sunlight that ran over her cheek made the gold of
one of her teeth glitter with a sinister deep cadmium fire. From the
silence that reigned in the house, Betka knew that Cécile Goudreau
must certainly have gone out. Without changing the position of her
body she stretched her foot so as to open the curtain slightly and get
a better view of the Countess's face which now became progressively
lighted until the whole was suffused by that wan tinge, which seemed
at moments to turn purple. She did not wake up, but brought her
hand to the breast which had not been amputated. Then Betka
again cautiously shut the curtain, leaving it open just enough to be
able to look outside, through the glass panes, at the sun – large, of
a deep opaque red and slightly irregular roundness, like the clumsy
contours and the thickly applied colour of the profaned and bleeding
hosts painted with such awe by the minor masters of the school of
Sienna. The rays of this fateful sun shed a light so materially scarlet
and so dense that instead of light it seemed like a thick liquid soaking
into and spreading over everything with a majestic and fascinating

malaise. Her stiffened leg emerging from her dressing-gown, Betka watched the serene flow of light rise to the upper end of her thigh which thus seemed soaked in red blood, to which the lingering beat of the sun still communicated that moist, somewhat sticky warmth, so characteristic…. She touched it with her finger: it *was* blood.

'That's all I needed!' she said to herself, lying down again and drawing the curtain completely with her foot. 'In five minutes I'll fix myself and go out.'

She wanted to enjoy a few more minutes of darkness. Before her closed eyes the empurpled Seine disappeared beneath the distant bridge of the Invalides. Then she saw the crowd filling the Boulevard Montmartre, in that first warm twilight of early summer, then again a river, this time the one in her village; her mother beating Volodya, her little brother, to punish him for having gone swimming, and each time the latter tried to climb up on the bank, wanting to get out, she would push him back with a black oar, beating him in the chest, in the face, and making him fall back into the water. Finally Volodya remained motionless, his tousled pussywillow-coloured head tilted on the running water… and suddenly one saw streaking away, a whirl of white foam, so white!, slightly rose-tinged, as if someone had spat out a mouthful of toothpaste. To Betka this cruel memory was charged with so much freshness, with so much of the incipient fragility of the countryside with those pale May evening skies, that as she deeply inhaled the rarefied atmosphere of the room, fragrant with the sweet and insipid smell of the opium, she thought she was filling her lungs with the pure air of the springtime of her awakened desire.

Betka found herself seated before the dressing-table in the bath-room, but she no longer remembered how she had come here. This bathroom was uniformly covered, floor and ceiling included, with immense squares of black marble. All the objects, even to the small-est accessory, were of gold. On the dressing-table everything was arranged with a perfect order and symmetry, in which one sensed the hovering presence of Countess Mihakowska's assiduous, scrupulous and maniacal attentions. Elongated flasks, all of the same pattern, were placed at regular intervals in rows parallel to the mirror in the order of their sizes; from the giant ones containing bath salts, passing gradually through the whole scale of perfume-shades, one reached the tiny vials for rare salves, to the last one, no bigger than a die, fixed and alert like the last piece in a game of Russian dolls. These series of flasks were arranged in several superimposed rows, all according to the same criterion of diminishing size. Betka, her face all pale, held herself motionless, her head slightly thrown back, her two hands aimlessly stroking the black marble in which the precious metal of each object was continued in the long, somewhat duller tubes of their reflections. A faint music was softly wafted from the Countess's room, and one could easily have imagined that instead of a girl at her toilet Betka had become a Saint Cecilia playing her golden organ, seated on a cloud, so weakened did she feel, so disembodied and as if helped up by the absence of weight which the almost absolute unconsciousness of her own movements imparted to her. She had the curious sensation, which she had never yet experienced, of perceiving the effect of her own movements only a few seconds after she had made them. Suddenly Betka felt a snowlike coldness invade her brow which but a moment ago was so warm; she lifted her hand to it, where it encountered her other hand which was already mopping her temples with an ether-soaked handkerchief. She further noticed, without understanding it, a mesh of cut hair in her hand – her own hair; then seeing the gold scissors she was holding in her other hand she said, with a feeble laugh. 'How silly I am!' After which she threw the scissors into the air. They described a broad arc in space and fell into the filled bath-tub. Betka got up and with fascination watched the scissors glitter at the bottom of the limpid water in which stirred constantly changing shadows from the iridescent streaks of pine-essence in suspension, slowly dissolving into capricious forms.

'Come now,' said Betka to herself, 'I'm not going to stand and look at that all my life! Let's proceed systematically. The Meyer method! The Meyer method!'* she exclaimed, imitating with her pale voice her mother's pitiless tone, which suddenly seemed infinitely remote.

Then she went back into the smoking-room, took several hundred francs in bills from the Prince of Orminy's polo 'trophy box', went and sat down before a large Venetian desk inlaid with mother-of-pearl which adorned the main wall in the hall, and wrote on an envelope, 'Mademoiselle Veronica Stevens, Hotel Ritz'. Then on a card of a thick, smooth whiteness like that of gardenias, '*Chère amie*, I was very sorry not to have met you at Solange de Cléda's the other evening. It is going to be difficult for me to see you for some time. I have found unhoped-for happiness. I shall not let it go. Thank you again.

Your devoted

BETKA.'

She reread it, added little quotation marks to frame the word 'happiness'. She slipped the card into the envelope, including the receipt for the telegram which amounted to forty-five francs, a fifty-franc bill and finally a part of her mesh of hair. Lastly she wet the gummed edge of the flap with her tongue and, her finger having encountered the roughness of an embossed inscription, she looked at it before shutting it, as if for verification. 'Yes, Cartier!' she said, definitely sealing her envelope. Having finished this first letter, Betka took a

---

* *Meyer method: A mnemotechnic method invented by the Viennese professor, Dr Meyer, which according to him economizes time and avoids all distraction in the problems of daily life. Betka's mother claimed to use this method in all circumstances, and even before punishing her children would exclaim, 'Come now, the Meyer method, the Meyer method!'.*

second envelope, hesitated a moment in embarrassment, for she did not remember his name-in fact, she had probably never known it. 'I'll deliver it myself.' And with this she wrote, in a telegraphic style, with capital letters and without signing, 'ASSUMING AT LAST THE RIGHT TO DO ANYTHING I PLEASE SHALL WAIT FOR YOU TONIGHT AT THE COUPOLE BAR AT MIDNIGHT'; adding the rest of the mesh of her hair, she sealed this envelope in turn.

'And now, let's be off!' she said to herself, ready to go out, but as she was about to open the door she saw rising from the depth of the reflections of the door-handle the flash memory of the gold scissors at the bottom of the bath-tub, and immediately thought, 'Cécile might hurt herself when she steps into the water.' She went back to remove them, but when she reached the bathroom she found Countess Mihakowska bending over the tub with her hand reaching into the water for them. Caught by surprise the Countess remained for a moment with the scissors in her hand, as if frightened. Betka could not resist the desire to embrace her, and going over to her she kissed her. The poor darling, in spite of everything she was still so beautiful! Mihakowska hurriedly went and sat down in front of the dressing-table, and as she was leaving Betka thought she guessed that the Countess was trying to conceal the involuntary weakness of a tear as, with lips compressed, she applied powder to her face.

Betka walked a few steps down the street and abruptly stopped. 'I've forgotten the main thing!' She raised her hand to her heart, where it encountered a hard object. 'No, I've got it!' she said reassured, and from the pocket of her fine linen blouse, of an almost masculine cut, like the ones Cécile always wore, she pulled out a little enamelled box wrought by Fabergé, wrapped in a silk handkerchief. Cécile had made her a present of it. 'When things look really bad, you just sniff a little of this,' she had advised her. It was nothing less than heroin. She smiled at this word. 'It's well named,' she thought.

Betka put her precious box back into the same pocket, shutting the snap with such force that she broke a nail; with the sharp pincers of her teeth she evened it, cutting with furious little bites a half crescent, perfectly regular and slender, that she spat up toward the very pale and sickly sky in which the last shreds of bloody clouds still lingered. After which she began to walk fast, straining all her movements, enjoying the sound of her joints cracking, so as to feel the pain of the pleasure of walking thus, the tips of her shoes striking the smallest stone that lay in her path with a vigorous and childlike thrust of her stockingless legs; she took deep breaths, imagining the distant hay of the countryside, and felt the moist and slightly choking breath of the recently sprinkled sidewalk rising up to her. She regretted not having been in the street earlier, while the sun was setting, so that she could have felt its blood-warmth and the coppery light of her hair set fire to her brain. 'Quick! Quick!' She wanted first of all to get rid of, to deliver, her two envelopes that itched in her hand; and after having finished with that, to be at last for the first time in her life without constraint and free to do whatever she pleased, whatever she felt like doing.

Reaching the Quai des Orfèvres, and the house where she lived, Betka ran up the stairs all out of breath, without stopping to pick up her mail at the concierge's where, for that matter, there was no one, and this gave her such a vivid pleasure that she quivered; yet she could not be cold; without stopping before the door to her apartment, she continued to climb up to the last storey but one. He was there. A streak of electric light along the bottom of the door indicated his presence. Betka hurriedly slipped in her envelope and ran downstairs again. By a stroke of luck there was still no one at the concierge's. For nothing would have been more painful to her at this time than to run into a person she knew and be obliged to 'pass the time of day'.

She started to run toward the Ritz but was soon so out of breath that she had to take a taxi. Her physical fatigue then combined with an atrocious fear of meeting Veronica, even if it should be merely by chance, just at the moment when she entered the hotel to leave the message for her; but she accomplished this with such lightning speed that the clerk, seeing the envelope drop on the desk, must have wondered if it had not been brought by a phantom.

Betka left the Ritz on foot, picking her course at random in the direction of the quays. As she followed the Seine, Betka met a tiny little old lady no bigger than a seal holding its head up; her outline was so sharp and determined that she had the personality of a salt-shaker, while the tip of her nose and her cheeks, set in a pale, taut-skinned face, were so red that they looked like three shiny cherries. She was selling cherries, and Betka bought two cornucopias of them from her and went and sat down on a nearby bench with such lightness and grace that none of the sparrows that were pecking on the ground were frightened. She felt exhausted, and to keep her head from reeling shut her eyes, squeezing them together very tight, and immediately saw springing from the depths of her orbits cherries of fire, that turned yellow, then black against a red setting and finally vanished.

Betka felt like laughing, her mouth consented to smile peacefully while her little bevelled nose stirred: in imagination she was savouring the effect which the two letters she had just delivered would produce, and for a moment she visualized Veronica's round forehead bowed over her letter, her two large locks of blond hair falling heavily on either side of her head, almost completely hiding her face. Then she saw the aviator reading his, probably laughing in silence over his easy and unexpected conquest. She still did not know this aviator's name, but she just now remembered his nickname – his 'bar surname', so to speak – Baba, by which he was known, acclaimed and toasted in the Champs Elysées bars. Aside from this she knew nothing about him except the fact that he had fought in the Spanish civil war, that he was tall, that he was attractive to her... and that he lived in the same house as she did, just two floors above her studio.

Baba lived there because of Madame Ménard d'Orient who sumptuously occupied the first two floors where she lived alone, surrounded by three or four servants and an old maid, a chambermaid, whom she had managed to get out of a convent. Madame Ménard d'Orient was young and fresh for her age, which was close to sixty, and she was always dressed in a foam of black and white lace. Cultivated and even erudite, she professed a real cult for everything that closely or remotely verged on the revolutionary pseudo-philosophies of the last years. The crystal and the fine silver ornaments of her table were often surrounded by the prestige of political émigrés who had sought refuge in Paris or who merely happened to be passing through, and the starched and embroidered whiteness of her napkins habitually served as cushions for hands which were too large or too small and which, by the dubious colour of their nails, revealed the somewhat verdigris moral patina of direct action and illegality.

Thus Madame Ménard d'Orient's apartment had witnessed the passing of a procession of semi-legendary beings, like the 'red priestess with the white hair' of Germany, Clara Zetkin, the 'comet without a visa', Leon Trotsky, and the Catalonian anarchist, Durruti, called by his followers 'the lion-hearted'. Now, since the beginning of the Spanish civil war, her house was even richer than usual in gatherings of weird specimens of men talking very loud, well shaved but with a blue cast to their chins, wearing highly polished white-and-yellow shoes with complicated tooling and ornamentations, ambling up and down the Boulevard Saint Germain as though it were the very *ramblos* of Barcelona, not forgetting a yellow tooth-pick nailed to their saffron-coloured teeth.

In the midst of all these oily, tortuous, rather base and excessively bilious Latins, what more startling contrast than that of Baba's nordic beauty! Of American descent, he was barely twenty-two. He was the youngest of the protégés of Madame Ménard d'Orient, who with a wholly maternal solicitude had fixed up for him a little apartment on the sixth floor where he stayed during his brief appearances in Paris. Baba had refined manners and loved luxury. His slightest gestures bore the mark of a somewhat pretentious dandyism that had clung to him as an inheritance from the period of his adolescence spent continually in London among the half-literary, half-crapulous circles of the capital. The day he decided to go and fight in Spain on the side of the Loyalists, his sceptical acquaintances were flabbergasted and his most intimate friends accused him of snobbery. Nevertheless, contrary to all appearances, nothing had been able to rob Baba of the granitic virginity of the fundamental virtues of his character. Blond and calm, he had the invisibility peculiar to heroes; his studied silence caused people to remark. 'How many fine things he doesn't say.' His presence was little noticed, but whenever he left a spot one felt oppressed by the emptiness which his absence had left in all hearts. It was then that each one understood that elementary, mineral force, fragile though it was and camouflaged with elegance, which constituted the irresistibly subjugating attraction of his personality; already reacting against the wave of opportunism which was rotting the foundation of most of the revolutionary movements. He had adopted for his own the motto of King Louis XIII, 'I can be broken, but not bent.'

How had Betka met Baba?

First on the stairs, where they frequently met and exchanged greetings, then....

On reaching this point in her reverie, Betka began to visualize in the slightest details what the scene of their first and only tryst would be like. During all this time her half-closed eyes had done nothing but observe the continual movements of the numerous sparrows that were pecking at her feet. This monotonous and ever-changing spectacle took on the character of the capricious play of shadows and lights appearing and disappearing on the cinema screen when, watching a film half asleep, the mind cannot grasp whether the white spot that has just appeared represents a car brought to a stop or a white door being shut. Thus there was established between Betka's more and more vague and nebulous outer vision and the inner cinema of her more and more precise memories, a kind of synchronic correlation which helped her, so to speak, to visualize better all that she was thinking-for instance, a crowd of sparrows suddenly grouped together formed the door, limited by its frame, of her apartment which the concierge came and opened. Then Betka saw the coalman enter, carrying a sack of coal on his head, stoop and deposit it by the stove near the entrance. It was at this precise moment that she had discovered the presence of Baba who had slipped into the room taking advantage of the presence of the coalman who almost immediately left without waiting for his tip.

Baba remained there, standing, motionless, looking at her intently, till Betka finally asked him in a friendly tone. 'Why do you look at me that way? It embarrasses me!' Then Baba smiled in the same surprising way that had struck her so much in Veronica, and that she now understood: it was hardness.

'If you turn me down I'll simply despise you,' said Baba as he nonchalantly seated himself astride the sack of coal, and trying deliberately by his tone to make himself as pretentious as possible, he continued, 'It's usually difficult for weaklings to endure the contempt of handsome creatures…. On the other hand if you accept… I can't promise you right away a great passion… but I can become very gentle, very "agreeably" tameable….' As he spoke he had picked up in his hands Betka's little white cat, who when Baba had sat down had begun to crawl up to him, fascinated by the fixity of the stare of his sapphire cuff-links.

'Come,' said Betka in a tone of amused impatience, 'what are you getting at?'

'I have calculated that you are going to give me twenty-five francs… for the Spanish Loyalists; you'll get your receipt, stamped with the committee's seal.'

While saying this, Baba nonchalantly went over to the table where Betka had had her breakfast and wiped away the breadcrumbs, using for this the little kitten, who mewed as she stiffened her tail. Then he opened his account-book, took out a metal box containing an ink-pad; finally, from his handkerchief pocket he pulled a stamper which he applied to the pad, and waited.

'Well,' answered Betka, 'you'll get the twenty-five francs, but I'll dispense with your making love to me, even though I find you very handsome and you're probably quite good at it…. How did you know I was an anti-fascist?'

'I carefully check your mail every morning at the concierge's,' Baba responded with great naturalness.

Betka felt an impulse of indignation, but she could only laugh at the dandyish tone in which Baba continued his sentence, as if trying to justify himself. 'You see. I've brought with me from London one charming and very English trait; I assume the right to do anything I please!' Then, going over to Betka, he took her in his arms. 'Be a sweet girl, and if some evening you feel yourself dying of boredom you can slip me a word under my door on the sixth floor. I have no telephone, and I don't like the concierge's indiscretions either… I'll take you wherever you want – for an ideological walk in the Bois, or do the chichi thing with champagne, or else something in the poor comrade style, a dubiously clean little twelve-franc hotel room where we'll make believe each pays for himself.'

Since that morning of their first encounter Betka had not seen Baba again. Hunted unceasingly by the cares of her daily life, she had not even had time to think of him except when she was reminded of him by her kitten each time it darted through a bright patch of sunlight after a fly, or repeated those quick movements of concupiscence with which it had clutched at Baba's cuff-links with its claws. She would then say to herself that he had been all ready to adore that angel of a kitten!

Now Betka felt herself delightfully chained to the rendezvous she had just made: midnight at the bar of the Coupole. And that still distant midnight began to glow, for already her desire, fumbling its way in the darkness of an unknown hotel room, had deposited its tiny wristwatch on the marble top of an after-midnight table…. Soon the hands would mark nearly one o'clock! Then that little figure 'one', barely perceptible, more slender than an incandescent flea, sufficed in Betka's faltering imagination to light up all her blood in a single burst, with an agony of honey and of phosphorus. The bag of cherries that she had just eaten had only excited her hunger; she thought of buying two more, but a sudden repugnance at having really eaten something solid assailed her, and she was terrified to think that she had sometimes been able to eat steaks as thick as dictionaries. It seemed to her now that her state of fasting was specially, wonderfully propitious to the kind of thing she wanted to do…. Nevertheless, in the first good café she came upon she would have an icecream. Before the hour of her rendezvous there were still six hours and a quarter. She had just counted and recounted them – quarter-past seven, eight, nine, ten, eleven, twelve. Meanwhile she was going to make the most of each of the seconds of that precious interval, of that stretch of free time which must be dense and sticky like a glue made of liquid amber and hardened cachalot's sperm.

Then Betka, getting up from her seat, with a pair of cherries dangling from her teeth, turned toward the west and went down the road that leads to the flesh.

She followed the course of the muddy river of human flesh in full ferment which filled the Boulevard Montmartre at half-past seven on this holiday evening. Each of these creatures bore inexorably attached to his person two ears, two cheeks, two hands…. She had never yet been struck by this double aspect of the anatomy of beings. Each human appeared to her now like those symmetrical and bloody blots that insects leave when one crushes them in the fold between the pages of a book. She in turn felt herself 'everywhere' double pressed, crushed by the animate and inanimate mass, thrilling to feel her desire become depersonalized in the swarming throng without distinction, beauty, age or sex; instead of one gaze, all gazes; instead of two bodies, all bodies, all spasms and moans at once. Betka, lightened by her fast, feeling as though she barely touched the ground, followed the heavy steps of this holiday crowd which appeared to her rather as one composed of grave and mystic peasants in a kind of grotesque and suppliant procession, of wretched and unsatisfied bundles of flesh in which each person carried in his left hand the painful heavy stigma of his cut-off right hand as an expiatory object, as his liturgical offering. She then imagined that avalanche of fanatics continuing to walk thus inexorably in the granite desert on which it would throw itself prostrate; and they would all pass, trampling her, the sinful Betka, fragile and facile, with their imperturbable step; asphyxiating her with their libidinous mass and crushing her till they caused the ultimate arborescent decalcomania of all her vital juices and plasmas to burst forth from the compressed tissues of her feeble organism so that at last, after the bestial passage of the humans over her minced body, the sun's rays might annihilate by evaporation the last liquid traces of her impurity.

Betka, carried along and rocked by this floor of grandiose and childish thoughts, disembarked, so to speak, at the entrance to a music hall all illuminated in red, situated on the confines of the Porte Saint Martin. She stopped before a large photograph hand-coloured in aniline tints representing the Three Montouri Brothers, 'fanciful athletes'; they all three appeared naked under their leopard capes and helmets; they had slim bodies with muscles carved out of steel, and only the one in the centre was slightly too corpulent. He had the head of a sphinx tattooed in the centre of his chest. The bill-board announced 'The Double Pharaoh Wheel'. The inter-mittent whirring of an electric bell with its insistent invitation to a continuous performance pecked like a sewing-machine needle on the rhinoceros-skinned neck of indifference of the crowd that filed past without even being aware of it.

Betka went in, took a seat at a table situated in a corner far from the orchestra and ordered a glass of vodka. The place was ugly and pretentious. On the floor a pair of dancing couples stirred like shadows. The show had not yet begun, the few spectators were scattered, so far apart and so hidden in the discreetly lighted corners of the loges that circled the floor that the place gave the impression of being almost empty. The syphilitic musicians, dressed like silk *gauchos*, attacked the Argentine tango 'Renacimiento' and the first notes of this melody provoked in Betka's weakened organism an emotive state similar to that of intoxication, which gave her sudden and irresistible urges to burst into tears. To prevent her tears from flowing, Betka pressed a cherry-pit that she had kept in her mouth for the last half-hour so hard between her teeth that it broke, severely biting her tongue. As the latter was bleeding a little she spat into the silk handkerchief that she had wrapped round her small gold box. She took advantage of the occasion to inhale a strong whiff of heroin. Then she emptied her cornucopia of cherries into a dish, began to eat some and, plunging her agile wounded tongue from time to time in the vodka as she watched the dancing, she gradually let herself relax.

Her impulse to weep now gave way to a state of acute lyricism that allowed her to contemplate this commonplace spectacle as imbued with an ultra-Romantic significance, and while trying to bemoan her own fate she compared the inconstancy of her broken life to the persistence of certain frivolous melodies clinging to the tottering walls of an epoch like ivy... 'Renacimiento'.... She had heard this tango in Roumania... then in Milan, during the troubled period that preceded the March on Rome.... In Barcelona on an evening of general strike. And as she saw the tango-dancing couples pass back and forth before her. Betka said to herself that in no matter what circumstances, whether it be war, pestilence, imperialist victories or the dishonouring defeats of country, there always existed in the shelter of history, in the twilight of a sophisticated and slightly tawdry setting, a couple of livid tango dancers, pressed cheek to cheek, their bodies united without love, aroused without passion by conventional poses in the rhythmic nectar of nostalgia, expressing all the condensed despair of the crowds of their time by a simple disdainful contraction of their superciliary arches. The handsome professional tango couples are the only ones who by their slow glides and mathematical stops know how to follow and to mark the slow-motion cadences that correspond exactly to the accelerated beats of the violent muscles of the hearts of those predestined to suicide. And this is why Betka watched the tango with complete fascination, with the hypnotic absorption of a paralysed bird following the languorous and precise movements of a snake. For she wanted to kill herself....

The music stopped, and Betka let a cherry-pit drop into a shiny black ashtray; this pit was clean and slightly greenish, and exactly resembled Countess Mihakowska's small head. Betka now dipped each cherry before eating it into the new glass of vodka that had just been brought her; soon the ashtray was filled with cherry-pits. She said to herself then, 'It looks messy!' And glancing about her to make sure no one was watching, she took all the pits in the hollow of her hand, wrapping them in her silk handkerchief, at the same time seizing the opportunity to open her box and take a new whiff of heroin that she inhaled till she was out of breath.

Absorbed by these small operations, Betka had not noticed the 'entrance' of the three Montouri brothers. When she looked up she was struck at seeing in the centre of the dance-floor, lighted by all the crudeness of the reflectors, the three Montouri brothers welded together in an act in which they seemed to unfold in the explosion of a single three-pointed star of flesh streaming with sweat and throbbing with arterial pulsations. The star suddenly fell apart, and three brothers stood in a row, motionless for a few seconds, panting in statuary poses, their arms raised in a Roman salute. All three were naked and wore only sketchy flesh-coloured trunks, very shiny and fitting their bodies so snugly that instead of dressing them they rather accentuated the impudicity of their appearance. Each time they were about to begin a new act, and while the strongest one took his stance in a rigid pose bordering on that of catalepsy, the other two approached, swaying in step to the muted strains of a little melody that the orchestra was playing, their eyes seeming to pick out the parts of their brother's anatomy to which they intended to join their own members. Then for a few seconds their iron hands gripped the supporting points they had selected to assure themselves of their solidity, immediately releasing their hold and saluting for the last time before finally giving themselves over to the execution of their act. One could then see, contrasting with the prevailing deep colour of their empurpled flesh, the pale yellow traces left by their holds. And it was precisely there, on the still livid flesh, that the hands of the two Montouri brothers now tapped several times in succession before seizing it and at last gripping it inexorably, with all the trembling and inaugural tension of their contractions. At this moment the taps resounded as lugubriously as a series of smacks administered to a corpse.

The acts continued before Betka's hallucinated gaze. Now the smallest of the Montouri brothers, the one she liked best, lying rigid on the floor, each of his muscles strained to the maximum, his two arms held tightly along his body, his feet engulfed between the thighs of his two brothers, raised himself slowly, slowly to the high noon of verticality while the other two, their torsos glued together and arched, their heads bent back, the veins of their necks swollen to the bursting point, seemed to be fused in a hideous mixture of quartered flesh.

Betka since her childhood had cherished a golden dream of being annihilated with the world in a cosmic catastrophe. Later, how many times she had identified herself with the mystics of 'the White Death',* the collective death by fire after collective pleasure. Repelled and attracted by the three streaming bodies of the Montouri brothers, she felt herself seized with the mad dizziness of wanting to throw herself, with her eyes shut, into the heart of the visceral wheel formed by all the intermingled steel muscles of those three athletes, so as to be caught in the cogs of their movements, crushed

---

* *The White Death: A former Russian religious sect in which thousands of adepts, living in common in piety and prayer, finally offered up their lives in sacrifice by letting themselves be burned alive in barns filled with hay. This burning was preceded by an orgy in which all the families belonging to their community gave themselves over, naked, to the deliria of fornication in a total promiscuity, without distinction of sex, family or age.*

by the fury of their contractions and ground by the frenzy of the shock of their bones into a hot and burning paste of 'White Death'.

The effect of the heroin had made Betka's glance bold and bright, and she kept it steadily fixed on the smallest of the Montouri brothers. The latter, who had not failed to notice Betka's preference, now threw his leopard cape over his shoulders and, leaving the centre floor, went and leaned against a column while he pretended to watch his two so-called brothers continue the performance – for there was no other kinship between the three than the animal one of their leopard skins. At this moment two lackeys appeared, dragging out onto the floor two large silver wheels between whose spokes were fastened a large quantity of contraptions containing rockets and Bengal lights. The smallest of the Montouri brothers, taking advantage of the suspense created in the hall by those two unusual wheels, went and sat down on the edge of the chair next to Betka, on the pretext of lighting his cigarette, and said to her very low and fast, in a metallic voice.

'My name is Marco, I'm through with my act. It'll take my two partners another twenty minutes to finish their "Pharaoh's Wheel" stunt. Do we skip out together?'

Betka did not answer him, but got up and followed him. Marco stopped at the door to his *camerino*. 'Wait for me here. It'll just take me five minutes to get dressed!'

Betka, without obeying him, followed him in and said drily.

'I'm staying here.'

At this moment she felt a slight attack of colic that made her thrill: she instantly remembered that her mother always forbade her to eat cherries, claiming that it would upset her; but in Betka's mind for the first time in her life the cherries that she had eaten were free of the little worm of remorse. Marco, disconcerted, hesitated to dress in front of Betka.

'Idiot!' she cried to him, seized with a sudden fury. 'In another minute you'll disgust me!'

'You wanted me just now,' answered Marco, nonplussed.

'And I do *now*', Betka burst out, 'but right away! Shut the door!' And as she spoke she whisked out her box intending to take a sniff, causing the cherry-pits she had kept in her handkerchief to fly out; the pits rolled to the cement floor in all directions. Marco thought she was going crazy, but he was seized by the contagion of desire.

'I don't have this room alone,' he answered, in an altered voice, prepared to obey her, '—they'll be coming in to dress presently.'

'Shut the door! Shut the door!' Betka repeated in a choked voice, while she went through the motions of beginning to unbutton her skirt.

Marco pushed the door, and there was a horrible grating sound; it remained half closed, jammed by a cherry-pit that had become wedged between the wood and one of the irregularities in the cement. Nothing would budge the door. Marco struck it like a battering ram, but at each new push the cherry-pit was caught more firmly, and the door which had closed only a few inches now remained solidly and as if permanently soldered to the floor, and could be budged neither one way nor the other.

'Cretin! Imbecile!' Betka cried in a fury. At this moment through the frosted and undulated glass panel of the door they both saw the rapidly approaching silhouettes of the other two Montouri brothers. Unsuspectingly they tried to push the door open with their thighs, but it did not yield. Then, flattening themselves to pass through the gap between it and the jamb, the two brothers squeezed their way with difficulty into the room, one after the other, each carrying in each hand two bottles of beer coated with a frosty film and specks of straw.

'Are we disturbing you?' said the tallest of the Montouri brothers, putting his four bottles on the floor and rubbing two long scratches that the wood of the door had made across his stomach. He looked at Betka.

'Excuse us – we have no other place to dress.'

'Are you an acrobat?' asked the second brother.

Betka did not answer. With a cigarette in her mouth, she was waiting for Marco to find his matches.

'She is a journalist,' said Marco, lighting Betka's cigarette with assurance. 'She wants pictures of us for a newspaper.'

'That's what we need,' continued the second brother, 'a pretty copper-haired blonde like you to complete the triple wheel of Pharaoh! We can kill ourselves putting on a good act, we can wear ourselves ragged-no chance of success without a pretty blonde!'

'That's an idea to be looked into,' said Betka in an amused and friendly tone. 'I've had some experience as a dancer.' But as she tried to get up on her toes her shoe slipped on a cherry-pit and she let herself fall into the arms of the tallest brother, who took her by the waist, exclaiming with stupefaction, 'Look! Never in my life have I seen a more slender waist!' To prove it he completely circled it with his hands, with the same elegance as a soldier taking a gun to present arms. And holding her thus, he cautiously lifted her till she touched the ceiling. Betka, having become gentle again, smiled throughout this ascent without ceasing calmly to smoke her cigarette. Now Montouri tipped Betka forward and she, holding herself rigid, passed her legs on each side of his head, opening her arms as if to imitate the wings of a plane. At this moment Betka distinctly heard gurglings in her empty stomach, and wishing to dissimulate them she burst out laughing, uttering crystalline cries as if Montouri's hands were tickling her irresistibly in this new position.

'Let's try the siren act,' said Marco, putting one knee to the floor and getting his arms ready to receive Betka's body. But Montouri, without obeying, made two dizzy turns upon himself and deposited

Betka on a couch. She was dazed, and she lifted a pale hand to her forehead as if to keep herself from feeling her head spin round, while she leaned unselfconsciously with one arm on the bare shoulder of Marco, who was kneeling at her feet. Betka was drenched with perspiration. How hot it was! And now she said to herself, 'Three more minutes to rest, and then I'm leaving.' But already she felt her members incapable of obeying her, bound to the couch by the lascivious chains of a triple desire. The tallest of the brothers had just seated himself close beside her, the third remained standing opposite her and all three watched her with a stupid stare, without blinking, like three dogs waiting to see which would be the first to catch a piece of meat. Then Betka's face turned pale, her little nose sharpened in the waxen transparency characteristic of the dead, and, as if obeying a command against which her will was powerless, she slowly passed her other arm round the neck of the tallest of the Montouri brothers, brought the heads of the two brothers together till they joined and, pressing them gently to her bosom she kicked off her shoes one after the other.

'Shut the door!' she said in a colourless and barely audible voice to the one who stood in front of her.

Then the third of the Montouri brothers staggered as if drunk over to the door and with a supreme effort of his athlete's shoulders, causing all the fibres of the wood to crack, obliged it at last to shut in a long and final grating.

... Three thousand pits of white death... three thousand triple cherries... three thousand triple Pharaoh's wheels... and two flakes of fine snow... in the hollow of her cheeks!

Thus Betka felt the coming of the dreaded cold. She was walking now in the night illuminated by the distantly spaced lights of the Quai Voltaire. Perhaps it was hunger – but would she ever eat again?... Each of her sore members was slowly congealing, while a kind of sleep without desire to sleep came over her... a light weight of winter on each eyelid, like crystallizations of frost deposited on the cornices of her gaze.

Toward the upper end of the Gothic Rue de Seine Betka gave fifty francs in alms to a poor legless cripple. She bent over and peered at him with an impure smile that would have wilted the freshest flower. The cripple looked like a noble Roman bust of a ragged old Aesop, and like the latter he was hunchbacked.

'You can touch my hump if you like,' snickered the old man, 'others do it without paying anything.'

Betka pressed the hump with her hand and felt his heart beating within it. Then she went on her way, but soon slowed her steps, realizing that she was being followed by the beggar who propelled himself forward on the ground by means of his hands. Betka imparted a lascivious lilt to her walk, and each time she stopped she heard the beggar's panting breath nearer to her, and now already he was beseeching her, drooling. 'Take your money back if you want, but come with me. Let me take you to Père Frandingue's. I've got a corner on his barge. I've got some money hidden! Let me take you to Père Frandingue's! I've got some money hidden!'

It was close to midnight on the Place d'Iéna. Huddled against the iron fence of the Luxembourg Garden Betka was weeping, pressing her turned-in lower lip with all her muscles in order to help make her tears flow in a continuous stream. 'All that is good! All that is good! All that is good! Provided I end it all!'

When Baba met Betka at the bar of the Coupole at midnight, she was so drugged that she barely noticed his coming. She began to talk as though they had been together for a long time. 'You won't go away from me any more now! Why did you leave me alone?' Betka complained in a honeyed intonation. For some time she had been deliberately exaggerating her state, now imagining she had become her kitten, now Cécile Goudreau, and now both at once.

'What's come over you? You're drunk!' said Baba severely.

'Why, of course I'm drunk – shouldn't I be?' asked Betka, dragging out her words, maliciously separating each syllable from the rest. Brusquely she got up and with a dramatic gesture hid her face in Baba's shoulder, exclaiming in a half whisper. 'I beg you, dear, take me away from here! Far from this horrible electric light – somewhere outside in the dark… with a lot of leaves… I want to catch cold! Feel, how cold I am,' said Betka when they were in the street.

'You're like ice, what have you been doing?' asked Baba, kissing her two closed fists.

'I've been playing… I've been playing… there were three of them,' said Betka, as if trying painfully to remember something pleasant; she smiled and went on dreamily, 'there were three of them…. Have you seen the triple Pharaoh wheel? They're all silver and all three of them catch fire at once!'

'Why are you crying?' said Baba, stopping her and pressing her cheeks as if to oblige her to confide in him.

'How do I know?' answered Betka, breaking away from the embrace and continuing to talk.

They went and sat down at a solitary café terrace opposite the Tour Saint Michel; the clock in the tower struck half-past twelve.

'At one o'clock,' said Betka to herself, feeling her throat tighten with the tyrannical pressure of her plan.

'There! This is fine.' Baba had said as he stopped. 'An icy nip in the air, perfect for you to catch your pleurisy, and here are your leaves, besides! Lots of leaves! With that old ivy-covered wall it's more like Oxford than Paris. Do you like the atmosphere?' As he spoke Baba tore off a long ivy branch which he placed over the quivering shoulders of Betka, seated on the grating skeleton of a white iron chair, her two fists resting in the very centre of the marble of the table. Baba now formed a hoop with another branch of ivy and cautiously placed it on Betka's head and said. 'And here we have a perfect Pre-Raphaelite crown to adorn your frustrations!' He mispronounced the word 'Pre-Raphaelite', and laughed. Betka pushed off the crown with a wretched movement of her closed little fist.

'I can stand it, I'm well dressed,' Baba said then, sitting down and raising his coat-collar, 'and I assure you,' he added, 'that tomorrow I shall leave for Spain without a cold… perhaps I'll catch just a little of your spring fever, then I'll have to scratch myself a little in the train. I'm as susceptible as you are!'

'You're disappointed to find me in the state I'm in this evening; you disapprove of me, eh,' said Betka with resignation.

'Open your hand,' Baba demanded, 'what are you squeezing in your hand? Don't be so tense all the time!'

Betka slowly opened her hand, which was filled with wet cherry-pits sticking to one another; she could not remember how long she had been holding them in this way.

'It's messy, isn't it? Does it disgust you? I know, I look like a madwoman….'

'And in the other hand? What have you got in it? Open your other hand!'

'No!' said Betka, pressing more tightly, 'that I won't show you!'

Baba, without insisting, was now wiping Betka's hand with his handkerchief.

'There—clean!' he said, as if arming himself with patience.

Betka then put her hand on Baba's knee and felt the angles of the bones that formed it, small and pointed, through the very light material of his trousers. Presently, with their hands joined, they looked at each other in silence and Betka discovered for the first time the infinite resources of tenderness that there can be in such a caress. Harried and distraught, always snatching frightful shreds of pleasure from a life gnawed by anxiety, she had had to feel the void of eternity open before her in order to experience at last the mystery of the passion of two hands that press each other, each of the naked bodies of the joints of each finger slowly shifting its position a hundred times, tirelessly interweaving in endless combinations, lubricated by tears, without relinquishing their hold a single moment.

'Tell me,' Betka repeated, 'tell me you disapprove of me.… But you promised me everything, you let me choose all the conditions of our meeting. Swear you won't leave me before dawn!'

Baba who had just glanced up at the time on the Tour Saint Michel clock, answered, 'I'll stay with you till half-past seven. My train leaves for Spain at eight, and if you were only able to listen to me I would persuade you to let me take you with me to Barcelona. I could make you a little red queen. You would wait for me in Cerbère just long enough for me to go to Barcelona and arrange for your passport, you would stay there with some friends of mine who would take care of you as if you were their daughter – sun, red wine, tiny little black olives…'

The waiter brought two more whiskys with Perrier water.

'You said yes, but you didn't swear you would stay with me,' said Betka without paying any attention to Baba's plans, to his seductive tone, 'I know, you cheat like everybody.'

'I swear to you! I shall stay with you till daylight! But don't expect me to console you,' Baba concluded harshly, slowly sipping his whisky. Then he went on aggressively, stopping at each sentence as if to give the passion that was beginning to inflame them time to cool, 'Pity is not my speciality. Early in the war – it was the hottest part of summer, sixty degrees centigrade – I had received my new

rata,* very ugly, but efficient. The village had just been destroyed and
Malaga was being bombed. Some hundred women had run out to
the airfield and surrounded our plane. They came followed by a
cloud of flies and carrying four or five children who had been killed,
wrapped in black coats. In their collective hysteria it was impossible
to tear them from the plane. They displayed their horrible burdens,
and kept handling them with fiendish insistence; they held up to us
pieces of bodies fringed with coagulated blood. *"Mira! Mira! Mira!"*
they cried in chorus, vying with one another in selecting the most
horrible exhibits, as if in this way the better to implore vengeance
for their dead. We had to take off quickly; there was no time to be
lost. My second, who had jumped to the ground twice to disperse
them, had had difficulty getting back in again. A bad wind coming
from the desert was already raising the dust in the plain, shaking
the distant olive trees. I yelled three times, "Get away! Get away!
Get away!" There was nothing to be done. The poor women clung
to the plane all the harder... like people drowning! Then I started
the motor, and the propeller of my *rata* put an end to the hysteria...
and to the rest! Never, never had I felt as I did that day when I was
face to face with the enemy how right I was. Since then I became
that indeterminate thing called a hero,' said Baba calmly, finishing
his whisky.

Then he went on, as he regained his coolness, 'There is no audacity
in heroism. Never do you think you're going to die. When you hold a
machine gun tight it's as if its jolts made the fleas of your fear jump
off... I miss my *rata* too much! The fog of Paris disgusts me even
more than that of London... it's more subtle.... Here people talk too

---

*   *Rata in Spanish means 'mouse'. The nickname given because of their speed and their
black appearance to the pursuit planes that the Soviet Union sent to Spain during the
civil war.*

much and too well about everything. You become monstrously intelligent, everything gets mixed up-the ugly seems beautiful, criminals are saints, or sick people, the sick are geniuses, everything is double, ambivalent! In the pitiless light of Spain it's different. Inside my rata everything again becomes inexorably certain; it must be the same for the others, for courage is equal on both sides – what does it matter? The important thing is to feel yourself become once more a drop of albumen, of instinctive and vulnerable life in the centre of a mica shell in the middle of the sky! Instead of thinking, your brain functions, the systole and the diastole of your heart, the chemical combustions of your liquids nourish the wings of your plane – well, all that is not literary! You feel really yourself, from deep inside your viscera to the tips of your nails-you are the eyes and entrails of your plane, and then there is no more Paris, nor more surrealism, no more anguish, do you hear? All your fears, all your remorse, all your theories and laziness, all the contradictions of your thought and all the dissatisfactions accumulated by your doubts disappear to give place to the furious jet of a single and unique certainty, the continuous and crackling sheaf of fire of your machine gun.'

Betka was not listening to him, but Baba's involuntary verbal exaltation was slightly repugnant to her. How many illusions! 'Veronica was colder than he,' she thought, observing him. Then she asked him, 'Do you know Veronica Stevens?... Not even from photographs?'

Baba looked at Betka for the first time with curiosity: she had paid no attention to him; she was thinking of something else.

'Who is Veronica? And why do you ask me that?' He was intrigued.

'She looks like you…. Oh, if you knew her! You would like her better than me….'

In fact the resemblance with Veronica suddenly appeared to her so striking that she could no longer distinguish in what respects they differed, and she remembered now Veronica's remark that had made such an impression on her on the evening of their dinner at the Tour d'Argent, 'I don't like myself, but I should like to find in my life someone who resembles me absolutely, to be able to adore him.' This being was Baba, she was certain of it, no longer able now not to imagine them together. And in no matter what context she tried to represent them to herself, whether amid the hundreds of vague and half-obliterated creatures of her memories or amid the crowd she had seen most recently, which had filled Solange de Cléda's drawing-room a few days before, the two haunting blond figures of Veronica and Baba stood out from all the rest, with the same anguishing fixity as the two figures of the famous 'Angelus' painted by Millet. One might say that around Veronica and Baba, too, there could be only silence and solitude, vanishing across the deserted horizontal line of fields.

Now Betka felt herself observed by Baba. Scrutinizing, silent, distant once more, he had shut himself up in the armour of his indifference and closed the chiselled visor of his silence through which the glitter of his eyes again appeared impenetrable. Betka now compared the hardness of Baba's gaze with Veronica's, just as one might have done with crystals, rubbing them together to find out which was capable of streaking the other. She felt those two gazes equally hard and hostile to hers, so feeble that it was about to close, voluntarily, forever. She compared her approaching end to Baba's; he at least was going to die in the heart of what he loved most in the world, his *rata*... spitting fire amid the clouds. 'I, all alone, in a twelve-franc hotel room.'

As she said this to herself she found herself reading and rereading over and over again the sign of the hotel across the street, 'Avenir Marlot'. The name could be worse; at least it was a future that meant nothing – a Marlot future! And as the clock on the Tour Saint Michel had just struck one, Betka said resolutely, and as if continuing her reverie aloud, '*Chéri*! I'm willing... now... take me.'

'You will? You're coming with me to Barcelona?'

Betka, as though she were unable to answer, shook her head and finally said in a choked voice, 'No, across the street!'

In the room Betka had a slight revulsion; sitting on the bed she imagined Baba and Veronica together after her death, and she felt herself grow faint with jealousy toward them both, but for the moment the fact of knowing that Baba was in the room seemed to her already a way of deceiving Veronica, of being unfaithful to her, of taking revenge on her. 'You'll see! You'll see!' she kept repeating to herself. But almost immediately Betka felt an infinite tenderness for Veronica being reborn.

At half-past one, Betka had swallowed some pills and was lying fully dressed beside Baba, who had reassured her once more, promising her not to leave her before dawn. In the darkness of the room each was absorbed in his own thoughts, imagining the hour of his own end. He with his long arms stretched over Betka's body, felt the shadow of the membranes of black wing-sheaths grafted to his shoulders with platinum roots springing from the depth of his heart. The moment the latter would be hit everything would contract, and it would be like two great hands of frost closing over him to protect him from the fire. For Betka-the opposite… the white death, and she now moved her head as if trying to draw nearer to an invisible flame; then Baba's long hands hovered for a moment over Betka's hair, as in a night flight, and came to rest on Betka's closed fist, inside which there was also death.

Baba could not unclench that hand. Betka was rattling in an incipient delirium, 'Don't leave!' She had just clutched Baba's hands, and bringing them to the back of her neck she begged him, 'Hold me here! Press here. Bite me here to make me die!'

'Go to sleep!' Baba repeated, warming the back of her head with his breath.

'What are my feet touching? I am walking on cherry-pits!'

'Sleep, sleep!…'

'I'll tell Veronica you spent the night with me.'

'Be quiet, don't move any more, *chérie*, go to sleep!'

'I know you're disgusted by my blood. Turn on the light, I want to leave.' Betka tried to get up, pulling the light cord and falling back on the electric light bulb that fastened itself to her bosom. Remaining thus motionless she felt that she could no longer make any movement. 'I'm better now,' she said feebly, and after a silence, 'where is my gold box? Cover my feet….'

'My love, my love, my love,' Baba was saying to her, close to her ear, very low, as in a whisper, 'You're going to go to sleep….' And by the way in which Baba leaned over her to kiss her she knew that he was going to leave. He too was cheating.

He did in fact leave after fifteen minutes, thinking that she was at last unconscious from the effects of the drug. But it was more than the numbness of intoxication, it was the beginning of the death agony. Betka now felt all her skin lifted by armies of shudders breaking in successive waves. She felt as if her whole body was bristling with an infinity of microscopic mauve hands, shivering, stretched toward her heart, the sole hearth that was still warm. She felt the latter becoming covered with tiny, very fine hairs…. There were even ears and whiskers, like her cat's warm little head! 'What have I done! Why are they punishing me? Goodbye, evil father and mother!… Veronica, angel!' She heard the horrible twittering of the awakening birds. 'I'm going to die!' she said to herself, and lost consciousness.

The birds, pretending to greet the rising dawn, were only intoning in Latin the psalm for the dead, '*Dies irae, dies irae, dies irae, dies irae, dies irae, dies irae, dies irae*….' 'Missssseerreerree,' growled the garbage-can down below, grinding its teeth against the sidewalk.

The sun was rising like a cherry.

Cherry-time was ended.

*

When Veronica read Betka's letter on the Sunday evening of her return from Fontainebleau, she said to herself immediately, 'It smells of suicide,' and remained for a moment holding the coppery mesh of her friend's hair and the blue telegram receipt with the tips of her long, curved nails. Instantly conscious of her mistake, she tried to reconstitute the circumstances of the telephone call during which this confusion had occurred, so that instead of sending the promised money she had sent the receipt. And to check the certainty of this fear, Veronica went and sat down slowly before the desk in the drawing-room and opened the envelope box. Yes, there were the five hundred francs she thought she had sent. 'It's frightful!' said Veronica to herself, immediately ringing for the secretary. Miss Andrews appeared, a lazy pallor ravaging her face and her dress rumpled by a barely interrupted sleep. Veronica cast her a withering glance which cut short the beginning of a yawn that Miss Andrews was obliged to compress by main force, hiding it inside her closed fist and trembling. In Betka's study the bell rang, without anyone going to answer it; then Miss Andrews telephoned the concierge; the latter had not seen Betka come in for five days and she had been taking care of '*la petite chatte blanche*'. Miss Andrews now waited for Veronica's fresh decisions. Finally the latter said, 'We shall probably have to spend the whole night looking for Mademoiselle Betka. I beg you to carry out all my orders to the letter. At the slightest initiative on your part you will be dismissed. First, you're going to go and eat.'

'I can do that later, I'm not at all hungry,' Miss Andrews blurted out, but immediately repented her eagerness.

'Don't begin to argue,' Veronica answered severely, and continued, 'Eat first, then you will go to the police commissariat of the Seine and arrange an appointment for me with the commissaire.

Just tell him that a person's life depends on this appointment being granted quickly.'

Five minutes later Miss Andrews was back, announcing that the appointment was made and that Commissaire Fourrier was waiting for her.

'You were very fast – you must have telephoned to gain time, didn't you?' Veronica asked with controlled fury.

'Yes, Mademoiselle,' Miss Andrews answered.

'Yet I ordered you to do it in person!' And as she spoke Veronica headed straight for the door to the adjoining room. 'Get out of here!' she cried.

Miss Andrews went as far as the door, then fell on her knees and said,

'Mademoiselle, I didn't dream of disobeying you, I beg your pardon....'

'Get out of here!' Veronica repeated, even louder.

Miss Andrews got up and left.

Veronica calmly let herself be dressed by her maid. Motionless, by the impassivity and the spirit of domination of her attitude Veronica resembled a blond Philip II of Spain, and she might have repeated to the woman who was dressing her the famous remark which he was in the habit of making to his valet on the eve of grave and decisive circumstances: 'Dress me slowly, because I'm in a hurry.'

Veronica knew that an evening dress and diamond rivières would be more effective in awakening zeal in the commissaire's imagination than clumsy insinuations as to her social importance, and at the same time would spare her from dwelling on the thorny subject of a bonus. At half-past ten Veronica was being escorted out to the door of the commissariat by Commissaire Fourrier who as he pensively rolled a cigarette assured her, 'If she's in Paris we shall have located her within three hours.'

Out in the street Miss Andrews was waiting for her, looking like a whipped dog. 'Of course you haven't eaten yet,' said Veronica in a tone of reprimand. 'Well, now it's too late. This is what you're to do right away.' She listed a series of names and addresses where she was to call – she was to inquire about Betka at various other police stations as a check on the official force; at the same time she was to let Cécile Goudreau and the Prince of Orminy know what had happened, for Veronica was beginning to detect the characteristic odour of opium in this whole business.

Betka was found toward three o'clock in the morning, and at the end of two days she awoke in the American Hospital at Neuilly. Her first sensation was that of summer, on catching a glimpse through the half-open door of a man wearing a straw hat. This disconcerted her for two long minutes; yet she knew that it *was* summer! A corpulent doctor, all dressed in white, came and sat down beside her, and resting his hands on both knees asked her, 'Come, now, why did you do it?'

'I was bored,' Betka answered.

'Well, well, she says she was bored!' the doctor repeated, with a harsh American accent, shaking his head and getting up to take the thermometer from the hands of the private nurse.

In the afternoon Veronica was given permission to see her for fifteen minutes. Her explanation was more than convincing. Betka accepted it as though it could not have been otherwise. She added merely, 'I no longer wanted to live in a world in which everyone cheats.'

The following evening, when she was moved to her apartment on Quai des Orfèvres, Cécile Goudreau came to see her. The morning after, Betka had a stormy telephone conversation with Veronica who tyrannically reproached her for this visit.

'I couldn't refuse to see her; she had sent me flowers to the hospital every day,' Betka protested.

'Shut up! I'm coming to see you!' said Veronica furiously, hanging up the receiver.

The sun appeared and vanished in the window-panes of Betka's studio apartment on Quai des Orfèvres. Veronica was sitting on the bed, and Betka was kneeling at her feet, weeping, and trying to keep her body upright, separate from her friend's. Veronica's hands were clasped round her neck, her cold fingers plunging into the copper-coloured hair and her nails digging into the hollow of the nape of Betka's neck, caressing it. Veronica let Betka struggle feebly, willingly following the harmonious generosity of her arms, the brusque gestures that her friend made to extricate herself. But at the same time Veronica held her prisoner, pressing her ribs with all the inquisitorial force of her slender muscular thighs.

'Enough weeping!' Veronica finally ordered. 'The meeting of creatures like us is so rare... we must cling to each other so close that nothing coming from us can ever disappoint us any more. Swear to me that we won't ever leave each other again, that you won't take opium any more!' Veronica commanded, relinquishing her hold.

'Yes, I promise!' Betka cried, raising her head and offering her double row of teeth in a fixed and resolute smile. Veronica slowly drew Betka's face close to her own and, pressing her lips to her half-open mouth, gave her a long kiss on her motionless, clenched teeth... and...

Three years passed – 1937, 1938, 1939...

PART TWO

Nihil

PART TWO

3

Postponement of a Ball

En este mundo troidor
nada es verdad ni mentira
Todo es sagun el color
Del cristal con que se mira.

CALDERON DE LA BARCA

. . . IN BETKA'S STUDIO-APARTMENT on Quai des Orfèvres the sun appears and vanishes in the window panes.

... Betka stands with her body inclined over Veronica's kneeling figure. The heads of the two friends are at the same level, pressed together cheek to cheek, their hair interweaves. Betka's bare foot rests on Veronica's unshod one, and both of them bend their bodies over the pulled-back sheets of the bed and look breathlessly at a child barely two years old, who with awkward movements of his plump and wrinkled little hands tries to unbutton Veronica's blouse, seeking the roundnesses of her bosom that Betka seems to want to offer him. This confusion charms the two friends, and each fresh effort of his is greeted with laughter.

After this play of maternal identification has gone on for some time, Betka with a proud movement unbuttons her blouse, baring her heavy milk-filled breasts which she dangles over her son's face; immediately the baby's hands reach up gluttonously to play with them, and at each grasp into the air or into her flesh Betka laughs with delight, as though the very proof of her maternity lay in the

149

turbulent avidity which she arouses in her child. Lovingly she flexes her arms, and her breasts, brought together by their own weight, slowly, slowly descend. For a moment the baby seems frightened by the sudden shadow on his face, but as soon as his mother's breasts graze him he no longer moves. Continuing to lower her bosom, Betka lets the soft fullness of her turgescent flesh rest more and more on her child's face, and he accepts the warmth of this heavy caress with a voluptuous immobility so ecstatic that the sight brings tears of tenderness to the two women's eyes – tears that immediately turn to those of wild laughter when Betka's son, choking, suddenly reacts with the baffled movements of a drowning creature, struggling with all the energy of his precociously muscular arms.

The sun, re-emerging from behind a cloud, shines directly on that glorious flesh, which becomes so dazzling that the whole room seems lighted by its reflection. Betka's breasts are elongated, with extremely prominent tips, such as one associates with the Roman decadence, and their skin is as glowing as that of polished statues and specked with highly pigmented freckles that look deceptively like the flecks of golden moss which, as it happens, cover the marble of certain fragments of sculpture left exposed to the inclemencies of the Pontine countryside.

A fly has just alighted on the tip of one breast, and none of the child's movements seem to distract it or make it leave that somewhat tumefied point of the breast which suckling has monstrously distended. A whole series of other satellite granulations, one-fourth as large, surround the central suction knob with brown, swollen protuberances in a fairly even circulary border. The child touches these supernumerary nipples one after the other, and sometimes presses them stubbornly with his small forefinger, pulling all the flesh in a rotating movement as though trying to make the whole turn round like a telephone dial.

Now the baby's hand rests motionless on his mother's breast, and the fly that clings to its spot between his open fingers leaves him indifferent, for he has just fallen into a deep slumber. Without apparent reason the two friends have suddenly become anxious and Betka, straightening her stiff back, utters a deep sigh. The fly has flown off, and the sun no longer beats down on the bed, but on the parquet floor beside it, where purplish little wads of dust emerge between the cracks.

Cécile Goudreau had kept as a memento of Countess Mihakowska a bizarre orthopaedic apparatus of black felt and gilt aluminium which had been used only for a short time to compress the tissues where the breast had been removed. This rather sinister object was now used as a vase in which the brightness of a few bizarre flowers would appear from time to time adorning a kind of little makeshift altar, in very bad taste, composed of the worm-eaten Polish icon and the portrait of the Countess dressed in riding-clothes, very Hollywoodesque, in a leather frame of a red so aggressive, new and bestial that even the dying light of the tiny oil-lamp which softened the whole could not humanize it. However, as the latter was no longer regularly tended, it would remain unlit for days and weeks on end.

From the time of the bloody events of the Sixth of February on the Place de la Concorde until the 'September equinox' when the Munich pact was concluded one might have said that nothing, or almost nothing, had happened. Everyone was absorbed, body and soul, in making the most of his minute allotment of felicity. Going out to a restaurant became a thing-in-itself. One no longer planned. One got up late to make the wings of ambition lazy and one dared not go to bed till even later for fear of awakening those of remorse. That cowardly feeling of being motionless, of curling up and turning round once more deep within the sheets of irresponsibility, became accentuated, assuming a tinge of perverse pleasure from the fact of knowing that one's historic neighbours of Spain were massacring one another in one of the most frightful civil wars of history. Everything was accepted and compromised for the sake of putting off an immediate decision. The important thing was to be able to add to the emptiness of one day the nothingness of the morrow. People cheated, took drugs, waited…. 'Things are very bad – if only they will last!'

And it was as though in those crucial moments one single being in the world, sucking the energy of all like a vampire, were capable of decision. This being was the great paranoiac of Berchtesgaden, Adolph Hitler.

As in the menacing calms that precede the violence of the unleashed elements, it seemed that each being remained paralysed and anaesthetized, as it were, by the crushing imminence of war. But this instant of electric tension which, before the breaking of great storms, arrests the majestic movements of the millenary oak and the awkward pecking of the newborn chick for the short interval of a few seconds, this instant had now lasted three long years during which the heart of Paris simulated death beneath the dangerously close jaws of the panting beast.

People immobilized themselves thus in the intuitive semi-consciousness of the catastrophe which must inevitably come while each one, beneath his inert aspect, slowly crystallized in the forms most apt to resist the ferocious and decisive constraints of the great ordeal. Each one, therefore, while obscurely transforming himself in the silent depth of his lethargic sleep, was only sharpening his peculiar mechanism of defence and perfecting the ruses of unsuspected systems of reaction, while with all the superhuman strength of his ancestral instinct of survival each one, with the avidity of a suckling babe, drew upon the unfathomable resources of that germ of common magic which is buried in the depth of the origins of all biology.

Confronting the hell of the inevitable reality each being, guided by his regressive desires of intra-uterine protection, shut himself up in the paradisaic cocoon that the caterpillar of their prudence had woven with the soothing saliva of amnesia. No more memory – only the chrysalis of the moral pain of things to come, nourished by the famine of future absences, by the nectar of fasts and the leaven of heroisms dressed in the immaterial banners of sterile sacrifices and armed with the infinitely sensitive antennae of martyrdom. This chrysalis of misfortune begins to stir, for it is getting ready to burst the silk walls of the prison of its long insensibility, to appear at last in the unparalleled cruelty of its metamorphosis at the hour and the exact moment which will be signalled to it by the first cannon shot. Then an unheard-of being, unheard-of beings, will be seen to rise, their brains compressed by sonorous helmets, their temples pierced by the whistling of air waves, their bodies naked, turned yellow by fever, pocked by deep vegetal stigmata swarming with insects and filled to the brim with the slimy juices of venom, overflowing and running down a skin tiger-striped and leopard-spotted by the gangrene of wounds and the leprosy of camouflage, their swollen bellies plugged to death by electric umbilical chords tangling with the ignominiousness of torn intestines and bits of flesh, roasting on the burning steel carapaces of the punitive tortures of gutted tanks.

That is man!

Backs of lead, sexual organs of fire, fears of mica, chemical hearts of the televisions of blood, hidden faces and wings – always wings, the north and south of our being!

*

Never has it been more appropriate than in this case to bring forward the Dalinian maxim that 'ideas of genius can best be illustrated by the most common images'. This is why it can be said without fear of banality that just as the future world conflagration was going to make the creatures that were to compose the fighting masses resemble those of the Martian world of insects, and just as the apocalyptic battles that would be lighted round the great fire of war would be comparable in their precision and hallucinatory cruelty only to those in the kingdom of the articulated orthopterans and apterous locusts, so the protagonists of this novel, subject to the inescapable laws of the great metamorphosis, would in turn be consumed as they approached the common stake of history, clothed and armed with their new entomological attributes and rising by that very fact to the category of epic characters.

At this moment, then, it will be easy for the reader to see the deep reality of each of the protagonists of this novel at a single glance by imagining them for a few seconds illuminated by the same flame....

Veronica and Baba appear as a pair of praying mantidae, in the role of Tristan and Isolde devouring each other; Solange de Cléda as a *Cledonia frustrata* with great white wings and a mercury body; Betka as a moth; d'Angerville as a gold scarab; and Grandsailles as the grey, nocturnal sphinx butterfly, the middle of whose hairy back is marked with a death's head. Spangling the serene sky of this novel, the six protagonists, in the sign of Taurus, will perpetuate the eternal myth of the rising of the Pleiades.*

Each of them will know the ravages of his strange passions, and while attaining the biological frenzy characteristic of the most ferocious insects, the orbits of their lives will always remain as distant from one another as the cold scintillation of the constellations.

---

* *The myth immortalized by Gobineau in 'Les Pléiades'.*

There then remains for the faithful chronicler of these lives only to describe their physical embraces with the objectivity of an entomologist and the conjunctions of their destinies with the mathematical coldness of the astronomer.

For three years, in the Château de Lamotte, there occurred no notable event to be recorded, except that the Canoness of Launay during this time lost the rest of her hair, which she replaced by a reddish-brown wig which left no doubt that tawdry cheapness had determined its purchase. For some time her hair, becoming increasingly thin, had been gathered at the back of her head in a little knot achieved by dint of ingenuity and skilful capillary economies; latterly the chignon had been reduced to the dimensions of a silk cocoon and the hair that held it up was so thinned out and fine that it seemed to stay on by a miracle. One windy afternoon when she was taking down the wash near the fig-tree a branch that beat against a low window grazed her head and completely tore off her chignon. She was grief-stricken, and she weepingly dragged herself about on all fours, trying to find her bloodstained roll of greying hair among the profusion of half-rotten figs with gaping red pulps which had fallen from the branches and lay scattered on the ground.

Aside from this event, Maître Girardin with his ant's patience and his militant honesty had succeeded in tripling the income from the Count's property. In Grandsailles' bedroom Saint Blondine's skull still continued to occupy the same place, and his violin beside it now flaunted a new red string. Since the evening when Grandsailles had performed the operation of changing this string, an infinity of tiny bright red silk threads that he had scratched away from one end remained in the room in spite of all the dustings. They appeared everywhere, in the ink, stuck to the ends of the clockhands, and often they could be seen flying across a sunbeam.

In the kitchen of the Château, the old servant Prince had aged by exactly three years. Béatrice de Brantès owned three large new yellow diamonds and had redecorated her apartment with immense white screens painted with milk, which had already turned yellow. Dick d'Angerville had acquired a large calendar-clock, executed by the famous automaton-inventor, Houdin, made entirely of crystal, and transparent.... And so on and so forth.

It was as though on the half-effaced background, as of an old tapestry, representing the confused and foggy life of all these beings, only the objects stood out with some sharpness.... Three years! An ash-coloured chignon lost among rotten figs, a bit of red thread that floats across a sunbeam, the hardness of a few new jewels, much hidden sorrow, an invisible clock, and a flow of milk to a mother's breasts. Three years! One does not see them but, transparent as tears, they nevertheless suffice to leave a bitter aftertaste that softens the faces and the gestures of friends, covering them with that slightly golden tint that was not yet a patina of sentiment but was already the light powder of poetry.

These three years that preceded the war left few traces, especially in the lives of the protagonists, and even the most attentive chronicler of the Parisian life of this period would have had difficulty in noting essential differences; if by magic one could have concealed from him this lapse of time he might very well on returning to his observations have been fooled and believed that those three years that had passed were but a day. If it is true that during this period several rather surprising changes occurred in fashion, it was also true that just at this moment certain characteristic styles of three or four years before, which had been quickly forgotten, had been revived; so that while living and being consumed in an actuality which had all the appearances of the most continual tension and spiritual invention, people did nothing but rotate the same elegances, the same literary styles, the same hidden passions, the same overt liaisons, the same perfumes, the same concierge odours, the same quarrels and reconciliations, the same gossip. The gossip of Paris has in its favour that solidly bourgeois, permanent something which, if it have ever so slight a foundation, one can count on for the rest of one's life.

The Count of Grandsailles had been ill with a prolonged attack of sciatica which had put the plan for his ball completely out of his mind. But people were talking of it again these days as of something imminent. Aside from the period when his illness had kept him riveted to the Château de Lamotte, the Count was almost continually going to London. Recently there had been much whispering, sprinkled with strange reticences, about two of his ephemeral affairs, the most permanent and least obscure of which was the one with the Honourable Lady Chidester-Ames. But whether the Count was at his Château or in London, ill or in the arms of his mistresses, Madame Solange de Cléda continued to receive flowers from him every day without a lapse during these three years, and the jasmines reappeared chronologically in their season, always in their ritual wrapping, like a veritable institution.

During these last years Grandsailles had seen Solange during each of his brief stays in Paris, but never intimately; as they met only in society, they never had a tête-à-tête which went beyond the limits of a superficial conversation. Solange, increasingly courted and admired, lived constantly surrounded by the crowd of her admirers, who proclaimed her to be the smartest woman in Paris. The Viscount of Angerville, in his effaced rôle of a Pygmalion, had succeeded in chiselling the atmosphere of Solange's salon on Rue de Babylone, which soon reached the height of refinement, luxury and wit. D'Angerville's almost continual presence might have made one assume that he harboured for Madame de Cléda a hidden passion restrained only by his certain knowledge of Solange's unalterable feelings for the Count. But in spite of the doubts and even the fears that the rumours about Grandsailles' latest bizarre liaisons had inspired in them, d'Angerville seemed on every occasion to wish to nourish in Solange's mind the hope of an eventual marriage with the Count.

One late afternoon in late August, 1939, the Canoness of Launay turned up in Paris. She got down from a second-class coach at the Gare de l'Est, wiping her right eye with the corner of her apron. The Count of Grandsailles was going to establish himself in Paris for a long season, and as usual the canoness arrived three days in advance to make the two residences ready so that the Count would find the indulgence of all his slightest manias maniacally prepared for on his arrival.

The first of these residences was, so to speak, the official one, composed of a rather melancholy suite of rooms on the fourth floor of the Hotel Meurice, that had been kept since the beginning by his valet, Grimard. The second was a small two-storey house hidden away in the Bois de Boulogne, in the Bois de Boulogne style – that is to say, no style at all-done in deliberately bad taste and often containing objects of great value which spent quarantine periods there before being sent to join the rare furnishings of the Château de Lamotte. The 1900 house in the Bois de Boulogne was surrounded by a dense little wood of chestnut trees which made it completely invisible and was of course intended for the Count's most secret rendezvous. But this address was also known to antiquarians, herbalists, dealers in rare books, in very special old works, and to florists. The canoness, who had her apartment on the first floor of this house, where she assumed the role of concierge, gave a particularly exacting and reluctant care to the upkeep of the luxurious and unusual details and complications of the second floor. She often sighed while she was about her chores, '*Seigneur Dieu!* What things haven't I seen in my long life!'

The boudoir reserved for the Count of Grandsailles' mistresses, which contained merely the usual toilet articles in addition to its furniture, was always prepared hastily, without negligence but only to the point of adequacy. On the other hand the canoness spent hours in the Count's bedroom and dressing-room, which were cluttered with intricate and esoteric pharmaceutical preparations that an alchemist would have envied: unguents with tenacious odours in vials of porous earthenware that had to be constantly wrapped in white cloth bandages which immediately became dirty and had to be changed frequently like a baby's diapers; heavy roots tumefied with purplish excrescences and black warts hanging from vine-stalks in the ceiling like bulbous hands afflicted with elephantiasis; cat-skins marinating in opaque glass crocks under a thick bed of mercury.... In the midst of all this confusion of heteroclitic objects, on the immaculate cloth of an out-of-the-way table, there always stood, arranged with the canoness's extreme meticulousness, two flasks of the same size but of different colour, one of red enamel, the other of blue, each respectively accompanied by a glass and a spoon which were also of fine enamel and in matching colours. These two flasks contained liquids of a resinous green turning to chocolate, both of them odourless, having violent and opposite tastes. The right-hand flask, the red one, contained a kind of thick, very sweet nectar; the one on the left, the blue one, held a very volatile liquid, whose taste was so bitter and nauseating that it was impossible to swallow it without vomiting unless its effect had been previously neutralized by a spoonful of the contents of the first. The canoness kept a constant eye on the relative positions of these two flasks, so that if the Count should want to use them in the middle of the night he could do so without mistaking them in the complete darkness and without having to turn on the light.

The Count, on the basis of personal experiments, considered the mixture of these two potions to have very special aphrodisiac virtues, while at the same time its frequent use acted as a powerful stimulant on other nerve centres, particularly the brain. A formula similar to his elixir, though less elaborate, is to be found in the Neapolitan Laporta's *Natural Magic*. It was actually but the love philtre of the Middle Ages, which according to him constituted the key, as it were, to that wonderful *Rêve de Polyphile*, brought into France by Béroalde in 1600 – the Count of Grandsailles' favourite book, his bible. Having a horror of all the rationalist and positivist tendencies of the eighteenth century, the Count had studied deeply the works of Albertus Magnus, Paracelsus and Ramon Lull, seeking their grandiose intentions everywhere in nature. He availed himself of the help of the old herbalist Guimet, a character whose picturesqueness verged on the absurd, who claimed not to have bathed for seven years, for strictly hygienic reasons, but who seemed to be familiar with the virtues of the most delicate and unknown herbs. Grandsailles, going beyond the esoteric side of his herbalist's superstitions, could not help becoming day by day more aware of the treasure of empiricism which these formulas infallibly concealed beneath their aspect of apparent trickery. What, indeed, was the most up-to-date pharmacopeia doing if not reactualizing under other names the mysteries that for a long time were attributed to the credulity of the Middle Ages? The influences and therapeutic virtues which the alchemists accorded to the mineral world of gems and precious metals had been so much laughed at! Well, was the use of gold salts not looked upon in our day as a powerful curative? And what about the direct application of certain living animals on an afflicted part of the body? Was not a toad or a chrysalis a charged and panting congeries not only of unknown electrical phenomena but also, and especially, of the still elusive ones of radio-activity, since their secretions and salivas seemed more and more to be proved to be in direct connection, not with the NBC short waves, but with the interplanetary ones of the music of the celestial spheres? As for the Canoness of Launay, if she had been told all this she would have listened to it only as to celestial music, and meanwhile this whole collection of drugs and disparate objects of unknown usage appeared to her rather to give off a demoniac odour of sulphur, especially since on a certain morning while doing the Count's room she had come by chance upon an open book exposing an abominable engraving of a succubus scene that illustrated the treatise written by Durtal* on Gilles de Rais' satanic practices. And since that morning, the canoness tried to avoid glancing at the pages of books left lying open, and more than ever she was careful to walk only on tiptoe in the upstairs rooms.

Since his arrival in Paris, the Count of Grandsailles seemed preoccupied and meditative. The final breaking-off of his last liaison with Lady Chidester-Ames had left his blasé mind a prey to an obsessing series of new fantasies, and now he spent most of his afternoons browsing in special bookstores in search of books and documents which could directly or indirectly provide a basis for those bizarre meditations elaborated throughout his monastic retreats at the Château de Lamotte and heated by the constant and overflowing imaginative ferment of his long daily conversations with Pierre Girardin. Moreover, the thought of Solange de Cléda, whose tacit availability had for four years eradicated from his mind all desire and lust to possess her, was now beginning to prod him anew, and her image seemed to incorporate itself in, and be destined to become the protagonist of, his new fantasies. But he still refused to contemplate this seriously, saying to himself. 'She will be mine the day I wish it.' Solange's image would feign to disappear and lose its obsessive

_____

* *An imaginary writer, the hero of Huysmans' novel,* Là-bas.

value for a few seconds, but suddenly he would remember the frank and noble inflection with which she had recently reacted to certain gallant insinuations of his. 'You know perfectly well – I want you so much!' Then Grandsailles would feel himself weaken and launch into unbridled purchases of more antiquities....

After nine days in Paris the Count of Grandsailles could no longer resist the desire to have a long tête-à-tête with Solange. It would be their first real meeting since the incident that had occurred in the Count's bedroom at the Château de Lamotte four years before.

As an appropriate setting Grandsailles had chosen a solemn restaurant with a high ceiling and fine crystal candelabra situated at the Porte Dauphine, a place that was deserted around tea-time; at the end of the evening they could go and dance a waltz in the Bois, at the Château de Madrid. Grandsailles took his car and called for Solange at her house on Rue de Babylone. When they reached the Porte Dauphine it began to rain. They picked a table near a large window, alive with wriggling rain patterns, and the Count gave the violinist a tip to make him stop playing for the rest of the afternoon.

'The progress you have been making in the last four years,' Grandsailles began, 'inevitably makes me reflect upon my own senescence. You have never wanted to show up in London, but your radiance was reflected from afar in all the salons, especially in the most hostile ones.'

'I have done all this only for you.' Solange answered, watching the downpour. 'Since the day when I sacrificed my pride by confessing my love for you I have wanted this love to be at your level.'

'Yet you won't deny,' said Grandsailles, 'that your new rôle as a social idol partly compensates for your pride, whose sacrifice I have never yet been willing to accept.'

'The glories of the world,' thought Solange, 'are like bubbles in the rain.'

'If we had the curiosity to try to observe the bases of our feelings objectively,' Grandsailles went on, passing his lighted cigarette to Solange. 'I am sure your pride might derive satisfaction from the present vulnerability of my desire – which, however. I should not dare to qualify with the same confidence as you by the name of "love", which is so easily uprooted. On the contrary, according to my Stendhalian methods of observing the famous "crystallization" of love, nothing indicates this in my feelings – absolutely nothing....'

'I know I have grown in your esteem; but why do you use the word "desire", when you no longer need it,' said Solange with dignity.

'I can't tell you how much I appreciate your present state of mind, which at last is going to enable us to talk over our case without blinding ourselves,' said Grandsailles, watching Solange attentively to assure himself that her calm was not feigned.

Solange looked at Grandsailles admiringly. 'It's wonderful,' she said to herself. 'So much calculation and hardness. He is already taking advantage of his flatteries to impose his plan on me – he would not even soften the word "nothing"; he had to emphasize it by the word "absolutely".... "Easily uprooted"... what a cruel phrase.... Uprooted!...' Solange repeated to herself, fascinated.

'I have no right to ask you the question I should like to ask. I can only draw on the credit of confidence you may be willing to grant to my imagination,' said Grandsailles, and waited to be asked to continue.

'One does not impose conditions on the vanquished who is able to remain on an equal footing – on his knees.'

'The beauty and nobility of your answer oblige me now not to conceal my shameful question from you. Would you be willing to step down from your present pedestal to become merely my mistress, even knowing that I don't love you?'

'I have already answered you – yes!'

'Well,' said Grandsailles, suddenly moved, 'it's even less than that! And it's also so much more! What I want of you....' and he rested his forehead for a few seconds in the hollow of his hand.

Solange gently drew his hand from his face. 'You are going to leave again.' she said reproachfully, 'without telling me what it is!'

'Yes! I can't today,' the Count answered, resuming his coldness, 'but I promise to tell you next time. Today I wanted to tell you about my liaison with Lady Chidester-Ames; this passion has left ravages in my spirit, of a kind I could never have imagined.'

Solange pressed the Count's hand imperceptibly.

'Yes, I know,' said Grandsailles, 'you want me to spare you this... I can reassure you, for that's all over now.... Yet it's rather too bad you won't listen to me.... All those stories about the perversity of our relationship are quite untrue; moreover, if you knew all the details of this passion, you would find what I want of you so much more human and comprehensible.'

'Nothing will appear incomprehensible to my love... provided you give my jealousy a little chance to slumber.'

'Then I shall not tell you about Lady Chidester-Ames,' Grandsailles answered. He looked at her musingly.

'Do you believe,' he said finally, 'that in the ideal physiology of love the orgasm must necessarily occur simultaneously in both partners?'

'I don't think it's an essential condition, though a very desirable one,' said Solange.

'Yet the whole orthodoxy of physical love since antiquity seems to revolve around that single question,' said Grandsailles. Then after a long silence, 'Certain very widespread practices in the Middle Ages set this as the final goal of the sorcerer's art in the realm of love.'

'You are referring to the phenomena of love-spells?'

'Yes,' replied Grandsailles, 'I am thinking of those beliefs, considered as dogmas for several centuries, in the possibility of employing magic processes to induce love between two persons purposely chosen as having nothing to predispose them to each other. Love was imposed on them progressively, like a kind of condemnation, or punishment.'

'Neither modern psychology nor certain recent biological discoveries would seem wholly to reject such magic processes,' Solange hazarded ingratiatingly, stretching the little white cat's paws of her erudition on the waves of feathers of the carpet of their fluid conversation.

'That's quite true,' said Grandsailles, 'I have just reread several tales that tell of such love-spells, the process and methods of which, quite apart from their astonishing poetic beauty, strike me as having a hallucinatory plausibility!'

Solange folded her arms across her bosom and pressed her shoulders with her hands, showing her readiness to listen.

'One begins,' Grandsailles went on, 'by choosing the couple destined to become lovers, preferably individuals having hostile tendencies. They must not be virgins, but from the moment the two have been chosen they are held to a complete chastity which must not be broken till the end. After several months of carnal abstinence, during which their bodies are nourished with food and drink in the preparation of which all the aphrodisiac sciences of herbs since the time of ancient Egypt have a part, and their imaginations are kindled unceasingly by appropriate tales, mostly borrowed from the dialogues of famous lovers and from the ardent maxims of Odoclirée, who unites lovers, then, and only then, occurs the first meeting of the couple to bring them under the spell. For this "presentation" they must encounter each other naked, adorned only with jewels composed of gems and precious metals selected according to the conjunction of their horoscopes and other favourable influences. During the whole course of this meeting, for which a rigorous ceremonial is prescribed, no word must be spoken nor must there be any physical contact. Any infraction of this constraint would jeopardize the ultimate success of the love-spell. After this preliminary scene their meetings are graduated with a refined art to awaken and stimulate their budding desire. But contrary to what one might expect, instead of progressing in the direction of normal physical temptations their relations only retrogress. Then the course of their romance enters what might be called a new phase of idealization.'

'Sublimation,' Solange suggested.

'After their second meeting, their nakedness is almost completely covered with interlaced leaves, at their fourth encounter they appear clothed in sumptuous garments, and their gestures, still regulated in advance as for a ballet, instead of being crudely immodest as they were in their first state of nakedness, become more pure, expressive of delicate feelings, unction and humility as they progress toward the final stages.'

'I can see,' said Solange, 'that this kind of exhibitionism in reverse might become a violent stimulus to the senses of those subjected to such ceremonies, to the point of arousing in them a wholly cerebral desire for each other. But does this frightful Tantalus torture of their flesh have anything in common with the sovereign and permanent feeling of love?'

'Yes, assuredly,' answered Grandsailles, 'or at least this is what the texts attest, on condition that the couple satisfactorily reach the end of their ordeal.'

'What happens when the spell is at last complete?' Solange asked, 'what is the final goal?'

'At the end,' Grandsailles continued, 'the two lovers are left alone, face to face, clad in veils which by their richness are suggestive of sumptuous nuptial robes. Both are bound separately to the branches of a myrtle tree in such a way as not only to prevent the contact of their bodies but also to maintain them in the most complete immobility. After a certain time, if the spell is successful the orgasm occurs simultaneously in the two lovers without any other communication between them than by facial expression. And it is said that this phenomenon is almost always accompanied by tears,' Grandsailles concluded, pouring Solange another cup of tea. There was another silence.

'These tears,' she said at last, 'and the expression of the faces with their capacity for infinite shades of pain and pleasure are undoubtedly what make the human act differ most from that of animals....' And as if debating with herself she continued, 'So it is possible to consummate a great physical passion without contact? This seems to lead inevitably to a wholly new theory of love which might in fact unite the conceptions of Epicurus and of Plato in a single idea.'

'In any case, it is at least a new perversion to consider,' said Grandsailles with reticence.

'But even so, do you seriously believe this kind of thing to be possible except for people having the extremely suggestible state of mind implied by the whole complex of mediaeval beliefs?'

'You are right,' said Grandsailles, 'such states of emotive hyperaesthesia could be achieved in present-day life only by creating real psychological monsters.... Nevertheless, modern psychopathology presents us every day with phenomena of the same order as those of witchcraft, in the seraglio of the hystero-epileptics who fill our hospitals. The hysteric arch which instantaneously bends a feminine body into a contortion which for a normal person would require weeks of acrobatic apprenticeship has the same spiritual origins, so to speak, as the spasms so well known since Chaplin, which enable patients to perform feats of coordination of which they are normally incapable. The floods of tears that great actresses are able to shed at will seem to produce nervous releases corresponding in every respect to those of true grief; here the limits of simulation apparently have the same medullary source as pleasure. The phenomenon of pleasure, in fact, though more independent of our will than that of tears, is all the more acute when it is dissociated from mechanical action and is produced more slowly, brought about by what might be called more spiritual means. I know that the word "spiritual" as I use it seems nonsensical and can only provoke sneers among the materialistic minds of our epoch. But the general conception of love as it has been presented to us since the eighteenth century strikes me as an aberration. The idea of "love at first sight" is a barbarous one which in itself is a serious symptom of the foggy decadence, the lack of contours and of details, in which the "dream" of humanity seems to be sinking. When one thinks of the Egyptians, of the men of the Renaissance who could dream of obelisks, of learned geometries, of mathematical proportions which enabled them to carry over into a waking state the application of subtle problems of architectural aesthetics which their oniric life had solved, the lack of rigour of the dreams of our contemporaries is a scandal, and their oniric episodes are barely to be distinguished from the wretched vaudevilles of their pitiful daily lives!'

Solange blushed, for she never dreamed.

'This same lack of rigour also annihilates passions,' Grandsailles continued vehemently; 'as soon as two beings want each other they rush to satisfy their desire no matter how, where or under what conditions – awkwardly, twisting their arms and choking each other with their saliva, only to satisfy their passing urges and their exaltations. All the love experience of my life condemns and rejects this orgiastic promiscuity! Just as the inspired poet* is incapable of writing beautiful poems, so a lover is incapable of building a true passion.... On the contrary, an almost non-existent initial desire can be cultivated, brought by a series of studied crystallizations from its confused state

---

*   *'The poet is he who inspires, rather than he who is inspired' Paul Eluard.*

of a sentimental murmur to the cold splendours of aesthetics, which are of a different order from the scrambled hash of the flesh. I want to build a passion like a true architecture in which the hardness of each rib shall sing with the precision of the stone-angles in each of the mouldings of the sonnets of the Paladian windows – a passion with stairs of pain leading to landings of the expectation of uncertainty, with benches on which to sit and wait at the threshold of the gate to desire, columns of anguish, capitals of jealousy carved with acanthus leaves, reticences in the form of broken pediments, round, calm smiles like balustrades, vaults and cupolas of enchanted ecstasy....'

By an effort of will Solange obliterated all the sounds around her the better to listen. Why, in Heaven's name, could she not be loved by Grandsailles? If each of his words could so overwhelm her, what would it not be to live with him always! And as she listened to him, Solange de Cléda kept repeating within herself, 'What is it that you do that makes each of your words secretly nest in my soul!'

But Grandsailles had slipped on his very narrow glove, and now made the reverse of it snap in a characteristic way that made him seem already far down the street.

'When shall we have our next session in sympathetic magic?' said Solange, laughing in her brightest voice.

'Do you want to meet me here, the day after tomorrow at the same time? Yes I know, I must tell you everything!' exclaimed Grandsailles; then becoming again the man of the world he added, 'You won't mind, *chérie*, if I don't take you now to the Château de Madrid, as I had promised? I am terribly sorry it's so late.'

'I should have liked to dance with you once more perhaps, before launching on this experiment; is that going to be forbidden us too?' said Solange, getting up and putting her hands on each of the Count's shoulders. The latter had only to turn his head to kiss Solange's left hand, and he said, 'It is a wonderful miracle that there has never yet been anything between us,' adding in a hoarse voice, 'let us swear never to do anything that can diminish our desire!' Then he kissed her other hand, said in a low, firm voice, 'We're going to bind ourselves together in a spell!'

'Can I be more under your spell than I am now?' asked Solange, her head stretched toward him.

'I want to be under your spell,' Grandsailles replied, looking into the depths of her eyes and taking her by the arm, barely touching her.

Before they parted, Solange reminded him, 'Tomorrow evening we are dining together at Béatrice de Brantès'. Since we are only at the beginning, may I still wear my most décolleté dress?'

The conversation with Solange had left the Count shattered and, feeling as if he had undergone a violent nervous shock, he had retired to bed very early in his house in the Bois. In bed he opened the *Annales de Démonologie* at random and fell on the very minute description of a curious case of a succubus visitation occurring in a waking state, of which a reverend Dominican Father, at the beginning of the fourteenth century, had three times been the victim, each time with a different subject. While sitting in the confessional, the demonic body of the woman he was confessing had broken away from her human body and, tying all his members, had subjected him to a horrible captive pleasure while during all this the conversation had gone on uninterruptedly with the subject's double who had remained respectfully and piously kneeling.

Grandsailles shut this book while with one hand he rubbed the back of his neck with his thumb and forefinger; then he opened the *Rêve de Polyphile* at a page marked by a ribbon, and read:

'The mouth of this last vase was heaped with a mountain, a mass of precious stones, all uncut and unpolished, tightly packed, crudely and without order, wherefore the mountain seemed rugged and difficult to scale. On the summit grew a pomegranate tree, of which the trunk and branches were of gold, the leaves of emerald and the fruit of natural size, the bark of unburnished gold, and the seeds of oriental rubies, all big as beans, and the membrane or film that separated the seeds was of silver. The gentle craftsman who had wrought this masterpiece had placed here and there split and half-open granates, and some of the seeds which seemed not yet to have ripened he had formed of large oriental pearls, a most superb invention that brought a blush to the cheek of nature.'

On reaching the word 'nature' Grandsailles put out the light and gave himself over to a deep sleep. He slept straight through and awoke only at eleven-thirty the next morning. As he was about to leave the house he passed the canoness in the hall and she said to him, as she stopped and scrutinized him:

'Monsieur should not overdo the green potion.... So many innocent little souls waiting in limbo to come into this world!' Then, seeing that Grandsailles was looking for his cane, she added without coming to his aid. 'No secrets for your canoness! She makes your bed!' And she went off, muttering, 'Poor angels! God be praised!'

During these years Solange de Cléda's dream of some day becoming the proprietress of the Moulin des Sources had not ceased to haunt her for a second, and today, crowning the fruit of her persistence, this once vague and chimerical plan was on the eve of being realized. It is true that Solange's desires could never have been realized by themselves alone, in spite of their vehemence, without the aid of a devout, prompt, constant and unconditional complicity. This she obtained through Maître Girardin's unparalleled devotion. In playing this role, the notary in no way thought he was committing the slightest disloyalty to the Count of Grandsailles, quite the contrary.

For if it was true that on Solange's explicit request his professional duty obliged him to maintain the strictest secrecy as to his client's intentions, it was no less true that he could imagine Solange's acquisition of the Moulin des Sources only as something equally fortunate for the Count. Not only would this property thus revert to friendly hands, eliminating all the fears of industrialization which haunted Grandsailles, but also the tacit community of interests which this transaction would create between Solange and the Count could only increase the likelihood of a marriage which he ardently wished from the depth of his modest heart.

Maître Girardin however, in spite of all his efforts, had been unable to obtain a reasonable final price, and he had definitely decided to advise against the purchase for the moment. In spite of the very considerable reduction from the original figure, the lowest price which Rochefort had been willing to accept was still more than twice the real value of the land, which with the most recent agricultural lay-out rendered the mortgaging of the investment extremely problematic. Madame de Cléda obviously had a right to spend almost the whole of her fortune as she pleased, but she had an eleven-year-old son in Switzerland, and it was the thought of him that awakened all the notary's scruples.

In this state of mind Girardin appeared for the conference which would probably settle the question. Solange de Cléda received him in the little drawing-room adjoining her bedroom where the first fire of the year had been kindled in the fireplace. Girardin kissed Solange's hand and said, 'Allow me to announce to you that England has just declared war on Germany.'

'This means,' Madame de Cléda said after a silence, 'that we shall inevitably be drawn into the war? France must follow this decision by only a few hours, and it may be that our declaration of war is being transmitted at this very moment....'

Out in the yard someone could be heard monotonously hammering nails. Girardin was burning with eagerness to launch into the subject of the purchase of the Moulin des Sources, but did not dare to interrupt Solange's concentrated silence. She paced back and forth the length of the little room, taking deep puffs of smoke through her long cigarette-holder. Then Maître Girardin moderated his impatience and calmly sat down. Thereupon he tempered his assurance by getting up again, and finally found his poise by leaning with both hands on the open folder which he had placed on the desk, bending his body forward and bowing his head over the documents which he pretended to consult, so that in this way his attentive waiting and even the advice he was preparing to give might appear less personal and more immediately related to the duties of his profession.

'Forgive me – I'm at your disposal,' said Solange as she came and sat down beside the desk in the depth of a large armchair. Then she continued in a tone which seemed irrevocable. 'I presume by your worried look that Rochefort persists in his price. It makes no difference. I have thought it over carefully and I wish the transaction to be carried through as quickly as possible – the war might give rise to new complications.'

'Precisely,' Girardin responded in a tone of moderation, 'the new situation is something to think about and we should be wise to wait while we observe how events develop.'

'No matter what turn they should take, I am firmly resolved to go through with this purchase,' Solange answered, with growing impatience.

'In that case, Madame, my professional conscience impels me only to call to your attention for the last time that the purchase of the Moulin des Sources on the present terms reduces your son's inheritance solely to this property, for even your two houses on the Boulevard Haussmann will have to be mortgaged for this purpose.'

Solange got up and again began to pace back and forth; but this time she had left her cigarette-holder on the table and she held her arms crossed over her chest in her characteristic way as if to keep from shivering. 'The Moulin des Sources properties,' she said, trying to convince herself, 'can easily triple their revenues by using new agricultural methods, and so my son would some day enjoy the benefit and be glad of such a purchase.'

'No, Madame, you must know that the purchase of the Moulin des Sources on Rochefort's draconian terms can be viewed at present only as the momentary gratification of a whim…. Nothing less than the possibility of reincorporating it some day in the whole of the Grandsailles domain could justify….'

'Do you assume for a moment,' Solange broke in sharply, 'that there is in this "whim" as you call it the slightest calculation on my part of a future marriage with the Count?'

'Proceeding from the most elevated feeling of love, it would be only legitimate if it were so,' answered the notary, respectfully bowing his head.

'It is not so!' exclaimed Solange, ready to burst into tears. Then, containing herself, she said resolutely, but with gentleness, 'I take on myself the responsibility as to whether or not this is an act of madness. I must have it. With a passion like mine, doomed as it is to unhappiness, if I don't carry through this "whim" my life is broken… without roots. My son will find it in his heart to forgive me when the time comes, and I shall answer for his future on my honour. In compensation, my devotion and my sacrifice shall be limitless….' She put her hand on Girardin's shoulder. 'You have just spoken against the Count's interests to defend those of my son, whom you don't even know. I thank you….' Then, laboriously but surely rectifying Pascal's famous dictum, she said, 'There are also reasons of the heart which the reasonings of the heart do not understand. Grandsailles does not love me. I have proof of this now by his own admission. Well, I shall become what he could have loved, esteemed. Grandsailles wanted the forest – I shall be his forest, I shall be *"la Dame"*. I have not become what I am in order to seduce him; I have become what I am in order to feel myself worthy, at the level of his indifference. And because everything that he wishes becomes a law of adoration for me, Grandsailles now admires me! Grandsailles can marry Lady Chidester-Ames. I shall be no less proud, and be his lady. I may not be chosen as his wife, his mistress or his slave, but I shall be the lady, the one who is engraved on his escutcheon....' She grew fervent. 'Yes, I love the Count. Yes, I am buying the forest because I love the Count and it is only in order to be able to feel myself at last inferior, but on his very land, planted in his earth!' She fell silent for a moment, then she said, 'Let me tell you this – I must surely be possessed by a demonic pride – I suffer from my unreciprocated love for Grandsailles, but his contempt would kill me!' She drew near the fire and squatted on the rug in front of it. 'If necessary, my pride shall be buried in his earth....'

Girardin was preparing to leave, and as he bowed he murmured in a low voice that she could barely hear, 'Madame, I know of your life only what I must, and what my respect allows to my deep affection.'

'Everything is sweet and bitter to me,' sighed Solange de Cléda.

The following morning the sale of the Moulin des Sources was decided on and the date set for a week from that day.

4

The Night of Love

IN BARBARA STEVENS' SUMMER VILLA, surrounded by old resinous pines. Veronica and Betka had spent the whole 'blond season', as the ancients called it, in the effluvium of an unbroken idyllic friendship, united flesh and nails with their small child. The two friends, blended into a single pink finger of destiny, day after day observed their little one, flesh of their flesh, growing apace with the tender July moons, the ripe August ones, and those of September, already hard, smooth and shiny like a fingernail. For the 'winy autumn', likewise so named by the ancients, had appeared, gilding the Bordeaux countryside with its honeyed light. An old Bordeaux sailor, ragged as a young Bacchus, could be seen these days carrying away, rolled up under his arms, the remnants of the last bath-tents from the surrounding private beaches, now deserted, hurrying before the still distant rumble of the first stirrings of the sea heavily awakening from its long slumber.

Toward the end of the first fortnight in September Barbara Stevens and her daughter Veronica once more started back for Paris, accompanied by Miss Andrews, leaving Betka and her son to remain another month in their Arcachon villa on the doctor's advice. Barbara Stevens had hastened her return because of the announcement – now at last official – of the Count of Grandsailles' ball, the date of which in spite of the war had suddenly and finally been set for ten days hence. On arriving in Paris Veronica, who had been speaking with her mother less and less, except when she needed more money, and who since she had been given her own cheque-book now hardly spoke to her at all, decided to leave the Ritz to go and live in Betka's studio on the Quai des Orfèvres. In so doing Veronica merely anticipated a secretly nourished wish of her mother's, who made only a feeble protest at her daughter's 'eccentricity', since after all the boon of this more independent arrangement of their lives freed her from a thousand precautions and concealments, opening the door of her apartment, in which until then she had had to play the rôle of a mother, to the generous hospitality of her new flirtations so prodigally launched in the course of the recent summer season. Veronica knew all this, but also she had convinced herself that she adored the atmosphere of Betka's apartment, the piping-hot and steaming café-au-lait in the morning, served in very thick porcelain cups with chips and cracks as fine, and of identically the same colour, as Madame Maurel's hair – it was she, the concierge, who served breakfast, and she was clean, but only moderately so. Also the purring of her friend's cat which had nothing in particular about it and was like any other purring.... And what else? Well – an undefinable something, which indeed and with reason seemed as if it must be 'precisely' the chief attraction, since it managed to keep her mind, habitually so calm, in a state of constant excitement.

After a few days, as though her vague premonitions were about to materialize, Veronica passed on the stairs a strange apparition that produced in her an indescribable malaise which she could not shake off for the rest of the day; it was a weird creature, tall and slender like herself, with his head and face entirely sheathed in a very tight white leather helmet which was broken only by a slightly V-shaped slit for the eyes and another one below, straight but much narrower, for the mouth. Edging these slits the leather had a triple thickness, reinforced as by cornices, so that one caught the glint of the eyes only as if behind a lowered visor; the mouth, disappearing in the shadow of the opening, was completely invisible.

Behind this shiny mask must be hidden some frightful disease or mutilation. Painfully the man with the hidden face descended the stairs step by step, treading unsteadily, helping himself with one arm violently clutching a crutch, while with the other he carefully leaned on the arm of Madame Ménard d'Orient, who was all dressed up in a straw-coloured gown. Once they had reached the courtyard Madame Ménard d'Orient's white-liveried chauffeur, full of ceremonious solicitude, helped the strange invalid to get into the car and be settled comfortably, while several children who were playing with the concierge's son stopped to watch this painful scene, silent, open-mouthed, without the slightest discretion. After the lunch-hour Veronica began to listen uninterruptedly, waiting for them to return, but she did not hear the car arrive and, reaching the landing too late to spy on them, she saw the invalid only for a second, just as Madame Ménard d'Orient's door was being drawn shut.

The ever-perspicacious reader will already have guessed that this astounding character, the man with the leather mask, was none other than Baba, whose *rata* had in fact recently crashed. He had had to undergo a gruesome trepanning operation on the spot without anaesthetics. This saved his life, but the shattering of most of the bones of his skull had left him completely disfigured. As soon as she heard the news Madame Ménard d'Orient had had Baba transported from Spain in an ambulance and had called in the best specialists to attend him. It was decided, as a daring but last expedient, to attempt to mend this mangled head by keeping it tightly compressed for several months within an orthopaedic cast of a kind which had to be created for the purpose. From then on. Baba's case became the chief topic of discussion for osteopaths, surgeons and orthopaedists, and Madame Ménard d'Orient's salon witnessed endless conversations of specialists on that little-known problem, ever surrounded by caprice and mystery, the resetting of bones.

For what is a bone? That is what all bone specialists were wondering, without being able to arrive at an even provisionally satisfactory solution. To some, bones were dismal concretions, as insipid and somnolent as those that are found in the deposits formed in calcified water pipes; others considered bones as the most atavistic personifications of ductile solidifications filled with opportunism and fantasy. For the most modern theorists of osteopathy had just invented, and put into practice, surprising methods which hastened the resetting of bones in certain cases of fractures that had been considered incurable. Old men unable to take physical exercise were made to relive former travels in memory, in order to provoke in them an imaginative fatigue that acted on their bones. So, if they had succeeded in resetting bones in old men simply by making them undertake imaginary voyages, this showed that bones were not so stupid after all!

It was Soler, the Catalonian, who was finally called in to create the new 'bone helmet'. He had been recommended to Madame Ménard d'Orient by Solange de Cléda because among his diverse activities he had devised a clever leather helmet, made with his own hands, which he used while driving his racing car. When the orthopaedist who gave Soler the order to make the helmet showed him the radiograph of Baba's skull. Soler was shocked. 'Good Lord! It looks like the bones of the feet rather than those of the head!'

But Soler, one hundred per cent Catalonian and a demon of skill, managed under the direction of the Italian orthopaedist Blanchetti to turn out an amazing apparatus. And Baba's helmet became a technical, even an artistic, triumph. The helmet was divided longitudinally by a network of geodesic lines marking the adjustable sections that supported the frontal and occipital bones, just as other sections, likewise joining in geodesic and transversal lines crossing through

179

the frontal ligatures, compressed the two parietal bones. Each of these meridian divisions was edged with holes through which passed laces of greased leather, as on a shoe. But by virtue of a number of metal adjustments one could, by tightening or loosening, graduate the pressure exactly on each of these sections of leather ingeniously fitting into one another and at the same time mutually adjustable and independent.

What might be called the frightful and metaphysical aspect of this helmet was constituted by its peculiar adaptation to the face. Here, aside from the disquieting element inherent in masks of every kind, a really horrible detail rendered the sight of it not only hallucinatory but even repulsive in the extreme. This detail consisted of a triangular aperture in the leather in the place of the nose, which was covered by a fine membrane of white kid stretched so tightly flush with the cheek-covering that there was no suggestion of a nose. On the other hand this membrane was pierced by two horrible round holes ringed with brass to allow the passage of air, so that in the act of breathing the membrane was kept continually fluttering, and these rhythmic movements, like monstrous pulsations, produced upon the spectator the same irresistible biological terror as is induced by touching one's finger to the soft part of the imperfect cranial suture at the top of a newborn baby's fragile head. But this did not complete Baba's metamorphosis, for even more paralysing was the strange fixity which the deep slightly V-shaped eye-slit of this helmet imparted to Baba's habitually hard and impenetrable gaze. Now that it barely shone in the depth of the shadows, yet was sharpened, as it were, by physical and moral pain, it had become doubly enigmatic and was in every respect like the fanatical burning gaze of a warrior of the Crusades. His mouth, barred by the chastity belt of silence, had become vehemence and his masked eyes a glittering dart.

*

'My dear Angel,' wrote Veronica to Betka, 'you will be flabbergasted to learn that 37 Quai des Orfèvres, in addition to your illustrious Veronica, has just become tenanted by the weird personage represented in the enclosed photographs. He is an aviator, horribly wounded in the face in the Spanish war, who after a year in the hospital now lives as a high-class protégé at Madame Ménard d'Orient's, who is watching over him as though he were the very pupil of her eye. He might just have stepped out of the most blood-curdling novel of terror, but in spite of the fright which he inspires at first, once you are used to him you can't help admiring the nobility of his slightest gesture, and the mask seems to enhance the beauty of his gaze.'

In this letter she enclosed photographs cut out of an article which had recently appeared in the magazine *Lu*. In these pictures, taken by Pagès himself, Baba appeared full-faced, in profile and from behind. They were accompanied by sensational captions, in which Baba was presented at the same time as a hero, as the man from Mars and as the incarnation of one of the impending miracles of osteopathy and of aesthetic surgery in general; for in the words of Dr Blanchetti, who was the specialist interviewed, Baba's face would eventually reveal no other disfiguration than light and inconspicuous scars.

When Betka received Veronica's letter she suffered dreadful pangs of jealousy that deprived her of sleep for several nights. She now understood the anxiety which had gripped her since Veronica's departure. Although she knew that Baba was in Spain, she had fore-seen something like this! She liked to repeat to herself that 'nothing that *could* happen ever happens'. Well, she was wrong! It did happen just the same! For after all, nothing is inconceivable. And her heart told her now that no mask and no repulsion would prevent Veronica from falling in love with Baba! Veronica's mere allusion to his eyes burned into her like a drop of boiling oil poured into the reopened wound of her jealousy. But Betka wrote nothing about the meeting

Veronica had announced. She repressed all her feelings, holding her child tight to her heart. Now, set off against the seared background of autumn, she saw Baba's tall figure bandaged in white, like the anguishing figure of Saint Lazarus, just resuscitated to interpose himself between her and her brief happiness. Whether by him or someone else. Veronica also would some day be snatched from her by passion. Sitting with her baby in her arms, Betka slowly watched the flowing resin of a pine-tree. 'All are drawn from the same sap,' she said to her son, as though the latter could have understood her. She took the child's hand and kissed his little fingernails one after another, and it was like the arpeggio of the gall-moon of her past happiness.

For three days it had not stopped raining. Grandsailles arrived a quarter of an hour early for his rendezvous at the Porte Dauphine, and Solange de Cléda five minutes late.

'You are ravishing,' said the Count to her, passing his hand lightly over her furs.

Solange was dressed from head to foot in blue fox, that is to say, not only her coat but her turban was of fox and her shoes were covered by tiny gaiters of the same fur, now all sprinkled with drops of water.

When they were seated, the Count of Grandsailles took up the conversation in a low voice.

'For some time,' he said, 'I have felt a more and more intense and dangerous eagerness to explore forbidden realms of experience.... You see, the idea that now we are coldly about to decide what we are going to do... while I have to control my voice to continue to talk to you....' Grandsailles broke off as if to recover his breath, and went on, making an effort to curb the emotion in his voice. 'The thought of this meeting has driven me mad! It's unbelievable, but

I'm trembling like a leaf… look!' He seized Solange's hand. He was indeed trembling, and his teeth chattered imperceptibly.

'*Chéri*!' said Solange, turning pale.

'You are my accomplice now,' said Grandsailles gently. 'You are going to obey and carry out the laws of my perversion to the last detail,' he went on, both gentle and tyrannical.

Solange gave a little affirmative and unhappy nod.

'The beginning will be a small matter for you,' concluded the Count, having again become wholly gentle.

Solange gave another little affirmative and painful nod, trying to smile at him sweetly. Grandsailles was for a long time silent in order thoroughly to cement by this silence the seeming compliance which he had drawn forth by Solange's second assent.

'But what? What must I do?'

Grandsailles had calmly written down the address of his house in the Bois de Boulogne on one of the pages of his date-book, which he tore out and passed to Solange with a sure hand. It was now Solange's slender gloved hand that trembled as it took this piece of paper, as if shaken by a fine and continual, almost electric nervousness. Grandsailles then gave his directions in short and steel-edged sentences, illustrating these by drawings which he pencilled on the tablecloth, going into details as to their execution, rectifying… before Solange's gaze. Her cheeks had become red-hot coals, while she felt her lips and her forehead turn to ice.

'There,' said the Count, 'this is the entrance gate to the little chestnut grove. It will be open. There you must get out. Cars can't go in. The house is at the end of the path. You will ring. The door will be open, but you won't see anyone, and no one will be there to show you the way. You will go up to the second floor. The first door to your left in the corridor – that is your boudoir. It will be lighted. There you will get undressed.'

'Altogether?' asked Solange.

'Yes,' said the Count. 'You will come into my bedroom and lie down on the bed.'

'How will I know where your room is?' Solange asked again.

'It connects with your boudoir, through the only door besides the one from the hall,' Grandsailles answered, caressing with his pencil the pale floor-plan of this boudoir which he had just drawn. 'I shall be in my room waiting for you,' Grandsailles continued, speaking more rapidly. 'When you open the door to my room everything will automatically become dark. You will remain motionless on my bed, in the dark, about fifteen minutes. When the clock strikes two you will leave again. During all this time nothing must happen between us – neither a touch nor a word. And afterwards we must never consider that we have the right to make the slightest allusion to this episode.'

'How am I going to reach the bed in the dark?' Solange asked, in a childish and worried voice, as if frightened at the possibility of making a mistake.

Grandsailles then severely repressed a smile that might have risked weakening the ascendant and triumphal march of his tyranny, and answered her as dryly as he could, 'I have foreseen that. My bed will be immediately behind the door. You will only have to take one step forward to reach it. There will be a very feeble night-lamp placed at the other end of your boudoir, whose light will enable you to find your way back when you leave.'

'Mon *Dieu*!' Solange sighed…. 'And when is all this going to happen?'

'Tonight,' said Grandsailles.

'At what time am I to come?' asked Solange, getting up and pulling back her glove to uncover a strip of her wrist for Grandsailles to kiss.

'Come at half-past one.' Then the Count, as if unable to resist a last whim, held her back by the hand for a moment and added, 'It would give me pleasure to know I could look forward to your coming to the rendezvous wearing the same furs that you have on now.'

Behind the great rain-streaked window the Count of Grandsailles watched Solange disappear, with the help of her chauffeur, in the depths of her Rolls-Royce. Then he pulled a slender, dry cigar from his pocket, vigorously bit off the end and spat it out with the same plebeian heedlessness as a peasant of the plain of Creux de Libreux might have done; out of a velvet case he took his diamond-studded obsidian cigar-holder on which were chiselled three hawk's claws with gold talons, put his cigar in it and had the waiter give him a light.

Sitting back in her car, Solange slowly relived the killing emotion of her laconic rendezvous with Grandsailles. 'At least,' she said to herself, 'he now thinks only of me; he spoke neither of the war nor of his ball....'

At exactly half-past one Solange de Cléda passed through the wrought-iron gate that formed the limit of the little chestnut grove, and when she was halfway up the path she saw the entrance door open. Someone must have been on the lookout for her so that she would not have to wait in the rain. She would not for anything in the world have had the rain cease. This persistence of grey, sombre weather enveloped everything that she had lived through with the Count of Grandsailles for the last three days in a kind of unreality and timelessness. Going up the stairs she felt her heart in her throat. She said to herself, 'I would rather die than falter!' But her feet seemed to have wings. She opened the first door to the left with a firm turn of the wrist, swung it into the boudoir and closed it again without a sound. She immediately felt dazzled and surrounded by a white, milky light, blended with an intense and intoxicating fragrance. The four walls of the boudoir were entirely lined with tube-roses.

This decoration, improvised that very morning, was the work of the famous florist-decorator Grimiert, the master of ceremonies of the official festivals of the season of 'la Ville de Paris'. The flowers were held up by a harmonious trellis of diagonally crossed white and green cords that spanned the walls and that were barely visible among the leaves; but at each intersection was fastened a little knot of gold cord, which gave to the whole a sunlike glitter. On the floor the tiling was covered with a carpet of dark, thick moss, giving to the whole the illusion of a uniform surface of velvet. The dressing-table was in turn entirely abloom with tube-roses and exactly in the centre lay a glittering jewel representing a small split pomegranate in gold and rubies, scrupulously executed after the description in '*Le Rêve de Polyphile*'. This jewel was accompanied by a little pearl-bordered plaque on which was written, likewise in pearls, the one word, '*Merci*'.

Solange, who had taken only a moment to undress, opened the door to the Count's room and everything was plunged in complete darkness; she took one step forward, and immediately her leg struck the bed; lightly, with an almost immaterial suppleness, she slipped on to the smooth, taut sheets and lay motionless, trying to moderate her breathing that seemed to rend her sides. She held herself with her face lifted toward the ceiling and her arms crossed on her chest, struggling to calm the tumult of all her senses, stubbornly imposing upon herself the fixed idea of thinking about the hour of her own death; it was thus that she was able to push back, step by step, the pleasure that she felt so close to the threshold of her immobility.

Outside could be heard the incessant scratchings of branches rubbing against one another beneath the Wagnerian sighs of the wind, the exasperation of leafy branches heavily soaked with rain striking systematically against the drawn shades of the window with the lapping sound of wet cloth.... When the clock struck two, Solange got up, light as a feather, but she restrained her impetus at once, leaning her knee against the edge of the bed for a few seconds before shutting the door again behind her, and lighting the flower-lined boudoir again in all its whiteness. As soon as she had put on her furs she took the gold pomegranate and the little plaque and slipped them into her muff, and presently, as though she had been whisked through space in a single breath by fairies, she found herself once more in her bedroom on Rue de Babylone, weeping in her bed.

As soon as Solange had left, the Count of Grandsailles turned on the light in his room. The sheets of his bed, imperceptibly mussed, barely kept the imprint of Solange's body, and her irremediable absence suddenly assailed him, haunting him and plunging his desire into a deep distress, in the heart of which the most contradictory feelings began to batter one another in a cruel struggle. First of all his bourgeois prejudices, startled into wakefulness, severely condemned Solange for having obeyed him so readily, and immediately the prod of his contempt painfully pricked through the still intact membrane of his esteem for the woman, who had needed so little urging to appear naked in his presence. But the pain was tinged with remorse over the hastiness of his, perhaps unfair, judgment and was instantly followed by a kind of infinite tenderness that found release in tears. For even in the total darkness he had felt Solange's nakedness like that of a martyrized, humiliated victim!...

But this feeling of compassion, in spite of its intensity, did not last long either, for now all the chaotic and ambivalent uneasiness of his thoughts was giving way to a single emotion, more and more clear, debasing, tyrannical and unendurable – that of jealousy. Yes, he was vexed at feeling himself, for the first time since he had known Solange, dying of jealousy! And the mere unfounded supposition that she might have belonged to another as easily as to him kindled all his blood. For that matter, this eventuality now appeared to him as an accomplished and inevitable fact. He instantly imagined Solange after

187

their 'spell' scene falling compliantly into the arms of the Viscount of Angerville, and this fleeting vision brought such a pang to his heart that he was obliged to raise his hand to it. 'I'm becoming maudlin, like a two-year-old,' said Grandsailles to himself ruefully, pressing the flesh on his chest with his contracted fingers. 'In fact this all goes together, with the recurrence of my complex of impotence.'

Filled with such thoughts, he made his way to the other end of his antechamber, and in the semi-darkness he poured a spoonful of his green potion into the glass and lifted it to his lips; immediately he spat out the liquid, retching with disgust and coughing violently. He had half-swallowed a spoonful of his bitter potion. He then lit the light. Was it possible that the canoness could have made a mistake? She had indeed, for the blue-enamelled flask was on the left in the place that should have been occupied by the red-enamelled flask: and the glasses were likewise turned around. This interchange of objects also struck him as a bad omen, and he rang furiously for the canoness.

He did not have to explain why he had sent for her. The glass on the floor and the Count's mouth, twisted with disgust, sufficed. For a long time the canoness gazed alternately at the two flasks, the flagrant proof of her mistake. In her consternation she could do nothing but shake her head in sign of contrition. Finally the wrinkles in her brow smoothed, for she had just snatched the cause of her distraction from the depth of her memory. She remembered now, and she was telling the truth: the last time she had prepared the Count's two potions had been the very afternoon when she had learned that war had been declared…. Such a thing had had to happen to give the Count of Grandsailles cause to complain about the order in which his familiar objects were kept.

'Well, my good canoness,' sighed Grandsailles, 'this war seems to me to be beginning with a very bitter taste!'

The canoness had already started toward the Count's door, and she had only to pass her gnarled hand once across the sheets to smooth them before opening the bed, then she went through the flower-decked boudoir without wishing to look and making a face as though she could not stand the smell of tube-roses.

'Confound Grandsailles,' she muttered, reverting to her fixed idea, 'it's not with flowers that one gets children!'

The Count of Grandsailles, though he was preparing to go out, was beside himself, and he paced his apartment aimlessly, unable to banish from his mind the Viscount of Angerville's elegant face with that vague, indeterminate moustache that could just as easily have been borrowed from the nonchalantly sporting face of a contemporary lord at the court of Saint James as from the discreetly malicious face of a councillor of the period of Richelieu. Presently d'Angerville's distant and outrageously gallant smile began to assume the hateful expression of perfidy. D'Angerville was his rival and, giving free rein to his imagination, Grandsailles treated himself to the sybaritic torture of supposing himself married to Solange, while d'Angerville continued to be her lover! It was as though the lions of love had been let loose in Grandsailles' brain, and the canoness who was watching him out of the corner of her eye, while she straightened the closets in the hall – she could hear those lions roar in his silence – was terrified to see the Count stop his pacing back and forth and go and fetch his revolver out of the drawer of his desk. This he habitually did each time he left for England, and he was in fact going to London the following day. Nevertheless this anticipated precaution, at this hour, meant that Grandsailles no longer intended to come back to sleep tonight. Moreover she did not like the obsessive way in which he so calmly slipped the weapon into his pocket.

'This nightmarish rendezvous was all I needed!' Grandsailles said aloud to himself as he got into his coat, alluding to the engagement in Scotland which he had accepted that same day, yielding to an inflamed and urgent appeal from Lady Chidester-Ames. This was a thing which, if possible, further added to the confusion of his feelings. It is true that he hoped for no reconciliation from this trip. Nevertheless the fact of going back once more to his recent, most adored mistress immediately after his first 'night of love' with Solange, which he would have liked to surround with silence and mystery for several days, added to his growing anxiety a fresh wrong on his part, a kind of disloyalty toward Solange, as though he were already deceiving her.

'In any case,' he said to himself in an almost delirious state, turning all his exasperation against a single being, 'd'Angerville is a man without honour!'

Tormented by such thoughts the Count of Grandsailles took a taxi to the heights of Montmartre to Florence's, which was the night club where Solange went almost every night. She was not there. Then he had himself driven to Maxim's, where he sat down at the table at which the sparkling mind of Béatrice de Brantès held sway. How he detested her this evening – her voice grated on him like a nightingale's! To make matters worse, they were speaking of Solange, who had not appeared for two days, and of d'Angerville who had just been there a while ago.

'I wanted to see him before leaving for London,' said the Count eagerly, 'at what time did he leave here?'

They consulted the *maître d'hotel*. D'Angerville had left Maxim's in a great hurry at precisely half-past two. At this moment Béatrice de Brantès told a lurid anecdote which she ascribed to the Prince of Orminy. The latter in his youth had witnessed the execution of the anarchist Gaillart, which had taken place at dawn as usual.... After it was over, happening to pass the house where his mistress lived, d'Orminy could not contain himself and dashed upstairs and awakened her from her voluptuous morning slumber by the most passionate embraces. He wanted to make the most of his nervous state, of his excitement at seeing a head roll.

'It's only nature,' said Saintonges cynically. 'Men come and go.'

The Count of Grandsailles spent the remaining hours until sunrise sitting behind the window of an all-night bistro where the truck-drivers from the Halles would drop in for a rest. From this point of vantage the Count could easily observe the two entrance doors to the Viscount of Angerville's private mansion, and the fact that the latter's car was parked in front of the door was an almost certain indication of what he imagined. He was watching for Solange to come out.... But as day began to dawn his situation struck him as more and more grotesque. He felt himself devoured by shame and had a homicidal urge to get it over with. He had made up his mind to provoke d'Angerville, and now accused himself bitterly of the sole and single fault of not having married Solange a long time ago. He could have adored her more than any other woman! Now it was too late. At half-past seven, no longer able to wait, the Count crossed the street to d'Angerville's house and rang the doorbell. The valet who opened the door, having been startled out of bed, seemed frightened by the Count's tempestuous appearance.

'It's very serious,' said Grandsailles, 'take me to the Viscount's room!' But being familiar with the house, he found his own way and broke into the room without waiting to be admitted.

'What's up?' asked d'Angerville, shutting the book he was reading and looking for cigarettes on his bedside table.

'You seem to be waiting for me, said Grandsailles, instantly recovering his naturalness. He was unprepared for the possibility of being mistaken in his suspicions and was trying now to gain time. 'Listen, my dear Dick, I didn't come here at this hour of the morning just to flatter you, but you're the only person on whom I can really count.'

D'Angerville, his long arms stretched on the eiderdown like slim greyhounds exhausted with melancholy, barely listened to him. Grandsailles continued:

'I haven't time to explain to you now. I'm leaving for London in an hour. I shall very probably be needing you there, and my mind wouldn't be at rest if I had to leave without your assurance that you will join me if I urgently need you.'

'I suppose it's about the mining concessions of Libreux,' said d'Angerville simply. 'Just send me a cable and I'll come.'

'Thanks,' said Grandsailles, avariciously withholding all effusion from his voice. 'At least I won't have the remorse of having waked you up. You were reading.'

'So I was,' said d'Angerville, 'I'm quite concerned about Solange de Cléda's strange state of nerves. I have never seen anyone passing so suddenly from one emotional state to an opposite one. I had left her late yesterday afternoon. She was eloquent, like a sheaf of fireworks, burning her furs. I had to promise to telephone her at half-past two in the morning to continue our conversation. Well, I had difficulty in hearing her voice at the other end of the wire, and she hung up before I finished talking to her.... It was not sleepiness – she was like someone under a spell!'

'She takes luminal to sleep,' said Grandsailles, wishing to reduce any mystery to this strictly pharmaceutical explanation. 'And what were you reading there?'

'It's a monograph by Janet on Raymond Roussel's neurosis – *From Anguish to Ecstasy*,' answered d'Angerville.

'A case of Clédalism?' asked Grandsailles, laughing a little sarcastically.

'Clédalism,' answered d'Angerville, delicately weighing the neologism as he picked up his book again, 'it's something even more obscure and beautiful than that.'

And he held out his lean, bony hand to the Count of Grandsailles' perfectly proportioned and muscled one.

The meeting (this time, surely the last) between the Count of Grandsailles and Lady Chidester-Ames, in the latter's castle in Scotland, was one of the most turbulent experiences in the Count's life; and now, on his way back, sitting in his compartment, enveloped by the anise fog of his cigarette-smoke, he watched the serene landscape of dunes roll past, congratulating himself on his wisdom and complimenting himself on having succeeded in not killing Lady Chidester-Ames. He savoured his heaven-sent good fortune at not having become a criminal. As he made all these reflections, the Count's eyes lingered in the contemplation of a great lead-coloured cloud whose contours resembled the outline of an ancient sarcophagus. Then Grandsailles indulged in the fancy of imagining, engraved in roman letters in the centre of this cloud, so appropriate as an epitaph of his liaison with Lady Chidester-Ames, the famous Latin inscription:

CADAVERIBUS AMORE FURENTIUM
MISERABUNDIS POLYANDRIEN,

which means

CEMETERY OF THE WRETCHED BODIES THAT
THROUGH LOVE HAVE FALLEN INTO MADNESS.

In the vagueness of a stealthy sleep the tomb, like that of Adonis, became a fountain. The train was now crossing the sinuous waters of a river. From the golden serpent, the faucet of Adonis's fountain, flowed the elixir of youth, and the great white cloud had become

Solange de Cléda's nuptial bed. Lady Chidester-Ames lay dead at the foot of their couch, metamorphosed into the animal form of a bloody wild boar.

The Count of Grandsailles was now firmly resolved to marry Solange de Cléda as soon as he returned. Her happiness at least appeared to him as the sole object of his life and all his recent dabblings in the occult field of love-spells appeared to him, in the new light of his budding passion, as merely the last painful residues of his infantile fixations, fading and vanishing one after another like the bats of his tortured celibacy before the limpid sun of marriage. He now understood how much Solange must have suffered from her unrequited love, but he consoled himself for this by telling himself that now her happiness would be all the greater and more unexpected, thus compensating her for all her past tortures. But instead of growing impatient the Count would have like his trip to continue on and on, to last as long as possible, so that he could intoxicate himself the more with the elevated and serene feelings that he had felt come into being in his soul after the nightmarish chaos and the distress of the violences and compulsions in which his spirit had been dangerously foundering in the course of this last week and which were in truth worthy of the *Annals of Demonology*.

It was now only a week before the day of the ball he was giving, which he had recently almost entirely forgotten and neglected. The circumstances of the war having inevitably linked this affair to pretexts of patriotic aid, the insipid taste of charity seemed to him to have depersonalized and dulled its strictly social brilliance in advance. But now once more his ball appeared to him dazzling as a shield. The Grandsailles ball would serve to announce officially his betrothal to Madame Solange de Cléda. No one was informed of Grandsailles' return to Paris except his notary, who was to come and meet him at the station in order to obtain and study the news he was to bring back from London regarding the mining concessions of the Libreux. Wholly absorbed by his affair with Lady Chidester-Ames, he had quite neglected to obtain the latest information on the subject. Yet knowing Maître Girardin's affection for Madame de Cléda as he did, he could not forbear smiling as he reflected that the announcement of his marriage would be more unexpected and welcome to his notary than any other news he could have brought back.

Thus it was in the best of spirits that the Count of Grandsailles stepped down from the train. After their effusive accolade he and his notary got into the car and drove to the Hotel Meurice to confer.

'I have great news to announce to you,' said Girardin, sparkling from the tormented depth of his anxiety.

'No more important or happy than what I have for you,' answered Grandsailles, 'but let's wait with this till we get to the hotel.'

Girardin bit his lower lip.

Grandsailles' fury on learning from his notary that Solange de Cléda had bought the property of the Moulin des Sources was indescribable, so laconically did his anger manifest itself, so completely without outward signs.

'Very well!' said Grandsailles dryly and without emotion, 'in doing this Madame de Cléda has lost my esteem and friendship.'

But by the gleam of hatred that shone in the Count's eyes, Girardin saw that the true and authentic Grandsailles, who had long disappeared, was again coming to the fore – the vindictive Grandsailles, with irrevocable decisions, with a pitiless heart and an elementary force sprung from an old stock of massive pride. Maître Girardin, filled with consternation, knowing beforehand the futility of making any conciliatory efforts, hazarded with the utmost prudence. 'Yet we cannot overlook the fact that the Count's greatest political enemy is made harmless by this sale. It brings the Libreux plain back to well-disposed and friendly hands.'

'Madame de Cléda is no longer my friend,' replied Grandsailles.

He had, during this time, been writing a note, in his tiny, precise and delicate handwriting. He handed it to Girardin in an unsealed envelope.

'You must surely be seeing your client soon,' he said, 'I beg you to hand her this.'

The note read,

'Madame,

'I have just learned through my notary, Pierre Girardin, of your purchase of the Moulin des Sources property. I must inform you that I disapprove of the motives of this purchase. Your fortune made it possible, but the heart of a Grandsailles cannot be corrupted by such means. This is why I beg you no longer to consider me among your friends.

Count Hervé de Grandsailles.'

When Solange de Cléda read this letter in the presence of her notary, she became so frightfully pale that Girardin, getting up from his seat, came over and took her free hand, pressing it between his own. Solange then passed him the note, and as Girardin protested, refusing to have knowledge of its contents, she said to him, 'I prefer you to know everything. The motives that the Count attributes to me are as far as they could possibly be from anything that has even entered my mind, and five minutes with him ought to suffice to dispel this misunderstanding. I authorize you to repeat this, if the Count asks any questions about me. As for myself, my dignity prevents me at present from asking for such a rendezvous.'

Maître Girardin, ever diligent, hastened to pay Grandsailles a visit.

'Count,' he said to him, 'Madame Solange de Cléda was deeply distressed by your letter.'

'Did she communicate its contents to you?' asked Grandsailles.

'No sir, she told me only that a horrible misunderstanding had arisen between you, and that five minutes with you ought to suffice to dispel it.'

'She shall have a rendezvous,' said Grandsailles, 'you may ask her to set it for any time she likes.'

When Girardin had gone, Grandsailles remained for a long time plunged in speculation. 'What could Solange possibly think up to try to justify herself? Surely nothing having the least validity as an argument; she will only try to devise makeshift sentimental subterfuges, to prevent at least the embarrassment of not appearing at the ball. What persevering ant's labour!' said Grandsailles to himself, at the same time underscoring his admiration for what he regarded as Solange's perfidy by a smile of contempt…. Ten years spent in pursuing day after day, by all human and superhuman means, that single goal: to marry him, to become the Countess of Grandsailles. First it had been a struggle of prestige, of pride; then when she had realized that he was still the stronger in this kind of method she had feigned to be the humble victim, and to resign herself to the tortures of an unreciprocated love with an ardour of sacrifice and a loftiness of soul that were without equal; all this in order to move him to pity. But at the same time she had not neglected society – on the contrary, she had climbed and climbed, animated by a demonic ambition and with the sole, deliberate aim of dazzling him. And he, the naive Grandsailles, no more wily than a simple peasant of the Libreux, had been within two inches of falling definitely into her trap, he had had pity on her. She had succeeded in dazzling him, and worse, in making him fall in love, in bewitching him. For even now, from the depth of his hatred, he continued to desire Solange. 'Her game has been perfect, without a fault,' Grandsailles said to himself, 'but she knew me so little that at the last moment she committed a crude, unpardonable psychological error in believing she had definitely sealed her influence over me by attaching herself to me through common interests. Well, she won't even get an invitation to the ball out of me!'

At this moment Pierre Girardin was back again, out of breath, and childishly ashamed of his eagerness. He had been unable to resist coming to inform him immediately of the time Solange de Cléda had set for her rendezvous with the Count.

'Well, when is that five-minute rendezvous?' asked Grandsailles testily.

'Ten days from today, at six o'clock, at her house on Rue de Babylone,' answered Girardin, making a note of it on a slip of paper. Grandsaillés was perplexed and repeated, unable to understand. 'In ten days?'

'It's quite understandable,' said Girardin proudly, 'Madame de Cléda surely wants to wait till the ball is over....'

'To be sure,' said Grandsailles, and without a word of leave-taking withdrew to his room vexed, outraged. What? Pride beginning all over again? Yes, that was it! She wanted none of his ball!

And so, at last, behind the protective opium of the ramparts of the Maginot line, the Count of Grandsailles' ball was held.

Those ten days of waiting for the meeting on which she pinned all her last hopes of happiness were the severest ordeal that a woman in love, in Solange's circumstances, could have imposed on herself; and, quite contrary to the interpretation the Count had given of it, she put off their meeting – which she might have obtained and would have wished immediately – only out of delicacy. She wanted no factors other than those of their own and true relationship to create the slightest misunderstanding at their meeting. In this Solange had only anticipated and come to the rescue of the weaknesses and evil thoughts that could not fail to arise in Grandsailles' spirit, too much inclined to judge the motives of each of Solange's actions as consistently guided by all sorts of aims and ambitions other than the very simple ones of her love.

But to make those ten days that separated her from her meeting with the Count flow by, what prodigies of will she had to summon up at each hour of her life! Less than ever would she have allowed herself to appear at the decisive moment before Grandsailles' eyes in a light unfavourable to her beauty, or to the integrity of her spirit. On the contrary, between now and then she was, more uncompromisingly than ever, going to impose upon herself the torture of becoming that fabulous creature invented by her burning imagination, to whom the Count had wished to be joined by a spell! Then Solange de Cléda's torture began without truce or pity, the torture of separating her soul from her body so that the torments of the one should not encroach upon and wilt the intact beauty of the other, so that she could reach the goal, those five minutes that Grandsailles deigned to grant her, and get down on her knees once more, as she had once said so sublimely, 'while remaining before him on an equal footing'…. But just as she had experienced no shame in accepting the humiliation of exposing her nakedness without the consecration of love, so this time she would not come down to earth again; she would remain kneeling on her pedestal, just as she had lain down without demeaning herself on the tomb of her illusion.

And as in this world the hours of circumstances can be extended and repeated, except for death whose hour is rigidly fixed, the ten fearful days flowed by and at last the moment of the rendezvous arrived. Solange was beautiful and dignified as a queen, clean in body and soul. What could one despise in her that was not her passion? The limpidity of all her intentions could not but disarm the Count's tortuous ones, whatever they might be. She had not learned by heart what she would tell him, for it was her heart that would speak for her. But the worst awaited Solange – though perhaps it was not yet the worst: at about six o'clock Maître Girardin came to convey the Count's apologies and to announce that the latter was unable to keep his engagement, having been urgently called to England. As his stay might be prolonged several months. Girardin was charged to advise her as soon as he returned to Paris. Several months! She knew what this meant, having endured each hour of the last ten days as though it were ten years of a calvary without resurrection. But as long as she had a single reason for hope she would live, she would continue to live by her despair. Then her permanent heroism of persevering in everyday life began again inexorably.

Wafted beyond the reach of her anguish by the effect of the luminal, she would awaken to it again every morning, benumbed by the amnesia of the drug, finding it all the more poignant in the crude and sudden revival of the memory of all her unhappiness. From that point on, while her poor soul crossed the threshold of the hell of her passion, she gave her lovely nude body over to the kneading, shaking, tapping, patting, squeezing, rubbing, twisting and pressing of the four bony and unsparing hands of her two masseuses; then food – surveyed, vitamined, tasteless, regulated and weighed in a scale, and while she automatically chewed with all the energy of the aching muscles of her jaws she would think only of letting herself die of fasting. Then the forced labour of measured rest periods, gnawed by the pecking of quarter-seconds, watch in hand.... Then the long sessions in beauty salons, in the mortuary atmosphere of which Solange lived through, one after the other, all the minutest ceremonies of her own burial with the paralysing realism of the choking and pressures of the winding-sheet and of the descent into the tomb so solemnly imitated by the shockless movements of the nickelled stretchers with their subtle mechanisms... and a little later, the horrible apparition of the first drops of the liquids, creams, balms and juices of her own decomposition that began to flow amid strong ammoniac odours.... Then the worst part of it, the resurrection, the monstrous ascension, the pitiless dancing lessons, with each whirl punished by a humiliating fall and each forward sweep by the 'fouettés' of the beat – torn by the spiked wheels of the pirouettes, crucified on the tiptoe, her open arms nailed to the knotty cross of rhythm, bound, stretched head down on the Saint Andrew's crosses of acrobatics.

Solange de Cléda, what are you doing with your body? What are you doing with your spirit?

No pity on earth for either, and so much base flattery from society for both! The painters and the poets go into ecstasies before the enigmatic expression of your glance, the ballet-master praises the flexibility of your entrechats, the make-up man the spotless purity of your complexion. But I see you on your knees, Solange de Cléda, in your room, when you are alone, with your head uplifted to your idol; you are like those mystic women, desirable and dying, painted by El Greco; like them, you have eyes made brilliant by the continual patina of timeless tears, hardened and barely translucent like the very shell of ecstasy. In the martyrdoms of your passion each of your gestures makes you tremble and each of your movements becomes a sharpened dagger falling into the sensitive emptiness of the moon-well of your anguish and remaining nailed to its bottom. This makes you cough, and the slit of your wound widens; then you cough on purpose, you cough with all your might to shake off all the swords stuck in your heart. Sometimes also you sigh so deeply that you are afraid to lose your breath, then you stop breathing altogether to stop living. The veins of your neck swell and your head trembles; each new second becomes a victory, but in the end you cannot help falling frenzied on the hard shiny tiles, your chest convulsed by the spasms of your frantic breathing, your sides aching with grief!

Solange de Cléda presents psychiatry with a strange case indeed, for even in the most painful aberrations of her mind, the very convulsions of her hysteria became for her a means of making her nervous centres more supple and her biological functions in general more regular. Becoming day by day more dual by virtue of the very nature of her somatic personality, she seemed to approach the absolute of that dualism, considered clinically impossible, of the body and the soul.*

Veronica stood on tiptoe the better to listen.... At the beginning it was like the thin insistent whine of a mosquito. Then the sound swelled and became more precise, and she turned off the gas and the electricity. It was in fact the air-raid signal, and by the sudden joy with which it filled her, she realized instantly with what secret impatience her unconscious had waited, night after night, for such an event to occur. The doors on the various floors began to slam, like blows of Hitler's fists angrily struck on a wooden table, and immediately the noises of the tenants, rolling like walnuts in an empty drawer, sounded in the well of the stairs. Now the siren bellowed powerfully, making the windows rattle. She was ready, her toilet articles too,

---

* *A remarkable fact is the capacity for endurance and even for 'health' that accompanies certain grave affections of the mind in well-determined cases of dementia. Thus in Napoleon and several other men of action I have been able to analyse vestiges of 'Clédalism' in which the mind seemed to function not only independently of but even in contradiction to certain laws of the organism, thus offering an exception to the old idea that the body is the mirror of the soul.*

Driving herself continually, with all the force of her paranoiac proclivities, to go constantly counter to all natural laws. Solange de Cléda while awaiting the Count's return was progressively and imperceptibly turning into a monster.

since for months she had been waiting only for this. Nevertheless she had been taken by surprise, and was wearing shoes she did not like. She rummaged about in vain. Finally in annoyance she slipped her gas-mask by its strap over her shoulder and went down into the cellar with a smile on her lips.

Everyone down here wore the same expression, impossible to repress in spite of the contractions that each one imposed on his lips to give himself a serious, if not grave, countenance – one more in keeping with the circumstances. The mingled illusion and anguish of this first alert seemed to make them all like children again. It had been said so often that modern bombardment would pulverize everything, that under the menace of external danger they all felt the intensely human pleasure of intra-uterine protection as they pressed and huddled together at the bottom of a dark and maternally protective cave. The people covered one another's legs with blankets, they brought cushions, crouched on sacks, seeking complicated postures for the wait. Madame Maurel, the concierge, did the honours of the cellar and served black coffee; a bottle of wine was opened, a box of stale crackers was passed around; the whole attention was concentrated on comfort and well-being.

Veronica alone would not sit down and, grown taciturn, stood waiting. She had on nothing but her white starched dressing-gown and had kept no other jewel than a little cross of pearls with three diamonds in place of the nails of Christ's crucifixion. This cross hung from an almost invisible platinum chain which held it resting, as in a nest of silky flesh, exactly in the middle of the soft hollow in the very pronounced bone of her sternum. When Madame Ménard d'Orient entered with Baba leaning on her arm, the latter might easily have compared Veronica's immaculate figure, framed by the blackness of the vaults of this late seventeenth-century cellar, to a legendary abbess rather than to a contemporary being.

Veronica now stood leaning against the damp, peeling wall. She had slipped off one shoe and placed her bare foot on the other. Baba looked for a long time at this arched foot, with its matt skin, its blue-tinged dimples, free of the stigma of the slightest redness touching or profaning its toes, of which each articulation of each phalanx seemed to rest on the ground beneath Raphael's approving glance, and as on the feet painted by him, the big toe was widely separated from the other toes, as by the effect of the strap of an invisible sandal. Baba looked, and one might have said that the weight of his leather helmet kept his large head bowed forward, obliging him thus to gaze down, so completely did his whole spirit seem absorbed in his contemplation. And it was in truth as though suddenly this being accustomed to piercing the clouds, equipped with helmet, gloves, micros, machine guns and carapaces, had discovered at last the beauty he had desperately been seeking in the sky in the simplicity of a bare foot resting on the ground in the depth of a cellar. After his deep plunge, like a diver who rises again to the surface, slowly Baba's eyes, followed by an upward movement of his helmet, scanned the whole length of Veronica's chastely covered body, but on reaching her neck his glance again remained fastened and as if crucified by the three diamonds on the little pearl cross. Veronica stirred, then, giving a fresh sparkle to her face, in order to break the fixity of that gaze which she wished at last to possess with her own.

Time sped fast, and their delight was like the glistening sting of their desire. They questioned the favourably menacing sky. When would be their next mute idyll? For the impassivity of Veronica's face was as hermetic as that of Baba's helmet, and her sure love no longer knew any fear or curiosity. She knew now that nothing beneath that helmet could modify the whole and continuous course of her emotions. If she wished to imagine him to herself, she had only to put her own face in place of his, for she – was he. And already her medium-like spirit traced their immediate future: 'This war will separate us... but at the end of a year he will return; it will be in America, in the winter.... He will have a few scars, but none could mar his eyes. Perhaps he will limp' – but then she thought of the arched postures of ancient statues in which the weight of the body rests on a single leg.

After this first descent into the cellar the tacit idyll between Veronica and Baba knew no other outward expression than similar scenes in the course of other alerts, and their frequent encounters on the stairs. As events were taking a rapid turn Betka came back to Paris, but at the prompting of instinct she waited till the last moment. On her arrival it was clear, though impossible to explain wherein the change consisted, that the friendship between Veronica and her had cooled. They continued to live together, but Betka refused to go down into the cellar during the alerts. Neither of them spoke of Baba. More or less surreptitiously Betka frequented Cécile Goudreau's group of friends, and began little by little to smoke opium again without Veronica's being too uncompromising about it, and this indifference deeply wounded her.

The Prince of Orminy, with the proselytism characteristic of drug addicts, had said of her to Goudreau, 'If we can manage to keep Veronica from taking her to America we'll have her for the duration of the war. But we'll have to find a home for her child somewhere. That will at least be easier than to explain him.' D'Orminy judged that Betka must be easy to corrupt and, vaguely lusting to have her as his mistress, was attentive to her, though through fear of Veronica he did not dare to overwhelm her with presents. It was in this anxious period of waiting (during which even Veronica's uncompromising character seemed to be weakening and she made no effort to check Betka's dangerous promiscuities as long as she herself was left undisturbed in her dream) that the German army, having flanked the Maginot line and finding no further effective obstacles in its path, began its lightning and methodical advance, and Americans received their government's official order to leave France.

In Barbara Stevens' apartment in the Hotel Ritz, Veronica was beating her mother. First she had forcibly snatched the telephone from her hand, then she had struck her a sharp blow on the hand with it, causing the pen to fly from her fingers, and finally she had knocked her down on the couch with her knees. Now the rôles seemed reversed, for Veronica was weeping and trembling with rage, while Barbara, frightened by her daughter's unprecedented fit of nerves, took her to her bosom to console her and begged her forgiveness. The violent scene that had taken place was but the culmination of endless dissensions which had set mother and daughter against each other during three long days of mutual exasperations. Veronica wanted at all costs to take Betka and the child with them to America. Barbara both wanted and did not want to, changing her mind every fifteen minutes, in a state of hysterical caprice which the gravity of the situation only sharpened. She insisted, in particular, that it would be impossible to legalize Betka's situation in so short a time. Veronica, with Miss Andrews' aid, had nevertheless imperturbably pursued the labyrinthine course of all the necessary routine to make Betka's departure possible; at last the miracle was realized and the visas and documents required to leave France and enter the United States were ready and on Barbara Stevens' desk.

It was just at this moment that Barbara, after a long embarrassed silence, came out stubbornly and uncompromisingly with her refusal to take Betka along. 'The most I'll do is to write her a cheque for a hundred thousand francs to rid myself of all worry,' and she picked up the pen and was about to fill out the cheque. Veronica said nothing, but went up to her mother with eyes blazing. As she saw her daughter approach. Barbara burst into a sharp, nervous laugh. Then, shrugging her shoulders and pretending to pay no more attention to her, she calmly began to write her cheque.

'I could never disappoint Betka in this way, and your money doesn't settle anything,' said Veronica coldly, and continued even more coldly. 'You know perfectly well the Germans won't forget that she used to belong to active anti-German propaganda agencies.'

Barbara hesitated a moment and answered, 'You don't dare to simply tell her my decision. Very well – I'll tell her myself!' And Barbara picked up the telephone and placed a call for Betka, who had been waiting downstairs for an hour to learn their decision. At this moment Veronica delicately placed her long fingers on the hand with which her mother held the telephone, and at this contact, pale as that of a caress, the latter trembled with fear. But, taking hold of herself, she pressed the receiver more tightly, trying for a moment to struggle – but in vain. For Veronica, turning into a fury, resorted to force. It was then that Veronica, wielding the telephone like a hammer, drove the iron spike of her will into the shimmying wood of indecision of her mother's hand. After the balm of Barbara's and Veronica's tears they telephoned to Betka, with the very same hammer, that she could come up. It had at last been settled that she was to go with them: they were leaving in three hours. With tears in her eyes Betka kissed the four hands of her two protectors, whose hollowed palms offered themselves to her welcomingly like the hull of a recently constructed ship with which she would at last be able to cross the ocean.

'I'll run and get the baby,' Betka cried, wild with joy.

'No, I'm going to fetch it.'

'I'll go with you!'

'No, you stay here,' Veronica replied categorically, pointing a finger at the couch. 'Miss Andrews will come with me.'

As she had foreseen, Veronica found Betka's apartment invaded by a group of her friends who, alarmed by the rumours of her possible departure, had come running and were waiting for her return to dissuade her from undertaking the trip and put a stop to the irremediable blunder, the virtual treason that she would be committing, according to them, by going to America. Cécile Goudreau, naturally, was there, and Soler, the Prince of Orminy and a *ménage* of two musician-pederasts who were in the midst of insulting each other furiously just at the moment when the entrance of Veronica, followed by Miss Andrews instead of Betka, restored a barely courteous icy silence in the room. It was broken only by the tinkling of the large snifters containing a fine Napoleon brandy which she had recently given Betka as a present and which this gathering of crows was now sipping.

Veronica went for a moment into Betka's room, and finding nothing else to take than the child, took him in her arms, handing him to Miss Andrews. She looked around for Betka's cat. But she was not in sight. Veronica decided to leave and crossed the room occupied by Betka's silent and sulking friends like a dandelion seed floating above the black and stagnant waters of a swamp. She walked down the stairs with her lithe antelope's steps to Madame Ménard d'Orient's landing. There she stopped, ordering Miss Andrews to wait for her a moment, and rang the doorbell. From the upper storeys could now be heard the confused sounds of dissension among Betka's friends, that had broken out all the more vehemently since she had left them. Each one was having his own particular fit of nerves; one could hear one of the pederasts weeping, uttering sighs punctured by reproaches, while the other brayed muffled invectives; a glass broke in a rage, and Cécile Goudreau's voice imposed silence with a Sophoclean tirade. Someone, probably d'Orminy, discreetly shut the door to keep the scandal from reverberating too loudly in the stairway.

The door to Madame Ménard's apartment was opened by a servant, and Veronica entered. The mistress of the house came forward holding out her two hands. Her lace dress bristling with shiny cat-hairs betrayed the fact that she had just been roused from a nap. Forgetting all propriety, Veronica merely said to her. 'Will you let me be alone for a moment with....' She dragged out this last word and left it dangling...., Taken by surprise, Madame Ménard d'Orient obediently opened the door adjoining the drawing-room without knocking, and after having assured herself that Baba was not asleep, she introduced Veronica, immediately shutting the door behind her and leaving them to themselves. Baba was sitting in an armchair with his back turned to her, but he saw Veronica advancing in the mirror opposite.

'This is how I shall see him arrive the day he returns,' said Veronica to herself. Baba got up with difficulty. He was surprised at the unexpected boldness of Veronica's coming, but he was grateful to her, too, for he had heard that she was leaving and knew that she had introduced herself here to say goodbye to him. Without hesitating, Veronica took Baba's helmet between her hands, pressed it to her face, and fastened her lips for a moment to the mask's mouth-slit. Then they remained facing each other, fixed in an absolute immobility – Baba, his head a little lowered, as if ashamed at not being able to respond more eloquently to her passionate effusion; Veronica, taller than he, rigid, tense in all her muscles. After a few moments of this unmaintainable state of expectancy, Veronica brusquely raised her long arms, joining her hands under her chin in the characteristic pose of the praying mantis. Then with her cold fists she clutched the cross of pearls and diamonds that hung on her neck and calmly pulled at the chain, harder and harder, until it broke. She gave it to Baba who barely moved. Then she left.

On the landing. Miss Andrews and Madame Maurel, the concierge, were growing impatient. 'If Veronica should miss the train, it might already be too late to leave tomorrow.' They gave a relieved sigh on seeing her reappear. At this moment an outburst of raucous laughter was heard from the top of the stairs, and one of the peder-astic musicians appeared for a moment wearing a small lampshade balanced on his head tied with a silk handkerchief of Betka's. He immediately disappeared, embarrassed. Veronica barely noticed this fantastic apparition. She was so absorbed, so much under the impression of the brief, poignant scene she had lived through in Baba's room, that she left without even saying goodbye to the con-cierge who, having just been handed a five-hundred franc tip by Miss Andrews, watched her go off with stupefaction, exclaiming as she crumpled the bill in her hand,

> *'Tant pis pour son cœur*
> *Ce n'est pas son pays!'*

Veronica Stevens turned her face toward America, but unlike Lot's wife she did not look back, for by her virginal nature she already possessed the same biological incorruptibility as the country, strong and intact, toward which she was travelling and which was her home.

On the eleventh of June, after several months' absence and on the morrow of his arrival from London, the Count of Grandsailles was awakened by his valet Grimard in his Hotel Meurice apartment. Grimard announced that the Prince of Orminy was waiting in the drawing-room and wished to see him.

'Have him come in,' said Grandsailles, raising himself and set-tling his back against the pillows, and as soon as Grimard had drawn the portières the Count found himself facing the yellow-toothed, somewhat horsy smile of the Prince, impeccably dressed in riding-clothes, with a polo whip in his hand.

'I have just spent the blackest white night of my life,' said d'Orminy phlegmatically, folding back the comforter and sitting down on the edge of the Count's bed. 'You see, from Olga's apartment on the Rue de Rivoli it's like a magnificent loge overlooking the Place de la Concorde to view the entry of the troops.'

'Imagine anyone being so reserved – Grimard, charming fellow that he is, didn't breathe a word about the Germans being here when he woke me up!' Grandsailles exclaimed, trying to take the whip from d'Orminy's hands.

'Well, old man, I saw Hitler's first soldier arrive,' d'Orminy began. 'He was of medium height, rather slight of build. It was about four-thirty in the morning; at that time the Place de la Concorde was completely deserted, there wasn't a cat in sight. Well, suddenly a cat, a grey cat, began to cross it, almost crawling, anxious, now and then looking toward the Rue Royale. Suddenly he broke into a run. Immediately there appeared a motorcyclist whom we had not heard, he made a wide circle in low speed, then stopped near the centre; there he got off, parked his motorcycle, pulled out a pair of signal flags that he carried rolled up in his pocket. He raised his arms, and, as though it were his daily occupation, gesturing like an orchestra leader, gave the entry order and began to direct the traffic.

'Then the advance guards of the Nazi motorized divisions began to arrive, solidly and uninterruptedly, tanks to the right, trucks to the left... my dear fellow, it was like filling a bath-tub, and it's been running right up to this moment, just as monotonously – you know? It was funny,' he continued, trying with his whip to hit a single fly that was in the room and that kept coming back insistently to the same spot on the eiderdown quilt, 'it was funny to see that little chap, an enemy – for he was an enemy, all right – all alone in the middle of the great square in the heart of Paris, within gunshot of any of the surrounding windows... I can't have been the only one to observe

him and to think of this.... Ah, my dear Grandsailles, when you see
that,' said d'Orminy with a long, discouraged sigh. 'What an ugly
colour all those tanks and trucks are: a dirty greenish-grey army –
too dark, too chemical. It doesn't at all go with that pearl-grey, that
imponderable shade, the swallow-dung colour of Paris' – and as
he spoke it seemed as if the prickling ammonia which this 'dung'
exudes, even in evocation, had the virtue of bringing tears to his eyes.

'Those German bastards have no tact,' said Grandsailles, getting
up and slipping on his bath-robe. Then he came back and sat down
on his bed, which d'Orminy had left to sprawl on a couch near the
window. 'At heart they worship us; otherwise, would they go to the
trouble of coming all this way loaded with cannon and with so much
good will? And doesn't the whole thing make you feel like committing
suicide?' asked Grandsailles.

'Don't joke about it,' d'Orminy answered, 'we're the ones who
always talk about committing suicide and end up by doing it. As a
matter of fact you hit it right, believe it or not. This morning I felt
like committing suicide, but it wasn't despair, for in spite of everything I can't bring myself to be as pessimistic about the situation as
all that... it's just that it's going to take so long.... This time it was
indolence, the indolence of having to run away, of stumbling into a
thousand difficulties, in short an insurmountable indolence in the face
of everything. When I went up to the mirror to shave, this operation
which I stoically undergo every morning struck me as superhumanly
boring, and impossible for me to carry through once more; I swear
to you I hesitated a moment whether to shave or to cut my throat.'

'Whereupon you decided to let your beard grow,' said Grandsailles.

'Quite right,' said d'Orminy, indulgently rubbing his chin which
was already rough, 'it's the first thing to do if you decide to carry on.
You can improvise anything in a passport, but a real beard takes time
to grow.... For the moment it's counterbalanced by my polo outfit,

which assures my being able to get around in Paris for today. My horses need me, or else the German army will need *them*. Tomorrow I'm leaving for Africa. When are you coming? My property near Casablanca is always at your disposal. My yacht is anchored just outside. If you're afraid of getting mixed up in the opium business all you have to do is set up your headquarters on the boat and you can make yourself at home on the property. Cécile Goudreau is going with me…. Don't forget that Africa will decide everything!'

'Decide!' Grandsailles raged, succeeding this time in seizing the whip and bending it in two.

'What's wrong?' asked d'Orminy, proud of the tumult that at last seemed to sweep over the Count, awakening him from his apparent apathy. 'Why, naturally nothing is decided,' d'Orminy went on in a tone of impatience. 'In 1918 Marshal Pétain stopped the Germans on the Somme, this time he has stopped them in Paris!'

'Enough joking, please!' said Grandsailles, giving him back the whip broken in two.

D'Orminy deposited it on the marble mantelpiece and, having removed the pearl pin from his tie, tried now to put it back exactly in the centre, biting his tongue in his concentrated attention. Grandsailles took the Prince by the arm, though he was careful not to distract him while he was engaged in this operation, and waited as he observed his performance in the mirror. When the pin was finally in place Grandsailles said, 'It's true that we have the fleet… and the colonial army. Weygand, Noguès…. What will Darlan do?'

'He's an opportunist,' said d'Orminy, 'but he has a rôle to play….'

'So have we,' Grandsailles concluded in a low voice.

Grandsailles had already headed toward the outside door and was waiting for d'Orminy, his glance resolute behind a film of emotion. Before taking leave of each other, the two friends kissed each other on both cheeks with unexpected force, driving their nails into each other's shoulders in a brief clasp as they agreed to meet in Africa.

That same evening, which was the first in Paris under German occupation, Grandsailles had a rendezvous at half-past six with Solange de Cléda at her house on Rue de Babylone. And as everything in this world, even the hours of circumstances, can be extended and repeated, everything except death, whose hour is rigidly fixed, Solange once more was ready for this visit of Grandsailles which she had been waiting for since the beginning of the war – nearly a year!

Through what emotions had her heart not passed, between the extremes of rebellion and suppliant tenderness! In the fragile condition which is that of lovers, how had the pure, warm egg of her generosity of soul not yet broken? If even the promptest relief seems too long delayed for the one who needs it, what an eternity it must have seemed before that which Solange was waiting for materialized! All she wanted was to have her love reciprocated. She was ready to ask his forgiveness with all her heart, no longer summoning her arrogant pride to her own defence, tyrannically submissive, belittled in every way? She could be oppressed, insulted, yes! provided Grandsailles did not find her ungrateful for all the benefits which his mere esteem could procure her. Solange, poor dupe, held no other grudges against her despot than those that were independent of his will – the excessively long time she had had to wait for this meeting through the fault of circumstances which the war had imposed. In the depth of her gratitude Solange went so far as to thank destiny once more for having tortured her thus in the interminable agony of her waiting, for nothing is too late at the moment when it occurs, and now at least their chances of reconciliation were assured by her total renunciation of all the residues of dignity and pride which had still animated her at the time of their last frustrated meeting and which might now have compromised her chances of success. At present she would know how to silence the protests of her human self-respect and trample it underfoot! No more levels, no more defence – a woman who gives herself, more beautiful than before, more pure in her intentions! With what eloquence she would now be able to beg him for mercy, with what prodigality of gradations her sincere regret would enhance each of her syllables, soothing to sweetness the last suspicions of Grandsailles' rancour. She had accumulated so much passion and tenderness for this single moment....

When Grandsailles rang the downstairs doorbell, Solange could not restrain her eagerness. She rushed out to the landing, stood there, tightly holding with her two hands the crystal ball that adorned the top of the ebony banister. Breathlessly she listened to the Count's footsteps as he began climbing the stairs with his swinging gait, that had the regular rhythm of a limping pendulum. It would take him at least a minute or two to reach the second storey, before his figure appeared against that last turn of the wall in greenish and shiny imitation marble on whose wavelike pattern Solange kept her eyes fixed. Standing thus, in the dim electric light that bathed this spot, her expectant figure resembled that of a chimera, a celestial Madonna's face attached to the equivocal, full-curved and half-animal body of a sphinx.

Grandsailles appeared, dressed in the uniform of a cavalry captain. Seeming not to notice Solange's presence, he continued to climb with the same pace till he reached the step below the landing where she stood. There he stopped. Solange had controlled an impulse to go toward him, and seeing that Grandsailles refused any friendly gesture, she drew back, making herself slimmer as she flattened herself against the wall next to the door, as if to invite him to lead the way across the threshold of her apartment.

'Madame,' said Grandsailles without moving, as if glued to the spot, 'our notary Pierre Girardin tells me that you claim that a five-minute interview would be all you needed to clear up our supposed misunderstanding. I am here to prove the contrary. You can't find a single word to justify yourself.... You have tried to force me to marry you,' cried Grandsailles. Then he added calmly, 'Tomorrow evening I am leaving for Africa.'

Solange's lips trembled several times as if she were about to speak, but she remained silent, while by an infinitely sweet shaking of her head she expressed, as no words could have done, all the injustice and the fatality of her unhappiness. Perhaps if Grandsailles had seen her expression at this moment.... But he was no longer looking at her. His eyes had alighted on the silhouette of his own shadow projected on the opposite wall and he was waiting only for the five minutes to pass. All the arguments, all the entreaties, all the ardent words that Solange had repeated to herself, day after day, were there hovering on her lips, but she said nothing. What was the use? Grandsailles turned his back and started down the sairs. At this moment Solange took a step toward him.... Grandsailles stopped short for a moment. Solange, clutching the ebony banister, waiting for the impossible, could barely hold herself upright.

'Take good care of yourself!' was all she said.

When Grandsailles had gone, Solange remained for a long time in the same position, her eyes fixed on the green imitation marble wall above that last turn of the stairway in front of which the Count had passed before he disappeared from sight. Solange de Cléda's face seemed to have become serene, but if at this moment someone had had the curiosity to draw near and look between her half-shut eyelids he would probably have been terrified to observe that they were without sight and that in the slits between her lashes, instead of fixed pupils, only the whites were visible. And it is in the whites of these eyes, smooth as those of blind statues, that Salvador Dali's imagination wishes to engrave, and thereby immortalize them at the end of this chapter, the Latin word, 'NIHIL', which means 'NOTHING'.

5

War and Transfiguration

O N ARRIVING at d'Orminy's villa near Casablanca and con-
templating the immense square of its whitewashed façade,
Cécile Goudreau had said, 'You can't tell whether it's the house that
makes the most of the moonlight or the moonlight that makes the
most of the house, so sweet does the jasmine smell here!' She had
taken a deep breath. It was in these fragrant and limpid moonlit
nights at the beginning of the North African November that the
most subtle and paradoxical villainies of the most dramatic shufflings
of contemporary politics were to struggle, unfold and be decided.
In these latitudes politics itself had entered a lunar phase, a phase
of shadows, of penumbrae and of fulgurations in which it became
difficult not to confuse the true sharp light of a friendly face with the
wan reflection of a spy's or a traitor's, so fierce and united were loyalty,
courage and treason, like Seraphis, worshipped by the Egyptians,
with its single animal head with three snarling mouths – dog, lion
and wolf – surrounded by the seductive serpent of opportuneness: all
in bright, solid gold, crowning a solitary trophy planted in the heart
of the desert and projecting an elongated and melancholy shadow
that vanished on the confines of the sand, which was parched and
avid of the new blood of history.

At the beginnings of this African 'intermezzo' everything became
ambivalent – difficult and easy, with nothing impossible. Merely to
be able to move one's little finger it was actually necessary to get
all the wrangling and conflicting powers in the world, if not into

agreement, at least compliant and tolerant of this little movement. But for anyone capable of manoeuvring with astuteness, suppleness and Machiavellianism this whole network, this complicated intrigue, this struggle of apparently irreducible imponderables could on the contrary be transformed into a favourable mechanism, and then the play of contradictory and simultaneous interests could become a powerful, formidable and secret master-lever, capable like that of Archimedes of moving the world by merely applying to it the pressure of a single little finger. But this required a special man, inflexible and fanatical in his decisions, suspicious of everything, trusting no one, possessing the science of provocation, as capable of concealing the ever-precise motives of his actions as the vague ones of his sympathies, and combining with the flashes of his anger the distant fog of an effaced and superlative elegance. This man was Count Hervé de Grandsailles, or at least he believed himself to be he, inasmuch as for a short time he really was. But if Grandsailles possessed to a superlative degree most of the faculties required to play an important rôle in this North Africa of the end of 1941, he lacked one, that must have been as important as the others – sympathy. Grandsailles succeeded in imposing himself, but his lack of sympathy immediately caused the objectives of his successes, too quickly attained, to crumble.

Grandsailles reached North Africa at the beginning of the month of November, and he immediately established his headquarters on the Prince of Orminy's three-masted yacht which was anchored in a small bay off-shore.

'It looks damned official!' Cécile Goudreau had exclaimed on seeing from the window of her room the outlines of two marines whom Grandsailles had obtained to mount guard on the bridge. Below deck the Canoness of Launay had succeeded in finding an adequate place for each of the Count's habits, setting up all his familiar objects in an order that to all appearances was the same as they had occupied at the Château de Lamotte or the house in the chestnut grove of the Bois de Boulogne, love philtres included. And just as in Libreux she might often have been seen of an afternoon surrounded by three or four peasants with one knee to the ground, their arms crossed on a woven basket, holding a piece of rough bread, reminding one of a Le Nain painting, so now it was common to see her in the winter sun with a newspaper on her head, surrounded by three Arabs squatting on their haunches, who came every day bringing provisions, reminding one of a Fortuny painting. But if the canoness always reminded one of a painting, the Count always reminded one of a third act, and while in Paris it was more or less Racinian, in Africa the curtain was about to rise on an astounding melodrama.

Since his arrival in Africa, the Count of Grandsailles seemed to have grown younger; his movements now were light and quick, and his limp had developed a special agility in getting in and out of the landing yawl, in going up and down the white marble steps to d'Orminy's house, barely grazing them with his spurred heels glistening with nickel, almost on tiptoe. He had grown thinner, and ate frugally. His outbursts of anger were lashing and brief, like the crack of a whip, and his expression was consumed by the fire of ambition. He appeared only in the evenings to dine in the company of Cécile Goudreau and d'Orminy, and at about eleven the latter would often accompany him back to the yacht where the two friends, the one in uniform, the other in mufti, would remain till three in the morning in deep conspiracy. This was also the time habitually reserved for rather shady visitors. D'Orminy, whose knowledge of law was far superior to the Count's, which was nearly non-existent, would help the Count to untangle and solve the complicated questions which he suddenly saw himself faced with and of which he had almost no understanding. And always the same scene would be re-enacted.

'I don't need to find out about the laws!' Grandsailles would bellow, 'I know everything! I have three thousand years of experience, I'm as old as the world!'

D'Orminy would burst into a yellow laugh with his yellow teeth, and before going off to bed would leave all the files in good order, laid out on the Count's table, ready for the latter to use the next morning to develop his plans. It is true that the use which Grandsailles made of all these documents the following morning was odd and unexpected most of the time. For according to him, and to use his own words, 'There was not a single law in the world which in the hands of a "real character" could not be used, without distorting it, for ends exactly contrary to those for which it had been created.' This essentially Jesuitical faculty that was peculiar to him for transforming all things, even the most adverse, to his own taste and use, Grandsailles called the 'touch of grace', the 'Machiavelli talisman'. And the latter's smile, which he considered the keenest of which man was capable, prevented him in his moments of success from registering his pleasure and enabled his set face to remain serious.

Grandsailles had been sent by Vichy on a special mission to negotiate an increase in imports from North Africa, especially of sugar and cotton: in this matter the backing of M. Edouard Cordier, who had remained in France, was inestimable, enabling him forthwith to represent the majority of the most powerful French industrialists, both morally and materially. All this endowed his person with a sudden importance in realms which he could never have suspected, but he valued his new power only as a means of carrying on his political intrigues more effectively. The moment came when, in order both to succeed in the mission which served as a front and to continue his more occult ones, circumstances made it necessary for him to go to Malta. The Count could barely contain his fury when d'Orminy began to list the insurmountable difficulties that seemed to lie in the way of this voyage.

'First of all,' said d'Orminy, 'there's the question of how to get there; you'll have to find a plane, and pilots....'

'*You* can take me,' Grandsailles broke in, slightly drawing back his face as if to avoid the Prince's bad-smelling breath, trying at the same time by this movement to arouse d'Orminy's acute sense of inferiority. He continued severely, 'Otherwise what's the use of your having been a pilot for ten years, and having a lieutenant's rank?'

'I'm no longer in the active service. My plane isn't at my disposal any longer,' d'Orminy replied.

'You still have your uniform?' asked Grandsailles.

'We'll look into all that later, but I don't think I'll be able to fly you.' As he spoke d'Orminy had been backing away from the Count and had seated himself with difficulty, as if in acute pain, behind the other's desk.

'The weather is good,' said Grandsailles, who had gone over to the cabin porthole, his face lighted by the moon. His hair, just beginning to turn grey, was silvered by its rays.

'I just had a glimpse of you as you will be when you are old,' said d'Orminy, looking at him with kindliness. 'You will hardly change, and only for the better.'

Grandsailles did not answer. He was thinking, 'I'll let you admire me for another few moments, after which I will insult you. You're just in the right frame of mind, exceptionally affectionate and devoted. You're feeling sorry for yourself, thinking you're going to die soon and imagining me surviving everything; you're even getting sentimental. So this is the moment to pounce on you mercilessly to revive your spirit of action, shake you to the depths, wind up all the springs of your energy so that your entire fund of resources will drop on all fours at my feet and you will flatten yourself out before my desires – flat as a carpet.' Then, imagining d'Orminy turned into a flying carpet taking him to Malta, he could not repress a smile, but turning it immediately into one of contempt, he broke his long silence and said in a hard tone.

'A truly courageous spirit would not in the present circumstances indulge in the kind of personal reflections that are passing through your head at this moment. Your suicide complex is of no interest to history. When you spoke, just now, of my old age you were only thinking of yourself. I esteem you, but your death will leave me indifferent. It will at least spare me having to listen to your foul-smelling secrets. I don't know if anyone has ever told you: you ought to have your teeth looked after.'

D'Orminy got up and left.

'Good,' said Grandsailles to himself, 'he'll go and weep over all this, like a child, with Cécile Goudreau. But I've got to catch up with him before he starts smoking opium.'

His teeth, dazzling white like gardenias, glistened in the moonlight, and he thought, 'Perhaps I went a little too far, but I can soften it in my letter.' He sat down at his desk and wrote at one stroke:

'My dear Prince: I deeply regret my insolence of a while ago. Few people can doubt your moral courage and your patriotic devotion less than I. I was unjust, but when you learn how important it is for me to get to Malta, it will explain the state of my nerves better than my excuses. I expect you immediately. Time presses, and for this I invoke only the friendship of your
                                        Hervé de Grandsailles.'

When the Prince of Orminy returned he coldly kissed the Count's cheek and once more sat down. The latter was disconcerted for a moment, for in observing d'Orminy on the sly he clearly saw by his eyes that, contrary to his expectation, he had not been weeping. However, the Prince's mood in spite of his attitude of reserve seemed as favourable as could be wished since it was he who immediately began to speak of Malta.

'I don't at all want to discourage you,' he said, 'but in order to succeed you will need the tacit or explicit permission of five countries; all must be and will be informed of your departure; all are more or less on a war footing if not actually at war; your mission must not be looked upon too unfavourably by any of them!'

'Not only that,' said Grandsailles, enjoying the complexity of the case, 'my mission will require everyone's collaboration.... Do you know what constitutes a statesman's strength? It's just the opposite of what people believe: instead of dividing further those who are already his enemies, he must unite them in some kind of collaboration. Two enemies whom you force to shake hands to come and attack you are defeated at the very outset, their collaboration will reduce them to impotence. But let's stop, for today, losing ourselves in speculations on the theory of action,' he concluded with a sigh.

'I am merely listening to you and submitting to the severe principles of your political action,' said d'Orminy indulgently.

'Then will you take some notes? I shall dictate to you the line to be adopted with the various powers, and afterwards we shall see who are the individuals best qualified to communicate my aims to them, whether officially or confidentially.'

D'Orminy unfolded a list which he had been fingering. 'I'll note everything on this list,' he said. 'Here – in the case of the British you'll have to deal with the Board of Economic Warfare.'

'You know that I am becoming pro-British and that they are the only ones who know it.'

'That goes without saying,' d'Orminy commented, and as

Grandsailles eyed him dubiously he added. 'You know that I feel exactly as you do about them.'

'How will the British react to this?'

'They'll let the Americans have their own way,' said the Prince.

'And what American agency might be expected to intervene?' asked Grandsailles.

'The State Department, and the American observers in North Africa.'

'Nothing could be simpler,' said Grandsailles then. 'America needs its observers in order to observe, and needs to observe in order to have its observers. So I'm going to provide them with a magnificent opportunity to observe and solve the Grandsailles case, a real test case by which they will be able to orient their future policies.'

'If they are interested in observing, they'll find nothing better than you,' said d'Orminy.

'The line for us to follow on this will offer no great difficulty,' Grandsailles went on, pretending not to have heard. 'Someone will have to undertake to announce the "secret" of my voyage to Malta in large, screaming headlines, as for a Broadway play,' and as d'Orminy went through the motions of making note of this Grandsailles stopped him, saying. 'Don't put any of that down – just the word: "theatre".'

'Comedian,' said d'Orminy.

The way in which the Prince uttered this word gave Grandsailles a start. Then d'Orminy continued, bitter and detached; 'You think that when you insulted me a while ago I didn't understand you were purposely putting on a comedy to make sure of keeping me here till four o'clock so that I would start running errands the first thing in the morning to arrange your trip to Malta for you? I know you too well by now! And it's a funny thing! No matter how hateful you make yourself, you still remain just as fascinating. You see, I'm not afraid to talk to you as your mistresses do. But you can't treat me like one of your mistresses without running the risk of making me your enemy.'

Grandsailles did not answer, realizing by d'Orminy's uncompromising tone that this time a quarrel might become irreparable. The Prince was immediately grateful to him for this.

'You see,' he said, 'though you haven't succeeded in deceiving me, you have at least succeeded in two things, one of which was what you wanted, and the other is a matter of indifference to you. The first – since you know that everything you wish must be realized – is to have won again my unconditional support for your plans; the second is that you have hurt me deeply.... How the smell of death has clung to me ever since I was a child!'

Grandsailles put his hand on d'Orminy's shoulder, and from the captain's star on his sleeve a gold thread hung quivering. D'Orminy removed his hand, and in a changed tone of voice returned to the subject of the future mission to Malta.

'With the Germans,' he said, 'we'll have to deal with the armistice committee.'

Grandsailles began to pace the cabin. 'It's simple with the Germans. They'll have to speculate on the necessity of strengthening the Pétain government.'

'And on the urgency of preventing an Arab revolt,' d'Orminy added.

'Yes, that's very important. I believe I have at my disposal the means of fomenting a small Arab revolt that we can control. I'm seeing Broussillon, the communist professor, tomorrow evening....'

'The Arabs won't move yet,' said d'Orminy.

'I say, a "small revolt". Broussillon has promised to provoke disorders in the Tunis markets the day I need them....'

'But besides the Germans, we also have the French to contend with; in their case we have to deal with the embassy, and the North African authorities.'

'You know,' said Grandsailles, 'it seems a paradox, but France is going to be the hardest. How am I going to convince them that I have to attend actively to the mission with which they have entrusted me in order to carry it out? That is in fact much too simple! And the Spaniards?'

'I'll take care of them,' said the Prince, 'I'm on the best of terms with them, and we have only to invoke a single word – "order"....'

'So you see,' said Grandsailles by way of summary, 'we're going to be able to present my mission in such a way that all the powers will in the last analysis be favourably disposed to it, while pretending to be not too well informed of my activities.' He fell into a meditative silence, then said, 'War, in the last analysis, is a state of things in which all parties are in agreement except that they fight, while peace is one in which they all disagree, but don't fight. The two are merely different phases of political life. And what have I done with my comb? I must have left it at your house – I had it last night!'

As he became progressively beset by difficulties, Grandsailles grew more and more capricious, like a pregnant woman, and now his repressed anger of a while ago in his conversation with the Prince seemed about to burst, judging by the hatred with which his eyes were injected.

'I can endure anything,' he continued in a rage, 'I can get along without the most essential things, but I *have* to be able to part my hair in an absolutely straight line with a metal comb!'

'A cold one,' said d'Orminy, smiling at him as though he were a child having tantrums. Grandsailles calmed himself.

'It's true though,' he added, 'with my hair mathematically in place and my shoes polished twice a day – with those two rituals attended to, it's as if all the stains of doubt and remorse are washed away and banished from my soul, and I feel myself again pure and worthy of communicating with action.'

'And the worst of it is,' said d'Orminy, getting up to retire, 'that what you're saying is true. Don't forget that tomorrow morning I'm arranging your interview with your new victim – Monsieur Fouseret.'

The following morning, while he began with a few telephone calls to lay the groundwork for his mission *for* Vichy, the Count of Grandsailles with equal zeal and no less actively was initiating the necessary subterranean negotiations that were to guarantee him the success of the second and chief objective of his trip to Malta: namely, that of plotting against Vichy, in pursuance of the revolutionary activity he had undertaken before leaving Paris, whose goal was to organize the future forces of resistance against the invader. Thus on the one hand he was trying to enhance his official prestige in the eyes of those who had confided this mission to him, bending every effort to crown it with a personal triumph; on the other hand, he was preparing to wage a merciless war against the very ones he was serving, thus betraying his hierarchical superiors, who had placed their confidence and their hope in his devotion. To succeed in his mission for Vichy, the Prince of Orminy's personal and unconditional aid would be about all he needed. The Prince, whose political position was close to the centre, had in fact a great influence in the most diverse official spheres, and could consider all doors open to him. But in order to dominate the situation in his new rôle as apprentice-conspirator, it was indispensable for him to establish contact with the extremes, that is to say, with the royalists on the one hand and the communists on the other. How was he to win simultaneously the support of both? This had been his almost exclusive concern for the last two weeks.

On one side Grandsailles had feigned a vague interest in a royalist plot in order to obtain the confidence of Fouseret, a very active royalist and a man of talent who was trying to create in North Africa a policy of direct understanding with England and America. At the same time the Count had made contact with the communist professor. Broussillon, who reportedly had maintained contact with the thirty communist deputies imprisoned in Paris and who knew all the devious paths of illegality. When Grandsailles felt he had gained sufficient ascendancy over Fouseret and Broussillon, he decided to resort to the same tactic with them that he had used the previous day with d'Orminy: suddenly to lose his temper and break with them. More naive than the Prince, and wholly unfamiliar with the Count's character, they would inevitably be taken in by his trick. Feeling that the moment for gaining his victims' confidence was ripe, Grandsailles calculated with staggering precision and utter disingenuousness the moment when he would make a show of anger.

'With Fouseret,' he said to himself. 'I'll get into a rage the first time he utters the words "à tantôt"; as for Broussillon, I'll politely show him the door the moment he utters the word "sabotage".'

Everything happened exactly as Grandsailles had foreseen. After the fear of a possible denunciation had robbed them both of sleep the aim of his stratagem was simple: to provoke Fouseret and Broussillon to join forces, as they inevitably would, in a conspiracy against himself, their common enemy; then stop this conspiracy at the opportune moment by becoming reconciled with his two enemies who, being mutual enemies, would from then on be bound and gagged by their own commitments. Thus Fouseret would live in the fear of being subsequently betrayed by Broussillon, and Broussillon, likewise, of being betrayed by Fouseret. Knowing their common secret, he could keep them both attached to himself, could manipulate them at will, stimulating their passions, exciting their ambitions, and make them simultaneously his involuntary accomplices, harnessed to the Machiavellian chariot of his plans.

'No, it's not so smart as all that!' said Grandsailles to himself, reflecting on his plan, 'but that's the way I've always managed to swim, and at the same time keep my clothes.'

The Prince of Orminy had indeed spoken the truth: Grandsailles' methods of political action scarcely differed from those he had so often used when confronted by the rivalry of his mistresses. Provoking a confidence of common jealousy and preferably even of hatred between two of them always assured his ascendancy over both. Fouseret and Broussillon were going to behave toward each other and toward him like two jealous mistresses! When Grandsailles felt that the union between Fouseret and Broussillon against himself was ripe he arranged to see the two of them separately the same day.

One of the marines introduced Monsieur Fouseret into the Count's cabin for the premeditated scene of reconciliation. Fouseret entered, bowed with respect and Grandsailles, getting up, gave him a military salute and gestured for him to sit down.

Fouseret was one of those men with misplaced cheeks on whose irregular geographic contours a celluloid red reached down almost over the jaws, while the cheek-bones, to which this colour belonged, were very pale. The excitement of the moment had exaggerated the effect of this contrast even further, the purple-streaked blotches on his face standing out sharply, while the upper cheeks, from which all the blood had drained, were such a livid yellow that it was as though one saw right through to the bone. He was dressed in a white suit, with a blue shirt, and his hair was red. Just as one could tell that he was intelligent, quick and bold, by the three wrinkles, deep as converging arrows, pointed at the outer corners of his eyes from each temple, so his somewhat flattened face, as if pressed against a pane of glass, was marked by that stamp of symmetry which makes the facial morphology of those predestined to a violent death so characteristically unmistakable.

Fouseret's scrutinizing and perspicacious air caused Grandsailles to be intimidated for a moment or two and put him on his guard. He said to himself, 'Let's be careful – he is a bird of prey!' This obliged him to make an effort, to surpass himself, and his handling of the situation was in truth masterful. First the Count sat down again, pressing his hands hard against his eyelids, then wiping his eyes with his handkerchief, he let his now haggard gaze roam over the horizon through the half-open door.

'I have been thinking things over,' said Grandsailles. 'I believe in your loyalty. After our last interview I could have had you arrested. Though I have not done this, your plans nevertheless continue to depend on my discretion, on which you have no reason to count. After our scene you might have tried to get rid of me, to plot against me. I have proof that you refrained from doing this. Otherwise you would not be here.' He smiled, then continued, 'Now you have nothing more to fear – on the contrary. France's situation has become aggravated, and I have had to revise certain legal notions which have been rooted in my mind for centuries.' At this point he uttered a sigh and said, as if painfully wrenching this confession from himself, 'Well, let me put it in this way: I don't approve, but neither do I any longer condemn political acts of violence!' As he said this he held out his hand to Fouseret. The latter accepted it, pressing his lips tightly together, and when he parted them they were white as a sheet of paper. 'France,' he said dramatically, 'will always be grateful to you for this.'

Grandsailles continued now in a calmer and more distant tone, 'I shall never participate directly in plots of this kind, however.... But I shall know how to shut my eyes to everything.' Then he suddenly assumed the tone of one who gives orders. 'In exchange I need you to accompany me to Malta. You will travel with me in the capacity

of secretary. In the meantime you must obtain the secret support of
your party for certain negotiations with the British. Tomorrow you
will be informed of the time of our departure.' Fouseret had become
glued to the wall, as if overwhelmed by the avalanche of the Count's
demands, which he felt he could not refuse....

'I have a panicky horror of flying.... It's pathological with me!'
Fouseret pleaded, his forehead beaded with perspiration.

'Let's not go into questions of personal taste. You may not like to
fly, but you also know that I for my part have no consuming urge to
crawl over the more or less criminal terrain of political assassination.'

'So much for the King's mail!' said Grandsailles to himself on
seeing Fouseret depart at last, his white suit standing out against
the blue sky, his two rigid arms held out a little from his body, symmetrically... like a heraldic fleur-de-lis.

Toward the end of the afternoon of the same day the cloud-
covered sky turned scarlet. 'Red sky – rain or wind,' the canoness
had said, bringing the Count a steaming cup of very thick chocolate.
Grandsailles, who was waiting for Broussillon, burned his tongue on
the boiling chocolate, and the falling of the barometer indicating the
approaching storm made him press his fist hard against his cheek to
control the pricking sensation in his old scar.

At exactly the appointed hour, Broussillon was admitted by the
marine. He rushed straight over to the Count, fell dramatically on his
knees, and with tears in his eyes begged him to intervene in behalf
of two communist students who had just been sentenced to death.

Broussillon was one of those shady characters who are to be
found on the fringe of every revolutionary movement. Undisciplined,
unscrupulous, vindictive, an irrepressible anarchist at heart, he had
become isolated from the membership of the party and had long
been on the verge of expulsion. Having lost all standing with the
leadership he had become the rallying point of a dissident group, and

he maintained a shadow of authority only by virtue of the confusion of the times. If he had been able so easily to misrepresent himself to Grandsailles as a responsible communist it was because Broussillon was the very incarnation of all his aristocrat's preconceptions.

Broussillon had a large, slightly monstrous head all full of bumps like a sack of potatoes. His weather-beaten skin was woven of coarse epidermis and his deep pores looked as though they were enlarged under a magnifying glass; the hair on his head, as well as the hard, greyish hairs of his beard, his moustache, his nose and his ears, grew rampant, and it was exactly as if the potatoes with which this face seemed to be filled were suddenly bristling with hard brush-hairs, and these hairs stuck out through the thick sack of his skin in all directions. Very delicate gold-rimmed glasses, and hands that were even more delicate, almost feminine, corrected his simian and hirsute appearance, imparting to him a servile, almost decadent character that betrayed every intellectual vice.

On his knees and with head bowed, he waited for the Count's answer. Grandsailles cautiously took a little sip of chocolate. Then in a blasé and inflexible tone of voice he said, 'Get up! I grant nothing by such means. Your supplications embarrass me. You're not a rag, you have backbone, and if I sent for you it was with a view to loyal collaboration. I regret to have to tell you that I need you just at the moment when you find yourself in this posture.'

Broussillon, stupefied, got to his feet.

'France's situation has become aggravated,' the Count went on, in the same tone in which he had spoken these same words to Fouseret that morning. Then he exclaimed, 'The hours are pressing and are becoming those of action! Yes! A hundred times, yes! Now I no longer shrink before the word "sabotage" which aroused my indignation and which caused our falling-out.' As he said these words he held out his hand to Broussillon, who seized it with a sincere and deep emotion, and just barely repressed an impulse to throw himself once more on his knees at the Count's feet.

'Let us speak quickly now. I have only fifteen minutes to give you,' said Grandsailles. Without sitting down, to avoid Broussillon's doing so, and in order to keep any sense of intimacy out of their conversation, which he immediately brought round to the strict terms of transactions, he continued, 'Today you need have no fear of asking me for what you hinted at in our last interview. It is granted in advance. In exchange all I want is an Arab revolt within forty-eight hours.'

'You shall have your Arab revolt,' said Broussillon simply, 'but it may cost the lives of several communists here, therefore I shall have to ask you for the name of some person in France who will answer for your word in all circumstances and to the last consequences.'

Grandsailles instantly thought of Pierre Girardin, but hesitated a few seconds. He knew that this Broussillon who just now had grovelled before him to implore pity for two lives was explicitly demanding a life in token of his good faith. The Arab revolt was too dear: he loved Girardin too much!

'Tell me first something about this. I do have in France devoted people who are willing to give their lives to obey my orders, but not slaves whom I could hand over to communist reprisals in case the mission with which they were entrusted should fail, or even if they should commit serious errors in carrying it out. You will have to accept without question the honourableness of the person I name.'

'That's understood,' answered Broussillon a little reluctantly, and added, 'You know about the vast plan for the industrialization of Libreux, which was put into execution immediately after the government had decided on the decentralization of the war industries?'

'I have been indirectly informed of this matter, though I have not actually gone back to my Libreux properties since the beginning of the war,' said Grandsailles, 'but I have followed all this via London, for it was the British who developed all those industrialization plans.'

'We need those plans!' said Broussillon. 'If we could successfully blow up the three inner dams on which all the electric power depends, we would have performed an act of historic sabotage.'

There was a long silence. 'Historic sabotage!' the Count thought to himself, 'what a degradation of a whole epoch!' The word 'sabotage' appeared to him almost as ugly and repulsive as the word 'broadcast', which he detested most of all those that had sprung up in the modern epoch. But suddenly this odious word, now destined to cleanse his beloved plain of the mechanical vermin of industrialization, sounded in his vindictive ears as a clarion-call of redemption. For the height of dishonour was that this vermin of progress now flourished in the hands of the invader. Sabotage! He visualized all the conglomerate ignoble matter of the five factories – cement, rubber, tripes of cables, skeletons of rails, whirls of wheels and constipations of cast-iron blown up in the flash of a single dynamite explosion. Sabotage! And at last the myrtles and honeysuckle might grow again on the spot where they had bloomed for three thousand years, healing over the scars in the mutilated earth with their perennial greenness. Sabotage! And the snails might again slowly glide over the backs of the same stones, that had remained in the same place since the period of the Romans!

Girardin now appeared to him as the man chosen by destiny, for not only did he possess all the necessary information but also, in obedience to his orders, he had succeeded in hiding in the Count's family vault the copies and duplicates of the plans for the industrialization of Libreux when the Germans had ordered all existing documents on this subject to be handed over to the occupation authorities on pain of death. Thus it was his notary, Pierre Girardin, one of the most traditionally conservative spirits of France, who was designated to carry out one of the most sensational acts of sabotage in this period of heroic resistance against the invader which was already beginning obscurely to germinate.

'I know the person who has a copy of all those plans in his possession,' said the Count at last, emerging from his meditation, 'and this person will deliver them according to my instructions. No!' cried Grandsailles, anticipating the request Broussillon was about to make, 'we shall speak again of your sabotage on my return from Malta. By then I expect the Arab revolt which you promised me to have shed all its blood, including the repression. As for me, I want no traces to remain. You have ten days in all!'

When Broussillon had left, Grandsailles remained for a moment leaning against the bulkhead, reviewing in his mind the results of the day's activities. He had just been handed a message from the Prince of Orminy in which the latter gave a detailed account of the day's progress, except in the matter of the piloting of the plane to Malta. For his part the Count had fully succeeded in his dark aims, and now felt that Fouseret and Broussillon were irrevocably committed to his hazardous plan. They had been so weak that they fully deserved, if need be, to be destroyed, sacrificed by 'all that'. Then he thought tenderly of Girardin. He saw him standing, at a great distance, in the courtyard of the Château de Lamotte, his bald head shining in the sun like a billiard ball. But it was tiny, the size of a vitamin-pill, like one of those melancholy pictures that one sees by looking through the wrong end of opera glasses…. 'I wouldn't want the Germans to shoot him for anything in the world,' he said to himself with a sigh. Then he visualized, like rows of Christ-figures in polished ivory, the decayed and uneven teeth of the Prince of Orminy whom he had so mistreated the previous evening – now unconditionally devoted to him.

Grandsailles tried to sum up his combined visions in a general feeling of pity, but failing to exalt his spirit in this way he felt instead an irrepressible thrill of joy run through his body and, reflecting pessimistically that man's love of power is limitless, he realized that he was hungry as a wolf. He had himself rowed ashore to go and dine in the company of Cécile Goudreau and the Prince of Orminy. Cécile Goudreau immediately struck him as reticent, and he was confirmed in his suspicion that she was upset by the tone in which she said, 'We can sit down to dinner. D'Orminy is not joining us.'

'What's going on?' asked Grandsailles.

'He has been working for you the whole blessed day. He is worn out.... But the worst of it is that he has also made his last flight: he has definitely been forbidden to fly.... You understand,' Goudreau went on, trying to soften her severe, almost spiteful tone by blending a little humour with it, 'you understand, the kind of life d'Orminy has always led, all his excesses – and especially his fondness for sport – there is nothing worse for the health. Polo, aviation, all those things are bound to ruin the constitution in the long run and affect the heart. Fortunately opium has helped to preserve him! He has had a kind of attack.'

'Idiot,' growled Grandsailles, who was no longer listening to Goudreau and was on the point of exploding. 'Who made him fly today? He knew well enough that I need him just now, every second, that my mission to Malta depends to a large extent on his activity!'

'Well, my dear,' Goudreau broke out full of indignation, crumpling her napkin and neglecting to eat, 'it's precisely for you that he flew, and he has just suffered the greatest disappointment in his life, for he had his heart set on piloting the plane that was to take you to Malta!' Goudreau looked Grandsailles straight in the eye. 'The war is making you terribly blind and ungrateful to those who are devoted to you,' she said in a tone of bitter reproach. 'You'll see, you'll see – you'll realize it when we have gone.'

'You're leaving with d'Orminy for America? That's it, isn't it? Why did you hide it from me? I should have guessed it!' said Grandsailles.

He did not frown and his voice had become indulgent, tinged with a melancholy contempt.

'Yes, my dear, d'Orminy is taking me with him to America in nine days. We are not people of action, and we would rather live in a friendly country than under a regime that becomes more like the invader's every day and where even conspiracy rubs elbows with treason and often becomes indistiguishable from it. What they have just done against the Jews is unspeakable! So you will be able to stay here, surrounded solely by your enemies, and expend on them all your gratifying precautions and your psychological subtleties!'

Grandsailles, who had rapidly devoured a broiled lobster, rose coldly from the table without waiting for Cécile Goudreau to finish and, considering his meal ended, was preparing to leave. 'I apologize,' he said, 'for leaving in this way, and I'm sorry you saw fit to start this unpleasantness, the first we have had.'

Cécile Goudreau in turn got up from the table. 'It's not for my own sake,' she said furiously, 'that I started this unpleasantness, it's because of the Prince. I know he's weak, and he is wrong not to rap the fingers of your despotism instead of staying upstairs weeping. But you've been merciless to him, and the way you have humiliated him is inhuman. Did you imagine the cruelty you showed him yesterday afternoon would be a treat to my cynicism?'

'Why did he have to come and cry to you about it?' Grandsailles asked, with a condescending sigh.

'He didn't cry yesterday, my dear, when you insulted him. That's what you would have liked. He is crying now that he knows he can't be of service to you! And he hasn't told me a thing, do you understand? He only said to me – and with what dignity – "Grandsailles just sent me away and told me that he won't be at all sorry the day I die, that my breath stinks, and that when I do die he won't have to listen to my foul secrets any longer!" And he just stood there without adding a single comment, up to the moment when you sent for him.'

'Let's forget that,' said Grandsailles after a brief silence; then in a tone of great gentleness, and holding out his hand, 'Come here, kiss this despot's fingers!'

Cécile Goudreau went up to him and Grandsailles kissed her demonstratively on the forehead. 'I am going with you to America. This was a part of my plans. But before this I must at all costs succeed in my Malta venture…. It's not my cruelty, it's Malta that cries out within me! If you knew how important this is for France!'

In his nervousness the Count put his hand to his hair to smooth down some strands that had been slightly mussed as he embraced Cécile Goudreau.

'Well,' she said, 'you'll have your comb. We found it and had it brought to your canoness. And you'll also have Malta. Once more, your Cécile is going to arrange things for you. I have to hurry. In an hour I have an appointment with a hero; that's just what you need at this moment, your gold comb and a man who, without knowing you, is willing to risk his life for you.'

'You're both admirable and terrifying, to know me as well as you do,' said Grandsailles.

'Did you ever hear of the American aviator nicknamed "Baba" in Paris?' asked Cécile.

'Baba,' said Grandsailles, exploring his memory, '… no.'

'Well, he is the one I have to convince, and get him to say yes this very evening,' said Cécile, winding a native turban round her head.

'I think I remember now.' said Grandsailles. 'There was a lot of talk about a helmet he had to wear for more than a year to reset his skull. Is he really well again?'

'Completely,' said Goudreau. 'The last time I saw him without his helmet, at Madame Ménard d'Orient's, just before coming here, you could hardly see any traces of his accident. Don't worry, he's the man for you.'

Thus Cécile Goudreau came to play an important rôle in this shady and dramatic conspiracy of Malta, by finding the exceptional being who would lend himself to this adventure and bring the Count of Grandsailles to the island. Baba, who knew the latter by his dazzling reputation as a social figure, was immediately flattered by the Count's choice. Besides which Cécile Goudreau's direct, acid and violent mind was one to fascinate and convince him.

'Listen to me, my child,' said Cécile to Baba, 'it's the combination of people like the Count of Grandsailles and you that will win us this war in the end. You know it better than I do. No matter how much of your merchandise of bombs you dump out it won't make much difference: you make a breach in the balcony of a failing bank, a rear balcony that nobody used.'

'Sometimes one does more than that,' said Baba, 'a few hundreds of thousands of balconies blown to bits!'

'Well, yes, *chéri*, but there are so many, many balconies, too many in the cities, that no one ever thinks of using,' Cécile exclaimed wearily, as if feeling suddenly oppressed by the weight of all the superfluous and useless balconies in the world.

'Sometimes it isn't only balconies, but factory chimneys that we smash.'

'Well, yes, my child,' she answered, conceding the point with condescension, 'but in our day this chimney that you blow up into a thousand pieces is rebuilt as quickly as though the film of your destruction were being run in reverse. Everything grows back again, each time more ugly than the last – that's undeniable – but each time also more efficient and modern and better adapted to war. On the other hand, flying over Malta and silently landing the Count of Grandsailles there seems like nothing. But you see, for the English especially he is a mystery – crafty as a Libreux peasant, with a sense of honour pushed to the extreme, as in a Spaniard. He fascinates people who, won over to his cause and prepared to join him in action, will enable him to sow in every French heart the ancestral germs of the forces of resistance which must in the end bring about the country's liberation. And the seed of Grandsailles is the very seed which produced the noblest and oldest oak-trees on earth....

'One forgets the oak-trees,' she went on, half-closing her eyes and looking dreamily into the distance. 'At the height of the grow-ing season, looking out over the fields, one is startled to watch the rapid growth, week by week, of certain plants that seem to leap right out of the earth with an expansive, luxuriant, Bacchic, imperialist vigour, that can neither be arrested nor controlled, peculiar to the "blitzkrieg" harvests of the bean family. While the growth is in full swing it absorbs and obliterates everything – that is Hitlerism, Germany, a biological, frenzied sprouting of beans and peas! One forgets the oak-trees. But suddenly one fine day that same trium-phantly erect stalk that supported the beans begins to look forlorn, the bean hangs its head, the season is over and in a few days there remain only brown and wilted plant vestiges on the field that but a short time ago was dazzling green. Then one notices that during all this time some oak seedlings have taken root among them and one lifts one's eyes to look once more at the venerable shapes of those that have seen these agitations and calms follow one another for two thousand years. The oaks are France. Roots also tear down walls in the end. You, I know, still feel yourself attracted to what appears new and stirring.'

'No,' said Baba, 'I too believe once more in the ineradicable forces of tradition and aristocracy, and today I feel my revolutionary illusions of the Spanish war days like a distant germination that has already been harvested in my life. A fresh craving for contours and solidity begins to possess us, and when I fly it is no longer, as before, the proud revolt of the archangels who are out to win a chimerical paradise. On the contrary, I am urged by a desire to reconquer the earth, the earth, in its hardness, its nobility... renunciation... to recover the dignity of bare feet resting on the ground. I know now that man must look at heaven with humility. You see, this war is making me a Catholic.'

Cécile Goudreau listened to Baba with pride, admiration, and as if just discovering with astonishment that besides being a hero he was intelligent and even capable of expressing himself.

'Why, my dear, handsome Baba!' she said to him, running her fingers through his hair.

'Don't call me "Baba" any more,' he said. 'I'm no longer the same man that I was in Spain or in Paris. Here I am only known by my real name, John Randolph, Lieutenant Randolph, and it isn't Baba who will take the Count of Grandsailles to Malta, it's me, Lieutenant Randolph.'

'I knew you would take him. That's wonderful!'

There was a long silence. Cécile Goudreau kissed Randolph's hand. 'I can take him there, but that's all,' the latter continued. 'I can't bring him back. I've obtained permission to make this flight provided I fly from there straight to Italy, where I have to drop two parachutists in Calabria.... And you see, Baba would never have been afraid of that, but I am. It's the first time I am afraid of an assignment. Italy has always brought me bad luck. I was once at death's door in Naples, with typhus – and worse things: my dog run over on the road to Venice.... In Venice, too, I had a fight with one of my best childhood friends....'

'Let's knock on wood,' said Cécile Goudreau, striking her clenched knuckles against one of the cross-pieces under the table, while Randolph, with a superstitious gesture, caressed the pearl-and-diamond cross hanging from his neck that his fingers encountered through the gap in his shirt.

'And what is Grandsailles like?' he asked.

'He is less tall than you,' said Cécile, 'but your eyes are alike in their fixity. His are less blue, but almost as bright. His hair is auburn. He is very, very handsome. He is even more handsome than you.'

'What is the Count doing afterwards? Is he going back to France?'

'No,' said Cécile, 'after Malta he is leaving immediately for America.'

'Perhaps I shall have something to entrust to him,' said Randolph, absorbed, falling into a reverie. Then as if pursuing his thoughts aloud. 'Yes, I shall have an object to entrust to him… it means a great deal to me… an object to deliver to someone in America. Tell him this from me.'

Two days later when Grandsailles, accompanied by Fouseret, climbed into the three-motored Farman that was to fly him to Malta, Randolph was already at the controls.

'This reminds me of my departures for London,' said Grandsailles.

'As a matter of fact it was these same planes that made the flight between Paris and London,' said Fouseret, 'only here we have a machine gun set up, with its faithful servant. Well, I congratulate you. It looks like a plane well adapted to the circumstances,' he continued with a joviality which was his characteristic way of reacting against fear and nervousness.

'What were you expecting?' asked Grandsailles. 'You probably imagined that a plane found by Cécile Goudreau would be a machine all covered with ivy, with old cracks between the interstices of the wings and oriental divans inside on which to recline and smoke opium.'

'I should not have dared to imagine that,' Fouseret answered, 'but what an astonishing image of the post-war, isn't it? – a sky covered with planes dashing in all directions at seven hundred miles an hour, filled with drowsing opium smokers who are going nowhere!' He laughed.

'This same unthinkable paradox of speed and immobility has already been invented and it takes the form of streamlined coffins!'

'What a frightful idea!' said Fouseret, turning pale. 'Do they really exist?'

'I saw them once in a catalogue. That's really how they were announced. The coffins had the same kind of curves as appeared on the new cars a couple of years ago.'

'Unbelievable!' sighed Fouseret.

Grandsailles continued, 'A thing intended for eternal enforced immobility having all the characteristics of adaptation to dizzy speed…. It's mad! It could only happen in our time!'

Fouseret had darkened.

'You shouldn't have brought this up,' he exclaimed in a bitter tone of reproach.

'Are you superstitious?' asked Grandsailles.

'A Spanish bullfighter never goes into the ring if he passes a hearse on his way.' Fouseret proffered by way of self-justification.

'You're neither a Spaniard nor a bullfighter,' said Grandsailles.

'But I am just as superstitious,' said Fouseret. 'Fortunately your presence reassures me.'

'You consider me so lucky?' asked Grandsailles.

'Don't you think this trip is rather incredible? You're being piloted by Randolph, the best pilot in Africa; you get me to accompany you, though I had sworn never to set foot in a plane again; you are the only authority to have succeeded in gaining the confidence of all political groups, and yet you have no well-defined policy. Does any of us really know why we are obeying you?'

The plane started across the field, and when it had left the ground Grandsailles said, 'Flying is not an aphrodisiac sensation as one might be tempted to believe. It is on the contrary an Apollonian emotion. With this magnificent weather and not the slightest jolt, it's as if we weren't moving at all. On the train there are always the passing telegraph poles to give us a relative notion of our displacement; here there is nothing. You're always left with the feeling that you're not moving, that you're going to get there late. The plane is a kind of anaesthesia of time and space; it is not a direction, an arrow' – and he recited, stressing each syllable – 'a pinned butterfly meditating its flight. It is a circle: Apollo!'

Fouseret, with the noise of the motors, had to make an effort to catch Grandsailles' words to which he listened full of admiration and although he only caught half of them he said to himself nevertheless, 'There is no resisting this man's ascendancy!'

A radiant dawn had risen. They were now flying over the Mediterranean, which was a cerulian blue, shimmering beneath Apollo's darts, covered with the scales of the immense, slightly curved back of the cold fish of the horizon. Light, fleecy clouds hanging very low, skimming the surface of the sea, seemed to be rising from it and floating upward, and their calmly changing forms peopled it like triumphs of blond Neptunes, violet nereids, dolphins and snow seahorses strung out in heroic poses and groups. Brief flurries of wind wrote shudders of joy in silver on the sea, and from a small torpedoed merchant ship rose a Solomonic column of very thick, pink smoke, dazzling like the colour of Venus's flesh. All around the flaming ship the sea was sprinkled with the tiny black dots of the struggling crew. Several patches of oil spread on the water formed what looked like large, very smooth grand piano tops, reflecting the limpidness of the sky. Fouseret wanted to call attention to the drowning men, but Grandsailles had gone to sleep and he did not want to wake him up. The assistant pilot explained to Fouseret that they had received a message about the sinking before taking off, but that a hydroplane was needed for the rescue. One would undoubtedly arrive before long, but there was nothing they could do to save the men. Grandsailles awoke only when the assistant pilot came bringing the oxygen masks. They were going to fly very high to avoid meeting Italian planes that might be coming from the direction of Pantelleria. At the same time he was handed the ear-phones. Randolph wished to speak to him.

'Hallo! Randolph speaking. I won't have a second to see you when we arrive in Malta. I shall hand you presently the object Cécile Goudreau spoke to you about. This is in case I should not come back from my next mission.'

'I shall never be able to repay you for the service you are doing me,' said Grandsailles.

Randolph now seemed to be giving orders to the radio operator, and the assistant pilot, having suddenly lost his temper for reasons which eluded Grandsailles, hurriedly helped Randolph on with his mask, then put on his own and relieved Randolph at the controls. Then the latter came and sat down beside Grandsailles, pulled from inside his thick leather coat a small wooden box that looked like a medicine box, tightly tied with several bights of red string, and handed it to Grandsailles along with a letter bearing his name on the envelope. Randolph and Grandsailles then looked at each other, and through the monstrous complication of their masks their eyes appeared alike, equally pure, and in neither case could one tell whether it was exaltation or coldness that gave them their greater lustre. With a single impulse the two men removed their gloves, and their hands clasped for a moment, like those of wrestlers. Then Randolph got up and went back to his controls and soon, as the plane dropped to a lower altitude, they were able to remove their oxygen masks. Having mussed his hair in the process, Grandsailles pulled out his gold comb and, using the glass pane at his side as a mirror, began meticulously to straighten his parting; suddenly the reflection of this white line seemed to burst into fire as if at the contact of his comb. It was a plane going down in flames only a short distance away.

'What is it?' Grandsailles asked Fouseret.

The latter, in great excitement, was moving his mouth rapidly like a goldfish out of water. Grandsailles had difficulty in hearing him and had to pull the cotton out of his ears.

'We've just brought down an enemy plane!' shouted Fouseret, beside himself.

'I didn't know there had been a battle,' said Grandsailles, finishing combing his hair. Then he asked Fouseret, 'We didn't forget the duplicates sent by Cordier?'

At this moment a violent jolt made the whole plane crack, like a nut that is pressed before being finally crushed, and Grandsailles, holding his comb in the air, saw Fouseret slump at his side. The assistant pilot and the radio operator both ran over to him. He was dead. The window above him was pierced by a curved line of sharp holes, like the tail of a frost comet. Fouseret was left where he lay. They merely covered him with the reddish robe that Grandsailles had had over his knees, and as Fouseret's hand extended beyond this improvised winding-sheet Grandsailles took hold of it in order to push it out of sight. The hand was plump and still warm. He pressed it with gratitude and held it. At this moment a hallucinating sight paralysed his whole attention. 'Malta!' They were flying at less than two thousand metres over the island that had just undergone a terrific bombardment. Malta the unconquerable! Brazier of British pride, edged with foam!

Randolph now appeared as if in a halo of divinity, made incandescent by the inner flashes of his rage, but the red light that illuminated him was only the glow of the anger unleashed in the outer world, like the fire itself. He had not turned his head – did he know

246

that Fouseret was dead? As much as fire knows of the dead! The swollen and irritated epiderm of the sky was still covered with the frightful eruption of the virulent anti-aircraft carbuncles, while the last searing machine-gun rays, hard and shiny like scalpels, flashed their deep incisions in all directions in the form of crosses, bursting the loathsome yolks of eggs fried in boiling oil with the tumours of explosions, bespattering the stars with all the thick pus of their dense and bloody smoke and smearing the clouds with the entrail-vomit of shell-bursts.

Below lay the mutilated city, fat whorls of smoke, like shreds of brains in brown butter, emerging from the split skulls of the big buildings, the houses with their eyes scooped out by the invisible spoons of the bombs. Here and there in the empty shell of one of these gaping orbits, the remnants of a bed stuck at a crazy angle as though the pupils of the buildings had contained carbon skeletons. There it lay entire, strong as the clenched fist of England, that no one would ever loosen, a single compact mass, not hard as granite, that breaks, but on the contrary fermenting like a great victorious wound, like a colossal and Dantesque Gruyère cheese of sacrifice, sulphur-coloured, each of its holes fecundated by death, each of its holes oozing with humours and swarming with subterranean lives and each of its lives in turn shot through with holes, in their souls and in their bodies; the first filled with the prodigal barbs of vengeance, the second by the sterile and avaricious ones of tetanus.

The Count of Grandsailles, suddenly conscious that his burning fist held a cold and disagreeable object, looked down: it was Fouseret's hand. He pressed it harder! Randolph had just given the landing signal.

A British lieutenant and second lieutenant came running up to receive Grandsailles. As soon as the latter stepped off the plane he said, 'We bring one casualty.' The soldiers stood motionless, at attention, till Fouseret's body was lifted out and put on the ground, while the darkening sky became flooded with the calm, interwoven sheafs of powerful searchlights, drawing immense crosses in whose intricate network one seemed to read signs of reprobation and pity for the turbulent passions of men. And it was as though from the heroic depths of the history of Malta two imperturbable and gigantic legs were rising to the centre of the celestial vault, the legs of the Colossus of Rhodes, long since vanished, from the depth of whose bronze chest one could hear a feeble, plaintive voice like that of an ailing old man…. The sacrifice having been consummated, the last distant sirens ceased their moans: the alert was ended.

The Count of Grandsailles remained one week in Malta without Fouseret's aid, guided by d'Orminy's prudent counsels. His plans, pursued with boldness and without the slightest outer restraint, through audacity and danger, were crowned with unqualified success. He was able to return to North Africa in triumph.

Randolph, after having succeeded in dropping the two parachutists over Calabria, had been brought down on his return, and the wreck of his plane, picked up at sea, had been identified beyond any possible doubt. The letter that Randolph had left for the Count of Grandsailles read as follows:

'I have a strong premonition that my Calabria assignment will be my last. Should this be the case I beg you, as soon as you reach New York, to deliver the cross contained in the box to Veronica Stevens, to break the news to her and tell her I had not forgotten her for a single moment. Veronica Stevens is not my mistress nor my fiancée and hardly even my friend, inasmuch as she only knew me when I was wearing my helmet and we met only casually during the repeated air-raids in the cellars of Paris. In the course of these meetings she seemed nevertheless to have developed a great affection for me. Thank you, good luck to us both.

John Randolph.'

Grandsailles arrived late at night at d'Orminy's villa. The Prince and Cécile Goudreau were awaiting him in a fever of impatience.

'My mission was completely successful,' said Grandsailles on seeing his friends again. And he added, 'Fouseret was killed on the way in our own plane. Randolph was brought down on his return from Calabria. But what's the matter here?' he asked, made immediately anxious by the reserved and almost indifferent manner in which d'Orminy greeted this sensational news.

'An Arab revolt repressed in blood,' Cécile Goudreau threw out tentatively.

'I know,' said Grandsailles, immediately suspecting the worst consequences.

'Broussillon is in prison,' d'Orminy sighed, deeply preoccupied and closely watching Grandsailles' reaction.

'That's bad,' said the latter dryly, and he added in a severe tone of reproach, 'You didn't have to tell me this news now. There is nothing to be done before tomorrow, and I absolutely must get some sleep. I am dead tired.'

'We had to tell you, to prevent your going to sleep on the boat. You must stay here purely as a matter of safety,' d'Orminy observed. 'We have been suspect and followed since you left. Arabs in the pay of the police are constantly on the watch around the house.'

'I'll sleep here.' said Grandsailles, 'on the boat I should feel myself a prisoner of my two guards.'

He went upstairs and retired. At eight o'clock in the morning he was up, and he went straight down to the yacht, resolved to dismiss his guards. Near the pier he found a kite lying on the sand, with its long string neatly wound by its side. Grandsailles, whose capricious character tended to manifest its eccentricities in an exaggerated form when under constraint, could not resist the temptation to pick it up. He gave a quick glance up and down the shore and, seeing no trace of the owner, seized the kite with childish avidity, got into the yawl and made for his yacht. There he dismissed the two marines, ordering them to leave their post immediately. Though they seemed surprised, they executed the order without ado, seeming to have received no superior countermanding orders.

A brisk little morning wind had risen, and the Count of Grandsailles, after the superhuman energy he had expended during the last week in Malta, though he kept telling himself that he must give thought to the admittedly grave situation, nevertheless found himself unable to concentrate or even to interest himself in it. Half consciously he unwound several lengths of the string attached to the kite he had picked up on the sand and launched it into the favourable wind. He let it out, pulled it in, let it out further. The serenity of the sky was absolute; there was no other cloud than the rhomboidal one, like a capricious flake, which he held on the end of his string, now wavering, now suspended motionless. 'Captive!' exclaimed Grandsailles, while thinking of other things, and he condescended to yield several more arms'-lengths to his cloth flier, as though the latter had long been begging him for it.

When the second mate came to advise the Count that the Prince of Orminy urgently requested to see him Grandsailles called for his canoness and told her as he entrusted his kite to her, 'Hold it while I go ashore – and don't get the string tangled!'

'Imagine Grandsailles! – I can't help admiring him!' d'Orminy exclaimed, breaking into Cécile Goudreau's room with his arms raised to heaven. 'Do you know what he is doing? You could never guess!'

'But do tell me!' cried Cécile, half frightened, half amused by a demonstrativeness to which the Prince rarely gave vent.

'Well,' he said, sinking into a deep leather armchair from old England, 'the Count of Grandsailles is flying a kite! Look, just look! It's not my imagination. I am quite incapable of thinking up such a thing,' and he pointed to the window. But Cécile Goudreau was already looking out at the yacht moored in the bay, and she exclaimed, 'Why, it's unheard of! But it isn't the Count, it's the canoness who is holding the string.'

'He handed it over to her, for I have just sent word for him to come here. He simply has to know the whole danger of his situation. And we haven't seen the end of it. This business of the kite, in fact, bids fair to drag a good, long tail. For Grandsailles took this toy without bothering to ask himself if it belonged to someone. And now we have in the kitchen a young Arab who sees his kite flying over my yacht and who is shrieking at the top of his lungs that it's been stolen from him and I'm just wondering if this youngster isn't one of those paid by the police and if he isn't using his what-do-you-call-it to signal the *gendarmerie* just across the bay....'

At this moment the Count of Grandsailles entered the room. 'You're really making a mountain out of a mole-hill,' he broke in, 'I've just given the youngster a hundred francs and he's gone off happy as a lark.'

There was an embarrassed silence, and d'Orminy said, 'I didn't want to tell you last night. The authorities have categorically refused to visa your diplomatic documents, making it impossible for you to leave with us for America. We must act quickly, for it's tomorrow night at five that the *François Coppée* sails for South America. I insist, do you understand. I insist on your going with us. For you to remain here would be suicide. Neither Cécile nor I will leave you here alone, surrounded by your worst enemies!'

Cécile Goudreau, who had been deeply shaken by Randolph's death, now fell to weeping silently.

'I don't know if it's right to leave!' she kept repeating, her voice husky, broken by sobs. 'This bit of Africa is still France!'

'We're no longer at home here since it's become impossible for us to act,' replied d'Orminy firmly.

'To stay here is like dying,' Cécile Goudreau muttered, 'and to leave kills me!' She sprang to her feet and cried in an unintelligible voice. 'France! What have you done with your sword!' and threw herself on the bed, racked by convulsive sobs.

Neither d'Orminy nor Grandsailles made the slightest move to go over and console her, for their eyes were suddenly lighted by the unalterable resolve to leave.

'I demand that you follow out my plan to the letter and to the end,' said d'Orminy, taking the Count by the shoulders; and he continued with unaccustomed energy, 'I shall countenance no discussion this time, for it is the only one to follow. In what I am going to do for you I risk my life. All I need is six pictures of you. The less you bestir yourself the better it will be. In fact, you can stay here with Cécile and wait for me till this evening,' And as Grandsailles mildly tried to protest, the Prince of Orminy smiled to him with the most human smile, the most saturated with feeling, that had probably shone on his face in the whole course of his life, and said, 'Stay, for once, and fly your kite.'

Late in the evening the Prince of Orminy came and brought news to Grandsailles. Both of them with Cécile Goudreau and the canoness, who also had to get final instructions for the departure, were calmly pacing the after-deck of the yacht, pausing now and then and starting off again. The full moon had just risen. 'It's so beautiful – it's like summer,' said Cécile Goudreau. All spoke in low voices. 'Listen,' said d'Orminy, 'I hear rowing.' All listened in silence.

'Natives,' said Grandsailles, as he made out a fishing boat. 'Yes, I know them,' said the canoness, 'it's old Batta and his four sons. They're going conger-fishing and are starting out so they will get there by the time the moon is down.' The boat glided off and lay steeped in a kind of supernatural peace... a milky silence.... One heard only a faint lapping of water against the keel, like a sound of lunar saliva. The moon-drenched kite lying against a bulwark looked like a stellar ray that had just dropped there like a sign of the Zodiac.

'*Mon Dieu*,' sighed Goudreau, 'this peace, all this beauty – it's more than one can bear, it's out of this world! Will we ever be able to leave?'

'Tomorrow at five o'clock,' said d'Orminy.

'If we're not all in prison,' said Graindsailles.

'The success of your mission to Malta will cause them to wait, to think things over,' d'Orminy answered.

'What a marvel Malta is!' said the Count, involuntarily raising his voice.

'Sh!' said the canoness, 'another boat going out for the conger-fishing.'

'I'm very much afraid Broussillon may turn informer when he hears of Fouseret's death,' said Grandsailles in d'Orminy's ear. The latter, who was deep in thought, did not answer and there was a long silence. One of the Arab fishermen was singing a plaintive song in Spanish. At each pause, when he stopped to take his breath, one could hear the water dripping from the oars:

> 'Se murio mi esperanza!
> Yo fui al entierro
> Y encontre mi amor
> Que hiva en el duelo!
>   Ay, oy, ay!'

Dead is my hope!
I went to the burial
And met my love
Who was in mourning!
Ay, oy ay!

'How is your foot?' Grandsailles asked the canoness.

'It still hurts,' she answered, trying to put her weight on her foot which had just suffered an attack of gout. Brusquely she struck this same foot with full force against the deck, shutting her eyes to control her pain, and cried, 'I can go to America on foot, even limping if necessary. Here even the smelts we eat stink of the Germans!'

'So you're happy to be leaving tomorrow?' d'Orminy asked, amused at her outburst of impatience.

'Tomorrow?' said the canoness, 'yesterday I want to leave!' she concluded in a comical rage.

D'Orminy, who had been absorbed in thought, now took Goudreau and Grandsailles by the arm and led them below deck, while the canoness, hobbling painfully, tried to catch up with them for fear of missing some detail of their conversation.

'Look,' said d'Orminy, 'beginning tomorrow the boat must remain without a crew on board, aside from the three of us and the three sailors who will bring us back to shore. At quarter-past three a special launch will come and fetch Grandsailles and the canoness to take them to the *François Coppée*, which leaves for Buenos Aires at five. The captain of the ship is informed of everything – bought very dearly, but trustworthy! You must leave here wearing my aviation lieutenant's uniform. Once on board the *François Coppée*, lock yourself up with the canoness in my three-cabin suite. On no account must you leave it. All you will have to do is to wait for us. Cécile and I will arrive only in the last moment.'

'Why must I disguise myself as you when I leave here?' asked Grandsailles.

'In order to escape,' answered d'Orminy. 'This very morning I put my house and my yacht at the government's disposal. Tomorrow a *gendarmerie* company will take the place over. We shall be observed. When you leave,' he said, addressing himself to the Count, 'they must think it is I. I gave my word of honour that you were staying, but in exchange I received the formal promise that you would in no wise be molested in my presence – they would spare me this and wait to take action against you till after I leave.'

'Then they have decided to arrest me?' asked Grandsailles.

'Just about,' answered d'Orminy.

There was a silence. Then Grandsailles asked in a sceptical tone, 'And what about you? How are you going to leave the boat at the last moment without being spotted? And how are we going to avoid the police inspection before the *François Coppée* hoists anchor? All this strikes me as sheer childishness!'

'That is my lookout!' said d'Orminy energetically, making an effort to stand up. 'Now remember what I've told you: the slightest deviation from my plan may mean my life, and anyway, devotion can go only so far. I loathe always seeming to speculate on my own personal danger!'

D'Orminy had sat down again and was pressing his forehead, puckered with fatigue, against the outstretched fingers of his weary hands that seemed mummified by discouragement. He remained thus for a long time. Cécile Goudreau had hung herself round Grandsailles' neck and was imploring him. 'Come, now, let him do it his way! Let him do it his way for just once!'

'All right!' said Grandsailles, 'I'll shut my eyes to everything, but I think I should tell you that this afternoon some gendarmes came with a letter for me from the *commissaire de police*.'

'What? And what did you answer?' asked d'Orminy, startled.

255

'Nothing!' Grandsailles replied. 'I refused to accept it, and I sent them packing.'

'It doesn't matter,' said d'Orminy, 'they'll be back again tomorrow in any case....'

Early the following morning the Prince of Orminy paid his last visit to Guillomet, the chief of police, whom he had known since childhood.

'Listen, old man,' he said to him, 'I don't want to keep you from doing your duty, but the Count of Grandsailles has been one of my best friends. Whatever may be your responsibility I ask you not to let anything happen before I leave. Also, as you promised yesterday, I don't want anyone to come and disturb us in my cabin on the *François Coppée*. The honour of the lady who is leaving with me depends on it. Cécile Goudreau is not going. I entrust her to you and leave her under your protection. She is an intimate friend of the Count's; she is the natural person to serve as a go-between for you and the Count – you know that he is impulsive and a little unbalanced.'

'I know,' answered Guillomet, 'yesterday he even refused to read the very considerate message which I sent him.'

At three o'clock a launch from the *Françoise Coppée* came to fetch the Count of Grandsailles and the canoness, and Cécile Goudreau and the Prince of Orminy remained alone aboard the yacht. The sea remained calm, smooth and burnished like a sheet of lead; the sky blended with the sea and the reflection of the mountain across the bay seemed as hard and corporeal as the mountain itself, as if the symmetrical excrescence of its double were but an inverted continuation of it. Only at long intervals would a *llissa* leap out of the water and shatter this illusion of the absolute, wrinkling the surface of the water with placid concentric circles.

'We still have two hours before us,' said d'Orminy. 'You won't guess what I've brought.' He went over to a cabinet, opened it and pulled out two opium pipes. 'We're going to smoke, it'll calm our nerves. From here we can see everything that goes on on the other side….' They smoked.

On the beach, before the Prince of Orminy's house, a group of gendarmes stood conversing. Among them were five civilians, three men and two girls. All were idle and restless, and they would sit down on the sand in uncomfortable positions only to get up again immediately; stooping to pick up pebbles which they would throw awkwardly into the water to make them ricochet; climbing up on a bank to take pictures of one another.

'What a capacity for sterile agitation human beings have!' d'Orminy exclaimed, possessing as he did the contrary faculty of being able to remain motionless as a mannequin for long hours at a stretch.

'Poor things,' said Cécile Goudreau, 'they're terribly ill at ease. They look as if they desperately needed to empty their bladders, but actually it's not their fault. It's perfectly clear. They have no opium! Now I understand Grandsailles. When you feel at the end of your rope, completely hopeless, what could be more exhilarating than to fly a kite!'

At a quarter past four, three of the police force climbed into a tiny boat, scarcely big enough to hold them, and began calmly to row out to the yacht.

'There they are,' said d'Orminy, 'they're already coming to bring Grandsailles their ultimatum. They think it's he who is here instead of me. You go out and receive them. Tell them that the Count is asleep, that you will give him the message and bring them his answer in half an hour.'

'And then what?' asked Cécile.

'I will tell you afterwards,' d'Orminy answered, and he went and shut himself up in Grandsailles' cabin.

Everything went as he had foreseen; the gendarmes delivered the message from Guillomet, their chief, and rowed away as they had come, lingering now and then to pick up a long red seaweed caught on the end of an oar, or using the latter to tap a piece of floating cork to try to make it sink. D'Orminy spent a long time reading Guillomet's message. The latter's manner toward the Count had become brutal. He called upon him to leave the boat and to appear before him. At the end of his message, however, he appealed to his patriotism and even invoked the tricolour. D'Orminy then went over to the little ship's bar, detached a small French flag pinned between two bottles of Amer Picon and surrounded by other flags of different nationalities, folded it twice, and put it into an envelope that he sealed with the official seal which the Count of Grandsailles had left on his desk.

'There, *chérie*,' said d'Orminy to Goudreau, 'go ashore and give them this envelope. Tell them you are coming back in ten minutes, but instead, without wasting another second, make your getaway; you'll just have time to get on board the *François Coppée*. There you will join Grandsailles right away and wait for me. I have things to finish here, but I'll follow you shortly, and I'll be on board the *François Coppée* half an hour after you at the latest.'

Cécile Goudreau went into the cabin a moment to get herself ready to leave; when she was already in the yawl she seemed to hesitate. D'Orminy complimented her on the adornment she had just put on – a 'damp stone' grey voile turban ending in a veil that reached down to her waist, encircling and clasping it like a belt.

'It's very "departurish",' said d'Orminy, 'but above all it's so Parisian. From where I stand, by squinting my eyes a little, it's exactly as if I were looking at a panoramic view of Paris.'

D'Orminy uttered these words as he stood leaning over the bridge railing, a little stooped, his torso projecting over the edge of the vessel like one of the beneficent gargoyles on the Gothic towers of Notre Dame. 'And now be on your way, *chérie*. I'll see you by-and-by!'

He grinned a goodbye as he watched her disappear, tightly clenching his teeth which in the already yellowish light of the afternoon sun appeared even yellower than usual, as though he were squeezing a half slice of lemon in his mouth, and even as if this fruit had managed in spite of the distance to squirt acid drops into the eyes of both of them. The half slice of lemon of d'Orminy's smile diminished progressively, and soon, of the Prince's whole figure, Cécile could make out precisely only the flashes of his gold ring shining in the sunlight, by which she could tell that he was still waving to her with his hand.

Cécile Goudreau pressed the rather plump envelope containing the flag with some uneasiness. The 'soft', unexpected contact caused by the contents produced in her an undefinably sinister sensation. Her launch, after describing a wide semi-circle to go round a group of reefs, headed straight for the beach where the group of gendarmes stood. Cécile Goudreau delivered the envelope, and almost immediately left, this time in the direction of the port of Casablanca, to board the *François Coppée* and join the Count of Grandsailles and the canoness, who must be waiting for her.

At the very moment when the chief of police Guillomet, having unsealed the envelope, was looking with stupefaction at the little tricoloured flag which he held up between his fingers and which was the sole response to his letter demanding that Grandsailles surrender himself, Cécile Goudreau, already far out in the middle of the bay, turned her head to look once more and for the last time at the Prince of Orminy's boat and she was paralysed to see the immaculate kite, warm with sunlight, soaring majestically over the yacht. Instinctively she thought, 'Something frightful is going to happen!' But she did not have time to crystallize the impression of her fear. A violent explosion rent the silence of the late afternoon, a black column of smoke rose in a whirl from d'Orminy's yacht which, after having dipped violently toward the bow seemed for a moment to have regained its stability while flames burst out from it in all directions, and it gradually settled on its side. D'Orminy had committed suicide, blowing up the engine-room with dynamite!

Cécile Goudreau kept her eyes glued to those flames, and to the soot-black smoke that now rose vertically very high in the sky, while she cried to her two sailors, 'Quick, Quick! What the Count of Grandsailles has just done is not our concern! Quick! I have to report this to the Prince.'

'It's I, Cécile,' she said, knocking at the door of Grandsailles' cabin.

Grandsailles opened. 'What's the matter?' he asked, immediately struck by Cécile's look of utter distraction.

'What's the matter?' she repeated in a fateful tone. She wrapped round him her arms that had become energetic as a man's and led the Count toward a lingering ray of light that came through the porthole.

'Come over here,' said Cécile, 'come here to the light. I want to see you, I am curious to know for once what your eyes are going to do when you hear what I have to tell you. Look at me... come, Hervé!'

The canoness, gripped by a recurrence of the gout, had drawn near by means of a series of painful but agile hobbles.

'Has d'Orminy been arrested?' the Count hazarded, and as Goudreau shook her head with a madwoman's terrifying smile, he immediately assumed the worst.

'I see,' he said, 'he tried to escape, he fired on the police and....'

Cécile Goudreau continued to shake her head, though more slowly and bitterly now, and said finally, hammering out each word, 'He killed himself in your place and scuttled his boat.'

At this moment the canoness let herself drop to her knees, uttering a plaintive wail that resembled the intensely human, almost childish cry of a dolphin that has just been pulled out of the water, and hid her face in her apron, trying to stifle a sob that she strung out in a succession of spasmodic, brief, diminishing jerks that would begin again with each burst of tears by the same initial moan. The better to give herself over to her despair the canoness let herself drop from her knees to a sitting posture. Cécile Goudreau, with an obsessive stubbornness which her recent dose of opium, no doubt, rendered even more exorbitant, had taken hold of Grandsailles' face, and with the claws of her hands she dug and pressed all around the Count's dry and dream-filled orbits as though by means of this kind of anxious massage she hoped to draw from him evidence of some weakness in his impassivity. She kept repeating, querulous, cajoling and suppliant at the same time, 'Come on, now. Weep! Weep! Why don't you weep!'

Grandsailles who had been enduring this outpouring with stoical indifference, abruptly stopped Cécile's hands, seizing her two small and livid wrists, which were only waiting for this, with a single authoritative hand, and said, 'Why do you want me to weep over an act that fills me with pride for my friend?'

Cécile freed one hand from the clasp, which had become affectionate, reached up and caressed a lock of the Count's greying hair, so seldom dishevelled, and with tear-filled eyes looking into the depths of those that refused to weep said to Grandsailles with an infinitely gentle note of reproach, 'Now you see.... Poor d'Orminy! We won't have to listen to his foul-smelling secrets any more!...'

Then brusquely she turned round and walked quickly to the mirror, adjusting her veil as though she were getting ready to depart.

'You're not going to leave me now?'

Goudreau turned her head slightly toward the Count, and looking at him through her veil that already covered her face, answered, 'Yes! I'm staying behind.'

'D'Orminy wanted you to go with us, we want you to come to America with us!' Grandsailles commanded feebly.

Cécile's modest reaction to this weakness was hurriedly to open the little bag she had brought and to pull out several fabulous pearl necklaces, which she threw on the bed with a gesture full of weariness. 'Here,' she said, 'put these on your canoness. They may be useful to you. I don't need anything any more. They were presents – d'Orminy's kind, you understand? They belonged to his mistress, the Countess Mihakowska; she gave them to me. You remember that poor angel? And you know the way she was forced to catch each of these pearls with her teeth!'

'Yes, I heard that story, but I never believed it.'

'Well, it's as true as the day. D'Orminy would tie her hands behind her back and she would get down on her knees.... What does all that matter to us, now or ever?'

Cécile Goudreau had become herself again. By making their conversation more casual and everyday, she hoped to make Grandsailles accept the pearls which he had put into her bag again and which she had pulled out and thrown back on the bed.

'It's no renunciation for me not to come,' she went on. 'my heart kept telling me the whole time, "It's not right! It's not right to leave!" I'm going back to Paris – my opium den – the green moss – my family vault! I'm not afraid of it any more. I'll stay with the dead.'

At this moment the siren wailed out the first signal of departure. It was long-drawn-out, and when it ceased Grandsailles said again, knowing already that his efforts to change her mind would be futile, 'Our leaving has already cost d'Orminy his life. You have only to take off your veil to change the course of your destiny. We are here in complete security. I spoke for half an hour with the captain. You won't be able to leave later, even if you wanted to.'

'I should not want to, I shall never separate myself from my feelings,' she replied, speaking hurriedly.

'I know,' said Grandsailles, as if trying to let himself be convinced, 'there was no sentiment to draw you to that country!'

Cécile Goudreau had come close to him, all ready to leave, and said with a disconcerting shade of coquettishness, 'What do you know about my feelings? Have you ever wondered if perhaps I was in love with you?' And she laughed at him with such candid sweetness that she seemed in a moment to have grown ten years younger. She pulled back her veil, 'Kiss me, anyway!'

They embraced fervently, and then she left. And Grandsailles realized that he had discovered just now for the first time that this autumnal being with her November irises could arouse desire.

The *François Coppée*, having left the port of Casablanca three hours before, was now sailing in the open sea beneath the first crescent of a hard, shiny moon, a little humped and chipped like a gypsy queen's casserole.

'I don't want to think of anything any more, I want to sleep till we get to Buenos Aires.... If only that canoness in there will stop her sobbing!' She had been so eager, had pestered him so much to be the first to leave, and since the ship had hoisted anchor she had started to weep all the more.

PART THREE

The Price of Victory

6

'La Forza del Destino'

D URING THE TWENTY-THREE DAYS' crossing from Casablanca
to Buenos Aires, the Count of Grandsailles almost completely
forgot, not only the episodes of the dramatic conspiracies and intrigues
which he had just lived through, but also the fact that the war itself
existed. Unable to see clearly what lay behind the total fog of his
future political activities, and with that capricious absolutism which
characterized the least of his absorptions and abstentions, the Count
decided to shut out of his memory everything that might cause him
the slightest displeasure, while slyly leaving a breach of tolerance
open to the representations of pleasure.

Thus in spite of having promised himself a restorative quiescence,
a vacation of 'vegetative amnesia' in the limbo of his brain, he was
soon assailed relentlessly by hallucinating and tenacious evocations
of his libido, too long waylaid by the fulminating risks of his daily
activity which had now suddenly ceased. Grandsailles' mind readily
became the prey and the 'pasture' of a series of interminable morose
reveries – translucent pebbles of the same great themes of sympathetic
magic and of succubus-possession monotonously rolled on the sand
by the waves as if to become perfected and polished... dull stones
that turn green like old sparkling ardours resuscitating from the ashes
of forgetfulness.... All the real or fanciful memories of his prolix
love experiences strewn in disorder along the semi-precious beach
of his life were now gathered together and arranged by his libido in
the great hierarchical and opalescent vase of his sybaritic egoism in

which he stored the treasure of secret pleasure. With the constant and skilful little blows of the hammer and chisel of his obsession and of his perverse abstinence, Grandsailles could strike at will more and more disquieting new magic flashes – obtained, however, at a loss of cerebral retina, of visual marrow and medullary substance.

It was as though Cécile Goudreau's last rapid kiss, which in spite of the dramatic circumstances of the departure had produced such a disconcerting effect, had stimulated and sharpened all his senses to the quick; and if in his memory of the Malta episode, but recently so dense with emotion, there now remained only a limp spider's web covered with dust and the three black and sinister stains of his three dead cohorts, all buried so to speak in a dark corner of the stable in which the domestic animals of his political instincts slumbered, Cécile Goudreau's unexpected kiss was still vivid, a sensation more real than at the moment when he had experienced it. It was as though each time he evoked Cécile's image through the grey veils which had fallen over her face since that moment, she had the power, in spite of time and distance, to renew the sting inflicted on his desire by a kind of invisible tongue, quick, ardent and cold as a snake's. How could Grandsailles ever have suspected such a thing? So many long evenings spent chatting with Cécile, the two of them alone together, without any other witnesses than the four heads of the four bear-rugs submerged by the satin of the propitious atmosphere of her opium den, and without a single spark of carnal lust having swept across the often dried-up hills of his prolonged continences.

Cécile appeared to him now clothed with attributes combining infinitely attractive shades of malice and pathos. With her faultlessly beautiful legs he often visualized her emerging, silent and obedient, from the places where his most gnostic imaginative orgies and bac-chanalia were consummated, and not infrequently at the climax of their troubling scenes it was precisely Cécile's face, delicately veiled in grey, that would in the last moment replace the usual one of the Honourable Lady Chidester-Ames who in turn had until then supplied the human embodiment of certain fauns with flawless legs and the ambiguous bodies of hermaphrodites, covered with soft, shiny fur.

But if Cécile's image now held the golden bridle of the extravagant cavalcades of his lasciviousness, harnessed to the mud-wallowing panthers of his perversity, one single being seemed on the other hand to detach itself from this part of himself, so tormented by base appetites, one single being emerging each time more victorious from each of the new ordeals of his more and more exacting desire, one single being who was beginning to appear to him as half-divine – Solange! Solange de Cléda who had found her way to him through all the walls of his pride, armed with the sole dignity and beauty of her image, her naked image, passing across the deep, thorny pits envenomed by the vipers of the outrageous injustice of the contempt in which the Count had tried to confine her. Yes! He no longer concealed it from himself now, since he had boarded this ship and his spirit, so long absorbed by the tragedy of his country, now again had leisure to dwell on her: he had become aware of a deep and sincere remorse over his inhuman, inflexible and pitiless behaviour toward the one being who, he knew, adored him with an all-absorbing passion.

Solange de Cléda! He visualized her now as perfect, as a transparent Louis XIV fountain, in which all the attributes of her personality were architecturally transformed into the precious metals on which her spirit was 'mounted' and which served her as an accessory and a pedestal. He would look at her and not see her: carved in celestial geometry, only the 'silks' of the rock-crystal of her soul were visible in her limpidness. But if Solange's spirit, because of its translucent purity, seemed to him more and more inaccessible to the senses, all that might be called the ornamentation of 'her fountain' now no longer appeared to him as light and virtual attributes. On the contrary each leaf of her modesty and each garland of her grace was chiselled with a minute detail and a refined art, as in a rare masterpiece of jewelry, so that the sculptured motifs, elaborately executed in the opaque metal of the border, only set off the smooth and unclouded diaphanousness of the receptacle that stood in the centre of her deep being. What uncompromising and gratuitous rigour he had shown toward her! She had wanted to marry him? What wrong was there in this, if it was willed solely by her passion? What would he himself not have done in order to possess a mite of authority in the soul of his country – which, perhaps to punish him for his pride, had in turn condemned him with equal injustice to the torturing elegies of ostracism!

Solange might have been an incomparable spouse, just as d'Orminy had probably been one of his best friends without his ever having suspected it, just as Cécile Goudreau possessed demonic-virtues as capable as Lady Chidester-Ames' of awakening the tortuous witchcraft of his vices.

The ship sailed on to the monotonous rhythm of its engines. His eyes that had always been sealed to the demands of his indomitable character had at last been opened by his recent experiences. But was it not too late? In the face of the miles of Atlantic ocean that were impassively devoured at each hour of their journey the misunderstanding with Solange appeared to him progressively as a drop of salt water, smaller and smaller and on the point of evaporating without leaving any other trace than a slightly bitter taste.

'I have never loved anyone but her,' Grandsailles would repeat to himself. And he promised himself that he would start a love correspondence with her as soon as he reached America. Would she be able to come and join him? And this man, who had not given a single thought to poor Fouseret, from whom d'Orminy's suicide had been unable to draw a single tear, now remembered with infinite emotion the last sentence he had heard Solange utter, when he had treated her so outrageously and started down the stairs without a word of farewell. 'Take good care of yourself!' Abandoning all effort to defend herself, she had thought of only these words, uttered in a tone so loving, so poignant and full of maternal tenderness.

And while the François *Coppée* left the ephemeral foamwhirl of the stages of its voyage behind it one after another the Count of Grandsailles, coming out into the daylight after one of his black and tyrannical sensual phantasmagorias, would imperceptibly move his lips to repeat to himself noiselessly, 'Take good care of yourself!' It had required a whole ocean of bitterness to moisten his eyes: 'The bitterness and dishonour of war had to uproot me to make me feel you taking root at last in my heart, Solange de Cléda!'

On the ceiling of the cabin the image of the sea-waves filed past upside down. The Count shut his eyes, and with an unaccustomed, hyperaesthesized visual acuteness, he saw cavalcades and triumphs similar to those described in *Le Rêve de Polyphile* and painted by Piero della Francesca. If he wished to examine a fragment of one of his imaginings at leisure he had only to tighten the muscles of his eyelids. This seemed to bring the optic diaphragm of his hypnagogic hallucinations exactly into focus, enabling him to decipher the enigmatic inscriptions of each trophy and to savour the chiselled floral motifs on the golden spokes of chariot wheels turning on hubs of black agate in which he distinctly saw a few white veins.

Thanks to this faculty of irritating his visualizations to the point of blinding clarity, he could thus by concentrating on a fleeting smile immediately see the curling lines of blessed turpitudes drawn as sharply as in a sculpture by Carpeaux and could individualize the minute anomalies of each of the pure, saliva-moistened teeth – his imagination in turn moistening, tooth by tooth. He could even distinguish through the veils over their bodies the various shades of salmon-pink on the tips of the breasts of dancing nymphs.

Each triumphal chariot of perversion passed across his vision, drawn by different creatures, by druids crowned with leaves bearing Arabic topaz vases of 'liquid desires', unicorns with feminine rumps, bulls white as foam, lions with the faces of angels... Cécile and Lady Chidester-Ames dressed in sea-cow skins opened the procession, applying their whips of myrtle branches that left myrtle-shaped marks on the innumerable flesh of the slaves of his mistresses, to whom Grandsailles now self-indulgently gave the names of famous lovers of antiquity – Celta Morgana who turned into a river of milk, Alimbrica with the white gums, the gentle Hemophia who loved blood, Corina with the breasts of a child, and Nacrea! But in the midst of this throng subservient to his specialized pleasures one saw a principal chariot which was at the same time a tomb and a fountain of Adonis. On this chariot lay a young horse of infelicity, all white, and on this horse Solange was seated like a queen, happy but a little terrified, her hands clutching the animal's mane for fear of falling on the host of her beautiful former rivals who were making elegiac gestures. Solange de Cléda wore a dress of blue gold and her chariot was drawn by six centaurs of the race of Ixion harnessed by means of strong flat-shaped bronze chains – God, how beautifully proportioned those flat-shaped bronze chains were! He had borrowed them from his Louix XVI clock, one of his last acquisitions before leaving Paris – the Count of Grandsailles had a habit of mixing up the mistresses he had possessed with the antiquities he had bought.

'None of my sentiments,' he would often repeat, 'but is capable of being carved in stone – they may be slightly hunchbacked harpies, if you will, but their hump forms an ornamental semi-circle, and the whole is set off by noble acanthus-leaves.' Solange de Cléda was now *the lady*.... He evoked her planted in the plain of Creux de

Libreux, the illuminated plain, and he thought of land while his eyes contemptuously watched the sea roll by.... The sea is bitter to some, to those who love it – the romantics; and some are bitter to the sea – the classics. Grandsailles belonged to the latter, and the ocean, knowing this, darkened with melancholy while the Count of Grandsailles smiled at the approach of the concise limits of the new continent.

Since their return to America, Barbara Stevens, Veronica, Betka and her son, accompanied by Miss Andrews, had been living on a property of Barbara's in the middle of the desert, near Palm Springs. There, around their hacienda-palace, there was no suggestion of the mossy and ordered vegetation of France – only space strewn with rocks in disorder looking up at the hard sky with their empty holes. And while Barbara, keeping constantly indoors, had to treat her aggravated heart ailment with delicate precautions, Veronica spent most of her time outdoors wearing out her heart galloping on horseback, trampling her heart, so to speak, beneath her horse's hooves that drew sparks of fire from the rocks, shattering them into fragments of rough tourmaline and frightening the great royal lizards that were soft as 'cheese of polished tourmalines', slipping without wounding themselves between the spines of old cactuses wounded in the flank. Each evening these cactuses formed groups of congealed gesticulations of '*viae crucis*' and of 'descents from the cross' silhouetted against the agates of the sunsets.

Veronica would ride her chestnut horse, her rounded forehead bowed like a menacing volute of obstinacy, the mother-of-pearl pincers of her thighs pressing the animal's flanks and blending with it in a pearly communion of centaur sweat. She lived thus, riding her chimera and preserving an absolute faithfulness to the image of the 'man with the hidden face', and between the dark, damp depth of the cellar of the house on Quai des Orfèvres where they had known each other and the calcinated, radiant mud over which the horse of her impatience reared its hope there was only desert, heroic aridity of love. Each evening the constellation of the three diamonds of the cross she had given him would appear quaveringly suspended in the sky. In what latitudes was this cross now sailing toward her? For it shone differently according to the indecisions of her heart. With all her curative saliva, dried by the violent exercise of riding, Veronica would efface, one after another, the traces of the scars that streaked the face of her hero so that it might soon be freed of the protective embrace of his helmet, which would open like an eggshell. Then he would come to her without any other stigmata than those of glory. (Gallop, gallop, gallop! Deliria of galloping, spurs, saddles of chastity, bitterness and wind – whip all this!)

Two curtains were now about to rise on the far horizon of Veronica's tragic life. The first of these was all black and bore the inscription: 'Nothing is more certain than death.' And this was the curtain of mourning for her mother, who died of her heart ailment the month after their arrival in America. The second of these curtains was a pure white banner; it had a strong fragrance of sandalwood, and one could decipher on it the four Greek letters formed of intermingled embroidered flowers – IMHN – which means *virginity*. This curtain was drawn before a fountain to conceal what was behind, and there was Veronica, her torn veil attached to the body of this fountain in human form which was Adonis. In an access of timidity and virginal modesty Veronica had scratched and bloodied his face, and he now kept it hidden in shame, masking it with two myrtle branches.

Barbara Stevens' death awakened Veronica's slumbering filial love by her absence of grief, just as church bells sometimes awaken one only the moment they cease to ring. Veronica now loved her mother because she had been so unconscious of her mother's life and was so little moved by her death. As her eyes were not blindfolded by the confusion of emotion, Veronica had been able to see 'what it was like' and death appeared to her similar to her image of the man with the hidden face. It was thus that her passion became dangerously morbid, her growing love and veneration for her mother now blended with her passion for him, and his existence appeared to her as certain as the death of her mother whose face, which had been a thing of such little moment, already tended to disappear while the sweetness of these two feelings appeared to her equal. The little cross became tinted with sinister reflections of eclipse and stars of Venus, and each of the little diamonds again became the nails of Christ crucified.

For it was as though Barbara Stevens' death, far from calming her daughter's impetuous anxiety, only accentuated her frenzy to the point of exaggeration, just as it sharpened the fixity of all her obsessions. Her unsociability, too, became pathologically irascible. In the evenings, when she returned from her mad rides across the desert, Veronica would rush up and shut herself in her room, as if afraid that someone would come and disturb her in her dream. Ignoring all conventions, she would cross the great covered patio crowded with lawyers, newspapermen and businessmen who waited day after day in vain for an appointment. As if possessed by evil spirits, her face frowning, Veronica would each time vanish like a gust of wind, barely acknowledging the presence of others with a wave of her hand clutching her riding crop. Fortunately Betka's entire and limitless devotion, stoutly seconded by Miss Andrews, partly made up for Veronica's utter heedlessness. Betka took it upon herself to look after the vast interests of the rich heiress and managed to guide her friend's interests with considerable wisdom. But Veronica, far from being grateful to her for her long hours of labour and her sacrifices, took umbrage at all this. Yes, Veronica developed a deep resentment against Betka: Betka interfered in her business affairs, even though Veronica knew this was done solely for her own good; Betka had a son and this son, Veronica claimed, detested her; Betka had let her breasts grow large; she tried to pry into Veronica's secret feelings; she was too fond of admiring her own body; she – above all Veronica resented the fact that the latter had always obstinately refused to share the confidences of her passion; never, never had she condescended to approach Veronica's incipient delirium.

In reality the one wrong which Betka was guilty of was that she had never lent herself to any of those outpourings of the heart which were the sole reason she wanted her for a friend. 'What stiffness!' Veronica would rage, and she would continually fret and say to herself, 'How she has always gone out of her way to avoid speaking of him – of the man with the hidden face!' Veronica for her part, out of sheer pride, would rather have died than take the least initiative in broaching this subject to which she felt her friend so bitterly hostile; it was as though Baba, thus excluded from their common life, had been Betka's own lover!

It was thus that their mutual and tacit silence on the one essential subject separated them, making their friendship ever hard and exalted, more exalted and acute even than before because it was more and more unsatisfied, bristling, precious and saturated with unhappiness like a diamond with a few drops of gall at its centre. Betka, in turn, suffered in silence, consumed with the thousand and one tortures of all jealousies, not toward Baba, whom she had forgotten, but toward that multiplicity of centrifugal pleasures of the blood-swollen arcs which make man and which she knew kept Veronica's alert, intact and pure biological organism in a permanently hallucinated state of expectation, while she felt her escaping from her own life more and more. Yes, the man who would appear at any moment could not but be the enemy of her who had renounced man for her friend – worse than her enemy, her executioner. Whether he was the impassive creature with obliterated features chosen by Veronica, or another with a more real face, did not matter – and how she already hated him! For this man, because of her friend's sense of the Absolute, was going to mark the irreparable end of everything between the two of them and this end would be the beginning of their hatred – she would hate Veronica – was it possible?

While waiting for the man to appear, Veronica and Betka were already quarrelling in silence over their child, Betka's child, and as the two of them sat in profile as in an ancient cameo representing a scene of circumcision, the one would hold the baby by the arm, the other by the leg, and their respective hands instead of offering the caresses which they simulated, seemed rather to press on the child's flesh like possessive claws. How were they going to share him who no more distinguished them in his affection than if they had been one? Two, who should have been one! One for him, and for themselves, two!

Between Veronica and Betka there was staged each evening a little drama, followed by a bitter tangerine-slice of reconciliation – a constant battle that was gradually getting the better of their friendship. On one of these occasions when Veronica had treated Betka most harshly, subjecting her to her extreme caprices, going so far as to put her out of the house only to beg her immediately to stay, making her weep, consoling her and making her weep again, Betka overwhelmed with despair finally exclaimed with rancour, 'There is nothing so fierce as a virgin!' She spoke the truth, for virgins have sharp teeth shaped like harpoons and their mouths are like nests filled with arrows that cupids carry in quivers carved out of fine mucus hanging from a strap across their shoulders.

On another occasion matters took an even more serious turn when Veronica struck the child's legs with a whirring blow of her riding crop. Immediately devoured by remorse she had run out, saddled her horse and ridden off into the night in a heavy sandstorm, and Betka in turn had to gallop after her, fearing that in her unbalanced state she might do something desperate. She finally caught up with her. Veronica, with her orbits bathed in the light of the new moon, seemed no longer to see, and her eyes were filled with sand. For the first time Betka had the courage to say to her. 'You will go to pieces if you continue to think of your frightful invalid. You know that I kept from you the fact that I know the horrible nature of your aberration, and you already detest us, my son and me, because of him, whose face you have never seen and whose voice you have never heard.'

'I know I am sick. I shall get a doctor for this, but not to have him cure me: to have him find me what I want! Mad that I am!'

Veronica had uttered these words in a burst of resentment, while at the same time growing calm like a red-hot iron when it turns white – quiet and concentrated, like a blind statue of folly, a riveted dementia that contemplates its chimera…. Then she repeated, 'My doctor will help me to find him! You stay here and take care of yourself and your son. You're stupid. I'll go off and try to find my frightful invalid… I feel a craving for fragmentation. Even when I was little I always preferred dolls without heads. Insects do the same – I've observed them in the desert. Mutilation – a beautiful mirage! Only broken gods, mutilated Apollos, and the noseless faces of philosophers have nobility. And as for yourself, like the Saint Agatha whom I look at every Sunday in the mission, each time I wanted to love you I have felt like cutting off your breasts!'

The following day Veronica left alone for New York, and Betka, the child and Miss Andrews remained in Palm Springs. She established herself sumptuously in the Park Avenue mansion which she had just inherited from her mother. It had always been too frigid, and now she wanted to surround herself with a caressing, warm setting, woven in little grasses of caprice and feathers of illusion. Her adolescent femininity leaned out of the windows of her soul. And the latter, like a turtle-dove, came and went, bringing back wisps of nuptial straw in its bill. It was as though Veronica were making her nest, and with her quasi-animal instinct she was in fact making her nest.

The antiquarians were like dry little birds, who wore tie-pins on their jabots and who ceremoniously helped her to make her nest, hopping about with their hands full of porcelains, like rare eggs, around her fortune, in minuets in which nothing was broken. The violent Amazon's life that she had recently been leading now seemed a hell of Tantalus, in which her impetuous body tended obscurely and desperately to tear itself apart without ever succeeding. Enough of pebbles sharp as knives! Enough of the desert of love! Free, free at last of Betka, of the child, of the horses, of the sun and of that calcinating wind that still tugged at the skin of her cheeks and made her teeth grate with the arid sand of river dreams, presaging the Nile of her dry season! 'Now I am ready for my mutilation. I want to be rid of "it".' But instead, war again won the day, this time involving her own country, and Veronica felt the cold dagger of Japan enter the flesh of her individual problem, opening a breach of icy water which closed the desired one of her deflowering.

Her nest was finished on the very day of Pearl Harbor. And in the whirl of black smoke, with the steel skeletons of the American ships, twisted and contracted like the arms of colossal dying starfish, capsized under a starless sky, Veronica felt the decision of her own sacrifice to her country graze her body with the flags of ancient victories and her will fluttered like the star-spangled banner. For she not only loved her country but identified herself with it. The fountain of Adonis? The tomb of Adonis? He and only he! Living or dead, real or unreal, he remained alone and unique in her thoughts, now especially since her own face was in turn going to be hidden by war, since at the moment when the slit of her mouth was preparing to open, it was to be covered by the white membrane of the hymen of sacrifice, by the panting mask which lends an occult touch to the faces of surgical nurses.

For she had decided to become a nurse, and specifically requested that she be assigned to the care of the severely wounded. She wanted to get close to the war, to the sharpest and most cutting that it had to offer. Besides, during the two months that she had spent in New York since her arrival, the city's resources of seduction had been quickly exhausted. How often she had told herself during this period, experimenting with a cynicism which did not at all suit her, 'At last I can give myself a rest from the exhausting torture of health and fresh air by upsetting my liver in good bourgeois fashion in the comforting and invigorating atmosphere of night-clubs, with a straw glued to the corner of my lips, sipping an alcoholic drink that turns my stomach but gives me the illusion for an hour and a half a day that I am intelligent!'

Now Veronica had just let this straw drop from her mouth with disgust, and instead of making the round of the night-clubs she began to see Dr Alcan, a psychiatrist, with whom she had struck up a friendship when they had met on returning to America on the same ship, the *Excalibur*. She wanted two things of him – help in recovering her moral equilibrium and connections through whom she might gain admission to a hospital.

Dr Alcan, without being handsome, could be seductive by the liveliness of his intelligence, giving one the feeling that one was constantly playing hide and seek with his mind on the too naked and flat expanse of his face, which was ennobled by the constant agitation of thought. But Veronica herself knew too much about psychoanalysis to be the dupe of her natural and inevitable tendency to 'transference' and was able to limit her need to see him constantly, sometimes twice a day, to a simple faithful friendship, a friendship however to which she knew she would be obliged to give a good deal of herself, perhaps even too much, as soon as the doctor should require it.

Everything that she had been dying to tell, but had never been able to, to Betka whom she adored and whom she was almost ready to hate because of this, she could and even had to tell now to Alcan, toward whom she felt no other inclination than that which the confession of her delirious fantasies procured her – always on her obsessive theme of the man with the hidden face. These confessions brought her daily closer to him in a promiscuity of confidential habits which in the end made their meetings more and more indispensable, and worst yet, irreplaceable. Who else, indeed, could have listened to her with so much acute comprehension? Thus when Alcan, in the course of the treatment, had to announce to her that he was shortly leaving for Africa to rejoin the French army fighting in Syria, this was such a blow to Veronica and her reaction was so great that she seemed unable to overcome her disappointment. To accustom her to the idea that their sessions must necessarily end, they decided to hold them at greater intervals, reducing them to a strict minimum. Veronica's melancholy then became illuminated by the open lights of those interminable sleepless nights in which insomnia with its eyes which never closed and in which hornets nested, sat beside her endlessly in its long-trained robe from which the beads of the hours dropped one by one.

Alcan had insistently advised her to return to Palm Springs, but now Veronica found herself more and more unable to think of the place where her mother had died without fright. What had become of the energy, the will, that spotless and prancing health of a thoroughbred horse, which had made of her an impregnable moral fortress? The will proposes and the subconscious disposes, and instead of the active courage which she had promised herself it was as though the towers of her soul had suddenly crumbled at the sound of war, just as the walls of Jericho had collapsed at the sound of the trumpet of Maccabee. For the faceless knight of the obsession that besieged her spirit had just completed the seven required circles around the stronghold of her virginity. Alcan's departure was delayed, put off from day to day, and this uncertainty became for Veronica worse than anything.

A year thus flowed by, and Veronica's mental state gradually became stabilized, sinking into a misty confusion of her memory and her imagination. These symptoms of endemic morbidity were becoming, according to Alcan, all the more alarming since Veronica seemed to be beginning to 'enjoy' seeking refuge in the arms of her own psychic malady as if on the consoling bosom of the sole solution.

At half-past twelve noon, the masculine hour for a quick drink in the King Cole bar at the Hotel St Regis, André Marion and Alcan had just met.

'What are you having?' asked Marion.

'I've just ordered a Dubonnet. What will you have?'

'I'll take an old-fashioned,' said Marion to Dominique, the bartender. Then, heaving a sigh and turning to Alcan, 'You see, I'm becoming adapted. It's whisky, water and sugar. It's not too nauseating, and it keeps its promise. I learned this a year ago.'

'But tell me, old man,' said Alcan, 'do you know who is here?'

'So many people!' said Marion sadly.

'You know who is here?' Alcan insisted once more with an air of excitement.

'Who?' Marion asked.

'The Count of Grandsailles!'

'I can't believe it!' Marion exclaimed.

'I met him yesterday afternoon at the Frick Museum,' Alcan answered triumphantly, quickly stirring his friend's old-fashioned with the glass stirrer.

'He was reported to be dead,' Marion objected, crunching a potato chip.

'I know, a Casablanca paper even published the news that he had blown himself up on board the Prince of Orminy's yacht.'

'Listen, old man, everybody has been dead, and everybody resuscitates, and sooner or later they turn up here. General Dutilleil was reported to have been killed in a plane crash. Well, it wasn't true. And Charles Trenet, the singer, did you know him?'

'What has become of him?'

'Nobody knows anything about him,' said Marion. They drank in silence. Marion looked at the hat-check girl and said, 'By the way, what is Grandsailles doing here?'

'He sees no one, he doesn't give anyone his private phone number, but he's living here. He must be on a mission. He told me he was leaving soon.'

'I have to dash,' Alcan said suddenly, 'I'm late. I'm having my last luncheon with Veronica Stevens. Are you living at the St Regis?'

'Why yes, for the time being,' answered Marion.

'Then I'll telephone you – we'll have dinner together. Don't tell me you're not free. I'm leaving in three days for Syria. I know a place, a kind of *bistro*, where they make wonderful tripe!'

'Give me another old-fashioned,' Marion told Dominique.

Alcan had told the truth, for just a week before, the Count of Grandsailles had arrived in the United States by plane from South America. He had taken two adjoining apartments, one for himself and the other for his canoness, on the nineteenth floor of the Hotel St Regis, and already the neat piles of several unopened packages from the shops of the best antiquarians cluttered his drawing-room. Since his arrival in America, on the pretext of wanting to break with his past and respect the democratic ways of the country which offered him its hospitality, the Count had formally renounced his usurped title of Prince of Orminy, and had kept for his daily use only the obscure and inconspicuous name of Mr Jules Nodier, d'Orminy's civil name. In certain circumstances he availed himself of the latter's rank of retired lieutenant and wore his aviation insignia. At the same time he had immediately hired two lawyers who were already fighting like two Japanese cocks to do him service and who were trying to release a part of the fortune which d'Orminy had transferred to the United States a long time ago.

The practical beginnings of his new life were working out pretty well, but New York had no charms for him. With the exclusiveness that had always characterized the Count's passions, he could see no other feminine faces than the remembered and now adored one of Solange de Cléda. 'Life is hard, bitter and a heavy burden far from Solange,' he would say to himself. He would drink now – though he had always been a model of sobriety – as though he were seeking in the fires of old armagnacs the taste of the earthly spirit of his absent and distant Libreux. 'There are two things that I can no longer put off doing,' he would tell himself every morning. 'One is to send Solange a long letter by diplomatic pouch to make up for everything; the other is to discharge my duty to Randolph as best I can, by announcing his death to Veronica Stevens and giving her back the cross. When this painful scene is over with everything will be better!'

It was through Dr Alcan that Grandsailles obtained an interview with Veronica. Alcan had warned Grandsailles, 'She is very irritable. Her nerves are in shreds, but her biological freshness is bound to save her. The people of this country are so intact that they can allow themselves to get out of order once in a while. When the time comes they never fail to mark the exact and pitiless hour of their decisions.'

'What I have to tell her is very painful for her and difficult for me,' Grandsailles had said.

'Whoever comes to destroy her dream can only do her good,' answered Alcan.

'I shall ask you one thing,' Grandsailles had said further, 'I beg you not to tell anyone my real name. I am here incognito, and all my undertakings might be jeopardized. Remember that I am just Nodier, the retired aviation lieutenant – even for Veronica.'

To Veronica Alcan had said, 'He comes from Europe, he has a message for you. He insists on telling you everything himself, even his name.'

Alcan was astonished that Veronica showed no reaction – she seemed to have expected this. Resentful of his departure, she had become coldly estranged from him and, with her mind roaming elsewhere, she even betrayed her impatience to bring their conversation to an end. Alcan was leaving for Syria the next day, yet Veronica hardly deigned to be aware of it.

Humanized, enriched and enlightened by the distant virtues of Solange de Cléda's loftiness of soul, the Count of Grandsailles felt the atheistic pettinesses of his character evolving toward the stable and central cross of mature faith. He was forty-five years old, and he was surprised now to find himself submerged by a feeling that was new to his heart – pity. It is true that this pity contained residues of his narcissism, for he began by exercising it chiefly on himself. He would say to himself, 'I'm getting old, and for the first time in my life I feel lonely; in my prolonged and quasi-monastic retreats in the Château de Lamotte Parisian society with its trivial passions sufficed to haunt my solitude, and the saturnalia of my mistresses would prowl outside, around my celibate's bed, under the watchful eye of that tearful bulldog, my canoness. Here no one knows me, and the few people I might have seen I must avoid because of the degrading infirmity of my change of personality. The canoness is sad; she hides it as best she can, but she is sad, and she has grown even uglier!'

Formerly the evolution of this ugliness, grown invisible through habit, had not been devoid of a certain diabolical seductiveness that exerted its fascination over him, but in his present state of mind Grandsailles could merely observe the monstrous growth of her ugliness objectively. He felt nothing but pity for her, and this was something he was not yet resigned to! No longer having anyone over whom he could tyrannize the Count suddenly believed himself to be a weak man. 'I know! I know!' he would repeat to himself, 'a crisis of Catholicism!' But instead of thinking of this development as he would have formerly, that is to say, fearing it as if it were an attack of sciatica, he now almost wished that the religious crisis and the sciatica would occur simultaneously, so that their combined physical and moral pain might offset the frightful emptiness of his life.

'In any case I've got a fine case of rheumatism,' he said to himself, trying to stretch his ailing leg which for several days had obliged him again to walk painfully and to have recourse to a cane. That afternoon, after his solitary meal in his room, he had slept a little and now he was thinking of the sad duty he presently had to perform: that of meeting Veronica Stevens to announce Lieutenant Randolph's death and give her the little cross of pearls and diamonds which the latter had entrusted to him. 'Where did I put it?' the Count wondered and, getting up, immediately found it in the first drawer he opened. 'It's touching,' he said to himself, picking up the little wooden box tightly tied with string, 'but I can't bring it to her like this,' and he tried to think of a case in which he could put it. Having untied it he took the cross between his fingers and examined it. 'I'll simply bring it to her in my hand, that's the most natural.' How he wished this business were already over! For nothing in the world was so depressing to him as scenes of weeping, the rôle of consoler, in which he had always felt himself awkward. Each time it was only with difficulty that he could repress a desire to become brutal, so as to have it over with more quickly.

Today, however, he had taken it upon himself to accomplish this Christian task with more resignation, and he seemed already to derive from it an imperceptible sweetness of recompense. After his apprenticeship as a conspirator, was he now about to school himself in pity? In any case, he felt that this second rôle was as foredoomed to failure as the first. Nevertheless he had just imposed upon himself still other duties of this kind – that of speaking to his canoness to try to help her overcome the melancholy in which he saw her sinking and to give her an opportunity to unburden herself of the reasons for her bitterness. Moreover, he reminded himself day after day of the moral necessity of writing to Solange de Cléda in order to make up for all the wrong he had done her.

'Perhaps,' he said to himself as he started out on his errand, 'Veronica Stevens is a pleasant person, and my visit may furnish me the occasion of a quiet friendship and provide me with the background of a discreet salon to which I can go from time to time and hold forth.'

When he got down into the lobby of the hotel the Count noticed that he would be fifteen minutes early for his appointment with Veronica. The stormy weather accentuated his thirst, considerably aggravated recently by his constant alcoholic libations. Just a while ago, in the depth of his sleep, benumbed by a stomach irritation, he had dreamed with delight of cascades splashing among fresh mosses and bare arms plunging to the shoulder in icy springs on whose edges grew tufts of mint. Grandsailles went into the King Cole bar, saying to himself, 'I am going to drink some very cold mineral water, but

I've sworn to myself never to touch another drop of alcohol.' The bar at this time was completely deserted.

'An armagnac?' asked Dominique, seeing the Count approach.

'Yes,' said Grandsailles, instantly yielding to temptation, 'it will bring my spirits back. The thought of this visit crushes me!'

'There's going to be another storm, and when there's a storm here it's really something!' said Dominique as he poured out the brandy, generously filling the wide-bottomed glass beyond the white line. Grandsailles unconsciously lifted his hand to his cheek to counteract the pricking sensations to which he was subject.

The outside of Veronica Stevens' private mansion was in the style of the most sumptuous old New York houses, but there was nothing to differentiate it from all the others. The trip in the taxi had chilled the Count to the marrow, and the biting cold of the New York winter made his skin numb and seemed to him to have covered his face with mutilations. The immaculately groomed English servant who came to open the door for him impressed him favourably. Grandsailles took delight in slowly removing his gloves, feeling himself appreciated for the first time in weeks, from the depth of the most impenetrable reserve, by this servant with lowered eyes. Preceded by him, the Count of Grandsailles passed through two feebly-lighted rooms, and was ushered into a long corridor that led to the drawing-room where Veronica Stevens stood, with her back turned, clad in her long starched white robe, surrounded by three black Afghans lying at her feet as if protecting her.

Veronica was facing the large mirror over the fireplace, and she watched his reflection as he approached. The corridor that Grandsailles had to pass through to reach the salon in which he came upon Veronica's calm figure was a kind of very narrow gallery of mirrors with a ceiling so high that it seemed to vanish in the darkness of the shadows. This gallery was very feebly lighted by rock-crystal wall candelabra placed every two feet, but the little salmon-pink shades of tightly folded silk which were further covered with several layers of voile of the same colour subdued the light, diffusing it so much that one might have thought oneself under water at the bottom of an aquarium. The corridor seemed interminable, and as if in a dream the Count of Grandsailles advanced, leaning heavily on his cane with one hand, walking painfully and holding the little cross of pearls and diamonds which he was to deliver tightly pressed in his other hand. At each step he felt all the barometric pressure of the electrically charged atmosphere weighing on his leg and to the benumbing indolence provoked by digestion was added the heavy fire of the glass of armagnac which had poured into his veins all the molten lead of his native land. The emotion of the impending scene made him weak and awkward; moreover, he had neglected to plan in advance how he should announce the dreadful news. His legs barely dragged him. If only he had another corridor like this one to pass through to give himself more time! But already he had reached the doorway and nothing could further put off their painful interview.

Here he stopped, surprised by the immobility of Veronica, who had not made a single movement. Was she observing him in the reflection of the mirror as he approached. Surely she was, for the moment she turned round to face him he had the impression that she had been watching him since he appeared at the end of the corridor and that she already knew him. Grandsailles had not had time to bow his head to greet her when Veronica had already come up to him very close and was looking into his eyes with an expression both of scrutiny and of deep shock. She seemed to sense or to know the news which the Count had come to announce.

Just as he was about to speak Veronica, without waiting for his words, flung her hands out and seized the one in which the Count pressed the little cross. Instinctively he held back in bewilderment.

How could she have guessed? But no word could have been at this precise moment more eloquent than the simple gesture of letting his hand open, and he did so. Veronica seized the cross and fell sobbing into the Count's arms. He pressed her to him with that enveloping and symmetrical suavity that he seemed to have inherited from the trimmed foliage of old French parks. His gestures were velvety and sober like those of a protective tree, and Veronica in spite of her bowed head and the effusions of her excitement seemed lofty and tranquil as a tower. Grandsailles, while waiting for this first outpouring of grief to cease, continued silently to hold her thus while with his distraught eyes, moistened by tenderness, he surveyed through the heavy strands of Veronica's hair that grazed his lips the rich and caressing ensemble of the drawing-room.

Outside the day had darkened and it was beginning to snow, while inside everything seemed to come to life in the warmth of the two black marble fireplaces that faced each other, crackling in unison with two symmetrically arranged wood fires. Over each of the fireplaces two oblong and parallel mirrors repeated to infinity till it became lost in a greenish haze the stereotyped reflection of the group formed by Veronica weeping in the Count's arms. Grandsailles let his gaze rest on this couple to which the flickering flames communicated a kind of life of its own, while seeming to unite them in a single tremulousness. The three black Afghans paced the room around the couple with movements that were melodic and velvety like the resonances of a cello, and their presence gave a strange sense of familiarity to the scene.

It was at this precise moment that something unforeseen suddenly occurred. Veronica had stopped weeping and had lifted her bowed head, and with half-shut eyes she brought her face close to the Count's offering him her lips. In a flash Grandsailles realized the frightful misunderstanding which his situation had created, and pushing Veronica away exclaimed in a muffled voice, as if to himself, 'Why, it's awful! It's impossible!'

As he spoke he quickly raised his clenched hand to his cheek to repress a smarting pain in his scar, while the abrupt movement he had made to break away from Veronica had caused his cane to drop noisily to the floor. Afraid that his rheumatism would hinder him, he did not try to pick it up, and without its aid he limped painfully over to a couch and leaned against its back. There he remained for a moment, with his head hanging, as if ashamed, his brain reeling with the tumult of contradictory ideas that assailed him. The clumsiness of all his last movements had revolted his pride, putting him in a humiliating posture in his own eyes – tortured with pain, bound and trapped by the embarrassing affront of a dreadful mistaken identity.

Veronica had not ceased to observe his slightest movements with an icy and inquisitorial stare, believing in turn that she completely understood his attitude – he was holding back because of his physical incapacitation! Invalid though he was, she but loved him the more. She took a resolute step toward him, and in a contemptuous tone that might have seemed the voice of fury if it had not been the much more imperative one of her passion, she said:

'If you had not come back, I should probably have died of the malady which has tortured my spirit for a year! Have you ever wondered what it is to love in this way? How can you be afraid that scars or any other injury could come between us – when I was able to love you without a face! Nothing can tear me from my dream now that I know my delirium was a reality. You cannot imagine what I have suffered. In my distracted condition I had lost even the memory of your gaze, and like a dreadful blind woman I could have recognized you only by finding and touching this cross that I gave you.'

Eagerly she raised the little cross to her lips, but in an instant all her violence seemed to drain out over the abrupt slopes of her spasmodic, exhausted energy and it was as though this violence had all gathered in the depression of her black despondency. She began to pace nervously across the room, followed by the anxious gaze of her three dogs, as though she were skirting the edge of a fit of madness, seeming to make a point of avoiding certain zones of the intricate ornamentation of the oriental rug whose prevailing colour and pattern were blood and lotus-blossoms. She now had an expression that was menacing, insulting, and childish at the same time and a delicate trembling like a down of fear ruffled the whole length of her body while she seemed to bend under the weight of her hair and be about to break in two. Finally, shaking these tresses with effort, as if to enable herself to talk – for she had become suddenly voiceless and could not make herself heard – she managed only to utter a sibilant and barely intelligible murmur that demanded a great effort, 'It's happiness that makes me weep this way – it's nothing! It'll pass...'

But her voice finally choked in an inarticulate, painful exhalation, and her face assumed a set smile that grew terrifying. Having abandoned her challenging attitude of a while ago she drew close to the Count, a little fearfully, as if imploring his indulgence for her state so that he would take her in his arms again.

'Alas,' said Grandsailles, 'and yet I have to tell you everything!'

'No! No!' Veronica managed to cry. 'No! I love you! No matter what I might hear!'

The Count of Grandsailles found himself again hesitant, holding Veronica's body in his arms, warm and desirable as the boiling, corrosive and ulcerating body of madness itself. As they stood thus, linked to each other by their evil fate, pressed to each other by the two-headed serpent of chance, Veronica found release in calm and beneficent tears whose sweetness seemed to bind them together in still more chains.... For Grandsailles remained criminally silent, and each new second that they lived thus in misunderstanding became more irreparable. Around them and in Grandsailles' suddenly lively and imperialistic eyes each knick-knack, each bit of porcelain, each rock-crystal ornament, each golden angle and each mesh of Veronica's hair began to glisten with the malefic and iridescent fires of an opal. In each object, from the lotus-blossoms on the carpet to the very heart of each of the abundant snowflakes that now were falling beyond the window, he perceived the sparks of his concupiscence flash and he felt them leave a searing mark – sparks in the depth of the six eyes of the three Afghans who were looking at him temptingly.

Now, like a coward, Grandsailles was asking himself, 'How shall I dare to tell this woman who has just regained her happiness that the man she believes me to be is dead and that instead of being the one to console her I am only an emissary of death! Why utter the irreparable word that will only destroy this great illusion without otherwise altering the course of destiny?' Why doom himself to sink by speaking when he had only to remain silent to save himself? Since Veronica was supremely beautiful – and even if she had not been, the fever of her ardour would have sufficed to make him desire her.... It was so good not to know which was in the other's arms, which was the more deceived... so great was the pleasure of their confusion of feelings and of personalities. There was so little of himself in the name he was using and in the false memory she had of him, without a face, so unreal.... Then, taking Veronica's face between his hands Grandsailles kissed her with all the sensual mastery of his consummate experience, and with the studied kiss of a usurper and a traitor sealed the charitable and supreme lie of pity on which they founded the union of their future life.

The next morning the Count of Grandsailles received a letter from France, from his notary Pierre Girardin:

'Dear Monsieur Grandsailles,

'By the time this letter reaches you the distress of our plain of Creux de Libreux will be at its height. In the relentless hands of the invader the progress of the mining developments and of the even more devastating war industries has already ravaged the whole region of the old vineyards, of the Saint Julien domains, as well as all the surrounding forests which were in turn cut down, not sparing the ancient spring that flows through them which, you remember, you like to call the "fountain of Adonis". All this has now become inaccessible terrain ringed and protected by barbed wire and high tension cables. What would have become of the Moulin des Sources properties if they had still belonged to Rochefort? The Moulin, as the key source of water-power, would no doubt already have been turned into a large electric plant. For the moment this seems an eventuality that might be spared us, or at least be put off.

'It is now my duty to inform you, in this connection, of the courage, the loyalty, the spirit of sacrifice and the faithfulness to all your ideas which in spite of the difficult conditions of the time have been Madame Solange de Cléda's sole norm of conduct. Each time litigious problems have arisen, Madame de Cléda has done me the honour of calling upon me and invariably has asked me this same and only question, "what would the Count have wished in these circumstances?" And I, making myself your modest interpreter, would transmit your wishes, the preservation of the plain of Libreux and resistance, and I was always obeyed without hesitation, blindly, I might say, and often without her even being willing to listen to my counsels of prudence when the objective could be achieved more completely.

'Immediately after your ball, Madame de Cléda came and settled at the Moulin des Sources and here she has remained ever since. The first thing she did was to give orders to replant the three hundred square metres with cork-oaks, knowing that the Count had so much wanted this. The planting was done in most favourable weather – little rains broken by spells of hot sun. The Martin brothers were in charge of the work, and they chose very young oaks from the Saint Julien grove which were transplanted, each with a great ball of clayey soil of the same rich consistency as that of the Moulin des Sources. All took root and in the course of these seven months, with the last growth of new leaves, they now already have the stature of little men. The father of the Martin brothers, who is now paralysed in his right arm, came to see them last Sunday and he says that if the winter is mild and "does not break the air" they will be ready in due time to be marked for the extraction of cork.

'Dear Count, I do not wish to assume the right to indulge in speculations as to the unhappy relations between yourself and Madame Solange de Cléda. My conscience would disturb me, however, if after what I have been able to observe of her conduct day after day and what I have known of her condition I were, through a criminal discretion, to keep from you this fact: Madame de Cléda is inwardly wasting away over your lack of clemency and of indulgence toward her. Never have I heard the slightest allusion to the nature of her sufferings, but from what we have kept of the peasant's discerning and wholesome eye we are able to recognize by a slight curling of the upper leaves, invisible to everyone else, when a tree is suffering from dry-rot. Madame de Cléda has the nobility to suffer without a gesture, like the most beautiful and fragile of all the trees newly planted on your land. Were it only as for one of these, I implore your mercy. *Prince maintient.*

'Please accept, dear Count, the unconditional and very affectionate devotion of your humble servant.

Pierre Girardin.'

The Count had no sooner read this letter from his notary than he sat down and wrote to Solange de Cléda, as follows:

'Chère Solange,

'No man can ever have been more humiliatingly and more cruelly bowed by his destiny than I am in writing you this letter. Yes, I am obliged to confess to you, at the very moment when I have become married to Veronica Stevens, that I love you. My love for you is now no longer the artificial product of the divagations of my brain. I love you as I should always have loved you, as a wife. And I must have the courage to tell you this abominable jumble of incongruity is no delirium. I, myself, have tried in vain to awaken from this nightmare. No, alas, my marriage is as inescapably real as my passion for you. However incredible all this may appear to you, the amazing circumstances under which insane chance has enmeshed my decisions would appear to you even more fantastic. But you must know that I esteem Veronica and that I have contracted sacred duties toward her whose fulfilment, by making her happy, will be my sole means of redeeming a double fault which I have committed against the person who shares my life and against someone now dead whom I betrayed and who had placed his trust in me.

'Dear, beautiful, beloved Solange, allow me to address you in this way for the first, only and last time, now that I shall begin to know the unhappiness which has been yours, now that your contempt will make you forget me, while I shall never be able to forget you! Black remembers white, darkness light, remorse conscience, and you have become my conscience, my illuminated land of Libreux, France Solange! Flower-lips – that is how I remember yours, on that evening of our separation when I condemned them to silence, so unjustly mistreating you. Lips of jasmine!

'Only one thing consoles me. I might have spared myself the shame of telling you that I love you, and I have not done so. This confession forever condemns and punishes all the fierce pride which has dominated my whole life. So be it. Not to have told you everything would have been too ignoble on my part. The true moral picture of me will wean you of your generous illusion. Know now that I am vanquished, still awaiting a word from you, if there can be such a word. If there cannot, I am resigned in advance to knowing nothing further of the only being I have loved in my life, and whom I adore.

'I greet you respectfully. Thank you, lady, for the oaks which you have planted.

Hervé de Grandsailles.'

7

Moons of Gall

THE OCTOBER RAINS of the second fall of the total German occupation had not ceased for two weeks, and had abundantly irrigated the plain of Creux de Libreux. The candle-lighted wakes were long as breadless days, the bread under the German eyes hard, the smile bitter, and deep in the wrinkles of the peasant's hands, rugged and as if momentarily ankylosed, some earth remained – enough to contain the germs of vengeance.

It was odd to see the swastika sewn to the sleeve of a real Nazi guarding a machine-gun nest built of sand-bags with a little roof of corrugated iron set up at the turn of the road to the old Libreux cemetery. Across from this protective post a little cabin of masonry sheltered two other German soldiers detailed to control the movement of peasants between Upper and Lower Libreux having to pass through this zone reserved for works that were in large part secret, in the full fever of war industrialization. It was odd to see this real specimen of a Nazi soldier whom they had glimpsed until then only in the half-blurred pictures in newspapers or in the more tantalizing ones in the rotogravures of magazines. It was really incredible. Yet the Nazi soldier was there, all right, sitting patiently, his plump back squeezed by the leather belt and looking from under his helmet at the rain falling on the road full of that earth, muddy, precious as gold, the secret of the fertility of the plain, but which he must have been considering with contempt as a disgrace to any civilized country as he contemplated it with his sky-blue eyes stained by the absence of

298

mud, eyes sterilized and castrated by the savage cleanliness of fascist motor highways. It was really odd, and even hallucinatory, to watch that Nazi, so out of place, sitting slumped before his weapon like a fat nurse busily knitting and mending the stockings of the invasion and the occupation.

And it was fine to see the two Martin brothers, so tall and jovial, passing twice a day to and from their work at the Moulin des Sources before the Nazi who, knowing them, no longer forced them to stop and show their permits. Each time, while the other remained silent, the taller of the two brothers with a sharp toss of his head would shout to the soldier – each day with more rancour – 'Everything all right?' while he seemed to assassinate him with his glance, which burned like a bite of garlic. The nightfalls were lugubrious in the countryside of Libreux, when in all the villages everyone had to be home. Even the little cafés that were once so animated had to be closed fifteen minutes after the ringing of the Angelus. But on the other hand the bonds of family which had tended to relax in the last years became knit once more under the coercion of misfortune and of the enemy from without, into a solid sheaf composed of roots, of the sweat of humanity and of domestic animality. It had the colour, the morality and the rough skin of a potato, as in the days of the Le Nain brothers.

Outside, beneath the sunless skies, the landscape of Libreux was absorbing the rain like a balm. The scars of the distant seasons of harvest and reaping were vanishing, while within each old farmhouse the walls were beginning to ooze through the poorly healed wounds of ancient cracks. Now a large damp spot had just entered to the very heart of the Moulin des Sources and appeared on the main wall, just at the intersection of the great vault that served as a ceiling for the dining-room, which at the beginning of the seventeenth century had been the refectory of the Jesuit convent of the 'Consolation'. In spite of several layers of whitewash, a great rectangular relief representing Christ lying with his face upturned, straight as an iron bar on his tomb, which bore the Latin inscription in indented letters, *Rígida Rigor Mors Est*, could be distinguished. The large spot of moisture that started from the intersection of the vault spread over half of this relief, extended vertically in a long narrow line down the wall to the floor-tiling, seeming thus to flow from the wound in Christ's side. What scenes must this vault not have witnessed, through the vicissitudes of time! Only recently the gossip of the plain had peopled it with the memory of the orgies of Rochefort, in a perpetual state of drunkenness, quarrelling and fighting throughout his Pantagruelian meals with his harem of rough, good-natured favourites with red eyes and hands, who were usually more or less pregnant.

The austere dignity of earlier times had been restored since Solange de Cléda's purchase of the Moulin. Reputed to be the smartest woman of Paris, she had shut herself off from society and retired here on the unhappy morrow of the Count of Grandsailles' ball, which she had not attended. Here she had been living in an almost monastic simplicity ever since. On this evening, towards six o'clock, Solange was sitting before the large round dining-room table covered with a blackish chocolate-coloured cloth. She wore a garnet-red dress and was weeping. In her hand she held the Count of Grandsailles' letter. Behind the door to the kitchen, always a little ajar, her maid Eugénie, who had just killed a rabbit, was observing her mistress while the blood flowed from the creature's neck into a glazed earthenware bowl. Génie, as she was called, had her sleeves rolled up and, looking now at Solange, now at the rabbit, was uttering expansive sighs of contrition. For her rigorously Catholic education had taught her that this world is a vale of tears, and she believed that these are as fruitful for the soil and tilling of the soul as rain for the countryside and the fields. The subterranean truffle truffled the roots of the oak-tree, the snail slavered, the manure manured, the cemetery rotted, the preserves preserved, the rabbit's blood dripped.... Solange ceased to weep, having heard the bell at the little courtyard gate awaken Titan's barkings, and the wooden shoes of one of the Martin brothers clopping through the mud to let the visitor in. Soon the Viscount of Angerville appeared in the dining-room, dressed in his olive-green velvet peasant suit. He kissed Solange on the forehead, on the palm of each of her hands, and again on the forehead.

'Will you allow me to go upstairs and lie down for an hour before dinner? While I rest I shall try to think of what we can do and what answer to give the Germans tomorrow. They can't be put off any longer. Maître Girardin seems to have received news and secret instructions. He will come at nine for coffee and spend the wake with us.'

'Yes, go, my dear. And I must write a letter during that time,' said Solange, again offering her forehead to be kissed. When he had left she drew the gasoline lamp close and with a hand that struggled heroically to contain the tumult of her passion, wrote the following:

'Dear Hervé – my – beloved – is it a dream to be able to call you this? Know, my beloved, that of your letter I have retained only your first words of love, which will remain engraved in my heart till after I am dead. Even when the worms shall have gnawed this heart away they will have to perish and be consumed in turn at the bottom of my coffin, curled up in the form of the letters of the inscription they have devoured, so true it is that this inscription must be and shall be the last reality that can be effaced from my existence! France Solange! Lips of jasmine! If the passion you express for me could become a certainty in my poor spirit that is still too incredulous, these beautiful words must suffice for the happiness of the rest of my life. I don't want to, and must not, utter any word of pardon. You are my master. If destiny has willed that Veronica should be your wife, not only do I accept it but also I shall be able to respect this marriage by my acts. But if your love for me is such as you say it is, since your unfaithfulness to her in thought cannot be aggravated by further letters, I dare to ask you to continue to tell me that you love me. Loving the plain of Creux de Libreux, I am learning to adore you the better. Just this morning I put on high black kid boots to go out in the rain and look at the young wood of cork-oaks; some of these have reached exactly my height.

'I beg a kiss for your jasmine lips of

Solange de Cléda.'

After the frugal and silent dinner with d'Angerville, Eugénie brushed the breadcrumbs into the hollow of her hand and folded the white tablecloth four times, leaving the table once more covered with the very dark chocolate-brown cover. Solange pulled out her sealed letter from inside the bodice of her garnet dress and passed it to d'Angerville.

'This letter,' she said, 'must reach the Count of Grandsailles as soon as possible.'

D'Angerville, as he took the envelope, kept Solange's hand in his, while Génie, looking out from the smoke-blackened depth of the kitchen through the half-open doorway, kept her eyes glued to the immaculate rectangle of the envelope on which Solange's and d'Angerville's hands had just met, seeming to maintain indefinitely a contact without a suggestion of a caress. The Viscount of Angerville lived at the Moulin des Sources. Three months before he had come to her post-haste, alarmed by an attack of deep despair which Solange seemed to have no will to overcome. Since then he had not left her. He would not have dared to, for Solange's spirit was subject to sudden extreme changes of mood, and the ecstasy of the periods of euphoria – a state of happy semi-unconsciousness – was almost as disturbing as the mood that would follow, in which her sense of the futility of life and her depressive anguish would confine her to her bed where she would remain for days with her shutters closed. Knowing that Solange wished to confide something to him, d'Angerville feigned calmness and indifference. As if brooding over other things he watched Génie watching them from the kitchen and preserved a long silence. It was also to help her that he had taken her hand. Finally Solange said in a low voice, 'The Count of Grandsailles has just married Veronica Stevens in America.'

Solange was looking into his eyes to discover his reaction, but d'Angerville's eyes still seemed lost in the indifferent contemplation of the kitchen. Solange followed his gaze, whereupon Génie drew the door partly shut and turned on the faucet over the sink.

'The Count has married,' Solange repeated, and she went on eagerly, 'but I am happy, very happy, for he has just written me about it – it was fate that forced him to it, but I'm the only one he loves! Do you hear?'

'I am still listening to you,' answered d'Angerville, 'but for some time now I have found that in listening to you I think of myself.'

'What do you mean by that?' asked Solange. 'Am I too selfish ever to ask you about your own feelings? Yes, that must be what you are thinking! But why, my dear,' she continued gently, 'don't you tell yourself rather that it is perhaps because I don't dare to ask you… that it is precisely because – I know!'

Then suddenly with her small fist Solange seized d'Angerville's shirt in the middle of his chest and pulled it toward her forcibly, as if to oblige him to confess, 'You love me, Dick?'

D'Angerville lowered his eyes to the dark tablecover, where they encountered the white envelope addressed to the Count of

Grandsailles, 'Yes,' he said, 'I have loved you eight years.' There was a brief silence, and when he spoke again it was as though those eight years had drained all emotion from his voice. 'It was only just now – when you asked me, 'Do you hear?' – that I understood at last with certainty that I can never have the slightest hope. But at least you must admit that since we have known each other this is the first time you have caught me being inattentive to you. You must forgive me! I have followed your love for Grandsailles day by day. I have even encouraged it, as much as was within my power, and while this was possible, but I had never yet seen your passion so glowing, seen it daze you so, as when you told me the news of his marriage! With what utter fanaticism you still persist in believing in him! And what right have I to dare talk to you in this way?'

'Come, dear,' said Solange.

He came close and rested his head on Solange's garnet-coloured bosom. Thus they remained without exchanging a word, as the light of the gasoline lamp began to flicker more and more feebly around its mantle, that hung crooked and half consumed. Before them the seepage of the rain on the wall shone like the slimy trail of a giant nocturnal snail. From the kitchen came the sound of the dishpan being emptied and of plates being piled upside down on the draining board. As soon as silence returned, Solange cried, 'Génie!'

'Yes, Madame.'

'You can bring the coffee.'

Génie brought the coffee, while Solange and d'Angerville remained in each other's arms until Génie had gone back into the kitchen. At this moment Titan barked in the courtyard and the bell sounded feebly.

'That must be Girardin,' said d'Angerville, giving each of Solange's hands a long kiss.

The door opened, and Pierre Girardin appeared. With worried little footsteps he entered the large, cold and inhospitable dining-room and after bowing with a courtesy which always seemed affected because of an excess of sincerity immediately sat down more familiarly between Solange de Cléda and d'Angerville, though not without an apology, 'I am sitting in the middle so that I can talk to you better.'

Génie immediately brought another cup of coffee for Girardin, and a bottle of old brandy.

'Génie can stay,' said Solange to Girardin. 'She can and should hear everything, especially since she and her son have risked so much for us for the place. Sit down, Génie,' she begged her.

Génie who had just poured the coffee and the brandy, sat down at the other end of the table, with two pins of concealed pride pricking her ash-coloured irises. Before he began his story Girardin rubbed his face violently with the palm of his hand, flattening his nose several times in every direction as if thus to gather all his thoughts in the blood that painfully swelled the veins in his brow and imparted a purple tinge to his face. Then, tightly squeezing his chin between his thumb and forefinger with a concentrated air, he became motionless and turned to Solange.

'This afternoon,' he began, 'through Broussillon, the communist professor, who recently escaped from Africa and has kept in contact with Mademoiselle Cécile Goudreau, I received two letters from the Count of Grandsailles. One of them Martin brought you, and the other was addressed to me. This one I immediately burned, after making careful notes. It contained secret instructions from the Count, which I shall regard as orders. By these orders I am required to deliver the copies of all the blueprints secretly in my possession to a communist organization in charge of sabotaging the whole plan to industrialize the Upper and Lower Libreux region.'

'I can see that this is going to complicate the situation as regards Madame de Cléda's property even further. Think of the reprisals,' d'Angerville objected, taking Solange's nervously clenched little hand.

'Allow me to say that I believe just the opposite,' Girardin calmly observed. 'What are the demands of the Nazi commandant of the province with reference to the Moulin des Sources properties? To surrender the three large sluices of the Moulin for the electrification of the plain. This, I know, represents a great force in the hands of the enemy, and until now, in the name of honour, I have advised categorical refusal and resistance, at the almost certain risk of immediate and relentless expropriation. But now, as I have just said, I am of a contrary mind, and in the light of the prospective sabotage in which we will all tacitly or directly participate, the eventuality of yielding to the enemy's demands becomes justified. Our seeming compliance toward him can only further and help to conceal the secret plans of the sabotage. For suddenly, instead of being treated with suspicion, as we have been until now, we shall be regarded and discreetly favoured as collaborationists, by virtue of which we may avoid becoming hostages. This will be our common alibi!'

'No,' said Solange, getting up, 'nothing that even faintly resembles collaboration! On the day of reckoning everyone will have some pretext or other on which to try to justify himself. I am a woman. I understand nothing of the intricacies of the political activity of men, but I shall never do anything that involves France except after the dictates of my heart: and I shall not surrender one handful of this earth of Libreux in any kind of compromise. They will have to tear it from me!'

At this moment Titan was heard barking.

'Who can be coming at this hour?' Solange asked with concern.

Génie went down to open and reappeared with the taller of the Martin brothers, followed by Titan. Martin, with his bloodshot eyes and his somewhat sagging cheeks, looked a little like the old Saint Bernard.

'Génie tells me you're holding a parley about the Boches. I have to talk to Maître Girardin, but only when you're through. What's first is first. I'll wait in the kitchen.'

'Sit down here next to Génie,' Solange ordered. 'My house holds no secrets for the people of Libreux when it comes to things that concern Libreux.'

She knew that Martin was one of the most devoted peasants of the region and that in his loyalty to the cause he was prepared for any sacrifice. Turning to Girardin who, though he knew Martin, seemed to hesitate, she begged him reassuringly but with a note of firmness, 'Go ahead-you can speak freely about anything having to do with my property and my situation.'

'I prefer to limit myself to the latter,' Girardin then proceeded, 'for it contains far more thorny problems than mere devotion to our country. If you refuse to surrender the water-power of the Moulin their first measure will be to cut down all your forests. This has already been announced in the provincial commandant's ultimatum.'

Solange gave a start, but remained silent.

Girardin continued, 'It is true that by surrendering the water-power you sacrifice at one stroke all the irrigated crops, nevertheless I am not unaware of Madame's sentimental attachment to those trees. But any and all of this – the cutting of the forests or the destruction of the crops – seems to me less serious than the pure and simple expropriation to which a categorical refusal would expose you. And in this connection my conscience will not let me forget the words *your* conscience spoke the day you decided to buy the Moulin des Sources, against my advice, when I permitted myself to invoke your son's interests. I remember every word, and what you said does you as much honour today as it did then.... "My son," you said, "will find it in his heart to forgive me when the time comes, and I shall answer for his future on my honour.... In compensation my devotion shall be limitless"!'

Girardin had repeated these words of Solange's in an exalted tone of voice, then he said very low, dropping his head as if asking forgiveness, 'If I have allowed myself, Madame, to mention your son on this occasion it is not in order to remind you of your love for your son, but of what raises you even above this – your love for France. Absolute resistance is absolute destruction, and the country, in spite of the occupation, must and shall continue to live!'

Everyone was silent, and now the rain could be heard coming down in torrents as though the sluices of heaven were being emptied. Solange had bowed her head, and with her hands held over her eyes seemed deeply absorbed.

'What would the Count of Grandsailles have wished in this case?' she finally asked.

'The decision is too serious for anyone to be able to answer for him,' said d'Angerville dispassionately, 'but all of us here will be able to testify to your exemplary loyalty to your country, no matter what our decision may be.'

'Madame… your son,' said Pierre Girardin in a low voice.

Then Solange de Cléda raised her arms, stretched them toward the vaulted ceiling and said, as if overcome, 'For my son Jean-Pierre, and for the little wood I have planted, I shall consent to letting the Germans use my streams for their electric power. As God is my witness, may the punishment of heaven descend on me and on my error, if such it is, like this rain that is pouring over Libreux!'

Now the violence of the downpour seemed to have increased two-fold.

'If it keeps on raining like this,' said Martin, 'by tomorrow we won't be able to ford the river to cross over to Lower Libreux…. For that matter, there is no chance of its letting up before the new moon….' There was a long silence. The peasants of Libreux regulated the calendar of their well-being by communion with the profane hosts of their moons.

But for Solange de Cléda all moons were full of gall! She knew now that her caprice in buying the Moulin des Sources had been a fatal error. This property would be her ruin and threatened to become her son's, too, at the least flagging of her daily tenacity in personally managing her affairs. It was for Jean-Pierre that she had embraced this life of heroism, it was her duty as a mother, and this duty she had scrupulously performed in spite of the torments of her soul. Never had she allowed herself the luxury of indulging the anguish of her afflicted spirit except after those endless sessions spent in pouring over accounts, distributing alms, attending to the problems and needs of the three hundred souls that constituted the strength of that bit of the land of France which she was determined to preserve. And how many times Solange had slumped with sheer exhaustion in the hard chair of her torture, of her labour, through which she hoped to obtain from her guilty conscience the redemption of her initial fault! To the property of the Moulin, Jean-Pierre's inheritance, she must make a total sacrifice. No! She did not have the right to die of love!

As if after due reflection, Girardin at last broke the silence. 'Listen to me, Martin,' he said, going round and drawing up a chair close to him. 'We are all going to have great need of you and your brother, for you are the only ones who are thoroughly familiar with all the little paths of Upper Libreux. Believing I was doing the right thing, I have perhaps committed one of the worst blunders in my life. Since the beginning of the occupation I have kept all the copies of the industrialization plans in the Count of Grandsailles' family crypt. The plans are still there, rolled round a pile of candles stacked beside the small altar.... This coming week we shall have to get hold of all those plans! How shall we go about it, now that the whole area of the old cemetery has been included in the guarded zone? I know of no other way of getting there than by passing over the main road, which is also being watched by the German control post.'

Martin was pondering and nodding his head.

'Yet there must be other ways of getting there – shepherds' trails…' Girardin insisted in discouragement.

'No,' said Martin, 'I have already got into trouble trying to take short cuts. All the passes and ravines are patrolled day and night. If you even go off the main road just to dig for a truffle you're sure to be arrested.'

Everyone, deeply dejected, seemed to be absorbed in listening to the rain, when Génie suddenly got up and went to pick up the broken handle of an old broom that lay between the front paws of Titan, who was slumbering at Solange's feet. The latter had sat down again and her tilted head rested in the hollow of her hand. Génie turned to Girardin, holding up her broom-handle.

'But Monsieur needn't worry about those plans!' she said. 'To get them back is simple as daylight. All Monsieur has to do is to go to the Count's crypt and roll each of the plans around a candle, like this – see!'

Génie had folded a newspaper into a narrow strip, rolling it round one end of the broom-handle. 'That's how the big candles are carried, with a strip of paper rolled around it so that the wax won't get on your hand.'

Nobody yet quite understood, and Girardin objected, 'But I can't pass under the nose of the Nazis carrying a lighted candle in broad daylight without their noticing it.'

'Why that's just it,' Génie exclaimed with an air both of triumph and of malice, arching her figure and resting her closed fist firmly against her hip, 'that's just it: in three days it will be All Saints' Day. They said this morning at the market the Germans have given permission to let the procession take the old cemetery road to the Saint Julien hermitage, as it does every year, where vespers will be sung at five o'clock. There and back with songs and music.'

'Now what do you think of that!' Martin exclaimed, digging his cap into his knees till the seams cracked, 'why, she's right, Génie is!'

Encouraged by the sly peasant smile that gave a faint glow to Girardin's tense face Génie, comically parodying the march of the procession, began to strut brandishing her broom in lieu of a candle as she passed back and forth in front of Martin.

'Martin is the Boche,' she exclaimed. 'Do you think he will ever be able to guess that the wax-spattered bits of paper we hold the candles with hide the contraband plans?'

'There will have to be six of us to carry all the plans,' Girardin rapidly calculated.

'Me,' said Martin, counting, 'my brother, Génie....'

'I too, of course,' said Girardin, 'it will be the first procession I have marched in my life!'

'We'll go to Saint Julien, too,' Solange said to d'Angerville, imploring his consent with the first amused smile he had seen her face assume since his arrival.

'Why expose yourself unnecessarily? Isn't the danger you expose yourself to every day already enough?' d'Angerville suggested, trying only half-heartedly to dissuade her and speaking, as it were, from the height of the walls of his melancholy, to which all access had been closed since Solange's admission that she did not love him had definitively raised the drawbridge of his hope.

'I want to go, dear,' Solange decided. 'If I have yielded on the main issue, I want at least to go on living by sharing the same anxieties and risks as all of you.... This All Saints' Day before the coming of winter will be the first distraction I have had since I have lived here as a recluse.' As she spoke Solange half opened her lips in a smile so strangely voluptuous that d'Angerville, astonished and disturbed, went and sat down close to Titan, making him rest his heavy head on his knees. From here d'Angerville watched Solange.

What had come over her? Grandsailles' letter had transfigured her, making her even more beautiful, though recently she had been surpassingly lovely and desirable in her grief. How was it going to be possible for him now not to adore her to the point of madness? A dog! Oh, just to be a dog! Old Titan!

Everyone was already on his feet. It was getting late, close to half-past nine, and Titan in turn stood up. But Girardin, before leaving, asked Martin: 'What did you have to tell me? You came to speak to me?'

'Yes,' Martin answered in embarrassment, 'but what is first comes first.... It's that the old man passed away this evening around six o'clock.'

'Your father is dead?' Génie exclaimed, making a sign of the cross before her face, while still holding the yellow broom-handle, with the lively movement of a ferret washing his snout.

'Oh, we were expecting it! Five days ago he took a turn for the worse, and wouldn't eat anything more. And he spent all his nights rattling in his throat and couldn't keep in the bed – he would throw everything on the floor. And so strong he was! Like a wild boar struggling in a sack, with his feet tied. It wasn't a pretty sight. The old woman cried and couldn't sleep knowing he was there next to her, dying. Then my brother and I took her down in the stable.'

'You made her a bed in the stable?' Génie cried, wringing her hands in consternation.

Martin dug his teeth into the edge of his cap and spat out a black stringy wad. 'No,' he said, no bed. And what harm is there in that? She sat up in her wooden chair the way she always has in the last two years. I tied her head fast to the back of the chair, and that way she sleeps nice and quiet, with her mouth open. Otherwise she would choke. It's like the old man, she can't breathe, but now she can't bend her back any more, either.'

'And as usual, with all that, no will,' sighed Girardin reproachfully.

'Come and talk in the kitchen,' said Martin to Girardin, taking him by the arm. There he shut the door, went and looked suspiciously out into the rain through a little low window before he briskly drew the red curtain across it and kicked aside the white cat, that scooted off into a dark corner from where he could observe them. Then Martin drew close to the notary and said in a low voice. 'The old man left us buried treasure. He explained everything to us two hours before he died. Be there tomorrow morning at nine, and we'll start digging. Even between brothers, you never know. We need a witness.' And, speaking even lower, 'There's plenty there, plenty,' and almost inaudibly, 'lots of gold!'

When they emerged from the kitchen, Solange went up to Martin. 'Tomorrow,' she said to him, 'Génie and I will come to your house to take care of your mother and watch over the body.'

When Pierre Girardin and Martin had left, Génie brought a last cup of coffee for Solange and d'Angerville, and immediately after went upstairs to bed. It was as though the two of them had only waited for this moment to be alone together once more, but it also seemed as if neither of them was ever going to be able to break the silence, so great was the timidity that had come over them. In the end it was Solange who spoke first.

'Listen, dear,' she said, 'I don't want my telling you that I don't love you to deprive both of us of the outpourings of tenderness that have made the bitterness of our lives bearable up to now.' D'Angerville had taken her by the shoulders and made her lie in his arms.,.. Solange continued, her voice breaking into a sweet quality that was full of the echoes of childhood, 'What can I do against a spell?' Then, suddenly serious, speaking in her deep contralto, 'For I believe in it, I believe in it now. I have had too many proofs that it exists.'

'What does? Tell me about it,' said d'Angerville in his most solicitous tone, as devoid as possible of irony.

'There is such a thing as sympathetic magic-love spells... I shouldn't dare to talk to anyone about this without fear of being made fun of, but it is time for you to know about the anomalies of my soul in order to silence your passion, were it only out of respect for it, for you know, without your friendship my life….'

D'Angerville's lips brushed against her forehead close to the hairline.

'Oh, I know, I never need to be afraid that you will disappoint me! But now I must tell you, dear, that just as surely as you are here beside me, holding me, the Count of Grandsailles comes and visits me. And his coming, each time it occurs, is preceded by a long period of signs and portents which seem progressively to take possession of all my senses, to benumb and bind them, without my will being able to do anything about it…. That is how I feel it periodically come over me…. And its intoxicating approach is always marked by a kind of torpor. Then everything changes, becomes transformed, as if by a magic art, no matter where I turn my tear-filled eyes…. Each time it begins with a mere nothing. I suddenly notice that the colours of a partridge feather are pretty, and then each time I think of this feather the memory of it fills me with a pleasure which is inexplicable to me, but so vivid!… After this I may think of almost anything – a chromolithograph of a hunting scene that decorated one of the walls of my room when I was a child – and immediately the reassuring smiles on the ruddy faces of the riders produce in me an indefinable sense of well-being, of love of life. A thrill of illusion and delight goes through and through me. This is only the beginning, for presently it is as if all objects, even the most dreary and prosaic in daily life, begin day by day to be metamorphosed…. You see this hideous chocolate-coloured tablecover,' said Solange, taking the material in her hand as if to demonstrate the revolting harshness of its colour, 'well, when I begin to sense that Hervé is going to visit me, in this same colour my eyes begin to discover warm, golden tones shining in the depth of this brown… and this garnet-colour that I am wearing – well, it seems to become transformed into a flesh-pink.'

Solange looked up. 'Even this vaulted ceiling which usually oppresses me like that of a tomb, when "he" is coming to me it begins to be delicately blue-tinged, like one of Tiepolo's pale watercolour skies.' Then Solage pointed with her finger to the relief that decorated the main wall of the refectory and said, 'Look, Dick, you see – even that body of Christ which looks as if it had been carved with a hatchet and is all straight lines – well, when I am about to be visited it, too, seems to become smooth and appealing as that of a recumbent Saint Sebastien, and his tomb then appears to me tender as a young tree. And even the inscription, rigorous as death itself, no longer arouses in my soul the fear which those chiselled letters were intended to convey. This means that Hervé is approaching, that he is coming to visit me! And it is never in a dream! I never, never dream! It always happens in the daytime! It doesn't matter where, nor when, nor in what circumstances. There's no way of foretelling it. If at least I could prepare myself for him – but no! He is implacable, inflexible, and it is as a captive that I must submit to a pleasure which becomes as inexorable and categorical as this same inscription, which I could translate, "Love is rigid and rigorous".'

Solange extricated herself with difficulty from d'Angerville's arms, and stood up, but immediately she seemed to get out of breath and, leaning against the table, she let herself fall back upon it with the full weight of her lovely body, and remained thus prostrate, her arms crossed over her bosom, looking up at the ceiling. 'Yes! I am under a spell,' she murmured, 'and each time I am a victim of my pleasure I have the same single image before me and the same cruel scene is repeated before my eyes – the bitterest moment of my life, that of our separation, when the Count treated me with contempt. What can this punishment be that couples in my poor spirit the involuntary tyranny of my ecstasies with the brutality and the humiliation unjustly inflicted on me by the man I love?

'Immediately after these visitations of Hervé's it's worse than ever and I have those death-wishes that you know all over again. Everything once more becomes dismal and contrary as before. This dress that I am wearing no longer has the lustre of flesh-pink, it again becomes the unmistakable garnet of a penitent's robe, and this chocolate-coloured tablecover on which I am lying also reverts to that almost black and unrelieved brown in which monks are shrouded. The roses themselves reek of prison, and only the little greening tips of the cork-oaks prick my hope.'

Without saying a word, d'Angerville forced Solange's eyes shut with his lips and taking her in his arms like a child, carried her up to her room and laid her on her bed. Then crossing the long corridor filled with pools of water from the leaking side windows, he shut himself up in his own room and spent the night reading. From time to time he would shut his eyes.

'It seems to be raining harder than a while ago,' he would say to himself from time to time, and also, 'Clédalism – a noble aberration…. God keep me from the temptation of trying to involve it with my own sorrow!'

The following morning the sky was even lower and more overcast, but the incessant rain seemed somewhat to have diminished, and still there was not a breath of wind. In an upstairs room of the Martin brothers' farmhouse, beyond drawn shutters, a woman from the neighbourhood was telling her beads aloud beside the body of Père Martin, lighted by a single slender candle planted in his two clasped hands. The evening before his old comrade, with whom he had used to go fishing every Sunday, had come to see the corpse.

'Doesn't he look as if he was alive – just natural?' the Martin brothers had asked him. And his old friend had answered, after considering him for a long time in silence, 'Why yes, natural as anything! He looks like he's fishing!'

Down in the stable old Mère Martin was mourning her husband, sitting ankylosed in a rigid blackish wooden chair, which one could tell by certain nicks must once have been painted blood-red. Mère Martin would often interrupt her sobbing to look open-mouthed at her two sons working, sunk to the waist in the manure, digging in the spot indicated by their late father – 'under the third cow'. Suddenly Pierre Girardin, who was standing with folded arms watching this scene, came hurrying up to the hole, while he pulled his glasses out of their case and adjusted them to his nose; for the two picks, striking a hard object, gave off almost simultaneously a dry, metallic sound that unequivocally betrayed the presence of the treasure they were seeking. Throwing down their picks the two brothers worked feverishly with their hands to finish unearthing the chest that contained the treasure and that in a few moments was brought to light. The three men huddled round it on their knees and began to examine it. Mère Martin desperately raised her head in a futile effort to see above their shoulders without managing to do anything but stretch the muscles of her neck, like cords of lights of veal, and hoist her old Adam's apple, hard, wrinkled and goitred, which remained immobilized in the upper part of that ravaged neck in a spasmodic contraction of salivary expectation.

The chest that contained the treasure was of pewter and as large as a small suitcase. Its cover was not fastened in any way and closed imperfectly, so that in order to see what it contained they had to pull out a lot of earth that had leaked in. There they found a pile of several hundred gold coins, some of which were wrapped and tied in small worm-eaten sacks made of striped ticking such as is used to cover mattresses. To be sure, the treasure was not as fabulous as imagined by the four eyes of the Martin brothers, injected with the fire of wonder; nevertheless, for poor people like them, living on the verge of indigence, this chest which they had just unearthed represented a fortune that would enable them to live in comfort for the rest of their lives.

'It will take us the whole day at least to make an inventory of all that,' said Girardin, his eye gauging the complexity of the different kinds of coins which the chest contained. But the elder Martin brother had got up and, bracing himself on his two legs, began to readjust his trousers, carefully rewinding round his waist a long black cloth sash which had come loose with the unaccustomed energy of his digging. This done, he turned his head to his brother who was silently watching him, propped against the wall with his hands in his pockets.

'Well, what do you say?' said the bigger brother, 'do we plug it up again? We don't want to touch it, do we?'

'I should say not,' answered his brother, as if insulted at being asked such a question. He had picked up a shovel, getting ready to bury the treasure again, when Girardin, who had listened in speechless amazement, objected: 'Well, at least we have to count it so as to leave a detailed inventory.'

But the smaller brother, without paying attention to him, had already tossed the first shovelful of earth on the treasure.

'Our father never made an inventory!' said the older brother. 'He lived his whole long life without touching it. In fact he added to it; all the little striped sacks were his. Well, we'll do the same! But be sure you remember what you've witnessed.' Then Martin spat into his hands and got to work. Soon the place where they had buried the treasure was once more covered with a thick bed of hay and manure, and the third cow nonchalantly went back and lay down in it.

'Well, my friends, you are the true forces of resistance! The Germans will never be able to conquer for long a country that

318

knows how to renounce and bury its well-being in the depth of its soil. They may possess and sully the body, but not the treasures of the soul of the nation!'

'It stays in the family, anyway,' said the smaller Martin brother, wiping his forehead with the back of his sleeve and trying with this observation to deprive their act of importance. The older brother, drawing close to the dingy light made even greyer by a regular curtain of thick spider's webs, rummaged in his pocket-book and finally pulled out a white sheet of printed paper folded in four, whose black, worn folds indicated that it had done a good deal of passing from hand to hand. 'Take a look at this,' he said, handing it to Girardin, 'I've just got one, and I have to give it back.'

'That doesn't matter,' said the notary, full of curiosity, and putting on his glasses again. 'I'll read it here.... Ah, yes! I've heard of this,' he purred, 'it seems that some outlaws, "men of the maquis" have infiltrated into the mountains of Upper Libreux.'

He glanced quickly through the document.

'This is dated August, 1943. It seems to be a circular addressed to these men of the *maquis*.'

He looked up at the two brothers. 'Shall I read it to you?'

They nodded. Girardin then adjusted his glasses a little selfconsciously, cleared his throat and began. His dry, official voice became warm and impassioned as he read on:

'*The Men of Maquis*. Every man who applies to become a member of the *maquis* in the united resistance is not only refractory to the German labour requisition but is also a volunteer and a guerilla in the French army.

'2. He agrees to submit to the very hard discipline of the maquis and to obey without question all the orders he shall receive from the leader designated or confirmed by the cadres of the organization of the *maquis*.

'3. Until the end of the war he will forego communicating with his family or his friends. He will maintain absolute secrecy as to the location of hideouts and the identity of his chiefs and his comrades. He knows that every infraction of this rule will be punishable by death.

'4. He declares that he understands that no special aid can be given his family without exposing it to his neighbours' jealousy and betrayal.

'5. He knows that no promise of regular pay can be made him, that his subsistence and even his arming are uncertain. He declares he understands that the slightest thing that reaches him will have been obtained and distributed only by a constant effort at the price of enormous difficulties and of extreme danger for all the upper cadres and the liaison organs. He will respect private property and the lives of French, allied or neutral citizens, not only because the existence of the *maquis* depends on a good understanding with the population but also because the men of the *maquis* are the élite of the country and they must give example and proof to all that bravery and honesty go hand in hand among true Frenchmen.

'6. The feeding and clothing of the *maquis* may oblige us to order pillaging operations on shops, on the Vichy police forces and even on their warehouses of food and clothing supplies for national aid or for prisoners.

'These seizures, which will be limited to what is indispensable to assure the subsistence of our members, will be executed by men selected with special care for their high moral worth. As soon as our arms-supply will permit, these operations will be carried out exclusively on the reserves of the army of occupation.

'7. Naturally no distinction of religious faith or political opinion is made in admitting candidates. Catholics, Protestants, Moslems, Jews, or atheists, royalists, radicals, socialists or communists, all Frenchmen who wish to fight against the common enemy are welcome among us. The volunteer will pledge himself to respect the opinions or beliefs of his comrades. Tolerance being one of the finest French virtues, only the lackeys of Hitler have tried to invent fanaticism in France. Not only will the man of the *maquis* respect the opinions and beliefs of his comrades, but he will be to them a devoted friend, a brother-at-arms. Upon this the safety of all depends and this alone can make life in the hideouts of the resistance endurable.

'Each one must forget his manias, his egoism and even his tastes. To sacrifice oneself for a comrade, to take his place at the task when he is tired, and in posts of danger on all occasions, this is the least that can be required of men in our situation. Never must one of our wounded be abandoned. The dead must be carried away and buried whenever humanly possible.

'8. The volunteer of the *maquis* will be armed only when his endurance, his training and his discipline make him worthy of receiving one of our scarce and therefore very precious weapons. He must take the best care of it, keep it scrupulously clean, have it always at his side or in his hand, except if he must give it over to the armourer of the camp.

'The loss of a weapon is punishable by death. This is a severe sanction, but it is indispensable to the safety of all.

'The volunteer will keep his effects and his body as clean as possible. Upon this depends his physical and moral health, which is precious for the safety of the nation.

'Every man of the *maquis* is the enemy of Marshal Pétain and of the traitors who obey him.

'France lives and shall live.'

'This is their rule and their law,' said Martin with pride.

'What are we coming to?' Girardin sighed, moved but also troubled. 'Shall we be able to avoid civil war after all this?'

321

'Now come along,' said Martin when Girardin had finished reading and given back the document, which Martin once more carefully
folded in four and put back in his pocket-book.

'Where?' asked Girardin.

'To the attic across from here. We won't have to go outside for
this. My brother and I have built a connecting passage.'

Girardin asked no more questions. Preceded by the older brother
they climbed up to the attic of the house. There, through a door
hidden in a closet, they entered a corridor built of wood, through
which they had to crawl on their hands and knees to the house
next door. Martin struck an agreed-upon signal and added. 'This is
Martin!' The door opened. Five men were in the room, smoking,
and the one who had opened carried a rifle in his hand. The older
Martin brother made Girardin sit down.

'We have to wait a moment for the chief to finish,' he said.

While he waited, Pierre Girardin could not detach his eyes from
the man with the rifle who had sat down right close to him, with a
modest and shamefaced air. Feeling himself observed he seemed not
to dare to raise his eyes to the notary's. The man with the rifle had
a wet mop of hair that completely covered his ears; and as it was
parted in the middle it had the effect of a woman's head-dress. His
face was covered with scabs sprinkled with a sulphur-yellow powder.
His muddy suit was so mended and dirty that it seemed woven of a
conglomeration of rotting moss and filth. On his chest were glued
remnants of spaghetti. But when one managed to meet his gaze one
discovered the most beautiful blue eyes in the world, the eyes of an
innocent, of a pure soul. And at this same moment one discovered
that under this manure also was hidden the treasure of a heart of
gold. The other men of the *maquis* seemed on the contrary and in
spite of their poverty to be neatly dressed, wore neckties and had all
shaved that same morning. Their chief was writing behind a small

marble-stand and seemed to be protecting his hand from the latter's coldness with a sheet of pink blotting paper folded in two which he slid along with the movement of his writing, controlling it with his little finger. This man had just condemned one of his comrades to death for having lost his weapon. The leader of the men of the *maquis* had close-cropped, grey-streaked brown hair that came halfway down his forehead, and he was only fourteen years old. When he had finished writing, Girardin went up to him. The leader stood up and cordially held out his hand.

When his interview was over Pierre Girardin, still escorted by Martin, went back on his hands and knees through the wooden tunnel, came out through the closet in the attic and went down again into the stable. There he found Solange de Cléda and Génie, who had brought feather pillows and with the help of the smaller of the Martin brothers were settling his mother more comfortably. Girardin could barely wait till he had greeted Solange to whisper to her excitedly, 'You must come with me. You can't stay here a second. It's dangerous for all of us. Please tell Génie, too, to join us without delay.'

Girardin took Solange by the arm and held over her his large mauve peasant's umbrella that supplemented the protection of her black woollen cape. When they were back in the dining-room of the Moulin des Sources Girardin said to her. 'Some of the men of the *maquis* have come into Upper Libreux; one of their leaders has just asked me for an interview with you. I was unable to refuse, for this leader is none other than your son.'

'Jean-Pierre-here?' exclaimed Solange. 'When am I to see him?'

'When he gets back from a short trip, on All Saints' Day, right after lunch. I thought this would give Madame time, if she wishes, to take part in the procession. Père Martin will be buried that same morning. We managed to put it off two days – that will enable us to get to the cemetery ahead of time and hide all the plans in the candle-holders.'

'Jean-Pierre here!' Solange repeated, raising her hands to her heart.

The morning of the All Saints' Day pilgrimage to the Saint Julien hermitage rose auspiciously without rain, though the sky remained overcast. At noon Solange de Cléda, sitting opposite the Viscount of Angerville, separated from him by the whole width of the big round table, was finishing in silence a light bread-soup shimmering with tiny grease-blobs and flavoured with rosemary. The sound of Solange's spoon striking disconsolately against her plate made d'Angerville look up.

'I can't eat anything more,' she said. 'I keep thinking about seeing my son again… I don't know what to think, I feel small and lost before him…. Shall I be able to speak to him as a mother should at such a moment and, at the same time, will I be able to hide the pride that I can't help feeling deep down in my heart at his courage – to be so young, and choose to undergo the hardships of an outlaw's life out of sheer patriotism!'

'Girardin showed me a printed circular addressed to the men of the *maquis*,' said d'Angerville, 'and it's really very impressive.'

At this moment Titan barked in the court.

'He's already here, it's he!' Solange, all pale, got up from the table. 'Please,' she said to d'Angerville, 'go upstairs and tell Génie to go up too. I want to be with my son alone and without witnesses.'

D'Angerville got up immediately just at the moment when Girardin broke into the refectory. 'Madame,' he said, running forward to kiss Solange's hand, 'your son is here, but he has come with an escort. I shall retire upstairs and wait to speak to you about last minute details. Everything is arranged, and the procession will start for Saint Julien in two hours.'

D'Angerville, Girardin and Génie hurried upstairs, shutting behind them the heavy oak door at the head of the stairway, which was usually left open. Solange de Cléda remained alone, waiting, and leaning against the edge of the table which had not been cleared and in the centre of which the soup tureen was still steaming. The door opened without any preliminary knock, and three men entered: the one in the middle was her son. He came forward toward Solange and kissed her on the brow, then said to her severely:

'Article Three of our statutes formally forbids us to communicate with our families. In my capacity as a leader I might have come without escorts. I haven't wanted to do this, for I am anxious to have witnesses to all my acts. If I am here it is not as a son but as an outlaw and a guerilla. I have come to demand that you shelter six of my men and hide them for two days, and to force you to perform at least a part of the duties which you seem to forget.'

As if wishing to reflect carefully before she spoke, Solange did not immediately answer. Finally she said, 'Jean-Pierre – so you *order* your mother to do a thing which you know she would not have refused – hospitality for you and your people, if they are in danger.'

'I know little about you, and the little I have learned is bad!' answered Jean-Pierre, while he signalled to the two men who accompanied him to withdraw and go and sit down at the far end of the room.

'What is bad?' Solange implored, feeling faint, then recovering her self-possession in an effort to summon a little courage.

'Having surrendered the water-power of the Moulin to the enemy, first and foremost,' Jean-Pierre answered.

'What do you know of the reasons I may have had for doing it?' Solange pleaded, feeling already nailed to the wall of her execution by the implacable answer she knew her son would make.

'No reason can serve as an excuse to betray our country!' cried Jean-Pierre.

325

'Listen to me, my son, in the Moulin des Sources I have, rightly or wrongly, invested all I owned and all you owned, and in doing this I took upon myself the whole responsibility for managing it, for seeing it through for the future.'

'The future!' Jean-Pierre repeated in a low voice, as if in a frenzy of hatred and contempt for this word.

'I was having you study in Switzerland, and just as your age had spared you the horrors of war I should have liked to spare you the terror and the indignity of the occupation as well. I had planned everything so that you could remain there comfortably. You ran away. You are extraordinarily young for the task and the responsibility you have assumed, waiving not only my permission, but even my loving counsel; you might at least have let me know as a friend, if you had made up your mind to despise my authority as a mother.'

'Yes, I despise your authority, and what affection have you shown as a mother or even as a friend? A week's routine visit every year to the school, and extravagant presents to appease your bad conscience. Well, let me tell you – I used to smash and tear them up, as if it were you they represented. Now I know the meaning of all that social glamour you built up around yourself in Paris. It was a symbol of the defeat of 1940!'

'My son, my son!' cried Solange, beside herself, her voice broken by sobs, 'if I wanted to keep the Moulin des Sources, it was for you, Jean-Pierre, for your future!'

'My future?' Jean-Pierre shouted, 'I am one of those whose only future is death!'

'How can we tell,' Solange moaned, 'what the end of this war will bring? What might happen to your inheritance?'

'I shall be dead before that,' said Jean-Pierre, still shouting, 'but even when I am dead, I shall inherit your shame!'

Humiliated and wretched, Solange drew close to her son. 'Look at me, my son, if you won't listen to what I have to say. At least look at me, so that you see in my face that I am not utterly contemptible! Look at my white lips, see how I suffer!'

'I have been looking at you, Solange de Cléda, and I see in your expression nothing but the remnants of the bewitching beauty with which you seduce your lovers, and if you are fragile and sickly it is only because you have been in the throes of your unhappy liaison with that Count of Grandsailles who has dishonoured you!'

Utterly dejected and at a loss, Solange slowly turned round, weeping, and staggered over to the great wall, where she buried her face in her hands and leaned with both arms against the rough stone. The moisture was still trickling down, and she pressed herself more firmly against it, feeling the cold water flowing and mingling with her boiling tears, and the voluptuousness of this sensation immediately became stronger than her own suffering. Ceasing to weep, Solange again faced her son. But now she seemed not to see him, and a mysterious smile of pleasure brushed her throbbing lips. This increasingly fixed expression must have been incomprehensible to Jean-Pierre.

'Why are you smiling like that?' he asked, both furious and disconcerted. 'Is it contempt? Are you trying to provoke me? Or have you gone mad?'

'Be quiet,' said Solange in a bare whisper, raising her hand and leaning it against the wall…. 'I feel him coming… I know it now, it began last night…. He is going to come and visit me…. It's he, the Count of Grandsailles, who wants to abuse me again. Everything is sweet and bitter to me for he is like you, inflexible, and he has no pity….'

Jean-Pierre, completely bewildered, made a step toward his mother, but she, as if to avoid his touch, nimbly eluded him and went and sat down at the table, lost in her dream and impervious to the outer world.

She was weeping softly, unresisting before the flood of tears, her bosom crushed against the table. The white cloth at such close range dazzled her, and she shut her eyes, hiding her face with one hand. 'You, too, have come to abuse me,' she said, 'leave me alone, leave me alone! You've hurt me too much!'

At this moment Jean-Pierre probably had an impulse of tenderness, for he reached out his hand and began gently to stroke his mother's hair.

'Go away, now, I don't need your pity any more!'

The hand stopped. Stung by the fact that her son was so ready to obey her, that his love was so easily discouraged, Solange insisted, 'Go away, I tell you....' And then she added, 'Now I refuse to shelter your men!'

At this moment Solange felt Jean-Pierre's nails dig painfully into her scalp, then his fist closed, pulling her hair excruciatingly, jerked her head back and flung it on to the tablecloth, where her cheek sank hard into the cutting crusts of dry bread. She heard nothing more. But when she opened her eyes there was no one in the room but d'Angerville, who was beside her. He kissed the corner of her lips.

'When your son left,' he said, the words blowing softly across her cheek, 'you fainted, with a blissful expression on your face... you did not cease smiling.'

'I remember nothing... but I know, he is going to come.'

Then she looked anxiously toward the half-open door to the kitchen.

'Everybody has gone to the All Saints' Day festival,' said d'Angerville. 'I locked the door downstairs, so that if anyone came he would have to ring. We are alone.'

'It seems to me suddenly that winter is over,' said Solange, 'as if spring had already begun. Take me away from here!' And, as d'Angerville hesitated, she repeated, 'Take me away from here, quickly, my dear; prepare the horses, I need fresh air. We'll gallop all the way to the Saint Julien hermitage, and we shall still get there in time for vespers.'

When d'Angerville appeared to tell Solange the horses were ready she was coming down from her room, and she stopped for a moment in the middle of the stairway, dressed in a svelte and close-fitting riding-costume that d'Angerville had not seen since their rides in the Bois de Boulogne.

'How far away Paris seems, doesn't it?' said Solange. She had gathered up her back hair under a tiny hat pinned with a fan of partridge feathers, letting it fall in loose waves behind her ears over her shoulders. D'Angerville went up to her, took her hands and separated Solange's arms, holding them thus for a moment away from her body, as if the better to appreciate the whole effect. 'How your hair has grown!' he said.

'Apace with my troubles!' said Solange.

'You have no make-up,' said d'Angerville, studying her closely. 'I've seen you once before looking as badly – and as divine!'

'I also remember that day,' said Solange, lowering her eyes, 'and how you must love me to be able to remember me as you do, in the smallest details and miseries. It was up there, in the Château…. I had been weeping then, too.' She raised her head and looked toward the Château through the narrow window. '*Bonjour tristesse!* Do you remember?'

'No,' replied d'Angerville, 'I said that to you the evening before, at the end of the dinner. But then I had been gallant with you, bolder than I would dream of being now; after which I called your attention to the fact that your eyes were red…. "Your eyes are red".'

'Let's go, shall we?' said Solange, taking him by the arm, 'we're going to gallop, darling. How is it we haven't thought of riding before this?'

In passing, Solange and d'Angerville stopped for a moment in the forests of young cork-oaks whose leaves after the last rains were tender and shiny as enamel. Solange broke off a young shoot and stuck it in the bridle to decorate her horse's head. Then they set off again. On reaching the Saint Julien hermitage Solange wanted to continue their ride, instead of going in to vespers, and they lost their way skirting a gorge at the bottom of which the red waters of an impetuous torrent swirled. Neither of them spoke. When they returned, they caught up with the procession just at the moment when it was about to pass the German control post, reinforced for the occasion by three squads of soldiers commanded by two officers in gala uniforms. It was a moment of intense excitement for Solange and d'Angerville. They held each other tightly by the arm, mounted on their respective horses at the edge of the road where they had stopped to watch the march of the procession. Advancing with stoic indifference under the scrutiny of the control, the crowd of peasants carried lighted candles and sang to the plaintive accompaniment of the bagpipe and the precise counterpoint of the tambourine that preceded the image of the Virgin of Consolation borne on the robust shoulders of the two Martin brothers and of two others, all four holding a lighted candle in their free hand.

'Breasts of live rock,' cried the boys.

'Tom, tom tom.'

'Legs of fresh grass!' sang the voices of the men.

'Lips of jasmine!' Solange repeated – 'it's all so beautiful it could 'Tom! Tom! Tom!' came the tambourine's accompaniment.

'Lips of jasmine!' Solange repeated – it's all so beautiful it could make one weep…. Look at Girardin, how small he looks…. He's singing, too….' Solange's eyes filled with tears.

'And back there, Génie – how dignified she is, how proud, in her old peasant costume,' said d'Angerville.

Just at this moment a frightful thing happened. Four German soldiers opened a passage through the crowd and stopped in front of Génie. Then, like a caterpillar of anguish, paralysed at the heart, the whole rest of the procession ceased to advance. As it had started to climb the slope of a hill, those in front could witness the scene from a point of vantage. The fears of the Martin brothers, Girardin and all those who carried the plans rolled in the holders of their candles can well be imagined! Solange, feeling tragedy imminent, shut her eyelids. But Génie was not alone in being subjected to this measure, for already other soldiers were searching other peasants to inspect what they were carrying in their baskets or their sacks. In Génie's case they suspected only her wide and unusual old-fashioned skirts, spread out at the bottom by the traditional armature of woven reed, now seldom seen, which the peasant women wore in former times. Instinctively realizing this, Génie acted with extraordinary coolness. To one of the soldiers who was trying to search her she handed her lighted candle, then calmly began undoing her skirts in front of everyone. When it became obvious that nothing more was concealed under the armature than a survival of folklorish under-garments, she slipped on her skirt again, with the same non-chalance, and took back the candle which the soldier courteously handed her and which naturally had attached to it the plans which he had been holding all this time in his own hand, duped by the Libreux peasant malice.

'Now that the danger is over and before it is too dark, I should like to return for a moment to the cemetery to place this new cork-oak branch at the door to the crypt of the Count of Grandsailles' mother as an act of gratitude. I noticed as we passed that the entrance to the cemetery was open, and it's just a short trot from here.'

When they reached the cemetery they got down from their horses and walked. At the end of the main avenue of cypresses stood the mausoleum, built in rose-grey Libreux granite, and Solange hung her branch between the points of the Count of Grandsailles' wrought-iron crown that was cemented to the wall and that had left streaks of rust in the stone.

'Now we can leave. Let's return quickly to the Moulin des Sources,' exclaimed Solange. But instead of going straight down the avenue by which they had come, and which was the shortest distance to the iron fence where they had tied their horses, Solange seemed to hesitate. As if overcome by a sudden indolence, she ambled down a side lane where the weeds, still drenched with rain, grew waist-high.

'Why don't we come here more often,' sighed Solange. 'Let's stay another moment. It's not here but under the vaulted ceiling of the Moulin des Sources that I feel as if I were in a tomb. I don't like to be shut in. When I am dead I should like always to have the open sky on my face!'

As she spoke she stretched herself out on an ancient sarcophagus between whose fissures grew fine, tall stalks of rye.

'Look at me, d'Angerville, how I will be when I am dead!' And, feigning to stop breathing, she joined her two hands symmetrically in the hollow between her breasts, but the expression of her face instead of conforming to the rôle she was assuming, took on a quite different expression and she seemed unable to control her lips as they half opened in an ecstatic smile. The moon, breaking through a shred of serene sky, glistened on the double row of her saliva-moistened teeth.

'Your hands are icy and your forehead is burning; you were all in perspiration from your violent exercise a while ago and you're going to catch cold!'

Solange tried to get up. 'My head is spinning, help me get down.' But the moment she stood up she collapsed in d'Angerville's arms, shivering with cold. 'Hold me good and tight, d'Angerville, it's horrible, but I feel it's going to come.'

'I know,' said d'Angerville, pressing her a little tighter. 'I know what you would like now. You would like me to abuse you too, and take his place. That's what you want of me?'

'Oh, don't! It's not a question of you or me now. It's our two separated loves that will do everything! Yes! I should like him to come and visit me…. Now, here! I have a horror of my room.'

'I'll bring the horses here, so that you can get back,' said d'Angerville, brusquely depositing Solange's body on the sarcophagus. One of her arms remained dangling, as if inert.

'But what is the matter with you? Do you really want it?' d'Angerville murmured, bringing his face close.

'Yes, I want it!'

'I'm going to get the horses,' said d'Angerville.

'First kiss me hard, way inside my mouth!' said Solange.

D'Angerville left without obeying her, but when he returned, leading the horses by the bridles, he found Solange lying as if really dead, not having moved a fraction of an inch. Then, falling on his knees, he kissed her on the mouth as she had asked him. Solange's body had become rigid as a piece of wood. D'Angerville took her by the waist, raised her with difficulty, and began to pull her off the sarcophagus. But one of Solange's spurs had become caught between two bricks. After a struggle they finally yielded, crumbling into a pile of clay. But d'Angerville lost his balance, and their two bodies, on the point of falling, collided violently against Solange's black horse, who reared and fled among the tombs, whinnying plaintively in the silence of the rising night.

'Stand up for a minute,' said d'Angerville, 'while I catch him for you.'

'I can't,' said Solange, 'lean me here against this cypress.'

D'Angerville did so, but Solange's body became ankylosed like that of a lugubrious manikin. Her head flopped into the branches

333

of the tree, which scratched her face, while in contrast to this her enigmatic smile of turpitude seemed to be accentuated in intensity and often she would violently contract her eyelids.

When d'Angerville had succeeded in setting Solange on his own horse, leading the other by the bridle, he galloped and galloped like a madman all the way to the Moulin des Sources, outdistancing the procession just as it reached the gates of the village of Libreux. He entered the Moulin dining-room carrying Solange's stiff body in his arms.

'Not in my room! Lay me on the table,' she said.

'The procession has just reached the village. Génie and Girardin will be here any minute,' d'Angerville shouted, his face for the first time becoming harsh and ugly.

Solange now seemed to be in the throes of death and her clenched teeth were bared in a smile.

The hooks that fastened her skirt had been torn off in the course of their wild ride. D'Angerville reached through the slit and felt Solange's bare thigh burning his hand, while at the same time her breast was icy. One hand in heaven and one hand in hell.

D'Angerville murmured a question in which only the word 'want' was audible, but by the way in which Solange's stretched throat contracted in the act of painfully swallowing, he knew that the flood of desire had already submerged her will.

He glanced toward the stairway, but she held him tight. She wanted it here, on this table of their abstinence, where for two years, at each meal, they had swallowed their desire the wrong way.

'But never again!' Her voice reached him faintly from the receding shore of the familiar world.

Downstairs in the courtyard someone was knocking with his fist, and Titan barked, uttering raucous howls. When d'Angerville went down to open he found Girardin, Génie, the two Martin brothers and the other two peasants who had helped to carry the Virgin of Consolation on their shoulders. All of them held the extinguished candles in their hands and were waiting, gathered into a compact group, gnawed by anxiety.

'I had to carry Madame Solange to her room,' d'Angerville explained. 'She seems very ill... she must have caught cold. Let Martin go quickly and fetch the doctor....'

Everyone went up to the dining-room in silence, each placing the remaining butt of his candle on the table and immediately withdrawing, all but Girardin who remained to gather all the plans, rolling them carefully round the longest candle-stub. D'Angerville helped him in this operation and asked Génie to bring a glass of hot wine for Girardin.

'I shall wait,' said the latter, 'to see what the doctor says.' Then he added, 'She must have been greatly upset by her son's visit.'

The doctor found Solange to be in an extremely serious condition. She was suffering from an attack of cerebral fever, and one of her lungs was severely congested. He left prescriptions and promised to return at midnight.

With all the plans rolled under his arm. Pierre Girardin then went to the Château de Lamotte, where Prince always kept a room prepared for him on the second floor for emergencies when he could not get back before dark to his little property in Lower Libreux. 'What a rain this has been, my good Prince!' said the notary when the old servant came and opened the door for him. 'Haven't seen anything like it in ten years!' Then he asked, 'Much trouble with the roofs? On my house down below it will take us a good two weeks to fix the leaks.'

'It's already taken care of,' Prince answered humbly.

'What?' cried Girardin, 'the masons have already found time to come?'

'In times like these,' Prince explained as if apologizing, 'I didn't want the Count to have anything like that to worry about. I got five sacks of cement… Monsieur will perhaps remember that every Sunday before the Rochefort purchase I used to do the masonry on the little fishing cabin near the large sluice-gate. It seems the Germans are going to destroy all that now.'

Girardin had removed his coat and his galoshes. 'You're wonderful Prince – you're carrying the whole weight of this old Château on your own two shoulders. And that fellow Tixier the Boche agent has he been bothering you with his investigation of the Count of Grandsailles' supposed suicide?'

'That's already taken care of!' Prince answered, 'He was found drowned in the course of a fishing "accident" – it'll be just two weeks ago.'

'And your son, Prince?'

'Still a prisoner in Germany. But he says he will be coming back soon.'

With a sudden sense of urgency Girardin said to Prince, 'I'll run up for a minute to the Count's room. Meanwhile fix me a little something to eat – you know I like warmed-over dishes.'

'I know,' answered Prince, 'I've been preparing some *tripes à la mode de Caen* for Monsieur since yesterday morning. I knew that the procession would end late and that Monsieur would not have time to return to Lower Libreux.'

Once in the Count of Grandsailles' room, Maître Girardin shut the door behind him and locked himself in. He immediately threw the roll of the plans on the bed, sat down a second in the chair beside it and after having rubbed his face with his hands uttered a long whistling sigh of relief. Then he went over to the tall mahogany chest on its Egyptian-style, long, narrow bronze feet. He opened the chest and took Saint Blondine's little skull between his hands, turned it over, and in the middle of the occipital lobe found the inscriptions in India ink which he had copied there, in accordance with the secret instructions received in the Count of Grandsailles' letter. He again copied the inscriptions on the back to his starched cuff and, making a line under the column of figures, he added it up just by way of precaution, to make it seem like a mere arithmetical addition, and then went and sat down at Grandsailles' desk. Now there was the long operation of concealing each of the plans, gluing them to the backs of the maps of an old atlas. Having finished all these labours, Girardin put down the butt of his candle beside Saint Blondine's skull, closed the chest, took the atlas containing the hidden plans under his arm, turned out the light, shut the door and went down to the solitary dining-room. The table was lighted by a masterfully chiselled naked Silenus holding a drooping, rough-grained candelabrum branch of oxidized-silver in his hand. Hovering like a benign spirit just beyond the sphere of light cast by the candles, old Prince was waiting to settle the chair ceremoniously behind him the moment Pierre Girardin, the notary, would be disposed to sit down and begin to dine.

A few days later Pierre Girardin was in Paris. In the little room of a hotel on the Rue Vivienne he carefully groomed himself preparatory to paying a visit to the communist group with whom he had arranged for an interview. His shirt, elaborately patched and mended, especially around the neck, nevertheless had a detachable collar, shirtfront and cuffs that were flawless and starched like armour, and with grey thread and stubborn fingers he resewed a loose button on one of his gaiters, which dated back to his marriage thirty-six years before, and to which this span of time had imparted an indefinable greenish hue, having an affinity to that of the mould of certain mushrooms evoked in memory.

337

Contact with these people whom he was to see, so oblivious of divine and human laws and of good form in general, was instinctively repugnant to him; likewise, and precisely because of this, he felt himself obliged to appear before them with the maximum of good form, for never so much as in the present circumstances had he felt himself become the symbol of the sanctity of property and the fanatical bastion of tradition. Respectful and devoted to republican institutions, but remaining a monarchist deep down in his heart, he execrated the internationalism and demagogic phraseology of people of this kind.

After passing, through a number of intermediaries, by a long and devious route, he was led at last into a subterranean room, dingy and lighted only by a metal-shaded desk-lamp, where he confronted the 'group'. Courteous and dry he spoke to them thus:

'Messieurs, in coming here to bring you the copy of the plans on the basis of which the Germans have undertaken the industrialization of the plain of Libreux I am, as you know, only strictly carrying out the order I have received from the Count of Grandsailles. The danger to which I and several of my friends have exposed ourselves in order to obtain these plans is fortunately already a thing of the past, but in their behalf as well as my own I shall ask you to forget you have ever known me the minute I go out that door, and never to send any of your people, on any pretext, to see me in Libreux. Our common enemy is extremely vigilant, every move I make is closely watched and any indiscretion on your part might jeopardize you as well as us. If the Count's orders should require it. I shall be the one to make the move and I shall come here again.'

'You're getting cold feet already,' said one of the men ill-temperedly. He was leaning over the table where, without once looking up at Girardin, he had been continually engaged in writing.

'Such a remark strikes me as obscure, to say the least,' said Girardin acridly.

'And yet,' put in Professor Broussillon, who was more conciliatory, 'the comrade said what he meant, and I shall now try to translate it for you in a language that is less brutal and shocking to your literary habits. The fact is that your bourgeois education – and it cannot be otherwise – is at the very antipodes of certain progressive laws of revolutionary ethics. It is Bukharin, I believe, who has formulated most clearly and boldly the principle that the free, though tacit adherence to any revolutionary action entails the duty to relinquish the claims of individual morality. Also in this connection, there are two long chapters in Plekhanov that are extremely enlightening in helping to understand that 'empirio-criticism', in the ethical and Hegelian sense of the word....'

'Gentlemen,' said Girardin, boldly interrupting him, 'all this in my bourgeois education is included under one word – "honour".'

There was a moment of embarrassed silence. Then Professor Broussillon, assuming a friendly but bantering tone, replied, 'Honour... that's a fine word, but it rather difficult to find specialized treaties in which one may may read and learn about it.'

'These things I learned from my mother,' answered Girardin, putting on his gloves again with elegance.

'Be that as it may,' said the man at the table impatiently, continuing to write with all the airs of a bureaucrat, 'goodbye, comrade! You're a good fellow and the party will not forget the service you have just rendered it.'

'I hope so – good evening, gentlemen!' said Girardin, bowing aloofly to the group and preparing to leave.

At this the bureaucrat flung his pen on the table, looked straight at Girardin for the first time, and exploded, 'Look here, what is this reticent way you have of calling us "gentlemen"? In this room we are all equal and alike – comrades! *Par exemple*! And you really ought to be just a little afraid of us!'

339

'Oh, what the hell, let him call us "gentlemen" if he enjoys it!' exclaimed one comrade who was reading a newspaper in the back of the room.

'Very well, then!' concluded the bureaucrat. 'Good evening, Monsieur!'

'Good evening, comrades,' Girardin answered imperturbably. 'When I came into this room I did so as an equal, but I am leaving it now with the conviction that if you are comrades I am a gentleman and that if you are gentlemen then I am a comrade.'

Broussillon bustled him out into the hall. 'Never mind,' he said, 'from now on the common enemy can be counted on to lubricate the still squeaking social unity of the revolution to come. But we shall all be grateful to you for the rest of our lives, and these are just the trivial grains of sand of different educations. Don't worry – we'll keep our word, nobody will come and disturb you in Libreux. Thank you, thank you.' And he pressed Girardin's hand.

After having spent several weeks in Paris, during which he received by letter somewhat more favourable news of Solange de Cléda's health, Girardin returned to Libreux. The first thing he had planned to do was to go to the Moulin des Sources to get news directly, and to pay Madame a visit, if her condition permitted. But while he was still at a distance on the road Girardin was greatly disturbed to see a light shining in the night which he thought he could localize as coming from one of the windows of the Château de Lamotte. 'Could the light possibly come from the Count's room?' He remembered so clearly having switched it off before turning the key, and the key was in his pocket! He quickened his pace and soon, reaching the last bend in the road leading out of the forest of cork-oaks, he realized that his fears were only too well founded. Perhaps Prince, having another key to this room, had had to go in there to see if any fresh leaks had appeared.... No, this was improbable. There had never been any leaks in the room. But imagine Girardin's stupefaction, when he reached the Château, at finding the main door slightly ajar. The thought of robbers crossed his mind for a moment. He entered cautiously, walking on tiptoe, climbed the great stairway like a ghost, and entered the Count's room. Seated at the Count of Grandsailles' desk was a Nazi officer, flanked by two guards. In a chair facing them sat Prince, who got up the moment he saw Girardin enter. The Nazi officer was holding the skull of Saint Blondine balanced on three fingers of one hand, and with the other hand he was gently fingering a candle-butt. The officer had grey, dreamy eyes and a ruddy face. His very pointed nose was pale as if all the blood had drained from its tip, and it was precisely in the cartilaginous tip of this nose that all his ferocity seemed to be concentrated. A soldier brought up a chair for Girardin, and when the latter had sat down the officer began to speak to him in fairly correct French.

'We need to have you furnish two explanations,' he said. 'First' (and with this he tossed Saint Blondine's skull into the air, adroitly catching it again upside down) 'first, we shall ask you to specify the address written in India ink on the underside of this skull' (and he pointed with the end of the candle to the minute figure that Girardin had recorded there): 'second, where are the copies of all the plans that were rolled round these candles?' and he cast a meaningful glance at the floor beside the desk, where lay a pile of candles that had been brought up from the cellar. 'You paid no attention to the fact that wax is extremely apt to keep impressions, especially those of heavy inks and of engineers' blueprints. Look yourself how well one can see the slightest details of the plan, pale though they are.'

Girardin took the candle that was offered for his examination. 'You're quite right!' he calmly answered.

'Just one more thing that may reassure you: your charming and patriotic plan of sabotage has been killed in the egg.'

'Well,' said Girardin, 'just try to imagine that my secret is composed of a tiny white box that opens but does not shut. An egg, too, you can break. The box, my secret, you will not be able to reconstruct, for my body and the secret are one. And inside you will only find a little yolk and a little white, a tiny bit of albumen, which is my poor little life. I make you a present of it.'

'Good. Think it over,' said the officer, seeming to want to put an end to this conversation. 'It's probable that neither of the two questions I have asked you interests us seriously as yet, and that we know all we need to know about both. Isn't this one of the plans that you handed over last week, for instance?' He opened the drawer and showed one of the plans delivered by Girardin, who could not help biting his lips imperceptibly.

'In that case,' he said, 'why do you insist on my informing on my comrades?'

'A matter of principle,' the German officer answered icily.

'Yes, I see,' said Girardin, 'the "principle of dishonour" – my principles are quite the opposite!'

'In principle,' the other officer resumed testily, 'your execution is set for three days from today. This might be attenuated depending on the degree of sentimentality and delicacy you care to show those who have put you in this situation. You must know that we discovered the whole plot thanks to one of your communist protégés who could think of nothing better than to compromise you by taking refuge in the Château when we tracked him down.'

'I couldn't refuse hospitality to a man persecuted by the enemy,' Prince excused himself, 'and I couldn't imagine that…

'Shut up! We'll remember that too!' said the Nazi officer, getting up at the same time that the two soldiers were arresting Girardin.

'I won't speak,' the latter said again as he passed through the door, and while he was being led away he muttered several times between his teeth, 'Damn empirio-criticism! Damn the comrades! Bah! I'll show them how to die like a gentleman!'

It was told in Libreux that Pierre Girardin was tortured, but that he did not speak, and on the day they received news of his arrest the Viscount of Angerville, after confiding Solange – whose condition was no longer serious – to the care of the Libreux doctor and of Génie, immediately left for Paris to do what he could through his connections and influence to save Girardin's life. But the date set for the execution of the Count of Grandsailles' notary drew near without any news of d'Angerville. What could have happened to him?

Thus it was that, with all hope lost, the day and the hour of Girardin's death arrived. At half-past five in the morning the roosters were already pecking at the crests of the dawn as the firing squad brought Girardin out into an empty field surrounded by young aspens. Dew-drops formed pearls on the steel of the guns and Girardin's gaiters were drenched from walking among the thistles. He was not afraid, but all at once he had to repress an impulse to weep-not for himself, but for Solange de Cléda and her illness; for he just remembered her and the fact that the Viscount of Angerville still had not returned and he feared the worst. Pierre Girardin then turned his head toward the Moulin des Sources.

'*Mon Dieu!*' he said to himself, 'how alone and helpless the living sometimes are!'

In the Moulin des Sources, at this hour, Madame Solange de Cléda's room must still have been steeped in total darkness, for the light of day, just breaking, was too weak to pass through the cracks of the closed shutters. But through the narrow dining-room window without shutters or curtains this wan, crude light, oblivious of tragedies, the same that shines for the first time on the faces of the dead, was beginning with its moving shadows inexorably to invade the great refectory and the round table covered with its

343

chocolate-brown cloth that seemed to grow larger as the dawn rose. The sky was again overcast and threatened more rain. Girardin let himself be blindfolded and cried, '*Vive la France!*'

In the afternoon the weather cleared for two hours.

It was like the most beautiful spring day. Great tragedies have always unfolded in a light of splendour that sets off the minutest details in sharp relief. The sun, the accomplice of all dramas, painted the six legs of each ant with the iridescent reflections of the landscape....

It was told later in Libreux that someone, in sign of vengeance, traced a swastika on a smooth riverstone with his finger dipped in Girardin's cold blood and that the ants held a Bacchic ritual and wound the rosary of their voracity around it.

On the evening of the day of Pierre Girardin's execution it began to rain once more, but this time wind and snowflurries joined forces with the water. Sitting in the kitchen, Génie was sewing and Martin the elder, sitting opposite her, was carving a pipe from a briar-root with his knife. Between the two was the long wooden kitchen table, and on this table, to right and left at equal distances, a black bottle of red wine and a chipped, earth-coloured plate containing white mushrooms tinged with blue and two truffles big as fists. Beside it was another white plate containing a rooster's two cut-off feet and liver.... This was the whole of France – the blood of the earth, the flowers of heaven and hell, flowers of the falling waters, black fire from below... and the rooster, the totem, the sacrificed 'chanticleer'.

Under the table, exactly beneath the white plate, the cat lay sleeping. 'I said on the day of the procession that the weather hadn't cleared,' said Martin, 'and that's when we should have had the wind that is beginning to blow now.'

'And still no news of Monsieur le Vicomte d'Angerville,' sighed Génie, looking through the half-open door at the round table in the dining-room, which now was always covered with its chocolate-brown cloth but which would have been covered with white cloths and set when Madame was well and Monsieur le Vicomte was there.

'If you ask me, I don't think we'll ever see the Viscount of Angerville again,' said Martin. Then he asked, 'And Madame Solange, is she at least feeling better?'

'She is better, sure she is better! Anyway she has no more fever now, but there's something wrong up here,' and Génie pointed her parchment-like forefinger to her forehead with its constellation of freckles, and she twisted her black-edged nail as though she were trying with the screwdriver of her finger to drive in the rusty heads of the screws of her freckles, which also somewhat resembled the grease-blobs of a very rich and golden sauce that had separated from the melted butter of her skin.

'Quit banging!' cried Génie.

Martin stopped striking his pipe against the table to empty out the wood-shavings that plugged the hole he was making and held it suspended in mid-air.

'What's the matter?'

'Nothing,' said Génie, 'I thought I heard Madame cry.'

Martin got up and went over to the window.

'There!' said Martin. 'I hear the same thing you did just now! It's as if all the dogs in Libreux were barking in chorus for some unknown reason. Listen, listen!' So indeed it was. 'You know, when that happens, they still say today it's Count l'Arnan riding through the sky mounted on his black horse.'

'Fairy-tales,' said Génie, 'you're trying to frighten me.'

The cat had just awakened and with a bound, as if frightened, disappeared in the direction of the dining-room.

'They also say that when he passes hens flap their wings in terror, sheep cringe in their folds, and children wake up in their cradles and begin to cry.'

'Be quiet, can't you stop it? What do you want me to do, give you a – glass of wine?' She poured out two glasses, and sighed. 'God be praised! When I think how Madame is going to feel when she finds out Girardin has been shot! We'll have to put off letting her know as long as possible – and I'm certainly not going to be the one to tell her. The curate will have to do it.'

A cry from upstairs made her start and spill the wine on the table. 'Sh! She's just awoke!'

'Génie!' the voice of Solange de Cléda repeated.

'Yes, Madame!' Génie answered, running toward the stairs and making the sign of the cross.

8

Chimera of Chimeras, All Is Chimera!

'To love and not know whom.'

CALDERON DE LA BARCA

IT WAS APPROXIMATELY seven and a half months – rather more than less – since the Count and Veronica had been married and had been living, immediately following upon their honeymoon, in the sumptuous hacienda-palace in Palm Springs, which in the time of John Cornelius Stevens had had a zoological garden of wild animals and a private airfield attached to it. With the war restrictions these two areas, bereft of lions and planes, had become overgrown with grass.

It was Sunday afternoon. The Count of Grandsailles was alone, sitting in the midst of the frigid luxury of the vast smoking-room whose imitation Spanish Renaissance furniture imitated the outmoded theatricality of a great Inquisition room.... The Count seemed sad and was watching a millipede that remained motionless in the middle of a white wall.

'If one day I decided to kill myself,' the Count reflected, 'which is extremely unlikely, I should choose the moment immediately after the radio, at no matter what hour of the day, has announced the despairing and inexorable phrase, "Bulova Watch Time"!'

Five o'clock had just been announced in this way over the radio of the immense room and once more the sempiternal 'Bulova Watch Time' had rung out those fateful and pitiless syllables on the anguishing stroke of five in the cloudless California afternoon. The

347

Count of Grandsailles would have liked to get up to go and turn off the radio which a servant had probably left on inadvertently, but he remained seated without moving, covered with the Sunday newspapers which he had been absentmindedly scanning while he was thinking of other things.

Far from his plain of Creux de Libreux, where the lifegiving rains must have begun to darken the fields, all that surrounded him here, and life itself, appeared oppressively monotonous and devoid of that imponderable element which constitutes the whole miracle – savour. With all his nails he clutched at memories. Sundays especially tugged at his heart, and if by mischance, as had happened on this particular day, the sinister and maudlin strains of a Sunday morning organ poured through the broadcasts had wounded his ears on getting up, it was enough to give him the blues for the rest of the day. But Veronica could not get along without listening to the radio. He had already endured it now for an hour; hence his hypochondria was already irreparably ensconced, transparent and heavy on his spirit, in his very own armchair; a little more or a little less of this fluff-music would make no difference, and thus it was that he had resigned himself to it, bound hand and foot by one of those fits of insurmountable indolence that enable you to endure, almost complacently, the enervating sound of a dripping tap or a banging door.

Yet the Count was at this moment far from being a prey to one of his habitual fits of moral depression, which used to assail him periodically in his Château de Lamotte with their hyperchloridic but hallucinatory torments. No, his conjugal life here with Veronica was obviously not heaven, but neither was it hell. It was a kind of purgatory, a pleasant purgatory, like a bath in a tepid lake, where time was Bulova Watch Time. Aside from this, and more importantly, the world seemed to him each day to be increasingly covered with the sordid moss of the dreary lack of the unforeseen. Everything was in decadence, nothing was worthwhile any more! The world news, too, with its often extravagant sensationalism, had in its turn ended by dissipating his passionate love of history. Since Rudolf Hess had thrown himself in a parachute upon Scotland – what a childish period!

Moreover, the war was becoming long-drawn-out.... He was looking now at an advertisement boasting of the progress of aviation, in which the world appeared progressively smaller in a series of pictures. At last it was so small that it could be held between the thumb and forefinger of a human hand, no bigger than a vitamin pill. 'What an aberration!' he said to himself in discouragement.

The geniuses of the Renaissance – Raphael, Leonardo and Michelangelo, the only ones who perhaps have touched God with their fingertips – had no other ambitions with their cosmogonies than to expand the world in the image of heaven. But today our horrible mechanical civilization means to reduce the terrestrial globe to the dimensions of a tiny pill which does not even have the virtues of a laxative! Man may achieve the feat of flying round the globe three times in a single day – what then? What a nuisance that is going to be! When one reflects that the swiftest minds, such as that of a Pascal, have conceived human wisdom as consonant with the ability to remain in a room without having a desire to leave it! And always the same things, the same images, but more and more insipid and commercialized. The same faces, all alike, the standardized sensuality of the movie stars; always the same Russian ballets, and – the new ones were even worse! Before, in the time of Diaghilev, they still knew how to dance, and even to fly, with the grace of fairies; today they had invented frightful new styles – such as he had just seen in New York – in which, instead of dancers, one saw creatures that might have come out of the nearest drug-store, dressed in street-costume, stiff and very constipated, walking with infinite precaution to avoid putting their feet in the muck.

Now he was thumbing through an illustrated magazine: lips heavily rouged, parted, and always those horrible smiles, those teeth shot by an explosion of magnesium against the wall of the zebra couches of El Morocco.... A soldier camouflaged as a feather-bedecked leopard-frog pouring coconut juice on the bare head of a bearded Canadian soldier, naked to the waist, his socks impeccably held up by a brand new pair of garters.... A lady with the face of a curate breaking a bottle of champagne against the prow of a new battleship.

'I shall have to plunge into my new books of demonology. There's no salvation anywhere. But I still believe, in spite of progress, that it is the succubi and incubi who can procure me the greatest consolation in this despiritualized world!'

And love with Veronica? Since the beginnings of their marriage he had not ceased for a day to want her. Like most Frenchmen, the Count professed a veritable fetichistic cult for divinely beautiful legs as well as a sentimental veneration for a vacant stare. Veronica possessed these two attributes to a superlative degree. She aroused him, he would look at her with the cold curiosity of a consummate voluptuary. He would surprise her by refined flashes of turpitude, he would artfully trouble her in the naked darkness of slow initiations. But between all this and loving her – no, he did not love her, did not love her at all, and from each of those nights, mornings, afternoons or evenings of love, the sole image that emerged more and more exclusive, victorious and strong, was the present and real one of Solange de Cléda. But the Count of Grandsailles was one of those who can easily give the illusion of a great passion, even while consecrating to it only a negligible attention. And on Veronica he lavished all his infinite resources of tenderness, attention and fluid, uninterrupted homages adorned with traditional courtly gallantry.

Thus Grandsailles lived, repeating to himself that only by trying to make Veronica happy could he eventually redeem the wrong of having usurped this marriage. And Veronica considered herself happy. If, in her heart of hearts, her old anxiety continued to be fed by her instinct, which also told her that Grandsailles would never give her the son she biologically craved, she was so dazzled by the discovery of the Eleusis mysteries of the flesh – two bodies and a single leg – that she could not yet perceive the Lenten ones with a thousand legs. For Grandsailles, beginning to moderate his ardours, had warned her of his need to go into periodic retreats, to remain sometimes for long days in succession withdrawn in his 'secret', in his books; and it was thus also that their single room became two and that they came to live apart in opposite corners of the big house, and that the distance which grew between their love was peopled with the coming and going of a thousand delicate, swift and imperceptible steps like legs of insects scurrying over the surface of the water of their habits that were so soon turning to autumn.

Grandsailles had, for that matter, gone as far in his sincerity as the integrity of his lie had allowed him to go. With a skilful and apparently crude two-edged frankness he himself had at the very beginning imposed the draconian conditions of his own marriage.

'I am not the one whose name I bear, but my destiny has willed that the one I am now must disappear forever or survive in hiding. You must give up all thought of finding out and swear to me you will never try to find out or let anyone inform you of my past and my true personality. This would be my undoing. My life is based on a horrible secret and the woman who shares the former can never share the latter. I shall often seem melancholy, and even more often you will feel that my thoughts are far away, that I live by your side like one obsessed. This will be because I am indeed obsessed. My life has condemned me to still other infirmities aside from those of my conscience. My organism also has its secrets and its reasons for being wasted and lessened. In marrying me, you, who are almost a

351

child, will be linking your life to that of a man criminally ravaged and scarcely more real than the one your own imagination has invented. Let us not get married!'

But aside from this last, Veronica accepted all Grandsailles' conditions without flinching – she who had believed herself capable of dedicating her life to cherishing an image of which almost nothing remained in her memory but the inscrutable white contour of its envelope now attached herself to a creature of flesh and bone, loved with the harmonious turbulence of all her viscera. But there remained within her a secret yearning on which the successive moons shed their milky light. With her initiation to physical love she was discovering that her true goal, beyond pleasure, was none other than the almost animal one of achieving motherhood. She now understood her delirious fixation on Betka's son.

She could also have understood the essential myth of virginity which is the white myth of Leda, laying ultra-white eggs. Then she might have seen that white, faceless head of her chimera emerging from the shadows of her conscience in the depth of the cellar of the Quai des Orfèvres house like a large egg ready to break, which would contain her child. For all virgins who, like Leda, are hallucinated by the whiteness of chastity marry the silver swan of Lohengrin in their dreams. Grandsailles, who was succumbing more and more to the vice of 'mythologizing', had discovered and analysed this myth as it manifested itself in Veronica, and he would say to himself:

'He – the white man with the hidden face – is still a swan. There are only white swans and black swans. I rather fancy myself as a grey swan – the colour of lead, like certain October clouds – but there aren't any such, and in my case, which is more to the point, I am not a swan.'

Then he would wonder anxiously if his sterility was not a result of the too frequent abuse of his aphrodisiac drugs, his elixirs of youth and his love philtres. For he, too, would have liked to have a son by Veronica and he knew that such a son would have been his, the child of his brain, the pure conception of Cléda – and, yes, he would have been the one for whom the canoness never ceased to sigh, the heir to the Count of Grandsailles, more and more haunted by her secret fears that he might remain without progeny.

This was the great problem, the great mystery in which he wished to plunge once more to escape from this period of egalitarianism and of de-hierarchization – the great mystery of progeniture, of heredity, of conception – for all the bases of aristocracy rested on this. He would leap forward several centuries by going back to the heart of the marrow of his beloved Middle Ages. In order to give himself over once more to ardent speculations of this kind he must get at two great trunks of books which had remained unpacked, among which the most esoteric ancient treatises of satanism and magic had their place alongside of the most rigorous scientific monographs of modern biology. There were also the great theological problems to which the subject had given rise, and especially that of 'mortal sin by representation' or by omission... and all those precepts preached in the epochs of inquisitorial Catholicism by the Holy Fathers of the church, precepts that were terrible and sometimes outrageously funny. Nightshirts with ingenious apertures to enable God-fearing couples to perform the act of procreation without sin; the explicit stipulation that the couple 'must not shut their eyes' during the act, and that they 'must look each other in the face, preferably in the nose, in order thus to prevent and avoid other representations and sinful memories of other persons'. And the forehead that must always remain moistened by a cross of holy water so that it may be preserved of all evil thoughts, in this way exorcizing the infiltration into the soul and the body of malefic spirits dangerously avid of possessing the flesh in such propitious circumstances. And also the constant

353

refrain of the terrible maxim, '*Pulva eris et pulva reverteris*' with which the fires of all uncontrolled lubricity were to be extinguished at the supreme moment on which might depend the engendering of a saint, a monster, an evil spirit... or a king. The Count of Grandsailles reflected that one had only to take these rich and substantial beliefs and superstitions of the church to the letter and to shed upon them the light of the special sciences of our time to see the dazzling path of Truth stretched out before one: mortal sin by representation!

'Indeed,' he would say to himself, 'if morality exists, the most terrible and reprehensible infidelities and adulteries are not those which are committed furtively and far from the loved being, but on the contrary, those which are committed in her very arms, in the moment of the act, by voluntarily or involuntarily representing to oneself the image of another, thus transmitting an impure life.'

From this faculty of dissociation and interdependence of the fundamental physiological and psychological functions of the human being arose all the theories of the body considered as a simple vessel, a receptacle of the spirits which, because continually present, communicating and in 'contact' through the power of evocation of the memory, could be materialized in blood, becoming then impossible to separate by any distance and any ocean. This idea of the numerously inhabitable body was rooted in the origin of all ancient beliefs of the Orient. What was it if not the splitting, reincarnation and transmigration of souls? But metempsychosis, which he considered a grave metaphysical error, was in his own experience a truth for everyday life. The Europe of the Middle Ages had, according to him, found precisely the most 'practical' solutions and the forms that were closest and best adapted to reality, those of the oniric world of incubi and succubi, whose secrets were compiled – with what minuteness of empiric details – in the annals of demonology and of the satanic practices of sympathetic magic. And the whole modern science of

354

hypnotism was already contained in these practices, since hypnosis is in effect but the hyperaesthetic manifestation of a permanent state of animism and of transmigration.

Yes! He was certain of the dreams that swept Solange and himself along the same current. Yes, in this he still thought like a peasant. And when a peasant of Libreux would say of a new bride. 'She's worried because she's afraid she will give birth to a child under the spell of the evil eye' – a future life depending on a distant glance that could sow disorder in its spirit – how close this way of understanding phenomena was to reality, or at least to what he himself thought. Yes! A hundred times yes! The enigma of procreation: what a wonderful medium, what a magic vehicle of satanism, of temptation and of damnation! – for damned he would be. What could be a more carnal enslavement of the spirit than to use pleasure as a means of obliging the cells, the plasmas and the viscera to create a physical resemblance in the eyes, the gums and the fits of anger of a hostile being who would be moulded in the image of a woman whom one had possessed only in the spirit? And was it so utterly demented to think of engendering a son of Solange de Cléda, across the distances of an ocean, by the body of Veronica? Yes, this was as possible as to receive Solange in his brain when she would come and painfully possess it, entering into all the folds of its circumvolutions with the imperial reality of her radiant image (an imperial reality, a radiant image: what words to describe poor Solange, sick in body and in soul, far away and alone!).

When the Count possessed Veronica in this frame of mind, did not she herself, with all her flesh, become the flesh of the other? Solange... far away and alone! But what was all this chaos of wild divagations, of impossible torments of martyred intelligence, if not the unsated and growing love for Solange that was making him delirious? With his clenched hands the Count of Grandsailles had rumpled his greying hair that fell over his darkened and stormy brow like a crown of silvery olive-leaves.

'The blood myth! And I possess you wholly, your whole soul! But it is your blood that I lack, and the day when I might have had it – with you stripped naked just for this – and I could have given you mine, I made you a present only of a half-open pomegranate with rubies, idiot of an aesthete that I was! For that, too, I will be damned! But even more idiotic are the doctrines that deny those still incomprehensible laws of 'grafting' by which the pulp of an orange has been forced to inherit the false blood of a pomegranate; yet it would be considered an abuse of credulity to conceive the grafting of an 'incubus' on blood, real blood, which is not only constantly agitated by the slightest representations but above all modified and poisoned by these to the point of provoking mysterious tumours and miscarriages of the false embryos of the vaginal fibroma that require surgical attention. Cancer strangely resembles an "incarnated incubus"!' exclaimed Grandsailles in the silence of his harassing and despairing meditations…. 'Yes, sympathetic magic, like dreams, is in the blood, and incurable. Solange de Cléda is like a fatal cancer that is in the process of devouring me and that is growing inside my brain!'

At this moment he felt something warm and blood-red press softly against his mouth. Veronica was timidly kissing him. The Count gave a start. How long had his wife been there beside him, probably anxiously observing him while he, plunged in his fantastic theories, had not even noticed her presence?

He got up unsteadily, as if he had awakened from a torturing vision.

'Our horses are waiting for us outside. Are you going to keep your promise of a ride in the desert?' Veronica asked him, with a touch of bitterness in her voice. Then she began to pace around him, like a docile lion. At last she said, 'I know that I can't ask you what you were thinking of… I am used to it now. I'm not complaining about anything, but I should like to help you. If we have agreed that I must never share the life of your soul, which is forbidden me, allow me at least to accompany it from time to time to make it gallop and tire your troubles, perhaps put them to sleep, just as I know how to exhaust your memories by my embraces.'

'If you were to approach these memories you would die of it, for they are naked memories without embraces,' said Grandsailles, who seemed only slowly to be returning to reality, while he combed his hair again with his gold comb.

'Oh, God!' exclaimed Veronica, unhappy and rebellious, shaking her heavy blonde hair, 'Why can't I ever make you happy, as you make me? Why can't my body serve at least as a dwelling-place for the spirit that haunts you? Yes! Why deny it! There is another woman in your life, who is far from you or perhaps dead. I shall never know, but since I have already accepted this from the beginning as a supposition, I should now like to become her in the flesh so that you might take me for her while your blood is still capable of being aroused by me... before the ardour of your desire begins its decline.'

Grandsailles sketched a gesture of protest and Veronica, drawing close to him, pressed her cheek to the Count's chest and said, 'Yes! I know it! You already love me less.'

Grandsailles answered her with a long kiss, and when he raised his head he saw the canoness cross the patio, casting a flashing, hateful glance at him as she passed. 'Why has she been looking at me that way recently?'

At the door that led out to the desert their two horses were waiting. The one was white as frost, the other black as sin. The white one was in the shadow and the black one lighted by a bar of sunlight.

'Which do you choose?' asked Veronica smiling maliciously, and answering her own question, 'I know – sin! He resembles the devil, doesn't he, that horse?' As she spoke she stroked the horse's muzzle.

'How graciously you remind me that you promised me to repeat our sin today!' said the Count to her in a low voice.

Veronica seemed upset for a moment. 'Why do you insist on calling that odd, but violent kind of love by such a name? For me, on the contrary, it is like fiery water from heaven, the golden rain of Danae.'

'What a desire to embellish, *chérie*,' said the Count, troubled in turn by the resolve to carry out a plan that had kindled in his brain.

'What need have you Latins, who are such aesthetes, to make ugly everything that pertains to the strangeness of desire? Does it matter through what gate one enters, as long as one reaches the paradise of the flesh? Why must you see the demon in all things?'

'Because the devil exists!' answered Grandsailles, mounting on his black horse and making him rear with a sharp touch of his spurs. At this moment the canoness who was squatting on the ground with her back turned to them, in the midst of cleaning a bird-cage, leaned far forward and perched on all fours, thus exposing her legs up to the thighs. Casting a last glance at the canoness's calves gleaming very white in the sunlight, the Count whipped his horse and set off into the desert at a full gallop. Veronica followed him, but she caught up with him only at the end of two hours. He had stopped to get off his horse on the edge of a small oasis which he had never discovered before. When Veronica in turn had got down she immediately came and threw herself in the Count's arms and they held each other in a long embrace while the black and white rumps of their horses steamed. Around them, within a two-hour radius, there was not a living creature and even the characteristic flora of the California desert was absent – nothing but a wholly mineralized terrain, without grasses or cactus, nothing but chunks of blackish and rusty rocks, like meteors that had burst into fragments and fallen from heaven, and the sky, smooth, ardent, like ignited iron oxide, calcinating and crackling all this with fissures of sterility from so much solitude…. And suddenly, in the midst of this vehement desolation of an extinguished planet, the frenzied twittering of thousands of birds that rose from a luxuriant, fresh and 'emeraldine' clump of centenary vegetation.

'It's a paradise,' said Veronica. 'Never on earth have I seen a more beautiful spot than here.'

They entered the oasis – a small pool of tepid water, so transparent that one could see the tiniest pebbles that formed its bed and also, at the spot where the palm-trees grew most densely, an old abandoned well. Veronica looked at the bottom and let a stone drop into it which broke the moon of sky that was reflected in it. The late sun was still burning and the Count had sat down in the shadow of an uprooted tree-trunk.

'Look, Veronica, how clear, how transparent the air is around that tallest palm-tree! There I seem to see an invisible tower – that of our bedroom.'

Veronica had taken off all her clothes and stood naked in the middle of the small pool, the long blonde columns of her limbs rising smoothly out of the water whose shimmering reflections, like tongues, lapped at the uptilted roundnesses of her breasts. She looked up to where Grandsailles pointed. 'Yes, I see it, too!'

The black horse who had come over to the edge of the pool plumped his right foot into the water and drank.

'We shall build the walls of the house all around these palm-trees like a belt. From the outside, to anyone coming upon it in the desert, its high circular wall broken only by little windows to make it secure against the wind will seem poor, like those of a refuge of beggars, anguishing as a barracks in which everyone has died of the plague, or like an asylum of lepers in the heart of the most ferocious sterility.'

'Or like a convent of swans,' said Veronica.

'Within,' continued Grandsailles, 'each of the rooms will open on this paradise of palms shuddering with fornicating birds and sparkling water.'

'And it is in this paradise that you dream of the hell of our sins,' said Veronica.

'Yes,' answered Grandsailles, 'the blessed have always occupied the middle, and so have the damned: hell or heaven is always in the centre. Here we are in the middle.'

'For me it will always be heaven,' said Veronica, looking at the sky.

'The acts of our passion,' Grandsailles added, 'are ashamed of the presence of the common which is always profane. How can what is unique belong to other than unique hearts?'

Veronica, cupping her hands together, scooped up some water from the lake and sprinkled the black horse with it, and he immediately shied away and stretched himself out on the moss. Veronica went over and lay down on him as on a living cushion.

'I told you that horse is the devil!' exclaimed Grandsailles, 'he makes himself so completely the accomplice of our desire.'

Playfully Veronica mingled her blonde hair with the black mane; she plunged her face into it, but it was rather to screen out Grandsailles' face, which now was close to hers and of which she would have liked to eliminate all but the eyes, and these eyes dazzled her so much that it hurt – as though the rays they shot had been sharp arrows to which Veronica's gaze served as a target for them to sink their points into one after another.

'Never have we been more alone than today. We might slit each other's throats, and no one would hear our cries.'

The Count enveloped her whiteness like a cloak, and they set free the lions of their love....

*

The silence was broken only by the occasional shudder of palm-leaves, the crackling of a twig, the deft movement of a light-footed, invisible creature. Then, between the arid sky – its deepening blue fading into the mineral yellows and oranges of sunset – and the parched desert, the sound of three crystalline splashes at tired intervals shattered the serenity of the pool, startling reflections so pure that they seemed to cleanse away all traces of the Count's depravity.

Stepping out of the pool, Veronica slipped into her clothes and mounted her white horse.

Twilight had descended, and before starting back Grandsailles said, 'We no longer seek each other, but let us continue to lie to each other. For no embraces can bring us closer, though we feel them in the very depth of our flesh. For we do not know who we are.'

'That's true,' said Veronica. 'All I have seen of you is your eyes, and that cross which I gave you and which you now wear around your neck. When you are too close for me to see it because it is imprisoned between our two chests or when I feel it dig into my back I shut my eyes and can still see it shining in their depths.'

'What a strange destiny!' said Grandsailles after another silence. 'We love and don't know whom we love.'

'Do I love you, or the one you were in my memory? Do you love me or her? I don't want to know – I want less and less to know; but let us both build something lasting around the precious uncertainties of our confusions. I want a house here!' Veronica concluded, pointing with her crop to the violent traces in the ploughed-up sand and the torn moss which marked the bed of the black horse after he had got up again.

They started back at a walk, each holding his free arm around the other.

'We touch the flesh,' said Grandsailles, 'and we embrace chimeras. We touch it to assure ourselves that we deceive and are deceived.'

'We embrace the unknown, we claw, seize and caress it, to assure ourselves that everything is chimerical,' concluded Veronica, 'and perhaps this is why we caress, embrace and claw with such violence – to see if we are capable of awakening to reality.'

'We walk beneath the same yoke,' said the Count.

'Yes,' answered Veronica, 'we don't see each other's faces, but when our two bodies touch they strike each other hard and persistently. I once saw oxen on the dusty roads of Portugal walking in this way, and their bony sides where they touched were all covered with ulcers.'

There was silence. The Count of Grandsailles plunged headlong into his thoughts of tenderness for Solange de Cléda and Veronica thought of the man with the hidden face of her memory whom she thought to be he, and thus, holding each other close, they went on into the deepening night as if joined and forming a single mass.

At dinner-time Betka was not yet back from her ride, and Veronica and the Count sat down at the table. This table was round and of about the same dimensions as the one in the refectory of the Moulindes Sources, but instead of being of plain and mouldy wood covered by a deep chocolate-brown cloth it was of frantically polished mahogany, in whose reddish grain the dazzling new silverware was pitilessly and savagely reflected. This loud ostentation was entirely Barbara Stevens' taste, but to a certain extent also it was what Veronica had inherited from her.

'For me,' said Grandsailles, 'luxury is absolutely the contrary of this fake place in which we are living, I have always dreamed of a house where all the door-handles would be of solid gold, but so oxidized and tarnished that no one would ever be able to notice it. Passion surrounded solely by oxidized aridity: that is luxury.'

'That is also how I wish you to build our walls around the oasis,' said Veronica. 'I feel utterly uncivilized next to you, with your refined tradition... I want to learn to see all the things you see. You have pointed to a tower in the sky and I have seen it. And everything you have told me – a tower for our common room, and tiny windows overlooking the reaches of the desert... I have seen our four eyes leaning on these like real persons dressed in white and crystal, looking out over the horizon. With your unparalleled gift of suggestion you have already erected before my waking eyes a dream more beautiful than anything which my own sleep could ever have invented for me.'

At this moment, through the tall windows overlooking the patio and barely distinguishable in the shadows, they saw Betka approaching on her horse, accompanied by a tall masculine figure, who was also mounted. Betka came and sat down at her place at the table after giving Veronica a hurried kiss on the forehead. She could hardly conceal her intense emotion.

'Who was your tall, gallant escort?' Veronica asked quizzically. 'Is he the same one who was with you yesterday evening?'

The oppression Betka had felt in anticipation of this question seemed suddenly to vanish. 'Yes,' she answered with steely assurance while she scrutinized Grandsailles to observe whether he would register the slightest reaction. 'He is the same fellow who went with me yesterday. His name won't mean anything to you – he is a captain of aviation who is back from Africa on a long furlough. I knew him in Paris. His name is John Randolph.'

'John Randolph,' Grandsailles repeated. 'No, I don't know him.' Then after a brief silence he asked Betka, 'Why don't you invite him for dinner tomorrow night? Veronica and I would enjoy it. We haven't the slightest desire to make you share our unsociability. The chair next to you is always frightfully empty.'

Veronica took Grandsailles' hand, pursuing his train of thought. 'And there will be complete happiness in this house only when this chair is permanently occupied by a creature as exceptional as Betka.'

'And as beautiful – I feel very strongly about that,' the Count added with an exacting mockery.

'A more handsome creature would be hard to find,' said Betka, half joking, eyeing Veronica while an irresistible smile pressed her mouth, like earrings of malice hanging from her dimples at the corners of her fleshy lips.

The following evening Betka and Randolph shortened their ride in order to await the Count's and Veronica's return from their second visit to the oasis, which they had already definitely decided to buy for the desert retreat which they would build there. Instead of cocktails Betka had icecold vodka and dubrovka with buffalo-grass suspended in it served before the fireplace, and the little Filipino servant also served some highly spiced anchovies on hot toast. Randolph's impassive face did not undergo the slightest deforming effect of intoxication as he calmly drank these burning beverages. He was one of those rare people not made ugly by fire. On the contrary the red reflections from the crackling logs, like anger, instead of carbonizing his face seemed to give him the ruddy purity of a rose – and who knows if the intact coolness of this flower is not precisely fire, cold fire and violence combined in a serene unfolding?

Betka, a very different Betka from the one he had known that night at the Hotel Avenir Marlot, appeared now before Randolph's eyes as a creature invested with sublimity. Over the copper of her flaming hair the passage from adolescence to womanhood had scattered the ashes of several prematurely whitened strands, between which the coals seemed to burn with even greater passion. Her large mouth, in turn, as if spiritualized by resignation, had kept only the tender grimace of the vestiges of her aching sensuality which was perhaps as ardent as before. She had become in Randolph's eyes a body as transparent as brandy, in which only the suspended aromatic herbs of her former vices were visible.... He looked at her, and he

364

scarcely saw her. He saw only through her. And through her he saw only Veronica for whom he was waiting, paralysed with anguish. She would arrive at any moment! As he waited for the sound of her horse's gallop, Randolph kept asking Betka, with the insistence of a fretful child. 'You are sure Veronica is happy? You are sure Veronica is happy? With what's his name, Nodier? And who is Nodier?'

'You'll judge for yourself if she is happy,' Betka answered. 'You'll see it with your own eyes, if they are not too dazzled by Veronica's enhanced beauty. But you have no right to cloud this happiness by reviving a distant memory. I love Veronica too much to allow you to do that. And it was only on your accepting this condition that I agreed to let you meet her.'

'I shall keep my word,' said Randolph with melancholy, 'I shall not make love to her.'

'But why shouldn't you try to make love to me?' Betka asked. 'We two have at least had one night of love together, haven't we?'

'And if I told you that I love you too?' he said suddenly, sitting down on the arm of her chair and putting his arms around her – but with his eyes lost in the darkness of the windows and visibly thinking of something else.

She lifted her face to him, bringing her lips close to his and said laughingly, 'I wouldn't in the least believe you!'

'And how right you would be,' said Randolph, kissing her between the eyebrows with tender friendship. But he added, 'Yet I could love you more and better than I did at our first meeting. It was your fault.... You were dead drunk – do you remember?'

He never found out that I wanted to kill myself that night, Betka reflected, and answered, 'Yes! I remember!'

It struck her that this was all like a dream, and Randolph as if continuing her thoughts aloud exclaimed, 'More and more I think I am the victim of my illusions, of an impenetrable dream. Sometimes

I force the skin back from my orbits to try to make my eyes open to reality, to find out where I stand in life. It's not so long since I was officially reported dead on the casualty lists, but I was only a prisoner of the Italians, and on my return to Africa I found out that the Count of Grandsailles had blown himself up with the Prince of Orminy's yacht. It so happened that I flew the Count of Grandsailles to Malta before I was shot down in Calabria. I immediately began looking for Cécile Goudreau to find out details, but she had gone back to Paris. Did you know the Count of Grandsailles in Paris?'

'No, never, but I knew Solange de Cléda. She was a love, that woman!'

'Her adoration for the Count became a legend,' said Randolph.

'It seems that the Count of Grandsailles was a very intelligent man, but cold and pitiless,' said Betka.

'It's funny, but I got just the opposite impression. He seemed to me a man of great passion. It's true that I only met him for a moment on an informal occasion, and at that I only saw his eyes. We were flying very high to avoid enemy planes that might intercept us from Pantelleria, and we both had on our oxygen masks....'

'They're coming,' said Betka, getting up. The galloping of their horses could be distinctly heard. 'You have given me your word,' said Betka, 'but swear to me once more that you will never tell who you are!'

'I give you my solemn word,' said Randolph. 'I only want to see her once more before I go back to Europe to fight again. I want to feed my dream, since it helps me to live. But don't worry, my soul has already been burnt out!'

Veronica and the Count appeared for a moment in the drawing-room before going up to change, and Betka introduced them:

'Veronica Nodier – Captain John Randolph – Lieutenant Nodier.'

Veronica came downstairs wearing a white moiré dress fitting closely over her hips, in which she made one think of an unruly white colt. And from her forbidding response to Randolph's first burning glance he felt the walls of an inaccessible tower rising before him. Dinner was served almost immediately and they took coffee and liqueurs in the drawing-room. Veronica and Betka played a game of chess while the Count of Grandsailles and Randolph conversed on the subject of the Napoleonic wars, one of Grandsailles' favourite subjects, in the course of which the writings of Stendhal and Alfred de Vigny came under discussion and the Count developed startling parallels between those wars and the present Russian-German conflict. Grandsailles could, when he wished, be a brilliant and captivating conversationalist.

'You give the impression of having lived in that period,' Randolph remarked.

'That may be,' answered Grandsailles. 'Napoleon was frequently inspired by my ideas.'

When it was time for leave-taking Grandsailles said to Randolph, 'I hope you're not going to leave us any more, and during the time you have left to spend here before you go back to Europe, if you are not afraid of always finding the same three people, we shall all be delighted to have you dine with us every evening.'

On the second day Randolph was already like an intimate of the household. Grandsailles had always felt the need of masculine company, that could better appreciate his gifts of speculative intelligence, and in Randolph – silent, sensitive and distinguished – he found an ideal listener. Moreover, the Count constantly feared that the secluded life which the three of them were leading might in the long run give rise to suspicions as to his identity. This handsome captain contributed to their group the charm of naturalness and, besides, his presence brought Betka a perfect opportunity for a flirtation. She had lately been abnormally attached to her son, with whom she had been leading almost a life apart, even keeping him more and more jealously away from any contact with Veronica. Thus he believed that Randolph's coming into their common life would normalize all their relationships and he therefore did everything to charm and make him feel at home. Nothing could have pleased Randolph more. He was madly in love with Veronica, and her coldness toward him only exasperated the growing feeling of frustration which her almost daily presence, with the torture of having to repress all his emotions at every moment, caused to break in black waves of pessimism on the very shores of delirium, spangling the churning waters of the dream of his life with the phosphorus of desire.

Veronica barely spoke to him, but if their glances crossed she would act as if she were offended, seeming to want to indicate to him his duty to be tender to Betka. Veronica's faithfulness to Grandsailles was so complete that it embarrassed her to be admired by others than him. Even Betka's adoration seemed to deprive her of that feeling of exclusiveness which was the very essence of her nature.

'Are you satisfied with my behaviour?' Randolph asked Betka on the fourth day. 'You see that I'm keeping my word.'

'You're doing nothing of the sort,' answered Betka severely, 'you keep staring at her as if you were going to devour her. But I won't take it upon myself to discourage you. She has a way of looking at a man that teaches him soon enough that he isn't always irresistible. And now answer me frankly, because I have a question to ask you, too: "Is Veronica happy"?'

'I can't tell you,' said Randolph, 'but one thing is certain: she idolizes Nodier, and I have to admit he has every fascination – a unique mind…. He is mystery itself. I give you my word that I have no intention of coming between them. Besides, I wouldn't have a chance, no matter how hard I tried,' he said in a tone of utter dejection, and he added, 'if only I could get Veronica to stop looking at me with her hard expression of reproach, if only she would show me a little friendship and warmth!'

'She has given you only what you deserve. Stop wanting her, try to be more attentive to me. When you have gone you will miss me. Besides, I am not so easy as that. I am no longer – polysexual, I believe was the word you used. There are only two beings in my life: Veronica and my son – and you, a little.'

'A little more or a little less?' asked Randolph.

'Just a little more – but you could never make me do anything foolish now.'

'I have better plans for the two of us than something foolish,' Randolph answered enigmatically.

Time flowed by peacefully and monotonously in the house of the Nodiers – of the Count of Grandsailles. Randolph was there continually now, and went with them to the oasis, and in the evening Veronica would sometimes play a single game of chess with him, which she almost always won; after which she would immediately go up to bed before Grandsailles who liked to drag out his conversations with Randolph and Betka, sometimes till three o'clock in the morning, when they would take their last Scotch, their 'night-cap'.

But now for two days the Count of Grandsailles had not come down into the dining-room, and neither had he gone to inspect the work on the tower in the oasis. He had buried himself in his new readings, and he himself said that on such occasions he was rabid as a dog with a bone and was apt to bite if anyone came and disturbed him. But this time he had reasons other than his speculative passion for retiring within himself. Again, more unmistakably than before, he had felt the recurrence of suffocating palpitations and other unequivocal symptoms of an incipient heart ailment. For nothing in the world would he have consulted a doctor, for he considered his own medical knowledge sufficient for his treatment. Besides, it was not his physical condition that concerned him most. For in the last few days he had been the prey to sudden dreadful headaches which seemed to pierce the back of his head as with a corkscrew, and these pains were accompanied by a whole cortège of bizarre psychological phenomena, elusive though quite unmistakable, and he knew that for these no doctor could be of the slightest assistance.

In the last analysis he was perfectly aware of what was wrong with him. Everything stemmed from the same source: his unsated passion for Solange de Cléda, which sooner or later must end by affecting his very reason.

Solange's letter finally arrived. He had begun to despair of ever getting an answer. But far from affording him relief, this letter only obsessed him the more, aggravating his pathological craving for seclusion. The thought of going downstairs and chatting with Veronica, Betka and Randolph was now almost more than he could bear.

'Randolph is keeping them company,' he would say to himself, 'and I really feel ill.'

Thus he spent day after day without being able to resolve to go downstairs. For a whole day he pondered his answer to Solange, and at about half-past five the following morning, no longer able to sleep, he got up from his bed and wrote:

'My beautiful, cherished, adored Solange,
'To what could I possibly dedicate the rest of my life if not to repeating to you constantly, each time with a different shade of feeling, that my love is even greater than my gratitude, which in all justice should at this moment be limitless, since you have expressed your willingness to grant me not

only the mite of esteem which I dared beg of you, but also to continue to favour me with your passion. For if I had never received an answer to my letter, my gratitude might perhaps have diminished, but never my love which constantly grows. Now, though this gratitude is of the highest, it is nevertheless far from reaching the heights of my love for you, so inaccessible will this feeling always remain to all others, including pity! I feel awkward and inept in my attempts to communicate with your heart through my poor love-letters. But with each passing day and in spite of the distance it seems to me more certain that my continual dreams of you cannot fail to pass into your spirit and take possession of your dreams. The magic of the science of incubi and succubi to which I have been subjecting all the disciplines of my mind in order to draw close to your spirit is none other than the science of dreams of ancient Egypt, the science of the real and tangible incarnation of the flesh-and-blood desires of dreams which end by covering the heart with "tissues of asphyxiation"... and paralysing it. Periodically, and quite beyond the control of my will, I feel as if all the convergent forces of my most secret organic being were gathering in my brain, provoking frightful headaches accompanied by bleeding of the ears as if, without moving, I were being subjected to unusual atmospheric pressures. As these symptoms multiply I begin to perceive images with phenomenal visual acuteness, while the area around my orbits begins to ache, as though they were being immersed in boiling water. Finally I see you as clearly as though you were standing right in front of me.

'I see you in instantaneous flashes, always outdoors and lighted by a bright winter sun, and these images are all the clearer if, at the moment when they occur, I press my shut eyelids with my handkerchief. I see you going down a ravine, wearing a bright red dress, near the newly planted grove, accompanied by the two Martin brothers. I see you leaning over to open the little wooden gate that leads to the back road, near the wash-houses. Titan watches you, motionless, and one of the brass studs on his collar suddenly flashes for a moment like a signal-light. Each of these images is accompanied by the sound of dear voices that talk to you respectfully, that of Pierre Girardin whom I assume to be your guardian-angel. Though I have a heart of stone, I am reduced to tears by the flash of a brass stud – because it belongs to the collar of a dog who looks at you – tears all the more burning because my eyes ache with the vision of you. And always at the end of this hallucinatory period I perceive of you the same final image – the most disturbing one – your face convulsed in a strange expression of ecstasy which is not solely that of pleasure, since it combines with one of anguishing and mortal terror which, I am sure, is but the subjective one of my own spirit trembling at having lost you, the wretched fear of my damnation alone bestially wrenching from me the pleasure you might graciously have offered me as the noblest of ladies that you are. My beloved Solange de France, lips of jasmine, my lovely, fragile young tree, I can feel each of your new leaves growing and pricking within the genealogical tree of my veins. If at least we could have had a son together! My thoughts are my hands placed like a crown round your brow, my memory is my mouth on yours, my desire the tissues of your entrails, my tenderness my arms! I kiss you all over, and I shall live only in expectation of your answer.

Your

HERVÉ DE GRANDSAILLES.'

In the days that followed Grandsailles obstinately continued his seclusion, and Veronica and her friends were beginning to be concerned, Nevertheless Veronica each morning received a few scribbled words from her husband, always with some lovely surprising thought on the subject of their love, which enabled her to live through the rest of the day and wait with resignation for the next. Each evening the game of chess between Veronica and Randolph seemed to be played by two phantoms. And seeing them so quiet, so close, facing each other, their heads slightly bent over the chessboard, like the couple in Millet's 'Angelus' in a sitting posture, Betka found it hard to believe that this simple scene was an authentic bit of reality. For Randolph, tall and melancholy, accustomed to setting planes afire, to flying beneath a shower of ashes and piercing through flaming clouds, now trembled with pent-up passion, with martyred desire, his heart impotent before her who without knowing it – even as he was unaware of it – obstinately rejected him precisely in order to remain faithful to him!

Veronica had loved Grandsailles, dedicating her life wholly to him, solely out of faithfulness to her delirious memory, that of the man with the hidden face in the depth of the cellar of the house on the Quai des Orfèvres; now this man whom she had waited for so long and so mortally was there, sitting before her, real – and precisely because he was visible she could not see him! Both of them were like pawns facing each other, isolated, unable to advance or retreat and as distant as two stars that seem to touch. But this was another game, and with a queen and a knight Veronica declared 'Checkmate!' Then she went up to bed. In passing the Count of Grandsailles' door she stopped and drew close for a moment. Above the door a streak of light showed that the Count was awake. She did not dare to knock.

'It's curious,' it suddenly occurred to her,' Randolph's face is covered with very fine, almost invisible scars. It's rather attractive, but why do I find it strange all at once?' She went and shut herself up in her room and no longer gave it a thought.

For weeks Randolph had spent several hours almost daily in Veronica's presence. His furlough would end and he would return to Europe without their having given any utterance to their emotions. There had been only that stubborn and merciless battle of eyes. And now that the time for leave-taking began to loom before him it seemed to Randolph that he noticed a change of expression in Veronica – a look, if not of acceptance, at least of compliance. Was it habit, or leniency inspired by the imminence of his departure? Probably both, and the first hypothesis displeased him as much as the second. Nevertheless the lack of charitable softness in Veronica's pitiless eyes had already upset him so much that he was ill from it. How could he resign himself to leaving her, perhaps for ever, without trying to obtain from her one single look of passion that he could carry away with him in his heart into the skies of war, like a shield for his wings? His furlough was shrinking like the famous wild-ass's skin described by Balzac and he superstitiously believed that if he were to try to snatch the slightest pleasure beyond what was strictly due him, if he did not preserve his silence before Veronica, the happiness of seeing her which had become the sole reason for his being would be brought to a premature end.

One evening Veronica and Randolph were sitting on the sand by the oasis, watching the tower which was nearing completion. They were alone. Betka was riding, some distance away, carrying her son on her own horse. The canoness, who had spent the afternoon putting away the linen, had gone off half an hour before in the supply truck, and the workers who had finished their day's work had also left.

Now that Veronica was sitting out in the open desert beneath an immense sky it was no longer possible (as when she was in Paris) to compare her gaze to the aridity of the desert and to the transparency of the azure sky, for her eyes were even emptier and more immense than these two elements of nature combined. Veronica had the clear eyes of 'frustrated yearning for motherhood'. She kept her head slightly tipped back so as to feel the weight of her hair blown by the breeze, and her whole body opened to the wind, like certain plants that are fertilized by this means. Sitting thus, she was oblivious of the potent challenge of her body's curves. Randolph held his head lowered close to her hair, and through its screen he riveted his eyes on one of her bare knees, which he saw both as Eve's apple and as Yorick's skull. No longer able to contain himself he began to speak, without detaching his eyes from the spot.

'It's only because you know the war is about to call me away again that you deign not to punish me whenever I can't help worshipping you in silence. It's only lately that you have begun to regard me with a glimmer of friendship. I've never gone in for inspiring pity. You've made me unhappy all the time!'

'You are wrong, John,' Veronica said calmly, without changing her position. After a long silence she passed her arm round Randolph's neck, 'I liked you the moment I saw you,' she finally continued, 'much more than I could have believed. I just discovered it a few days ago. No one in my place would talk to you so frankly as I am doing. You must be equal to the confidence I show you in telling you this, but listen to me....'

Randolph remained as if paralysed. Painfully swallowing his saliva he lowered his head still further without, however, changing the direction of his gaze, and as the sun was now setting, the tip of Randolph's ear had begun to cast its shadow on Veronica's bare knee.

'Yes, listen to me, John: though I have a very strong feeling for you, Jules is everything in life to me, and I mean to be absolutely faithful to him until I die.'

'You're contradicting yourself frightfully,' said Randolph.

'No, I am only following my nature and my destiny. What binds me to Jules is far above any feeling that can be expressed. It's not just to him that I am being faithful, it's much more than that. Through him and beyond him I worship a far-away image, and this image has raised my love to the realm of the absolute.'

'What is that image?' asked Randolph.

'You wouldn't understand,' answered Veronica, 'and one must never speak of what is unique to oneself.'

'You are deceiving yourself with words,' Randolph exclaimed, then he said in a low voice, 'At first I believed you were happy with Nodier. Now I know you are not!' He had uttered the last words with vehemence, while he pressed his cheek against Veronica's head.

'I am the happiest of women,' Veronica retorted, 'by virtue of the very fact that I must share the tormented life of him who is dearest to me in all the world. Don't press me so with your arm. If I have been frank it was not in order that you should take advantage of it and spoil our illusion!'

Randolph released Veronica from what had been the beginning of a passionate embrace, and now the shadow of his ear reached the exact middle of Veronica's knee.

'May I,' he said, 'at least be allowed to caress you with my shadow?'

With this he lowered his head so as to make the shadow of his ear slip down the whole length of Veronica's leg; then he made it glide slowly, slowly up again as far as her knee. There he paused for a moment and slowly, ever more slowly, he began to move it higher, encroaching upon the very white flesh of her thigh, up to the edge of her skirt. 'Your life is a desert!' he exclaimed with irritation. 'Nodier will never give you the child you yearn for. I know everything – you are like those hallucinated creatures dying of thirst, who fill their mouths with burning sand, not knowing that one elbow-length further down there flows a spring of fresh water that could save them.'

'And are you that spring?' Veronica asked mockingly, throwing her head back to look at him squarely.

'Give me your mouth,' Randolph commanded, clasping her in his arms and snatching a savage kiss.

Veronica let herself be kissed without kissing in return, then she got up. 'You've satisfied your little urge. Now leave me.'

'I am desperately looking for a little gentleness in you,' said Randolph getting up in turn, 'and now I shall have only your contempt. I know I've spoiled everything by letting my feelings get the best of me. I shall leave tonight.'

'You won't need to,' said Veronica, in a frightfully detached and icy tone, 'for tomorrow morning Jules and I are coming to live in the tower. It's your duty to remain with Betka a little longer, if only to keep up appearances. But never again expect of me the look of friendship and tenderness, and perhaps something more, which I foolishly let myself convey to you. You did not deserve it.' Veronica got on her horse and set off at a gallop.

Grandsailles had come down from his room for the first time in a fortnight. He took Veronica in his arms and held her in a long embrace.

'Today,' she said, 'I would like to stay in my room!'

'I'll keep you company,' he said. 'I have so many, many things to tell you. It's as if I were returning from a very long voyage.'

'For me it has been an eternity,' sighed Veronica, 'a real desert!'

'And tomorrow the oasis,' said the Count, his lips brushing away a large tear that flowed down his wife's cheek.

The following morning before the departure Betka came to see Veronica in her room. 'John has told me everything – what happened between you last night. He is utterly miserable, and he wanted me to ask you to give him a chance to ask your forgiveness.'

'I don't want to see him again,' said Veronica. 'My forgiveness he has. For that matter, he kisses like a child! It can't even be considered a sin.'

Betka felt somewhat offended by this slight to Randolph's powers of seduction, 'You surprise me,' she remarked, 'you make it sound like a case of sour grapes.'

Veronica pretended not to notice the challenge, embraced her as usual and left.

In the oasis tower their projected Paradise Regained was beginning badly. For the first time since their marriage, Veronica seemed distant and listless in her husband's presence; she was dreamy, answered without listening and spilled the bag of millet seed on the floor each time she went to restock the bird-cage.

'Aren't you happy here?' the Count asked her as they finished dinner on the third day.

'Why yes, I'm perfectly content!' Veronica answered.

'Be frank,' Grandsailles rejoined, 'for you act as if you missed someone.'

At these words Veronica, who never blushed, turned so red that the rush of blood to her habitually pale face made her eyes weep for pure shame, while her brow and the area around her lips became beaded with a perspiration of anguish. Her bosom swelled with resentment at feeling herself thus betrayed in her feelings, and she lost all countenance. 'Don't suppose that for a moment,' she exclaimed, thinking to forestall the suspicions under which she assumed Grandsailles to be smarting, 'there is nothing between John and me!'

'I should never have thought of asking you that,' answered Grandsailles, approaching her and trying to embrace her. But Veronica, who had suddenly become irritable, eluded his clasp, mounted the few steps that separated her from the door to the tower where their room was, and before she disappeared turned round to face Grandsailles, 'But there is someone we miss,' she said, and there was hatred in her voice, ' – our son!' Then she shut the door noiselessly behind her.

At this moment the canoness appeared, carrying the bird-cage in her hands, and Grandsailles turned to her. 'Did you hear that, my good canoness?' he said. 'You hold it against me too, don't you, that I have not had a son, but you, I know, would have preferred him to be Solange de Cléda's!'

'As long as it's a boy I don't care whom you have him by – even if it were the devil!' Thereupon the canoness blew on the feeders filled with millet seeds to get rid of the chaff, but she blew so hard that it flew into her face and some of it got into her right eye, the one that was always running. She put the cage down on a table for a moment and with a corner of her apron tried to remove the particle.

'The devil,' Grandsailles repeated dreamily, 'perhaps he is the only one by whom I could have one. Have my black horse saddled – I feel like riding. I couldn't sleep now.'

When he was gone the canoness picked up the bird-cage again. 'It's white flesh he should be mounting,' she said 'but according to the law of God and in obedience to his dictates.'

The following evening Veronica and Grandsailles had a worse scene than the night before. The latter must have behaved violently, for as they both left their room in the tower, Veronica said to him, 'From now on, I don't want you in this room any more. It used to fill me with such high hopes, and now it means only disappointment. After this the room shall be consecrated to my solitude. You have asked my forgiveness a hundred times. Well, I forgive you on one condition: give me the key! I want the key to this room, which is now the room of my sorrow and where you will never have the right to enter on any pretext. You must respect this solitude whenever it needs me, or I need it. You have a secret which you have kept in your heart-and this I have countenanced. But you have also locked the door to our room without my permission. All right! I never told you that I didn't have a secret, too. I am going to become suspicious, like you!'

'I won't go into your room if that is your wish. I promise you,' said Grandsailles, and he went and sat down by the fireplace. A moment later Veronica was sitting close beside him. She put her hand on his.

'Thank you, darling,' said Grandsailles, taking it and pressing it.

The canoness entered, bringing a new bellows and a box with giant matches. She got down on all fours and began to light the fire. The kindling that she arranged in peasant fashion around two large logs began instantly to crackle joyously, but soon a thick puff of smoke blown down the chimney entered the room.

'That's only because the chimney is cold,' said the canoness, her irritated red eyes streaming with tears. She added wood-shavings, fanned the fire with the bellows, and now the flames, enveloping the two logs, rose high. But suddenly, as if blown down by a gust of wind from the outside, another, much thicker puff of smoke entered the room. Grandsailles got up, coughing, and went to open the window.

'The chimney is surely stopped up,' he said, 'we'll have to call the mason tomorrow and have him attend to it.'

'Just leave it,' said Veronica to the canoness, 'it won't burn. We'll wait till tomorrow.'

The next day the chimney was checked by the mason, but he claimed that everything was in order, that nothing obstructed it. Nevertheless he had a man climb up inside it and install a little revolving tin vent at the top to protect the chimney from counter-draughts. 'It must surely have been the wind,' said the man to the canoness, 'but with the little cap I put on you won't have any more trouble with smoke.' Then the man had left.

But in the evening when the canoness got down on all fours in front of her fire, again great puffs of smoke blew, one after another, into the room.

'And today there is not a breath of wind,' the canoness sighed in utter bewilderment, and straightening up on her knees, with her hands on her hips, she exclaimed. 'It looks like the evil work of sorcery.'

Sorcery or no sorcery, and however incredible it might appear, the fact was that in spite of the masons' consultations and altera-tions, at the end of a week the fireplace in the large library adjoining Veronica's tower-room still worked no better than on the first day.

It must have been at about half-past eleven in the evening that the Count of Grandsailles and Veronica, sitting before the extinguished fire in the fireplace, were finishing a game of chess. Veronica had just picked up a black knight with the pink, blue-tinged pincers of her long fingers, and at the moment when she was lifting it slowly from the chessboard in deep thought she suddenly became motionless. She turned her head toward the door leading to the patio, which had unexpectedly opened. In the doorway stood an old cowboy dressed like a beggar, his grey moustache drooping over his lips, his eyes smoke-coloured, his skin very wrinkled like an Indian's, his hat respectfully held in front of his chest while with his other hand he held a gnarled stick. At the end of this stick dangled a little bundle wrapped in a very clean white handkerchief.

Grandsailles and Veronica looked at him questioningly and the man finally said in a far-away voice, full of tenderness, 'I am the smoke-man! I have come a long way, and I always travel on foot.'

'You're what man?' asked Grandsailles, not quite sure he had heard right.

'The smoke-man,' he repeated.

'The smoke-man,' Veronica repeated in turn as if it were more natural to her.

Grandsailles got up and had him sit down, shutting the door that the smoke-man had blithely left open.

'I passed through this way because the servants would not have let me come in. I heard in the village that your fireplace doesn't work.' He cast a glance full of malice at the extinguished fire, and it seemed as if in the depth of the misty smoke of his eyes sparks of fire were kindled in the exact centre of each of his pupils. 'I am the smoke-man – I get rid of the smoke in fireplaces when no one else can. I know the winds of this region. My aged father died in this very oasis. He used to have an adobe hut here, and I lived here till I was thirteen. He taught me everything. He would make fires in the desert, and from him I learned to observe how the smoke rises, what kind of humidity and land winds – the eddies of unfavourable moons, the hot sunset gusts and midnight dews – make it go down; and how to set up the strong draughts that suck it straight up into the sky.'

Suddenly Veronica and Grandsailles had the feeling that all their hope lay in this smoke-man who seemed to have descended from heaven, and they called the canoness to have her bring him a glass of sherry.

'My good man,' said Grandsailles, 'you can begin your experiments with our fireplace whenever you please. The masons have in fact experimented and exhausted the resources of their science to no avail. I am quite convinced that this all has to do with some unique, imponderable climatic anomaly of this locality. I myself have already wondered about the concentration of moisture that must be created by such a small oasis surrounded by the reverberating mineral desert, with the rocks that keep their warmth far into the night.'

The smoke-man nodded his head benevolently and smiled as if Grandsailles had been no nearer to the truth than other mortals.

'I shall begin my work tomorrow – but on just one condition,' said the smoke-man, 'and that is that Monsieur shall pay me nothing, not a single cent, unless I am completely successful. The cement, bricks, hardware, tools – all are to be at my expense. I don't eat much, and I can sleep anywhere. I want to set an example for those in the village who make fun of me! When you no longer have any smoke you can reward me as you see fit, and I shall be satisfied.'

They were entering the second week since the smoke-man had begun his labours and he was still struggling unavailingly with the obstinate smoke in the library fireplace. Nothing, nothing, nothing worked!

'I feel sorry for the poor fellow,' the canoness had confided to the Count. 'I've been observing him. I can see him getting thinner every day. He no longer eats, he no longer sleeps, and what is worse, he spends all his meagre savings buying funnels, extension pipes, wire – and I'll telling you, he'll never succeed in getting that confounded smoke out of the chimney!'

'We'll let him work two more days. He has already done so much damage that a little more won't make any difference. We will reward him for his work just the same. We might have suspected that he was a little crazy.'

'But it's a fact,' replied the canoness, 'that the others weren't able to get rid of the smoke either.'

The smoke-man would pass from a state of exaltation, of almost delirious hope, to prostrations of despair, lashed into a new frenzy by an idea that would keep him awake all night. Early in the morning, sometimes at dawn, he was already on the job, appearing on the scene loaded with heterogeneous objects that he had had made at a metal-shop in the village, building little supplementary chimneys within the chimney itself, as if to lead the smoke to the roof by stages and there expel it definitely, once and for all, into the free air. That confounded draught! How it was going to draw now – this time it could not fail. Then he would drop to the floor on all fours to light the fire, his hands trembling as in a fit of epilepsy, crumpling up newspapers, striking matches, burning his fingers. The fire would catch in whirls of flame, rise victoriously as if sucked up by a powerful siphon. His heart would pound, savagely thumping his old man's chest, and he would hold his breath in anxious expectation. Yes! This time it would work.... But no! Suddenly an ignominious puff of grey, thick smoke would, as on all the other occasions, come and spit in his face, and the tears of his fathomless bitterness would add their sting to his smoke-scorched eyes.

Finally one evening Veronica and Grandsailles entered the library on tiptoe, followed by the canoness, who also wanted to spy. The room was submerged in a soft, very faint grey smoke that never left it, like clear water clouded by anisette. But in the fireplace the smoke was even denser, so that one could barely see through it the outline of the smoke-man's legs, from the knees down, inside the chimney where he was standing. He was stamping his left foot in sign of discontent and aggravation like a restive horse, while the hearth was covered with half-extinguished coals and pieces of burnt newspaper. Suddenly the smoke-man emerged from under the chimney and stood there before it, discouraged, his arms dangling, with a face like a Greek tragic mask. The Count, Veronica and the canoness withdrew to the end of the corridor to avoid being seen.

'I'll talk to him,' said the Count, going in and shutting the door behind him.

At dinner Grandsailles explained the situation to Veronica: 'The smoke-man began to weep like a baby, and he begged me on his knees to give him just one last chance to carry out his final experiment.'

'Well, let him, the poor man,' said Veronica.

'But the trouble is that he is asking something impossible,' Grandsailles objected.

'What does he want?' Veronica asked, with a smile of tenderness.

'He says now that he has to make a hole through the ceiling of your room – that it's the only solution.'

Veronica considered this eventuality for a long time. Then, taking the Count's hand she said in a gentle tone that masked her bitterness.

'Perhaps it's a solution, for by now the smoke has also invaded our hearts and it is the torch of our love which is in danger of going out.'

'I wanted in fact to suggest to you that we leave this spot and return to Palm Springs,' said Grandsailles.

'We shall leave the day after tomorrow,' Veronica decided, 'after the smoke-man has made his hole.'

Then they called the smoke-man and the canoness, and Veronica gave her instructions: 'Have the big bed taken out of my tower room, and the curtains and the white feather-rug.' To Grandsailles she added, 'I don't want anything to be left except the four mirrored walls and the marble-tiled floor. Let the smoke-man make his hole in the ceiling as he wishes. After that the house will be locked up and we return to Palm Springs. Besides, the walls here are too new and it's damp everywhere.'

By the following evening the hole had been made in the angle of the ceiling and the chimney wall. If the experiment worked it would only be necessary to install a permanent chimney-pipe that could be plastered over and made relatively inconspicuous. But this new experiment failed like all the rest, and this time even more spectacularly than before. After the fire had crackled in the fireplace for a few minutes and at the very moment when it was belching smoke into the library as on all the previous occasions. Veronica's room suddenly seemed about to catch fire. The hole in the ceiling spat out several consecutive sheafs of sparks whirled up by the draught, as well as whole bits of flaming wood-shavings. And all these flying cinders after whirling for some time in the air, reflected to infinity in the four mirrored walls, at last settled calmly on the tiles where they slowly died out one after another.

'In any case,' said Grandsailles, 'we could ask for nothing better in the way of fireworks. Where is the smoke-man?'

'He wants to leave,' said the canoness. 'He has already put his little bundle tied in a handkerchief to the end of his stick out on the chair.'

'Have a first-class supper made ready for him in the kitchen,' Veronica ordered, 'and we will see him afterwards.'

She and the Count went into the dining-room in which they were to have their last meal. When the canoness returned, Veronica asked her if all was well.

'I set everything out for him on the table. He has everything, a real feast-stuffed turkey, a bottle of French wine, dessert-but he just sits in front of his plate and he doesn't eat.'

'Go and see,' said Veronica anxiously.

A few moments later they heard the canoness utter a cry of astonishment. They both ran out into the kitchen. The food was on the table just as it had been served. The smoke-man had vanished without having touched a thing. They ran out and called in vain. The canoness thought she could make out the bundle of his white handkerchief tied to the end of his stick, but it was only a road-sign. 'He's old, but I've seen him several times when he was in a hurry. He can run fast as a rabbit.'

The following morning, before they left the oasis for good, Veronica opened the door to her tower-room for a moment. The ceiling, all around the hole, was blackened by smoke and the marble floor was entirely covered with a layer of ashes. She locked the door and kept the key.

No sooner had they settled again in Palm Springs than Grandsailles, who could but ill conceal his irascibility, went back and cloistered himself in his room, pleading his recurrent headaches as an excuse.

Veronica was standing before the lighted fire in the living-room and looking at herself in the minor above it. Pensive, with a deep line of melancholy between her eyebrows, holding an apple in one hand and in the other a knife, she seemed unable to make up her mind to cut into the fruit. She was so absorbed that she saw a figure approaching her through the mirror almost without noticing it. It was John Randolph. The moment she became aware of him he was already beside her. For several seconds Veronica was overwhelmed by a strange sensation. 'Why, I've lived through this before!' Veronica turned to him and Randolph lowered his head as if in shame, while Veronica instinctively lifted her hands to her neck. They remained thus face to face, motionless, like two anguishing figures.

'I have a favour to ask you,' Randolph said breathlessly. 'Give me just one hour. I must explain to you. Tomorrow is my last day! I have waited for the two bitterest weeks of my life to ask you this!'

'I want to, too,' said Veronica.

'Where and when?' asked Randolph eagerly, so close to her that without shifting his balance he was able to apply a kiss to each of her two fists which she continued to hold clenched as if clasping something under her chin.

'This afternoon at five o'clock at the oasis, in my empty room in the tower!'

At about five o'clock Veronica and Randolph reached the oasis on horseback by different roads, meeting as if by chance. Veronica had arrived first. She ran up to Randolph. 'Did you see?' she said, 'someone is following us. He's coming this way.'

'Yes, I noticed,' said Randolph getting down from his horse and looking into the distance to follow the movements of a trotting horse and its rider. 'I think it may be Betka. She is the only one who knows of our rendezvous – I had to tell her so she could warn us in case your husband took it into his head to come here for a ride.'

'But it's not a woman – it's a man's figure,' Veronica answered, 'my heart tells me it's Jules! You shouldn't have said anything to Betka!'

'You don't mistrust Betka, do you?'

'Not yet,' answered Veronica, shielding her eyes from the sun with her hands as she continued to watch the approaching rider.

'Do you want me to go?' asked Randolph.

'No! He would see you leaving the oasis in any case. Bring our horses and shut them up in the stable; then come immediately to my room in the tower. There I'm on my own premises – he promised me never to violate its privacy. If he knocks at the door he will have broken his word.'

Randolph presently joined her, but the time of his absence seemed to Veronica like a century. When he returned, she said to him, 'There is no longer any doubt. It is Jules, and he is galloping this way. Betka has betrayed us.'

'Yes, it's he,' said Randolph, going up to the window. 'Let's not stay in this room. Let him find us outside, near the pool.'

'No!' cried Veronica in a fury, 'we're staying here, in *my* room,' and she went to the door, locked it and came back to the window.

'In that case let me talk to you.' Randolph begged her.

'I don't want to hear anything from you now,' Veronica said irritably, 'you've made me do something wrong! The first thing I have ever done to him that is wrong!'

With her hands clutching her throat she paced back and forth like a hunted animal and at the same time proud as a queen. 'Why did you come into my life – do you call that courage? You should have had the dignity to keep your emotions hidden. Jules and I are absolute beings. The misfortunes you have just brought down on our heads will also be absolute. Is that what a creature who soars on wings is like? You will see – how I am going to hate you!'

388

'I can more easily set the whole sky on fire than put out the fire in my heart!' answered Randolph.

'Be still now! He is coming,' Veronica ordered, holding her breath in anguishing suspense.

Nodier had calmly got down from his horse and tied it to a ring in the wall. Briskly he climbed the few steps that led to the little side door in the court and from there entered the library that adjoined Veronica's room. He went straight to the fireplace and Veronica, hearing the andirons being moved, immediately understood their situation. 'If he lights the fire we are lost!' she exclaimed in a low voice, glancing up at the hole in the ceiling.

Though he did not follow her meaning, Randolph drew Veronica to him in a protective gesture. 'Whatever happens,' she said, looking hard into the depths of his eyes, 'you must not call out!'

Grandsailles had lit a fire and thrown into it a sheaf of documents which he wished to destroy. Almost immediately the hole in the ceiling of Veronica's room belched forth a whirl of sparks. Then as on the night before, the furious draught in the chimney made bits of burning shavings fly all about the room, Randolph pressed Veronica's head between his arms while a fine rain of fire fell on them. At the risk of burning her face Veronica looked up: a glowing cinder had just alighted on Randolph's forehead. 'You, who have set the heavens on fire,' she murmured between her teeth, 'must now endure being branded by a spark!'

After its first burst the fire in the chimney went out, and the Count of Grandsailles left.

'I'm convinced it was a pure coincidence,' said Randolph, examining the remains of the bundles of carbonized papers. 'He came here only to burn some secret documents.'

'We shall soon know,' said Veronica in a meaningful tone, and her face was sombre and severe as she mounted her white horse.

That last evening of Randolph's stay in Palm Springs the Count of Grandsailles, Veronica, Betka and Randolph were dining together round the highly-polished mahogany table in which the sparkle of the ostentatious and pitiless silverware was savagely reflected. It was exactly nine o'clock in the evening, and no one spoke.

'One would think we had formed a conspiracy of silence!' said Grandsailles at last with great naturalness. He had just finished his last mouthful of consommé, and the only response was the sinister clinking of the silver against the plates. Then the Count took a pear from the fruit dish in front of him and began to peel it as if in nervous anticipation of the dessert. But immediately recovering his calm he went on, 'This silence can only be interpreted as the sorrow we all feel over the departure of our friend Randolph, who might be said to have dropped from heaven just for the purpose of sweetening our excessive solitude, for which I am wholly to blame. I was thinking of you, Randolph, all afternoon,' the Count continued looking intently at the aviator, 'I rode out to the tower in the oasis, for I wanted to burn some secret documents in that confounded fireplace that chased us away from there. What about you? What did you do this afternoon?'

Randolph did not flinch and he answered, 'Are you putting me on my honour to answer truthfully?'

'Oh, not in the least,' Grandsailles replied, 'it was just a question like any other.'

'Then,' said Randolph, 'just imagine, if you will, that I spent my afternoon as I always do, smoking cigarette after cigarette.'

'That isn't good for your hero's heart,' Grandsailles replied.

Veronica seemed to become hypnotized by a Lilliputian reflection in the silverware on which she had kept her eyes glued since the beginning of this conversation, and Betka, terrified and pale, was looking at Veronica.

'A curious country, America, don't you think, Randolph?' said the Count of Grandsailles, making a face after biting into a piece of pear impaled on his fork, and putting down his implement on the edge of the plate. 'Its fruit has no flavour, its women have no shame, and its men are without honour!'

Randolph jumped to his feet as if released by a spring. Betka tried to hold him back, but he had already rushed toward Grandsailles who, without moving, sat carefully wiping his lips with his napkin after having moistened it with orange, as if considering his dinner over. He added, 'I call your attention, Randolph, to the fact that you have let some of the fire from your cigarette drop on your shoulders, which is strange, and also on your forehead, which is still stranger. You've got a burn there,' and he pointed to a reddish swelling close to the hairline of Randolph's head. Grandsailles let his vague gaze roam lazily to Veronica, who still did not stir, seeming absent and not paying the slightest attention to Randolph's more and more threatening attitude.

'The fruits of our country,' said Randolph, measuring each syllable, 'have the flavour of liberty and hospitality, which you have basely taken advantage of to feed yourself and your secrets; our women are those whom you try unsuccessfully to corrupt, to pervert and make sterile, and our men are those who have the honour of sacrificing their lives in that Europe of yours to redeem the honour which you weren't men enough to defend and shamefully lost to the enemy.'

Grandsailles was now struggling to his feet, but before he could get up he received a terrific blow of Randolph's fist full in the face, which made him roll to the floor with his chair.

Veronica rushed to Grandsailles where he lay and tried to revive him with Betka's aid. The Count could scarcely lift one hand to his heart, while one finger of his other hand fumbled feebly at the collar of his shirt, as though he were choking. Betka undid the knot of his heavy silver-speckled tie, ripped open the buttons of his shirt, and bared his chest. Randolph's bloodshot eyes then fell on an object that left him breathless with shocked surprise, and for several moments he thought he was suffering from a delusion. For there, hanging by a little chain round his rival's neck, was the cross of pearls and diamonds that Veronica had given him in Paris and that he had entrusted to the Count of Grandsailles on their flight to Malta! This mysterious Nodier could be none other than the Count himself.

'Veronica!' Randolph cried, 'the cross that man is wearing is the one you gave me!'

Returning slowly to consciousness some hours after his heart attack, the Count of Grandsailles remained a good fifteen minutes with his eyes shut, pretending to be still asleep. But he knew that Veronica was there, sitting anxious and loving by his bedside, observing him attentively, for a moment ago he had looked up furtively between his eyelashes. He relived now the violent scene with Randolph, and he felt Veronica's love redoubled in his favour by the brutal way in which his rival had treated him in spite of the delicate condition of his heart during the past weeks. After this squall, he enjoyed the sensation of coming back to life again in the warmth and comfort of these surroundings, his head nestling in a downy convalescent's pillow. And as never before he understood the full value and meaning of a wife, of a spouse. It was a joy, now, to wake up gently, gradually, and through the shadowy blur of the thick lashes of his lids calmly and voluptuously opening, he began to perceive more and more distinctly the figure of Veronica who must only be waiting, with her heart in suspense, for him to wake up in order to rush forward and bend over him, to press her brow to his brow and her hands in his hands with that violent tenderness which since their marriage had not ceased to be the almost constant pattern of their relationship.

392

But Veronica, instead of stirring and coming over to him when she saw him wake up, did nothing of the kind. On the contrary, it was as though her immobility were assuming an aspect of terror, and her fixed gaze struck him as hostile, ferocious as an animal's. The Count, chilled by Veronica's incomprehensible attitude exclaimed, 'Why do you look at me like that?'

'I'm not looking at you, Count de Grandsailles,' Veronica answered, calling him for the first time by his real name, 'what I am looking at is the cross you are wearing around your neck. It does not belong to you. You have usurped it, stolen it from a dead man – from Randolph, whom you thought dead.'

The Count of Grandsailles, seized with a feeble convulsive trembling, which was a complete confession of his longstanding lie, brought his two hands to his neck as if to protect the cross from Veronica's concentrated and ungovernable fury. But with a move-ment that nothing could restrain she seized the cross, wrapped it in her fist, and pulled it toward her slowly, slowly, with all her strength, until she finally broke the chain, and then went off with her sure step, entered her room and hung the cross above the head of her bed. Then she removed from her finger the engagement ring she had received from Grandsailles and put it away in her black velvet jewel-box. There now remained no other evidence of their encoun-ter than this ring, which in its miniature night was like the annular eclipse of their conjunction.

'I don't want to live with anyone. I want Grandsailles to leave my house. I want Betka and the child to leave my house. I want the devil's canoness to leave my house. I don't want to see anything more of Randolph. I want to live alone again with him, with the white swan of my memory.'

As soon as he had slightly recovered and the condition of his heart permitted, the Count of Grandsailles went into retirement and seclusion with his canoness for a certain length of time in the refuge of the oasis, but he had previously assured Veronica by letter that he would always respect her room in the tower. Into his retreat he also took Betka's son to live with him – and this, too, constituted a dark mystery between Betka and the Count: the 'bending of blood,'as he called it. Since his marriage he had, in collusion with Betka, laboriously, furtively, done everything to wean Betka's son from Veronica's influence. To what end?

Betka left for Africa with Randolph. There was no thought of marriage between them, but they could not get along without each other. Grandsailles had entrusted Betka with a mission, and for this she had to meet Cécile Goudreau in Tangiers.

The day the Count moved back to the oasis he said to his canoness, 'I want the child to live and be treated as a prince. He will occupy the whole second floor of the house. He must never leave the enclosure of the oasis. He has a dreadful but precious blood disease. With him I shall risk what little is left of my soul. This will be the great experiment. Nothing exists that is not in the blood! I shall live in a single room, and I want you next to me, canoness. You will pray for Solange.'

He forbade any cleaning to be done in his room, which became like Faust's study. And for the first time in his life his hair remained ungroomed through the long days, matted and snarled by the choleric insomnia of his interminable nights. He wrote profusely and incoherently, drawing up human and divine laws. He deflected blood from its natural course. France and Solange became a single divinized being in his delirious brain, he lived alone with her, turning into a living madman, yes, a madman! The Count of Grandsailles! 'Old fool! Old fool!' the canoness muttered within the caverns of her ego, 'God will punish you!'

*

In the plain of Creux de Libreux the persistent November rains were followed, after the mists and snows and sunny days of winter, by the March downpours. Beneath the Germans' yoke Europe was rediscovering the tradition of its ancient catholic unity through the community of suffering, and in Libreux the Middle Ages were being reborn with their springtime of superstitions. At the Moulin des Sources Madame Solange de Cléda had come down to the refectory for the first time in three months. It was still cool and she kept a footwarmer full of hot coals under her feet and a white wool shawl over her shoulders. Her head, resting on three fingers of her left hand, was bowed over the table with its dark chocolate cloth, while two fingers of her other hand lying on her right knee held the Count of Grandsailles' letter, folded in two, which she had received that morning. Behind her stood Génie, with one corner of her apron pulled up and tucked into a belt of thick cord from which several old keys hung down to the middle of her belly. With her arms folded and one finger to her mouth, she had just turned her torso in the direction of the half-open door to the kitchen where the older of the Martin brothers was sawing wood. When the latter had stopped his work and silence returned, Solange said, 'I now have every proof that the Count came again and possessed me during the whole period of my illness.'

'If it is as Madame claims, it can only be by the demon's art,' answered Génie, keeping her eyes fixed on the opposite wall as if in these circumstances a glance cast by chance upon her mistress might in turn bewitch her.

'You know, Génie, when the Count comes and visits me he sees me not with the eyes of his memory, but with his own eyes, and then his eyes hurt him. Do you hear, Génie? And his head feels as if it is going to burst. He tells me this in his letter, Génie! He says he has seen me with a scarlet dress opening the gate to the back road. That's

395

my garnet dress! It was the day I went to the clearing to watch the men working. Titan was with me.'

'The clearing will be good for pasture now,' said Génie, following her own train of thought. 'Madame ought to go walking in the clearing often, and not stay away from church too long. Everything that happened to Madame during her illness I'd swear was only evil spirits.'

'The Count was not a believer,' said Solange.

'By thinking of your soul perhaps you will prevent his from being damned,' replied Génie.

'I know,' said Solange, 'since the Viscount of Angerville did not come back and Girardin was shot by the Nazis. I have felt as if these frightful misfortunes were my fault!'

'Madame!' Génie exclaimed.

'Yes, Génie! I know what I am saying. All these things that are happening to me are very ugly sins.'

'Think of the Count's, Madame. I know a woman of Lower Libreux who had just the same thing happen to her, just the same as you. Well, it wasn't her fault, it was a man who had her under a spell. She became pregnant and her belly got big, just as if they had really been together. Well, in spite of all that she was cured and she even became a kind of saint.'

'Yes, I've heard about her. And it was the tanner who exorcized her,' said Solange. 'I know what you're getting at: you would like me to go and confess to that fellow – priest, shepherd, tanner or whatever he is.'

'Why, yes, all of us would like you to. Since he's no longer a tanner he never wants to go into houses. He says mass out of doors and he confesses and gives communion with real bread to those who go to him out in the fields. Today nobody can believe in real curates any more. It's all right for us peasants to help load a truck with potatoes for the Nazis if we have to, but priests have no business hanging around with them the way they do.'

'But how can I go and meet the tanner, since they say all his movements are watched?'

'I can arrange that,' said Génie, 'I'll have him meet you in the clearing.'

'And how will I recognize him and know that he will listen to my confession?' Solange asked with childlike concern.

'Just as it's always done. He will make you a sign when you are to come to him,' answered Génie.

'You are right, Génie. I must confess myself to the shepherd-tanner and pray God to forgive me my sins and the Count's, so that he may visit me only in his thoughts, and so that he may see me in his memory but not with his eyes. And just as he has had the power to abuse my poor body from afar with the demon's aid, so may I, by the force of my virtue and with the aid of God, be able to save his soul.'

When Solange de Cléda reached the clearing of the Moulin she sat down on a rock and waited. About a hundred paces away she caught sight of a shepherd who was whittling a branch to make a stick with. The plain was illuminated and a broken rainbow remained suspended between Upper and Lower Libreux. The clearing was strewn with white stones lighted on one side and casting long black shadows. Each of the spaces that separated one stone from the others appeared to Solange to be infinite, and she felt surrounded by a limitless expanse, so true it is that when hope pacifies souls the things of the earth begin to resemble those of heaven. Everything was separate, clear, imbued with that melancholy serenity that the planets would possess if it were given to man to see them closer as solid bodies, each one lighted on one side and projecting a long black shadow on the immense metaphysical mineral of the firmament.

The shepherd had just stood up and, cutting a low branch from an oak-tree, tied it with a bundle of fibre in the form of a cross close to one end of his stick. Then he climbed a small hummock covered with wild mulberry and turning in Solange's direction raised his rustic cross above his head. Solange had risen in turn, and the two figures could be seen crossing the clearing and going to meet each other.

EPILOGUE

The Illuminated Plain

Epilogue

All things come and go. Years revolved round a fist more and more obstinately closed with rage and decision, and this fist, since the character was sitting in a large armchair with his back to us, was the sole thing which it was given us to see.

From the adjoining room a strident music, monstrously amplified by an unknown device, reaches a brassy intensity that is so vibrant and furious that it seems as if its sole effect on the human ear must be to draw blood. And day and night this powerful apparatus wearilessly repeats the same selected pieces from Wagner's *The Valkyries*, *Parsifal* and *Tristan and Isolde*, repeats them over and over again. Suddenly the closed fist tightens even more and its bones seem about to cut through the skin and its knuckles are livid as cherry-pits. It strikes on the arm of the chair once, twice, three times, four times, five times. The fifth time blood begins to flow. Then it strikes once more and once again with even greater force. Again it remains motionless for several hours, and as the blood coagulates it becomes dark and almost black, like a very ripe cherry.

Nothing surpasses the honour and supreme glory of blood! Why did not destiny allow Jesus to live in my time of domination, so that I might have strangled him with my own hands! The dirty, snivelling Jew, the cowardly masochist, the disgrace and shame of strong men! You would have deprived the world of the sole thing that is capable of making man resplendent – blood! You would have spared man the sacred treasures of the blood that was given us by God to shed! Only the cringing race of Jewish curs could have invented that degrading incarnation of the idea of God and steeped it in the degenerate blood of the sickly body of that lackey of pity, of that prophet of remorse, Jesus Christ! All that is unstable, dishonouring, infamous and sullying I include in that name, Jesus Christ! Ah, he who should come, sword in hand, to open a breach of fresh, pure and regenerative blood in the virgin heart of paganism, in the depth of the grottoes of live rocks of the race, of the Olympian mountain of Venusberg, and kill the vile dragon of Christianity....

At this moment the first echoes of the crescendo in the death-scene of *Tristan and Isolde* resounded stridently, painfully, in his harassed tympana and the thought of his own death assailed him, acerated and sharp, as though a silver sickle were cutting a low swath across the floor on which his eyes were fixed. He lifted his feet nimbly as if to avoid the stroke. For the last six days he had been subject again to a new maniacal and obsessing fit of cleanliness. He lived in horror with the thought that death might overtake him while any part of his body had not been washed and washed again several times during the day with perfect scrupulousness, and any of his mucous parts had the least suggestion of an odour.

For some time he had been voluptuously inhaling a warm redolence that emanated from the somewhat rustic tanned calf-skin of his Tyrolian boots. Suddenly his heart received the shock of a frightful doubt: had he washed his feet again in the course of the day, as was his habit? For it did indeed seem to him that, mingled with the effluvia from his boots, he caught a faint suggestion of an odour from his feet. He tore off one boot and sock; the moment his very white foot, slightly moist with perspiration, was liberated from its sheath, he pushed his forefinger between two toes, lifted it to his nose and inhaled: his face turned purple with rage and hate. Yes! It smelled! He rushed to the bathroom and, not wanting to lose a second by running water into the bath-tub, immediately plunged his foot into the washstand under the faucet in an uncomfortable and strained position. He washed his foot ten times, a hundred times, the interstices between his toes were becoming red, but always there remained an offensive residue of odour that would make him begin all over again, tirelessly and obstinately. When one of the feet was thus washed, he unshod the other one and washed it in turn with the same care.

Having completed this operation he went back into the large room which he had just left and sat down again in the armchair. Then one saw that this character was Adolph Hitler. Likewise, by the long rectangular window looking into space one recognized that he was here in his retreat of Berchtesgaden. Before sitting down again Adolph Hitler stopped in front of the large Vermeer abducted from Count Chernin's collection (the most beautiful painting in the world, according to Salvador Dali), that he had kept here since the occupation of Vienna. Hitler's hand seemed to caress the canvas, barely grazing it, and lingered briefly on the laurel-crowned young woman's face, slightly averted in a divinely graceful movement. At this moment his fingers contracted and remained convulsed and stiffened like a claw. Then the hand relaxed and became limp, pale and as if filled with tepid water, and he went back and sat down in the armchair.

One perceived then that this armchair was surrounded by the greatest artistic treasures in the world. Raphael's 'Betrothal of the Virgin', from the Museum of Milan, Leonardo's 'Virgin of the Rocks'... Piles of the rarest and most priceless manuscripts, and over there, behind him, in the half-light in the centre of the room, the 'Victory of Samothrace' – the real one, the one from the Louvre Museum, but looking in this horrible rigid room like a bad reproduction.

Six days previously, Hitler had blown up the single elevator by which his eagle's nest could communicate with the rest of the world. If they should try to destroy him, they would be forced to destroy with him the most sublime dreams and creations of civilization.

Before Hitler's eyes, lost now in the mists of the Valkyrie that rose from the rains sweeping over the plain, night had conjured up the vertical forest of black cypresses of Boecklin's 'Island of the Dead'. One might have said that these same cypresses were growing now within his own room as it became progressively flooded by the velvet darkness of another night of nightmares and delirium. His visions were about to begin. And already the familiar phantoms were arriving, each in turn, to take their places in their habitual spots. The fluid and purple-streaked melancholy of Dürer at his left, and at his right old Nietzsche, all transparent and visible only by the frightfully sharp points of his moustache and the two deep holes of his orbits, desiccated by the malign fever of his brain. To his right, and in a solitary corner, the Mad King, Louis II of Bavaria, dressed in ermine and azure-blue, the flaccid and wet umbrella of his onanism riveted to the middle of his chest like an arrow.

Then followed the procession of Prussian generals, the only free men on earth, for being without conscience or pity, equal to the implacable gods, they had been entrusted by destiny with the mission of spreading the *Furor Teutonicus* of German blood throughout the world. 'Yes, we have lost another war! I shall win the next one! For I am indestructible and invulnerable. They can tear me from my people, uproot me, but never destroy me, for like a cancer I am in the blood of the German people, and the blood of the German people is indestructible and eternal, and like a cancer I shall sooner or later end by reproducing myself again inexorably in the soul of the entire German people! It is neither an ideology nor a "Kultur" that I have defended. I am proud of having proclaimed the death of intelligence. It must some day be annihilated by the German people. I do not have to give ideas! I give to the world pieces of my soul, which are pieces of the soul of the German people, and this soul shall triumph!

'But what about the body? What about the body of the German people?'

The body of the German people was standing before him, the Pontius Pilate of a new dispensation, on the expanse of the infinite snows of the Russian steppes. It was all covered with black veils, and its feet were frozen – and odourless....

There were heard the canticles of a land of saints. The Red Army, an army of unbelievers, sustained by the prayers of their white ancestors as on a bed of snow! Their dispossessed ancestors still had the treasure of their ancient faith to give them and thereby save their souls!

'The bending of blood! The bending of blood! A chimera? That which cannot be?' Thus that other madman, the Count of Grandsailles, kept endlessly repeating enigmatic words, hammering his dusty table with his closed fist as he sat in his own seclusion – his oasis.

'The moment is at last approaching when I can return to the illuminated plain of Libreux after the long darkness of my exile and bend the rainbow of the old blood of Grandsailles on the body of Solange de Cléda. The war is ended!'

During all these last years, since Solange had gone to the clearing of the Moulin and confessed herself to the tanner-shepherd on a serene late afternoon in March, she seemed indeed to have been exorcized and freed of all her ills. The Count of Grandsailles' spirit had ceased to visit her in a manner outrageous to her modesty. Nevertheless he did not for a single moment leave her thoughts. But she let her spirit dwell on him only to pray day and night for the redemption of his soul. At the same time she practised charity and she had Martin and Prince rebuild the old chapel of the Moulin, where the tanner-shepherd would secretly come and say mass. Her orgasms, that used to occur in the midst of the most excruciating tortures of her spirit, were succeeded now by mystic ecstasies suffused with the beatitude of her purified soul and of her body's calm. But furthermore God had rewarded her, bestowing upon her the greatest of all happiness, which she would never have dared to ask or to hope for: the Count of Grandsailles, divorced from Veronica, was at last in reality going to take her for wife. Here were already two letters from him which she read again and again, sprinkling them with tears of joy. Now all the sufferings she had endured throughout those long years of the occupation appeared to her negligible.

But would she still be beautiful? Yes! For the mark of suffering had only further ennobled her. As there are wines that age well, so she had suffered well. For in her suffering there was no alloy of pettiness. Only little worries and base, mediocre fretting make faces ugly and shrivel bodies, great martyrdoms never. For these convulse and deform only the muscles tense with passion of the Apollos of anguish shining like snow-white bones through the burning wounds of crucified Christs. Solange de Cléda, lovely martyr without any trace of the sword! And what a pent-up treasure, what an intoxicating murmur of intact desire was that of the resurrection of her flesh, and to what mortal had it ever been given to approach the miracle of this woman, elevated to sublimity by deliria of abstinence and the holiness of prayer!

How could Solange de Cléda, in her state of pre-nuptial euphoria, have perceived or fixed her attention on the little reticences full of bitter and fearful innuendoes that Génie and the Martin brothers, since the end of the war, had constantly introduced into their least remarks. Yet the isolation, as of a plague-centre, created by the fermenting atmosphere of civil war of Libreux with its venomous and baleful whisperings, was daily growing more dense round the Moulin des Sources and its streams that had been deflected by the enemy and remained like a burning and ineradicable stigma. But she was a woman, only a woman, knowing nothing of politics, and all that she had done, and done solely in order to safeguard the interests of her ungrateful son, had been governed by the advice of Maître Girardin who had died so nobly for his country! How then could they hold it against her that she had acted in the light of the experience of so exemplary a citizen?

'Génie can say what she likes,' she would argue with herself, and then turn to Génie: 'The Count of Grandsailles is a just man. He is perhaps already on his way here to join me. My poor Génie, the people of Libreux will have to listen to him. He is their master, Génie!'

'Times have changed, Madame. Madame doesn't know, as we do. We hear things. You never go out of the Moulin des Sources, and perhaps it is better for us all that you don't!'

'Will the peasants of the Libreux forget all the charities and the help they have received from me during these winters? Have they no longer any heart?'

'I am afraid not, Madame. Evil winds are already raising the dust of the plains, and as for hearts – the Germans have worn them thin!'

'You must be patient. Génie, as I am, and let us pray that the Count will bring reconciliation to the bosom of each of our families and between each of our families. May Catholic France once more achieve the pacification of blood.'

The Count of Grandsailles was of the breed of men who come into their own during troubled periods of civil war. Vindictive by nature, his spirit prematurely afflicted with twilight delirium was injected with a new and final exaltation of avenging patriotism by the war's termination, and he planned to return to Libreux in the rôle of a judge. He now repudiated the life of shameful compromises and of usurpation which he had led during these last years. His would now be the probity and inflexibility of an exemplary Spartan, for his beloved country was once again menaced by death – this time in the form of anarchy.

'Girardin, it is on the ground on which your body fell that we shall now shoot our traitors!'

Approximately one month before the Count of Grandsailles obtained permission to return to France he was visited in his Palm Springs oasis by Broussillon who was on a confidential mission, having become the leader of a new political party. For after Girardin's death, having assumed too individual a rôle in the sabotage plot of Libreux and broken the discipline of the communist party, he had at last been expelled from it. In retaliation he had committed the infamy of betraying former comrades, and his inordinate ambition, as well as his anarchist aspirations, led him at once to form a new independent party of reactionary colour, though adapted to certain extremist 'civil war' tendencies that were opportune at the moment.

Broussillon had come firmly resolved to link the Count of Grandsailles' future political activity in Libreux with his own. But Grandsailles, as hostile as ever to any plan involving the industrialization of Libreux, was bent on converting it back into an exclusively agricultural region and presently it was Broussillon himself who was impressed and contaminated by the Count's political plans and who began to yield to him in everything. The growing influence of his authority over his compatriot's ideas, which had at first seemed so firmly rooted, reawakened Grandsailles' love of action, still intact and more exasperated and impatient than before.

But on the third day this state of effervescence and impatience was shaken, as if deliberately, by the greatest despair in Grandsailles' whole life when, still unbelieving but thunderstruck with grief and anger, he received from Broussillon's lips a detailed report of Madame de Cléda's conduct during the period of the occupation. With fiendish cunning Broussillon had waited for the opportune moment when Grandsailles already felt as though he were returning to his country of Libreux in the rôle of a redeemer, as though he were biting into the thirst-provoking apple of his power – the domination of Libreux – with all its juice and its skin, so ardently craved during his long absence from his native land, during the long, dry desert of his emigration. Then Broussillon half-casually remarked. 'It will be difficult, if not impossible, to aspire to the slightest influence in Libreux if you see Madame Solange de Cléda when you return.'

The list of accusations against her was detailed, minute – a refined and overwhelming torture. The apparently irrefutable proofs that Broussillon offered regarding the permission given the Germans to divert the Moulin des Sources streams reduced him to a tense, dreadful silence: a collaborationist.... But Broussillon had, as if carelessly, kept an even more searing accusation for the end.

'In Libreux it is no one's secret,' he said, 'that for more than a year Madame de Cléda lived quite openly with her lover the Viscount of Angerville, who later mysteriously disappeared. That's something the devoutly Catholic peasants of Libreux will never forget, and it is on the revival of this religious feeling of the people that we largely have to count today. Besides, the clergy of Libreux have kept Madame de Cléda completely isolated, going so far as to accuse her of satanic practices with a charlatan tanner who claims to be inspired by God.'

'D'Angerville! D'Angerville! I should have guessed it,' Grandsailles repeated silently to himself. Yet he could not swallow, much less digest, these accusations that came as such a sudden shock to the salivary and gastric juices of his hopes, lovingly secreted during all these months. And served by Broussillon, whose person now appeared to him in all its sordid shabbiness, they were revolting to the point of nausea.

'Get out of here!' he broke out hoarsely, 'I don't want to believe you nor see you again. Madame de Cléda is the being I love most in the world. It is from her alone that I wish to know the truth and it is her alone whom I will believe. She will tell me the truth. Even if all Libreux rises up against me. I shall listen only to her.'

Broussillon, muttering inarticulately, bowed and stumbled his way out, and Grandsailles immediately sat down to his desk to write the following letter:

'Dear Solange:

'I have on several occasions in the past done you great wrong and have despaired of your forgiveness. But I could never lie to you. And this is why, when destiny involved me in the greatest lie of my life, I confessed everything to you – my marriage with Veronica and my then hopeless passion for you. I might have said nothing at that time, since we were not morally bound to each other and our relations had even been completely broken, but I preferred to risk losing whatever respect you might have for me to hiding my true feeling from you. Your response to this was so generous and fine that I have looked upon you since then as a divine being.

'But our relationship is in the realm of the absolute and only there can we maintain it. Now, on the sordid plane of contingencies, I am being asked to believe, with plausible supporting evidence, that during all this time you lied to me! In only a few weeks I leave for Europe. But before this I must have the truth from you on two matters. One is that you make no mention in your fervent letters of your relations with d'Angerville, and the other, that when you informed me of the progress of the growth of the little forest of cork-oaks

which you planted for me you said nothing of the Moulin
properties under the occupation.

'On these two matters, both equally decisive, I shall believe
no one but you. Has d'Angerville ever been your lover? Did
you yield the water rights to the enemy? I appeal only to your
sense of honour to answer me, but if the answer to these two
questions is yes, never again expect my forgiveness. I shall
not grant it.

Still your
HERVÉ.'

A week before the date set for his departure for Europe the Count
received one of the first cables from the other side of the ocean to
be made available again for the use of private individuals. It said
merely. 'BOTH ACCUSATIONS TRUE – SOLANGE DE CLÉDA.'

The morning for the Count of Grandsailles' departure from the
oasis was like an image in which a fleeting mood of curious malaise
has been captured. Even without knowing wherein this mood consisted one felt that enigmatic and unavowable bonds had linked the
Count, Betka's child and the canoness in a new mystery consummated during their long seclusion. The Count, who from complete
lack of exercise was now able to walk only with a faltering step, as
though he had just risen from a long illness, had aged by five or six
years and his face bore the imprint of a superhuman determination. He was frightful to behold, especially in the analytical and
unretouched light of the California sun. Beside him, always a little
behind and unable to catch up with him, walked Betka's son, also
limping, with the help of a crutch. He was pale and beautiful as a
wax doll, wore black stockings on his legs that were thin but curved
and modelled like those of a girl. From time to time he would lift a
little lace handkerchief to his nose as if to examine whether it was

bleeding. Two paces behind them followed the canoness of Launay, and it was she who was the most horrible to behold, for she seemed rejuvenated! And a spark of crabbed and vindictive voluptuousness rendered her gargoyle's ugliness even more perfidiously demonic.

On the ship that was bringing them back. Grandsailles was almost constantly in the company of the renegade Broussillon. He liked to dictate laws, to linger over the formulation of laconic maxims on which the fate of the fatherland were to depend.

'You will tell me later, my dear Broussillon, the incidents of Betka's death in Tangiers. It consoles me nevertheless to know for the moment that she died in the arms of Mademoiselle Cécile Goudreau, who is a great friend of mine. It is fortunate that Betka left me her son – it is as though she had a premonition that she was going to die...' Then he would go on and expound further laws, his upright jurists's reveries and the new legislative prescriptions, half bucolic, half ascetic in the manner of Saint-Just, which were to be engraved in the future rose-grey granite of Upper Libreux. But at times he became a man of empire, and nostalgically parodying Napoleon, about whom he was reading a book at the moment, he would say, 'To a weak and devoted man I would try to offer reassurance; but to you, Broussillon, who are a man of strong character, I shall speak differently. We don't know what awaits us in France. We must know how to be both aggressive and compliant, our rôle is to dare and to calculate, not to shut ourselves up in a fixed plan but bend to circumstances, let ourselves be guided by them – to profit by small occasions as well as by great events: limit ourselves to the possible, but stretch the possible to the limit. We must be pitiless – suppress the loose-tongued and the corrupt who already threaten France with anarchy and complete ruin. Sacrifice all that may still remain of memories and past sentimentalities. I am building myself a soul of marble, a soul that is unassailable, a heart immune to common weaknesses. But you, Broussillon? You are not initiated to the mysteries of the "bending of blood", and only those who have painfully passed through this are tempered for all the ordeals of moral endurance. Yes! I shall have a son – a real son of my own! With my blood! A son procreated by other laws than those of nature! The "bending of blood"!'

Broussillon was only waiting for the moment when he could feel firm ground under his feet and plunge into action, and meanwhile let himself float on the morbid fascination of the Count of Grandsailles' delirious ideas. Hour after hour as they paced the decks or leaned over the railings, their two pairs of eyes devoured the anxious distances of the ocean beneath the starry vaults of early April, in which the snow of each star had already melted and was replaced by a warm touch of the sun.

'It's the same illness, the same kind of attack that she was seized with the day of the procession,' said Génie to Martin, 'but this time Madame will die of it.'

On the very evening when Solange answered the Count of Grandsailles with the laconic confession of her faults she had had to take to her bed, a prey to the same cerebral fever that had already once kept her ill for several months. But the doctor immediately noted that her condition was much more acute, for Solange was at the same time seized with convulsions which racked her body and only yielded after euphoric climaxes to states of such utter supineness that for several hours she might have been thought to be really dead.

Grandsailles had dealt Solange a deadly blow. She had understood immediately, and the figure that rose before her inward eye, fiercely intact and full of rancour was that of her enemy – the

413

authentic Grandsailles. He was her enemy and had never ceased to be. What could she answer to his letter? Their love, after all the martyrdom she had endured, could no longer be based on the plane of bargainings, and of excuses even less! Was she to explain to him that d'Angerville had been her lover on only one occasion, under circumstances in which his, Grandsailles' image had possessed her exclusively? That she had paid dearly for this by a frightful illness and that it had happened at a time when he was constantly unfaithful; that she had no reason then to hope that his marriage to Veronica would some day be broken?

And why should she have marred their correspondence, revealing a love that seemed so absolute, with the avowal of her infidelity, so difficult to tell about from a distance in a letter, which she would have confessed to him face to face and which she knew had left in her mind no other traces than those of a nightmare! The injustice was too great for one woman's heart. And then the matter of the water rights of the Moulin yielded to the invaders! Well, the Count wanted her to die: she would die without complaining.

Thus she began to die. But death was difficult for a body prepared only for the consummation of a long-sought happiness. Her will did not command unquestioning obedience and her body at last revolted. The chaste, ethereal smile that had but recently mirrored the serenity of her soul now became the horrible frozen smile of her morbid ecstasies from which the tanner-shepherd alone had been able to deliver her. Now the Count's vindictive violence had entered the most delicate parts of her flesh like an iron rod, constantly prodding her old wounds, giving her no rest. Time after time, inexorably, she was forcibly subjected to pleasure in an interminable torture of mortal voluptuousness. 'It is the Count of Grandsailles who has come to visit me again,' she would cry in her delirium. 'Already I hear the hooves of his black horse beating upon my heart... and his arm is raised with the red sword of his vengeance to punish me! I am going to die, and never was the air so filled with birds!'

This was true: through the wide-open window, beneath the white-washed porches, under the tiled cornices of the Moulin and on each of the budding branches, never had so many different birds been seen or heard, twittering and singing, pressing against one another, as in that first month of the April of victory. Génie wept in silence, her two hands joined, and the older of the Martin brothers, like a faithful Saint Bernard dog, watched his mistress with a look of grief more ancient than tears.

'I don't want to stay in this room when I die,' said Solange de Cléda. 'I want to be taken down immediately and I want my coffin to be placed on the cover of the dining-room table where I sinned. Leave the coffin open so that I can see the prostrate figure of Christ on the wall, and don't nail the lid down before I myself tell you to!'

At half-past five in the afternoon the tanner came to give Solange extreme unction. But it was a painful scene to witness, for the demons would not abandon her body, and Solange cursed the rustic cross that the tanner held with his trembling fist close to her face. Late in the afternoon of the following day she began her agony. In her delirium Solange de Cléda spoke again, 'How many days have I been dead?' she asked, 'Five – I know – five. They will have to begin to bury me. I make the air bad, my flesh is spoiling... until today I could still be visited, but now everybody is beginning to be afraid of me. Why is my coffin all filled with bones, and whose bones are they?'

Then she held out her hand that was delicate as a fairy's.

'Let everyone leave here! I want to stay alone! He is coming, he is going to come one last time to visit me in my coffin before they nail me down. Stop! Wait just one last moment before nailing me down!'

'Poor thing,' said Génie, making the tanner and Martin leave the room. 'She hears the hammer-blows of the masons who are tearing down the German constructions at the Moulin. She thinks they are already nailing down her coffin. I told them this morning to wait till Madame Solange was dead, but they all hate Madame now.'

At this moment they heard a spasmodic rattle in the midst of which Solange cried out, almost unintelligibly, '*Je suis la dame*!'

The tanner half-opened the door. Solange de Cléda had breathed her last, her arms were spread out wide like the branches of a tree, her head was thrown back and her face remained taut, her lips parted in a beatific smile.

'That is how she died;' said the tanner. 'How she must have loved him, for not only did she give him her life – she wanted also to give him all the eternity of her soul. She refused God in order to receive him, to the end! But God is merciful!'

Génie shut Solange's eyes, of which only the whites were showing. They folded her arms across her chest and made her hold the rustic cross in her hands. Several times Génie tried to close her mouth, but it refused and continued to remain a little open, and between the parted lips her small, even teeth continued to shine in a pure, child-like smile. They had to wait six hours before the coffin was ready. The cabinet-maker, who had heard that Solange had died possessed by devils and who suspected that the tanner had had a hand in all this, had his wife give the excuse that he had gone out to work in his vineyard in Lower Libreux and that he would not be back till the following day. Then Prince came and took measurements of Solange's body and in the little carpenter's room in the cellar of the Château de Lamotte proceeded to build a coffin. He used boards of very fine lemon-wood that had been cut a long time before. When the coffin was finished he carried it on his own shoulders to the Moulin des Sources, and at half-past ten in the evening they put Solange in the bier which was placed, in accordance with her wish, on the round table in the dining-room, and they began the prayers for the dead, while the wax of four large candles spattered on the chocolate-brown cloth.

Two days later Solange was buried by the two Martin brothers, the tanner-shepherd, Génie and Prince in the Moulin des Sources chapel. And after the long night of waking, Prince returned to sleep only two hours, for this was Sunday morning and for nothing in the world would he be late for the first mass. With the tanner it was hard to tell.... After all, it wasn't regular.... For some time, as he himself said, Prince's life had hung only by a thread, but he was born to serve with resignation. To the death of his only son in Germany, which it had been impossible to keep from him any longer, was now added the death of Solange de Cléda, whom he had venerated all these days and months in the silent but fervent concentration of his respect. His house in Lower Libreux had also been destroyed by the enemy during the evacuation. And still the Count had given no news of his return. How changed he was going to find the country!

Prince, the Count of Grandsailles' old servant, awoke with a start considerably before the hour and dressed in his best holiday clothes. He was one of the first to get to church. He went up close to the altar where the Holy Sacrament was exposed, and humbly bowing his head said, 'Lord, here I am, this is Prince.' Then he prayed for the grace of Solange's soul and for the Count's prompt return.

During the time that the Count of Grandsailles was homeward bound, Randolph was sailing in the opposite direction, toward his native land, America. He had been among those whom destiny had chosen as a hero to carry out the grandiose prophecy of Nostradamus when, symbolically designating the countries of Europe, he predicted that they 'will feel the yoke of "the Beast of Blood".' But just as it seems on the point of dominating all, the Beast will be subdued by a young people come from beyond the seas to redeem and deliver with its new blood the faults of the ancient people that has spent itself in the excesses of science and of sin. Thereupon, like armies of sons returning blindfold to meet their naked white-haired mothers, enriched by the science of blood which they have drunk at its venerable source, those who do not remain buried in the millenary earth will return beyond the seas to the young country whence they have come and with their own women will bring forth children of a new breed.

Thus Veronica also was included in this prophecy; for she became a mother. Like a warrior after the battle, the man with the hidden face of her chimera at last raised the visor of his helmet, and she saw him.

All were becoming visible again, who had been creatures without faces, creatures of dissimulation, of camouflage and treachery.

And what is peace if not the rediscovery of the dignity of the human face?

All this time – while the methodical Teuton in his rapacity was turning the course of the streams to wrench the metals of war from the bowels of the earth of Old Libreux and empires were crumbling; while the immutable snows were burying the victories and defeats of the Russian plains; while mimetic men devoured one another like carnivorous plants in the depth of the jungles; while the whole action of this novel was unfolding – the wood of young cork-oaks that Solange de Cléda had planted on the morrow of the Count of Grandsailles' ball had been growing. The wood had grown, and now each of those trees, instead of reaching the stature of a little man, had reached the stature of a little giant.

Last Sunday as the two Martin brothers were passing through the grove toward three in the afternoon on their way to vespers, the older one said to his brother, 'Lend me your knife. Let's see what we can tell about the cork.' And taking the large knife that his brother unsheathed he went up to one of the oaks that stood approximately in the middle of the wood and that was smaller than the others. He sank the blade hard into the softly squeaking bark and, cutting through it the shape of a large rectangle, he slipped the fingers of both hands into the upper slit which he had cut wider so as to get a good grip, and slowly and firmly began to pull. After a few moment's effort the sheet of cork gradually peeled off till it came loose in his hands intact and without a break. Such had been the custom since time immemorial; this was the mark by which the cutters would know that the cork of this wood could be gathered in due time.

In the place which the strip of cork had left bare in the middle of the tree-trunk now appeared a kind of delicate skin – silky, tender, sensitive and almost human, not only because of its colour which was exactly that of fresh blood but because these trees stripped of their costume of cork strikingly suggest the bodies of naked women with their arms raised to the sky in the noblest attitudes, and by their bold lines and the smoothness of the rounded reliefs of their trunks they imitate the most divinely and ideally flayed anatomies in the world of sense perception, while yet they have their deep roots in the earth. The mere presence of a naked cork-oak in a landscape suffices to fill the evening with its grace.

The two Martin brothers drove the carriage down to the Libreux station to fetch the Count of Grandsailles, the child and the canoness, and Grandsailles realized by the reserved attitude of the peasants whom he met there that the country was hostile to him. Also, in the course of the short ride to the Château de Lamotte he learned that Solange de Cléda had died just a week ago in the Moulin des Sources. At the Château Prince came and opened the door with his usual self-effacing, timid air, as though the Count had only been away overnight. Yet tears were streaming down the creases on each side of his nose. 'My good old Prince,' he said 'what you must have suffered and endured!'

'That's all over,' Prince replied modestly and, visibly eager to break away from the embarrassment of such effusions, he hurriedly gave orders for the placing of the baggage in the rooms that he had had made ready.

Betka's child was exhausted, and the canoness immediately put him to bed while the Count, who had just entered his room, remained in the centre looking vacantly at each piece of furniture, not knowing what to do. How long did he stand thus? When the canoness came in to announce that dinner was ready he gave a start and said. 'It's about time we changed the electric bulb in this room. It hardly gives any light....'

'One would think winter was coming back,' said the canoness, 'do you hear? What a wind!'

Seated in the dining-room the Count watched the canoness bustling about. 'Where is Prince?'

'He isn't feeling well. The excitement of Monsieur's return... and Prince is very old!... But he left everything prepared and I will only have to serve.'

The Count could barely swallow his meal. His eyes burned. Each of the delicate attentions that Prince had shown in the dishes he had prepared for him.... For in this meal there was everything that Prince knew the Count loved best in the world. How had he managed to keep his best wines for him? Mon *Dieu*! How bitter all this tasted today! And the canoness came and went. She did not let him out of her sight for a moment, but though her eye was attentive its sparkle, as he knew, was kindled by rancour.

'Why, my good canoness, do you insist on looking at me as you do?' he asked toward the end of the meal. 'Don't I deserve pity like the rest? And haven't I kept my promise to bring you back to your beloved Libreux?'

The canoness placed one knee on the chair and riveted her wicked eyes on him. 'Pity for you?' she said with sudden fierceness, 'pity for the Count of Grandsailles?' She shook her head with a frightening smile.

'What's the matter with you, canoness, how dare you talk to me in this way?'

Then deciding to unburden herself once and for all of everything she had carried locked away in her heart throughout her long life, the canoness slowly came round the table and by some fiendish chance sat down beside him on the very chair which Solange de Cléda had occupied several years before, on the one occasion when she had dined there.

She assumed the most comfortable posture, as though she had been alone in the room, half-opening her fat legs in an attitude of complete relaxation and abandon, and in her characteristic way picking up the corner of her apron and holding it to her eye which was running as much as ever. Her hunched body, tightly squeezed into an old alpaca dress with an irridescent sheen like a fly's wings, began to shake with irrepressible little squeals of laughter.

'*Seigneur Dieu*! Pity for the Count of Grandsailles!' Then she darkened and added, 'We are back in Libreux. What else was left? Now we have only to die here.'

Yet Grandsailles for the first time in his life was pitiable. He tried anger, but he could not even change the shameful expression of his blighted face. With his bowed head he resembled the bare field of Libreux in winter covered with grey stubble.

'You succeeded in fooling everybody, but there are no secrets from your canoness. The Prince of Orminy... Fouseret....' the canoness began to reel off implacably, like a judge pronouncing sentence.

The Count looked at her, terrified, as though his own accusing conscience had just awakened and become incarnated in her.

'Yes, you know it, Grandsailles! And that saint, Solange de Cléda, that angel of heaven, you killed her, too. Slowly, slowly, slowly – only one of the race of the Grandsailles could have done it in that way. You tore away all her living skin bit by bit over the long years of her martyrdom. And at the end, when she thought you were going to make her happy, you gave her your last knife-thrust in the middle of her noble bosom!'

'Shut up, canoness!' Grandsailles growled hoarsely.

'A despot! That's what you are – the blood of Girardin! For him, too, you are to blame!'

'Shut up! Get out of my sight, your ugliness fills me with horror,' Grandsailles shouted, his threatening fist seizing the naked Silenus that formed the stalk of the silver candelabrum.

But instead of obeying him the canoness only drew closer, kneeled on her chair, leaning her elbows on the table and as she bent forward without the slightest embarrassment the gaping neck of her dress exposed her bosom far down, with her two breasts, withered, elongated and dangling like a goat's, but white as milk. 'Well, no,' she said in a low voice, throwing her hot breath full into his face, 'I won't leave the handsome Grandsailles, and certainly not before I have told you everything – the main thing. For your greatest crime of all is not having made a child. Always in your family one like you has been followed by a virtuous son, and only a son could have made up for all the evil you have done on earth.'

'Shut up. Shut up! What do you know about those things? I shall have my heir!'

'Who?' the canoness exclaimed diabolically, and she raised her arm and mockingly pointed to the floor above. 'The poor martyr who is sleeping upstairs? You old lunatic! You've made a cripple of him! And you might be locked up in prison for the rest of your life if it was found out! You old lunatic! You have deserved nothing. And you have only what you deserve. You have had the skins of the finest and most beautiful women of your time, and you weren't able to have with any of them what the peasants of Libreux have the very first time – a son! And now you couldn't have him even if you wanted to, because you are almost impotent. No secrets from your canoness. But she is closer to your bed than you think, and I know that you could still have this son, but only with me – yes, with your canoness!'

'Horrible old madwoman! I'll punish you! Just wait!'

'I am only sixty-five years old. I seem to be a thousand because I've been living by your side, and you're a dog. But I am still able to bear a child, and I can prove to you that what I say is true!'

At this moment a strange phenomenon must have occurred in Grandsailles' harassed and delirious brain, for in the depth of his anger he was seized all of a sudden with an incomprehensible attraction which seemed to be born precisely of everything that was most abominable and repulsive about the canoness – her eyes edged by her chronic conjunctivitis, like red wounds, appeared to him suddenly precious like those of a divinity, set in rubies; her evil drooling mouth with its crooked teeth seemed to him a stream with the wheels of a mill of temptations that was pulling him into an abyss of ignoble desires; and the foaming saliva that thickened like a yellowish-white paste at the corners of her lips hallucinated him like drops of an aphrodisiac and deadly pus. Standing before him in its reality was the frightful succubus dream that had haunted him all his life, incarnated in the decrepit and familiar flesh of his canoness. And it was not a dream!

'It is Solange de Cléda, eternally damned because of me, who has entered into the demon's body of my canoness to be with me once more! The devil take you!' roared Grandsailles, lifting the silver candelabrum threateningly.

423

'Wretch! It's the devil who brought me here and all hell is speaking to you through my lips!'

'You're going to get it now!' Grandsailles roared in a paroxysm of hatred, 'but once I start, I'll hit again a hundred times till your face no longer looks like anything human.'

Then the canoness began to retreat, but continuing to hurl invectives at him all the while, as if thereby to attract him, backed away to the end of the corridor where her room was. The Count, like a somnambulist, entered after her, still holding high the silver candelabrum with which he was threatening her. The door closed behind them and presently there was heard the sound of two dreadful blows followed by an absolute silence, a thousand times more sinister than any sound.

At about this moment Betka's child must have awakened, for he came out of his room, limping on his crutch, wearing his long nightshirt that reached to the floor. He went down two steps, and hearing nothing more went back to bed. One also had the impression that all the dogs of Upper and Lower Libreux had conspired to bark together at this same hour.

The following morning the canoness of Launay, sitting on her bed, wept uninterruptedly. In the dining-room the Count of Grandsailles, his head resting on the ebony of the table, has just awakened. He seemed to have aged by several more years. He got up, and with the aid of his cane stalked down the long corridor, without stopping before the canoness's room to console her. He went up into his room and headed straight for the balcony door which he opened, stepped outside and sat down on a little stone bench adorned with chimeras. His heart contracted at the sight of the deep black forest of young cork-oaks that had grown during his absence, and he could not avert his eyes from the realization of this old dream.

In the centre of the forest he could see the oak which the elder Martin brother had marked last Sunday. It was the living symbol of

Solange, martyrized by the war, flayed alive by the peace, dead and buried behind those trees. Solange de France, breasts of live rock, lips of jasmine! For how many years Grandsailles had lived in a state of hallucination, waiting for this moment when he would again see his beloved plain of Creux de Libreux, the illuminated plain! Already he could feel it, without yet seeing it – just a little higher, above the tree to which his gaze had remained obstinately riveted. Obscure sounds of carts, to the left, in the direction of the Moulin, attested the whole earthy and sacred reality of this soil…. But instead of looking up, the Count of Grandsailles bowed his head and hid his face in his hands.

RENOVABITVR

THE END

THE STORY OF PETER OWEN PUBLISHERS

Peter Owen founded his eponymous publishing house in 1951. From the beginning he championed major but little-known international authors including Hermann Hesse, Shusaku Endo, Anaïs Nin and Tarjei Vesaas, often publishing them in English for the first time. Hesse's Siddhartha *was one of the first novels he published, buying the rights for £25. The company helped to build the British writer Anna Kavan, as well as Margaret Crosland, who published 25 books with the firm – translating 18 titles from the French, including works by Jean Cocteau and the Marquis de Sade, as well as writing seven books of her own. Peter Owen also published Salvador Dalí's only novel. The list eventually included ten Nobel Prize-winning authors, earning Owen an OBE for services to literature.*

Born in Nuremberg in 1927, Owen moved with his British-born mother to London soon after Hitler came to power; his German-Jewish father joined them a year later. His first job was as an office boy at The Bodley Head, and, after a brief stint in the RAF, he used an armed-forces paper quota and capital of around £800 to set up his own publishing company, aged 24. Several years later, an aspiring novelist named Muriel Spark came to work for him as editor.

Peter Owen was one of a kind; a maverick, a pioneer. Throughout his seven decades in publishing he was known as much for his flamboyant shirts and snakeskin ties as for his dogged persistence and dedication to high-quality literature in translation. Independent to the end, Owen ran his publishing house until he died in 2016, aged 89. His memoir, Not a Nice Jewish Boy, *appeared shortly after his death. Pushkin Press acquired the company in 2022.*

AVAILABLE AND COMING SOON FROM
PUSHKIN PRESS CLASSICS

The Pushkin Press Classics list brings you timeless storytelling by icons of literature. These titles represent the best of fiction and non-fiction, hand-picked from around the globe – from Russia to Japan, France to the Americas – boasting fresh selections, new translations and stylishly designed covers. Featuring some of the most widely acclaimed authors from across the ages, as well as compelling contemporary writers, these are the world's best stories – to be read and read again.

MURDER IN THE AGE OF ENLIGHTENMENT
RYŪNOSUKE AKUTAGAWA

THE BEAUTIES
ANTON CHEKHOV

LAND OF SMOKE
SARA GALLARDO

THE SPECTRE OF ALEXANDER WOLF
GAITO GAZDANOV

CLOUDS OVER PARIS
FELIX HARTLAUB

THE UNHAPPINESS OF BEING
A SINGLE MAN
FRANZ KAFKA